Lexi was about to wrangle *in his surf.*

But she had no choice. He may well be Jazi's father, and the only person with the power to grant her custody.

A confirmed bachelor, he'd stated in one article that he never intended to have a family. According to him, he took a satisfaction in his work that he'd never found in a relationship, so why force something that wasn't meant to be?

Lexi hoped he believed what he said. Jazi's and her futures rested in his hands. But she needed to confirm her hunch before she put her proposition to him.

She made her way to the bar, a room dressed in dark leather, light wood and shining crystal. And there he was. Seated at the end of the bar in a custom-made tuxedo that emphasized the broad reach of his shoulders, showcasing his tall, lean frame to perfection. His brooding expression kept everyone, including the bartender, at bay.

A shark surveying his territory, there was nothing subdued about him. His hair was nearly black, his eyes dark and piercing, though the color was indiscernible at this distance and angle. Features a shade too sharp to be considered classically handsome

She was had to check. He may well be. Yeah
father that he only pays a ... little money to save
... for another ... she was a week to have

A cautioned the book he'd ... saved to one ... and
in the week needed to time seems to expedite
to time he took ... panics him in his work that
... of money to aid the desired days ... with there
committee... he wasn't mean to be.

I ask inhaled he believes that he shut. His hand
then raised listen in his hands, this he meant to
confirm but in ... of ... there she ... he ... required him
require...

She made her way to the face in confident within
day reaching light work and some unrecognised
there he was ... Seated at the end of the ... bar in a
otherwise quiet ... that emphasised the broad
reach of his shoulders, ... was conscious his him, to
than to continental in his brooding expression very
between ... without the outer ... hat set...

... of ... a ... during the barstool there ... he kill the
column or part him. His red was a very dark hair,
of ... rate. The ... of any ... graphic its grip was
discernible at this distance and angle. Features
shade too sharp to be considered classically
handsome made him all the more compelling

THE CEO'S
SURPRISE FAMILY

BY
TERESA CARPENTER

First Published in Great Britain 2016
By Mills & Boon, an imprint of HarperCollins*Publishers*
1 London Bridge Street, London, SE1 9GF

© 2016 by Teresa Carpenter

ISBN: 978-0-263-92017-8

23-0916

Our policy is to use papers that are natural, renewable and recyclable products and made from wood grown in sustainable forests. The logging and manufacturing processes conform to the legal environmental regulations of the country of origin.

Printed and bound in Spain
by CPI, Barcelona

Teresa Carpenter believes that with love and family anything is possible. She writes in a Southern California coastal city surrounded by her large family. Teresa loves writing about babies and grandmas. Her books have been rated Top Picks by *RT Book Reviews*, and have been nominated Best Romance of the Year on some review sites. If she's not at a family event, she's reading or writing her next grand romance.

To my readers. Thank you for taking the time to find me and read me. And a warm hug to those who go to Amazon and Goodreads to leave reviews. You help other readers to find me. Bless you.

CHAPTER ONE

LEXI MALONE'S HAND shook as she touched up her lip liner. She met her gaze in the gilded ladies' room mirror and saw nerves reflected in the blue depths.

"For Jazi," she breathed and capped the liner.

The reminder chased the shakes away. And most of the nerves. She'd do anything to get her twenty-three-month-old goddaughter back. Accosting a man in an upscale restaurant to determine if he was the child's father was nothing. And it may not come to that. Tonight was a fact-finding mission.

At the theater where she'd used to dance strange men had approached her all the time. She'd learned to handle them long ago. Of course, the Golden Link was a well-respected private club at the Golden Cuff Casino and security had stood ready to protect her if things got out of control.

Here all the security belonged to Jethro Calder, a top executive of the Pinnacle Group, and owner of the restaurant she stood in. The Beacon mixed old-world elegance with modern efficiency and hearty fare. And it was housed in the Pinnacle Casino and Hotel where Calder had a penthouse suite.

She was about to wrangle a shark in his surf.

But she had no choice. He may well be Jazi's father, and the only person with the power to grant her custody.

She'd done her homework once she realized his possible relationship to Jazi.

One of the "Fabulous Four" to take Pinnacle Enterprises to the top of the fiercely competitive world of digital gaming, Calder was known as the Dark Predator. Few went up against him without feeling his bite.

A confirmed bachelor, he'd stated in one article that he never intended to have a family. According to him, he took a satisfaction in his work that he'd never found in a relationship so why force something that wasn't meant to be.

Lexi hoped he believed what he said. Jazi's and her futures rested in his hands. But she needed to confirm her hunch before she put her proposition to him. She needed to see his birthmark for herself.

"So stop stalling." She scolded her reflection, earning an odd look from the woman next to her at the vanity. She offered a small smile but the woman tucked her lipstick away and left the bathroom. "Good job, Lexi, you're scaring the tourists."

She sighed, fluffed up her shoulder-length red hair, lifted her chin and followed the woman out. "For Jazi."

It seemed prophetic that today was Alliyah's birthday. Lexi hoped it meant she'd be lucky. She made her way to the bar, a room dressed in dark leather, light wood and shining crystal. Alliyah, Lexi's best friend and Jazi's mother, had been a dancer too. Unlike Lexi, Alliyah had made extra money by being an executive escort. When men like Calder needed a date for an event, they called the service and Alliyah got an expensive night out on the town and earned the money to buy whatever she had her eye on, which could be anything from diapers to a new designer purse.

Sex was not part of the service. But occasionally Alliyah hooked up with her dates. Jazi was the result of one of those hookups. As soon as she'd found out she was pregnant Alliyah had quit the service. Unfortunately, she hadn't been sure of whom the father was. Or more probably she hadn't wanted to share Jazi. Whichever, she'd been closedmouthed about the baby's father, even to Lexi. When she'd died in an automobile accident, her silence contributed to placing her daughter in foster care. A system Alliyah had despised, having bounced around in it for a good part of her youth.

Lexi supposed she could thank her mother for being spared that unpleasant experience. No, Lexi had longed for a little neglect in her childhood. Instead, every moment of every day had been structured, filled with practice, schooling, practice, regimented exercise, practice, scheduled meals, and more practice. All under the strict eye of her mother.

Oh, yeah, Lexi had prayed for time alone.

But that had been a lifetime ago. Now she just wanted custody of her goddaughter, and Jethro Calder was her ticket.

And there he was. Seated at the end of the bar in a custom-made tuxedo that emphasized the broad reach of his shoulders, showcasing his tall, lean frame to perfection. His brooding expression kept everyone, including the bartender at bay.

A shark surveying his territory, there was nothing subdued about him. His hair was nearly black, his eyes dark and piercing, the color indiscernible at this distance and angle. Features a shade too sharp to be considered classically handsome made him all the more compelling.

Pretending uninterest, she studied him in the mirror as she walked up to the bar. "A dirty Manhattan, please," she ordered from the attentive bartender. She held her breath—no going back now. The drink order was a signal to Jethro Calder that she was his date from Excursions.

After reading the article, she'd contacted Sally Easton, the owner of Excursions. Lexi had met the older woman several times when Alliyah worked for her. Sally had even tried to recruit Lexi more than once. Lexi had explained she needed to talk to Calder about something important but when she tried going through his company she got passed on to a lower executive. Sally put Lexi off not wanting to jeopardize his business with Excursions. But today she'd got a call that Jethro Calder's date had to cancel. Sally was giving her this one chance.

"May I buy that for you?" A man old enough to be her father slid onto the stool next to her and leaned into her space.

She controlled the urge to flinch away from him. Why did a miniskirt make men lose all sense of propriety? Before she could politely refuse his none-too-subtle come-on, a tuxedoed arm threaded between them and a deep male voice declared, "She's with me."

A strong hand settled over Lexi's and Jethro Calder assisted her from her seat.

"You're late," he said.

She froze. Then forced herself to relax. She meant to observe him tonight, try to catch a glimpse of the birthmark on his wrist to confirm his link to Jazi and get to know him a little better before retreating to plan her next course of action.

"Right on time actually."

Her gaze went to the mirror making sure no one spotted her for the fraud she was. No one appeared to be paying particular interest in them except a familiar brunette who was lovely but about ten years older than Calder, who she knew to be thirty-five. A cougar on the prowl?

"No way, Calder." Her would-be suitor protested. "You're always claiming the young, pretty ones. If she were with you, why didn't she join you?"

Calder ignored the man. Instead he addressed the bartender, who arrived with her drink. "Sam, Madison's tab is on the house tonight."

"We're having a bit of a tiff." Lexi curled her arm around Calder's. Hard muscles flexed under her fingers.

Slightly mollified by Calder's generosity, Madison's scowl deepened at her gesture. Not wanting his annoyance to turn to suspicion, Lexi grabbed the drink from the bar.

"There are lots of beautiful women here tonight." She set the glass down in front of the brunette whose hair Lexi had styled less than an hour ago. With a smile she announced, "This gentleman would like to buy you a drink."

The woman frowned. The man sputtered. And Calder led Lexi away.

"You're late," he repeated, his breath whispering over her ear, his deep voice shivering over her senses. A warm hand in the small of her back directed her to the elevator that would take them down one floor to the casino floor. "I'll let it slide because watching you hand Madison's ex-wife that drink was the most fun I've had all day."

She eyed his solemn expression. This was him having fun?

"That was his ex-wife?" No wonder she seemed so interested in their interaction.

"Yes. She eats at the restaurant every Friday night after her spa treatment."

"And he comes in every Friday night to pick up pretty young things in front of her?"

"Every week for the last six months."

"People are strange."

"You have no idea how strange until you've lived in a casino."

"Believe me, working in a casino is as close as you need to get to see strange." She'd learned that as a dancer. But that was in the past. Now she cut and styled hair, a day job so she could be at home with Jazi when she got custody.

His eyes narrowed on her. "You work in a casino?" They were a dark, twilight blue. Her heart pounded. She'd only ever seen one other person with eyes that color. Jazi had his eyes. She swallowed in a suddenly dry throat. She'd found Jazi's father.

A hundred emotions rushed through her, love for her goddaughter, hope, fear, anticipation, trepidation. But she forced herself to concentrate on the conversation. "Hasn't everyone who lives in Las Vegas worked at a casino at some point?"

"That doesn't answer my question," he stated.

"I work at Pinnacle's actually. At the Modern Goddess Salon." She wasn't surprised he didn't know her. The spa rented the space. "Is that going to be a problem?"

His brows contracted and she realized he was actually thinking about it. He sighed. "No. It's not a problem."

"I was a last-minute replacement." Lexi advised him, sticking as close to the truth as possible. "I'm afraid I don't know anything about where we're going."

"I never reveal the destination until we're en route."

Of course not. Everything she'd read on the man indicated he was a very private man. He walked with purpose and speed. Luckily her dancer's grace allowed her to keep pace.

"Hmm. Kind of makes it hard to know how to dress."

The fact he wore a tuxedo meant the occasion was formal. She tugged at the hem of her black minidress, hoping she met his requirements.

"I provided the information that it was a formal event." His dark gaze ran over her, the intensity in the navy depths sent a shiver down her spine. "You'll do."

"Good to know."

She'd gone with the classic little black dress. Wide band sleeves rested just off her shoulders and flowed to a vee in front showing off a hint of cleavage. The material clung to her curves in a loose fit, allowing her to move. It was more provocative than sexy. And because Lexi liked sparkle and shine, the fabric glimmered with every step she took.

The automatic doors swooshed open to the glittering entrance of the casino. There were lights and movement everywhere. People, cars, taxies and valets flowed in a ballet of arrival and exits backlit by a cascading water feature.

A car waited for them and a valet rushed over to get the door. "Good evening, Mr. Calder, Lexi."

"Hi, Miguel, how's the new baby?"

A huge grin lit up his face. "As pretty as her mama."

"Miguel and his wife just had a baby girl a month ago," Lexi told Calder. "Her name is Saralynn."

There was no change to Calder's expression, but he nodded at Miguel. "Congratulations. Lexi," he gestured to the open door, "we have to get going."

"Of course."

Cold fish—check.

Strangely disappointed, she slid in and across the seat. When she glanced back, she saw Calder tip Miguel with a couple of hundred dollar bills. She perked up. Maybe not so cold after all. He joined her, his large body taking up most of the space. She suddenly felt crowded and overly warm. Definitely not cold now.

She might panic—if she were the type to panic—if he didn't smell so good. No fancy cologne for him. He smelled of soap and man. And he made her mouth water.

Rein it in, girl, you're on a mission here.

As a distraction, she focused on his generous gesture. It gave her a sense of hope. He'd stated in more than one article that he didn't want kids or a family, that he didn't have the patience or skill set for a long-term relationship so why set himself up for failure. Her plan rested on the fact he meant what he said, but it helped to know he wasn't totally dispassionate about kids. She needed him to care enough to act.

"How do you know Miguel?"

Jethro ground his teeth, annoyed he let the question slip out.

How she knew the other man didn't matter as long as she was a pretty armpiece and was able to intercede when required to redirect the conversation.

A task she should have no problem with since she'd been chattering ever since they met.

"Just from working at the Pinnacle. I've been at the spa now for a month. I like to talk to people so I've met a lot of the Pinnacle employees."

Yes, he could see her as a people person. Where he was not.

"Miguel treated his wife to a day at the spa after Sara-lynn was born. I thought it was a wonderful gesture and suggested to the owner that she put together a package just for new mothers and publicize it throughout the casino and hotel. She agreed to give it a try. We've had quite a few women come in."

"So you're in marketing?"

"Oh, goodness, no. I'm a dan—a hairdresser."

His head swung around and he rolled his gaze over her, accessing every curve. The escorts at Excursions were a mix of entertainers and professional businesswomen. He'd made it clear he preferred the latter. He had more in common with a businesswoman. And the one time he took a date to the next level had been with a dancer. He'd regretted the slip.

He preferred to keep his social and sexual encounters separate. He prized the discretion and privacy Excursions' services provided. He liked that sex wasn't part of the arrangement. The last thing he wanted was for the line between social and private to blur. That could only lead to complications and expectations he had no desire to deal with.

He never lacked for partners when he needed sexual release.

Casual dates with no promise of a follow-up were harder to come by until a friend recommended Excursions.

Having a new woman on his arm on a regular basis gave him the image of a player. He didn't care. He wasn't out to impress anyone and it gave warning to those who would expect more from him, all the better.

He'd made the mistake of sleeping with a date only once. She'd been a stunning woman of mixed race and he'd been out with her several times. Her intelligence and grace made him the envy of every man at the foundation dinner they'd attended. He'd been receiving an award and drank more than usual to offset the attention. Being in the limelight tore at his nerves but his date thrived on it. She'd been the perfect person to have on his arm that night and the high of the event had carried them upstairs when she made her interest clear.

Alliyah was gone in the morning and the next time he contacted Excursions he asked for a professional woman so he hadn't seen her again.

Excursions' quality control was slipping if they'd sent him a dancer. And he didn't even have her name beyond Miguel's addressing her as Lexi. He usually got notice and a new profile when he was getting a replacement date. He liked to know something about the women he spent time with even when he paid for the pleasure. He sent off a text.

"A dancer." He repeated.

"No. I told you, I work at Modern Goddess. I used to be a dancer." She licked her lips drawing his attention to the sultry lines of her mouth, the perfect bow over a plump bottom lip. "Now I do hair at the spa. I just thought pampering a new mother totally made sense. I remembered how tired and stressed my roommate was after having my goddaughter, Jasmine."

"Hmm. What's your name?"

"Oh, goodness." She laughed—an infectious sound that filled the back of the car. "We kind of skipped that part, didn't we? I'm Alexa Malone, but you can call me Lexi. And of course you're Jethro Calder. I read the article in the Pinnacle newsletter where it showed you and the other executives holding up the lifetime award of excellence for the Pinnacle game. That must have been exciting."

"Yes, it was a nice acknowledgment for the success of the game."

"I should say so. A top ten seller for ten years, that's awesome."

"It's actually been for fifteen years and more than half

those years it was in the top three, but they wanted to have wiggle room for future awards."

"What's it like working with Jackson Hawke?"

He frowned. He got that question a lot, mostly from people trying to angle through him to Jackson. But there was nothing in her tone or demeanor to indicate anything other than simple interest.

"He's a brilliant programmer, but he leaves the finances to me."

"Of course." She nodded and pointed at him.

She used her hands a lot when she talked. He couldn't decide if he found it charming or annoying. Whether he found her charming or was just attracted to that luscious mouth.

"We all have our talents, don't we? Mine is music. So, Jethro, where are we going?"

Music, he noticed, not dance.

"We're going to an event at Caesar's Palace." His phone buzzed and he read the text. "At least I am. I'm not sure what you'll be doing." He held up his phone. "Excursions doesn't have your name on file. Who are you?"

CHAPTER TWO

OOPS. LEXI BLINKED at Jethro. She'd been caught out. She shifted her gaze to the phone he held aloft as evidence of her culpability and her eyes went wide.

The position of his arm caused his suit and shirtsleeves to slip down revealing his wrist and the tip of the birthmark. Enough for her to see it matched Jazi's.

The mark reminded Lexi of a dragonfly with a curled tail only kind of blotchy. She'd been stunned when she saw it on Calder's wrist in the picture accompanying the article she told him about. The top execs of Pinnacle had all been holding the award aloft. Calder had been standing closest to the camera and there on his wrist was the same birthmark as her precious Jazi's.

Lexi had known instantly that he had to be related to the baby, most likely her father. When she'd read his stance on never having a family, she firmly believed it was a sign. With his help she could get Jazi back.

Between the matching eyes and the birthmark, Lexi had all the confirmation she needed that Jethro Calder was Jazi's father.

"Ms. Malone?" Fingers snapped in front of her eyes.

She blinked and focused on the man next to her, staring into his unreadable features, into Jazi's blue eyes. Thoughts of how important he was flooded her mind, crippling her with fear. If she blew this she'd never get Jazi back! And she was about to blow it. Big-time.

Stop. Get a grip.

She drew in a slow, deep breath, released it around a

sheepish smile. She only had one option now. She looked him right in the eye and confessed. "I'm sorry. You're right, I don't usually work for Excursions."

A dark brow lifted at her easy admission. "So you were just at the restaurant to shanghai a date with me?"

"Oh, gracious, no." Now his other brow lifted. Had she offended him? She half shrugged. Best to stick as close to the truth as possible without getting Excursions in trouble. "Today was my best friend Alliyah's birthday. She used to go to work for Excursions. She passed away six months ago and I needed a distraction tonight, so I called Sally and asked if she could hook me up with a date. She said she had a cancellation and here I am."

"A cancellation?" Suspicion dripped from the question.

"Yes. You can call her if you like." Lexi held her breath—the last thing she wanted was to cause trouble for Sally.

"You recognized me."

"Yes, from the article. Why, did you know Alliyah? Alliyah West?"

He looked away, but nodded. "We had a couple of dates. You said she passed away."

"She was killed in an auto accident just over six months ago."

"I'm sorry to hear that. She was a charming companion."

Lexi glanced out the window and saw they were cruising along the dazzling Las Vegas Strip. "So listen, I'm sorry I'm not what you were expecting. You can let me out anywhere along here. I'll catch a cab back to the Pinnacle." She batted her eyelashes at him in an obvious ploy. "Unless you still need a date for the evening?"

"Now you're propositioning me?"

"No." She rolled her eyes and shook her head. "You know you can be a bit of a stuffed shirt. You might want to watch that. I'm offering—free of charge—to go with you to whatever thing you have going on so you don't have to find a replacement date."

"You're willing to spend the evening with a stuffed shirt?"

"Hey, I've been out with worse. At least you smell good and have a nice ride. But if you're not interested, just have the driver pull over and drop me off."

"Let's say I agree to allow you to accompany me, I'd prefer to pay you for your time."

Lexi blinked at him. "Why?"

"Because I prefer to keep our association on a professional level."

"You want me to cut your hair?" She said it just to rile him. The man had no sense of humor. Or sense of fun.

"What?" His brows drew together in a scowl. "Why would you suggest such a thing?"

"Because I'm a cosmetologist and my profession is to cut hair."

"That's not what I meant." His shoulders were razor sharp against the black leather seat. "More, you know it wasn't."

"You're right, I'm messing with you, but you deserve it for being so pompous."

"A stuffed shirt and now pompous," he muttered.

"They're nearly the same thing. And obviously your comfort zone."

"I merely wish to keep things clear."

"Oh, I get the point. It wouldn't be a date."

"That is correct. And as I value my time, I feel it only fair to pay you for yours."

"Very gracious of you."

He sighed and relaxed slightly.

"But forget it." She patted his knee and flashed a bright smile. "We'll just go as friends."

He practically choked on his own breath. "We are not friends. I barely know you."

"Sometimes people just click and are friends for life."

"There was no click."

"We even have a history." She talked right over him. "We both knew Alliyah, were friends of hers." If anyone needed a friend, it was this man. He was so cut off from everyone around him. For some reason, Lexi felt compelled to be there for him tonight. Perhaps because he was Jazi's father or maybe just because she hated to see anyone so alone. "Close enough, don't you think?"

His hand closed over hers on the seat. "You miss her very much don't you?"

Tears threatened. She nodded, and without thought turned her hand over in his to give his hand an answering squeeze. "It would be payment enough to spend the evening with someone who knew her."

"Then that's what we'll do." He pulled away from her. "As long as it's understood that it's not a date."

"Understood. There will be no good-night kiss."

He gave a shake of his head. "I may be a stuffed shirt, Ms. Malone, but you are outrageous."

"Huh. You say that like it's a bad thing."

He dropped his head forward as if he'd reached the end of his patience, but she thought she saw just the tiniest of smiles at the corner of his mouth.

"The event at Caesar's Palace is an art showing at the Maxim Gallery."

Interest flared in her bright blue eyes. "Oh, that sounds like fun. I've heard of the Maxim. I'll warn you, though, that I know nothing about art."

"There's no need for you to have knowledge of art." Jethro assured her.

He was still wondering at himself for allowing her to join him at the opening. It was unlike him to make impulsive decisions. And he didn't reward dishonesty. She may be from Excursions, but she was unlike any of his previous dates. And a former dancer. That alone should have been enough to drop her off along the strip as she'd urged him to do.

But there was a lightness about her that appealed to him, a genuineness that intrigued his jaded soul.

Outrageous was an understatement. No one talked to him like she did. Stuffed shirt? Pompous? He'd fire anyone who dared say such a thing. It didn't matter that it was the truth. That he worked hard to maintain a hand's distance from everyone around him. He wouldn't be disrespected.

Coming from her it rang of the truth, plainly spoken.

"Good. Because my art appreciation is limited to knowing what I like, which could be anything from a good Elvis painting to a portrait of an old woman smiling. And I never know if there's any importance attached to the piece."

"Well, it's highly doubtful there's any significance to a velvet Elvis painting."

Soft laughter trilled through the air. She nudged his shoulder with hers. "I know that much, silly. But he was a huge contributor to the music world and I like the colors. When I look at the painting, I like to think he found peace."

So did Jethro. Elvis was a favorite artist of his. One more thing linking him to this woman when the softness of her was already too dangerous. She didn't fit in either of the two categories he allowed in his life.

"So you don't believe he's living a secret life somewhere?"

"No." Sadness briefly dimmed the animation of her delicate features. "Much as I'd like to believe he's still with us, music was too much a part of his soul for him to stay undetected all these years. He'd have to perform, and if he performed he'd be found."

Disconcerted because he held the same belief, he went on the offensive.

"How old are you?" he asked derisively. "Twenty-three? Twenty-four? You're too young to be an Elvis fan."

"Please, great music transcends age. And I'm twenty-seven. Old enough to know my own mind."

Not as young as he'd feared—or should that be hoped?

Against his better judgment, he'd decided to indulge himself tonight and enjoy a bit of light company, but having a few elements that put her beyond his strict restrictions would be helpful.

"We're here." The car rolled to a smooth stop. Jethro pushed the door open and stepped out.

"Good evening, Mr. Calder." A valet immediately appeared to greet him. "Welcome back to Caesar's Palace."

"Thank you. We're here for the Kittrell showing."

"Very good, sir. We've had a steady stream of arrivals for the showing tonight."

"That's good to hear." Jethro tipped the young African American before extending a hand to assist Lexi from the car.

"Sean!" she exclaimed and gave the valet a warm hug. "I'm glad to see you're back in town. How is your mother?"

Sean shifted, uncomfortable under Jethro's stern regard, but the smile he turned on Lexi was full of warmth. "On her feet again. The knee surgery was just what she needed to get her pep back."

"I'm glad to hear it. She's too young to be sitting on the couch. You tell her I said hi."

"I will. And I want to hear what's going on with you." Sean discreetly nodded in Jethro's direction. "We'll talk soon."

"Yes, I'm off to view art." She glanced his way, and Jethro absorbed the impact of her laughing eyes. "See you soon." She bid her friend goodbye and made her way to his side.

He claimed her hand. "Do you know every valet in Las Vegas?"

"I know a lot. For all the tourists, Las Vegas is a small town. At least when it comes to the world of entertainers. Valeting is a common way to pick up extra money or pay the bills between jobs."

"I see."

"Is there a problem?"

"No."

"Something's bothering you," she insisted. "Does it upset you that I stopped to speak to them? Because it would be rude to ignore the fact I know them."

"It's their job to provide discrete service and fade into the background. I'm sure they respect the dynamics of the job."

"You're saying it's okay to be rude."

"I'm saying, they're working."

"So you're a snob."

He sighed. "I'm not a snob. I just like getting where I'm going without a lot of meaningless chitchat."

"It wasn't meaningless." She protested. "I was genuinely interested in how his mother was doing."

"That's not the point."

"Then what is the point?" She easily kept stride with him as he led her toward the famous Caesar shopping mall.

"The point is it's rude to be making a fuss over other men when you're out with a man."

"But we're not on a date." She reminded him with a tad more satisfaction than he cared for.

"We're together. That's what counts."

"So it's okay for me to be rude to them, but not to you?"

"Correct. No. Stop messing with me. You're giving me a headache."

She grinned, obviously pleased to be called on her teasing. "If you loosened up a bit, you wouldn't get headaches."

"Woman, you are a headache."

"Ah, you say the nicest things. Oh, it's the thunderstorm. I love this. Do we have time to watch?"

Without waiting for a response she skipped—yes, *skipped*—forward to perch on the stone bench of a fountain. He found himself following her, taking satisfaction in indulging her delight. She patted the space next to her inviting him to sit.

Suddenly an uncertain expression crossed her face and

she popped to her feet. "Sorry—my *oops*. I know you want to get where you're going."

"Sit. Enjoy your show." He sat. "And when we get to the showing, you can do something for me."

"Ah." She resumed her perch, her knee touching his, her gaze focused above on the changing skyscape of the indoor mall. The sunny day had darkened to gray clouds with flashes of lightning. "The job your dates perform for you."

The comment annoyed him. So what if he wanted his companions to provide a service while they were with him. He paid good money for their company. And tipped well.

"You really are a pest. If you don't want to do it, you don't have to."

"Don't be so touchy." She bumped his shoulder. "Ah." A gasp escaped her pretty lips when thunder boomed in the background adding audio to the overhead show. "I do love a good thunderstorm. I don't get how all these people can walk by as if nothing is happening right over their heads."

"Maybe they've seen it before. Or they're caught up in the moment or the conversation. Or simply need to be somewhere." Personally he couldn't remember the last time he'd paused to notice the movement of the mock sky in the shopping mall. He had to admit it was pretty cool. It certainly added to the overall effect of a Roman city.

"What have you got?"

"I'm thinking this might be something to consider for Pinnacle for our next revamp. We could have simulated battle scenes."

"Oh, and flames like the city is burning. With the postapocalyptic theme you could do all kinds of things with the skyscape, extreme sunsets and meteor storms, flash floods. You could even bring it down on the walls though that might compete with the casino action."

"The tourists would love it. It would give them the sense of being in the game even more than the decor does now."

He liked the creative way she thought. All tossed out so

artlessly. Right. In his experience, nothing, not even ideas, were given away free. She wanted something.

He'd bet his life on it.

Above them, blue skies began to ease out the clouds and lightning. Lexi stood and smoothed her dress over her hips.

"It's a great idea, but what I was actually asking is what would you like me to do for you at the party?"

CHAPTER THREE

PARTY? BLAST IT. In order to get his mind functioning again, Jethro dragged his gaze up to her face, not daring to linger on the intriguing hint of cleavage or her luscious lower lip.

She meant the showing. He'd almost lost his desire to attend the event tonight. But as owner of the gallery and the artist's patron it would look bad if he didn't at least put in an appearance. Plus, he believed in the man's talent.

He and his friends made a great team evidenced by their huge success with Pinnacle. Yet the last few years, he'd felt compelled to prove he could succeed on his own. The gallery, like the restaurant, was his attempt at diversification.

"It's nothing too difficult." He stood, his hand going to the small of her back as he directed her along. "As a high-ranking officer at one of the premier entertainment conglomerates in the world, I get approached by a lot of people with ideas for the next best whatever. I'd like you to run interference for me."

"I can see where that would get old." Sympathy shone from eyes the color of the pastoral sky above. "Sure, I can handle that. Tell me about the artist."

"He takes parts of photographs, layers them together and breathes life into them with an editing software he created. The end result is stunning, the colors vivid."

"I can't wait to see his work. It sounds unlike anything I've ever seen."

Jethro must be impressed with the artist. Talking about him was the most animated she'd seen him all night. Though, to be fair, he had loosened up from his stuffed-shirt status by allowing her to watch the sky show and by sharing his thoughts about revamping the Pinnacle.

At the gallery the crowd overflowed into the mall.

"Well, I'd say the showing is a success." Lexi wrapped her arm around Jethro's to keep from being separated from him. "And it's such a crush nobody's going to hear anyone in here. I don't think you need to worry about being approached by any wannabe gamesters."

He grunted. "You underestimate the zealousness of programmers, songwriters and other assorted artists the world over. A crowd like this just allows them the opportunity to get up close and personal."

Actually she knew full well the zealousness of artists. No one knew better than her how one-dimensional they could be when it came to their art.

"Maybe it's your warm personality," she suggested.

She grinned when she received an arch stare over his shoulder. "You like to live dangerously don't you?"

"Sorry. I can't seem to resist." And she should. Her every action counted toward the future and his willingness to help her. But she'd been restrained for too many years not to be herself at all times. Plus, who knew he'd be so fun to tease? Or turn out to be such a good sport? "Take heart, you're bearing up under the challenge."

Right inside the door hung a huge picture that was gorgeous. A tropical location brought to life in vibrant colors. The nose of a small plane bobbed in the cove and on the beach a gazebo with fluttering curtains housed a table, chairs and a meal awaiting missing lovers. To the side of the print were a picture of a lagoon, the plane and a gazebo. The title was *Escape*.

"I love it," Lexi breathed. "Don't you just want to be there?"

"It's inviting."

"Inviting? If that's all you've got, I'm going to have to find someone else to go with."

"Someone with a sense of adventure," a man said behind her.

"Yes." She agreed, moving to include the tall, stylishly dressed man. He had long dark hair, green eyes and a confidence he wore as comfortably as his fitted jacket. "And a sense of romance. Someone with a thirst for life."

"Exactly the mood I was going for." The man grinned and held out his hand. "I'm Ethan Kittrell."

"Ethan is the artist." Jethro shook hands as he introduced Lexi.

"Calder, I'm glad you made it. And for bringing such a lovely companion."

"Are you flirting with my companion, Ethan?" There was no emotion in the question, which only served to make it more menacing.

As if she belonged to him. Not likely. She'd fought hard for her freedom. And wasn't he the one to insist this wasn't a date?

But truthfully she wasn't even tempted by the handsome artist. For all his eccentric cleverness, he paled next to the sheer presence of Jethro Calder.

Good thing this wasn't a date. Because, her independence aside, she'd be way out of her element.

No, tonight was make-believe, just an opportunity to observe him in his world. Which meant she could be herself. As long as she didn't alienate him, she could relax and have fun.

"Not tonight, I'm not." Ethan held up his hands in surrender and shifted ever so subtly away from her. "Just a little harmless admiration for a beautiful woman. I wouldn't want to do anything to upset my patron."

"Wise move." Jethro directed her farther into the gallery, pausing to study each new piece they came to.

Patron? No wonder he'd been hot to get here. A patron to the arts, hmm, seemed there were unexpected depths to Mr. Jethro Calder. Still, being a patron was no excuse to be rude.

"Pay no attention to him." She rolled her eyes at Ethan. "He's still learning his people skills."

"Sweet thing, people use skills on him not the other way around."

"So he tells me." She surveyed Jethro's profile, and observed the pinch at the corner of his eye, a sure sign he hated them talking about him. This was a big night for him as well as Ethan. "He practically gushed while describing your work."

"I have never gushed in my life."

"You were quite animated. With good reason. I love, love, love these pieces." She leaned in close to a picture of an old firehouse with a clock tower. Beside it were photos of a barn, a fire truck and a watch with exposed gears. "Is it a stippling effect?"

"Very perceptive. I'm a master of shadows."

"Really? Shadows." She stepped back and looked at the picture again.

A hand at her waist drew her in front of Jethro. He followed the line of the fire truck with his finger. "The shadows disguise the layering and add depth and dimension." He spoke right in her ear, his breath blowing over the sensitive skin. She shivered and fought the urge to lean back against him.

"Yes. I can see the shadows are key."

"Ethan, there you are. And Jethro, you finally made it. Excellent." A woman with pale skin, black sharp-edged hair and bright red lips swept up to them. She wore a black suit that flowed around a reed-thin body. Hooking her arms through each of the men's, she led them away. "The press are here. Time to make nice."

Lexi followed as best she could considering the crowd quickly closed around her now she didn't have the almighty Jethro Calder with her. When she got cut off, she decided to look around at more of the art. The woman obviously worked for the gallery and it sounded like Jethro would be busy for a few minutes, so he shouldn't miss her.

As she strolled around, she encountered several people she knew. The director of her last dance review at the Golden Link and his wife, a pit boss from Pinnacle and his partner, and a client of hers from Modern Goddess. She chatted briefly with each making sure to talk up the artist; she even influenced a sale with the director.

She kept her eye on Jethro in case her duties were needed but the dark-haired woman, whom she'd learned was Lana, the gallery manager, guarded him like a lioness with her cub. No wannabes were getting through her.

Ethan found Lexi by the buffet table.

"Hey, I've been racking up sales for you."

"I'm glad to hear it." He grabbed one of the fancy bottles of water. "And I'm glad I caught you alone."

"Ah-ah." She shook her finger at him. "You promised Jethro no flirting."

"He's who I want to talk to you about. I want to thank him for his patronage by giving him one of the pictures. I thought you could help me choose one for him."

"Oh, goodness. We really haven't known each other that long."

"Maybe not, but you obviously have his number. And he likes you."

What an interesting comment. She wondered what made him think so. She laughed. "I think we both have you fooled."

"No." Ethan shook his head, his green gaze serious. "As a photographer and an artist, I've learned to read people. I'll admit Jethro is tough to get a read on because he doesn't show much emotion. Most people don't even try unless they want something from him."

"That's just sad." She dismissed a pang of guilt. He couldn't miss what he didn't know he had.

"Yes." Ethan sipped the expensive water. "But it's a persona he fosters. He doesn't let people close."

"You're just proving my case."

"I'm proving my case. Because *you* see the man. You recognized his excitement for my work. You tease him." He shook his head. "Seriously, I've never seen anyone talk to him the way you do. And he takes it. That's how I know he likes you."

Okay, he'd made a couple of good points, but Lexi still wasn't convinced. She'd love for Jethro to like her. It could only help her case, make him predisposed to help her. But the evidence seemed pretty flimsy to her.

"That and the way he looks at you. He hasn't taken his eyes off you all night."

Of course the comment had her searching out Jethro, and sure enough he looked right at them even as he talked with an elderly Japanese couple. She waved and he cocked a dark brow.

"This should really be your choice." She told Ethan.

"I'd still like your help." He insisted.

"Okay, but I should get back to him soon."

"This won't take long," he assured her. "And he's busy taking care of business so we have time."

"Business? You mean patron stuff?"

"No. He doesn't have to do much with that except praise my work."

Uh-oh. She sought him out again. Had she misread the Japanese couple? Could they be overeager gamesters she should be saving him from?

"He's dealing with boring owner stuff." Taking her arm Ethan led her to the first picture. It already had a red dot indicating it had been sold. "There's plenty of time for you to help me."

"I didn't know Jethro owned the gallery. Is he going to be moving it to the Pinnacle?"

"He hasn't mentioned any plans to do so. And it has a following here, so I wouldn't think so."

Interesting. Calder was associated so closely with Pinnacle, she found it difficult to think of him branching out to other casinos. But then Pinnacle wasn't just a casino but part of a huge entertainment conglomerate. The company started out creating and distributing video games. The hotel and casino were decorated based off the first game, a postapocalyptic world where everyone fought to survive.

The diversification made her wonder if he might be considering breaking away from Pinnacle. When she got the time, she'd have to think of what that might mean to her plans.

"Has Jethro shown an interest in any particular piece?" she asked Ethan. "That might be a place to start."

"Good idea. Let me think." He stopped and propped his hands on his hips. His gaze ran over his work displayed on the walls. "No. He's shown general appreciation but not for any specific piece. As I said, Jethro doesn't give up a lot about himself. That's why I was hoping you could help."

Lexi spied a picture of a smoking cigar in a crystal ashtray next to a bottle of aged bourbon in the forefront of an old-fashioned parlor. The colors were muted but powerful. She thought of the old-world elegance of Jethro's restaurant and knew he would appreciate the piece.

"That one." She nodded toward the painting. "It would fit nicely in his restaurant so it's something he'll like."

Ethan considered the painting and then nodded. "You're right. It fits him. Let me grab it before someone buys it. Thanks." He dropped a kiss on her head and strolled off.

"He's still making moves on my date," Jethro drawled close to her ear. "I might have to have a talk with him."

Lexi jumped and swirled around. "Geez, how long have you been there?"

"I just walked up. Why? Something happen you don't want me to know about?"

"Nope. You startled me, is all." Looking to divert his attention from Ethan, she gestured to the crowd. "You must be pleased. Ethan told me you own the gallery."

"It's a recent acquisition."

"Calder." Her former director and his wife came up to them. They made a stunning older couple. "You're doing a great job here at the gallery. Ethan Kittrell is quite a find."

"Thomas and Irene." Jethro offered his hand to the couple. "Thanks for coming. We're always pleased to provide something unique for our collectors."

"Indeed. Irene fell in love with a couple of prints we'll be taking off your hands."

"Irene, I've always admired your taste."

The older woman beamed under his approval. "And you've redeemed my opinion of yours when it comes to women. Oh, I know how you young men like to play the field, but I hope you realize what a treasure you have in this girl."

"You know Lexi." Jethro's expression went blank.

Oops. Time to do her job. He was either insulted, and trying to find a nice way to tell a good client to mind her own business. Or counting to ten before blasting her, with no consideration of future relations.

"Irene, you're going to make me blush." Lexi interceded before Jethro could react. "There's actually nothing romantic going on. Jethro knew Alliyah and today was her birthday. We're just celebrating her together this evening." She smiled through the sadness. "She would have loved this."

"Oh, my dear." Sympathy filled Irene's brown eyes. "She would indeed. My apologies, Jethro. Such a tragedy to lose her so young. Do you know how her—"

"Family is doing?" Lexi quickly interrupted before Irene could mention Alliyah had a daughter. "Yes. Everyone misses Alliyah terribly but we're doing as well as can be expected."

"Good, that's good. She's lucky to have had you for a friend. You let us know if we can do anything."

"Absolutely," Thomas confirmed. "And remember, you're welcome back with the troupe anytime you want."

"Thank you both. You have a good evening now." She gave them both a peck on the cheek and sent them on their way.

"Sorry about that." She patted Jethro on the arm. "But no harm done."

She hoped not anyway. She wanted to be the one to tell Jethro about Jazi. To gauge his reaction and sway him to her cause. He was a sharp guy; she didn't want him to be wondering about a child in Alliyah's life and start counting down the months.

"What are you after?"

"What?"

Jethro's firm grip on her arm gave her no option but to join him in a dimly lit hallway.

"Hey." She tried to shake her arm loose, but he held on.

"Who are you?" he demanded.

"I don't know what you mean. I'm Lexi."

"How is it that you know everyone?"

"I don't know everyone. That's crazy." She pulled against his grip. "You're hurting me." Not really, but he had her unnerved and that was close enough.

"Quit squirming and it won't hurt." His fingers loosened but he retained his hold, forcing her to follow him down the hall.

"Let me go and I'll quit squirming."

He opened the door of a well-appointed office. It had a feminine feel and Lexi guessed it belonged to Lana, the gallery manager.

Jaw clenched, he released her. Then frowned at the red marks on her skin. "Your skin is too delicate."

She rubbed her arm singeing him with a reproachful glare. "Apology accepted."

She dropped into a visitor's chair and crossed her legs.

"Sorry," he muttered belatedly, grudgingly. He sat on the edge of the desk. "Now tell me how you know so many people. I saw you talking with people all over the gallery."

"Just because I talked to people doesn't mean I know them. Is this about me not protecting you from the madding crowd? You seemed fine whenever I glanced your way."

"Mocking me will not save you. Answer the question."

"Save me?" She laughed.

He didn't.

"You targeted me, Ms. Malone. I want to know why."

CHAPTER FOUR

LEXI PUSHED THROUGH her front door, slammed it shut behind her and threw the bolts. Unable to shake the sense of being pursued, she backed away.

Pull it together, girl. The man had better things to do than chase her down.

After Jethro dropped his question bomb, she'd slipped out when Lana and Ethan walked in carrying the piece Ethan had chosen for Jethro.

Best timing ever.

Okay, she'd panicked.

She hadn't been prepared for his questions.

In the bedroom she grabbed a nightgown—a lavender bit of silk edged in black lace—and headed into the bathroom for a shower. She'd bolted. What else could she do? He thought she was some femme fatale intent on getting something from him.

And, in a way, she was.

He'd been so intense she didn't know if she'd ever be prepared to face off against him.

But she would. For Jazi.

Lexi clung to the fact he gave Miguel a healthy tip when he learned of his new baby. It showed he had some sensitivity for kids. Right?

During the cab ride home she'd decided she needed to call tomorrow and make an appointment with Jethro. She'd see him before she went into work and get this all straightened out.

Stepping under the spray, she rinsed her hair, letting the

hot water soothe her. As plans went, it lacked finesse and relied heavily on his willingness to see her again. But what she'd learned of him tonight told her an up-front, honest approach was her best bet.

All the things she could say filtered through her head as she dried off and applied a tropical-scented lotion in honor of Ethan's *Escape* painting. The silk of her nightgown glided over her skin in a sensual fall, ending at midthigh. She continued to ruminate while combing and drying her hair. The thick auburn tresses were still damp when she thought she heard a knock on her door.

Flipping off the hairdryer, she listened and the knocking came again. She wrinkled her nose. The last thing she needed tonight was the distraction of a friend coming over for gossip and coffee, something dancers liked to do. Since she'd left the troupe, she often had people dropping by.

Or maybe that's exactly what she needed. To just get out of her head and focus on someone else for a while. By the time she reached the door, she was ready to embrace whoever stood on the other side.

She swung the door wide. "Hell…"

Bug-eyed, she stared at Jethro Calder.

"What? How?"

His navy eyes swept over her darkening to near black by the time his gaze met hers. Who knew black could show such heat? He stepped forward, crowding her.

Instinctively she backed away.

He kept coming and she kept retreating until he cleared the threshold. He closed the door behind him.

"Are you crazy?" he demanded. "You don't answer the door without knowing who's on the other side." His gaze made another journey over her as he continued to stalk her. "Especially dressed like that.

"How are you here?" She meant it as an accusation. It came out in a whisper as she continued to dodge his pursuit. She hit a chair and sidestepped.

"Does it matter?" He caught her elbow when she tripped over the ottoman and nearly landed on her rump. "You wanted me and, sunshine, you've got me." Lifting her to her toes, he lowered his head and slanted his lips over hers.

Her hands landed on his chest ready to push him away. But oh, my...

For all his ferocity, when his mouth took hers, there was no anger, no punishing assault on her senses, nothing but pure passion, undiluted desire. The soft pressure of his lips lured her into opening to him.

Oh, he took, with a seductive demand that had her lifting farther onto her toes and looping her arms around his neck. Her mind was lost, transferring the cadence of his touch to notes in her head. Grip, glide, soft, firm, thrust, nip—the heat built in body and melody to a place she'd never been before.

He whispered erotic threats and words were added to the song in her head.

As she floated on sensation, he became her rock, hard, solid, grounded. His arms were a haven of safety and the orchestrators of the sensation and rhythm surging through her.

She wanted more. Now. More of his taste, more of his touch, more of his heat. More.

And then her knees hit up against something and she sat. She blinked and her bedroom came into focus. He'd moved them down the hall and into her room without her even noticing they were moving.

Eyes liquid with arousal, he watched her as he unbuttoned his shirt. He'd lost his jacket somewhere along the trek to the bedroom.

And OMG, she'd lost her nightgown. She sat in front of him in nothing more than a rosy blush of need.

Sanity came rushing back with a roar.

"Stop. Whoa." Grabbing the edge of her sunny yellow comforter, she wrapped it around herself. She wasn't modest, a dancer couldn't afford the luxury, but she felt too exposed under his ravenous regard. "I'm sorry, but this is not going to happen."

His fingers froze on the last connected button. "Excuse me?" Dark brows lowered in a fierce scowl.

Intimidating, much? Oh, yeah.

"I'm sorry," she said again. And she meant it. He'd just lit her up like a torch in every way imaginable, body, mind, soul. And he couldn't be more off-limits if he were the Pope. "This isn't what I intended when I sought you out."

If anything the scowl deepened. "Explain."

The demand was nearly a growl. It occurred to her she should be afraid, but she wasn't. She'd been in his arms, felt his body resonate with hers. He'd never hurt a woman. Not physically anyway. He had too much control. But there were worse ways he could make her pay. Her mind raced. This needed to be handled carefully.

Feeling at a disadvantage, she inched to the side and stood up. He stepped back giving her some room. She breathed in relief. "I'd prefer to get dressed for this conversation if you don't mind."

It wasn't a question and still he looked ready to protest, a signal to her that he was in charge of what happened here. Never mind it was her apartment. Clearly the man was used to being in command wherever he went. Finally, he gave a brief nod and left the room.

Okay, in no way did his silence reassure her. Anger defined the rigid line of his shoulders as he strode away.

"There's wine in the refrigerator and glasses in the cupboard to the right," she called out, then bit her lip. This wasn't a date, but she knew if he left, she'd lose all chance of ever talking to him.

Ready or not the time had come to plead her case.

She grabbed clothes from the dresser and hurried into them, soft gray sweats and a baby-blue sweater cropped at the waist. In the bathroom she tamed her hair into a ponytail and noticed the pants clung to the curves of her butt and the sweater played peekaboo with her belly button. Dang. Time didn't allow for another change.

Tugging at the hem of the sweater she went to wrangle the shark in her living room.

He leaned against the counter of her kitchen island, sipping a glass of wine. His dark gaze ran over her making her senses tingle.

"You have five minutes," he stated in that near growl that just added to his effect on her body.

Ignoring the urges she could never act on, she helped herself to some wine. She perched on one of the bar stools at the island and took a sip.

"Four minutes. Don't try my patience, Ms. Malone."

"I really wanted to do this differently. I was going to come by your office—" She slanted him a wry glance and reached for a picture frame at the end of the counter. Handing it to him, she said softly, "Alliyah had a daughter. Her name is Jasmine. She's twenty-three-months-old."

He refused to accept the picture, didn't even glance at it. "What does that have to do with me?"

"You said I targeted you. This is why. In the article I read about Pinnacle, there was a picture included. You and the other executives were holding up the award. I saw your birthmark."

One dark brow lifted. "You targeted me because of my birthmark?"

So cool, so unaffected when her whole life weighed in the balance.

"Yes." She hesitated, prayed this was the right decision, that she wasn't risking losing Jazi to the one person Lexi could never get her back from. "Because Jasmine has the same birthmark."

Okay, she had Jethro's attention. Truthfully, she'd had his attention from the moment she walked into The Beacon in that snug little black dress and he hoped she'd be his date. But never in his wildest imaginings had he considered the night would end up here. He'd been suspicious of her, enough to follow her here.

The sight of her draped in damp silk, white teeth biting her lush lower lip, had sidetracked him for an irrational moment. A hot, blow-his-mind moment that should never have happened. The lack of discipline was in no small part responsible for his…mood.

No one ever accused him of being dense. She meant to suggest Jasmine was his daughter. And he dealt with numbers every day, so he could do the math. The timing fit. But not the circumstances. He never had unprotected sex, never.

"Coincidence," he stated.

She groaned and shook her head. "You don't strike me as a man big on coincidence."

She wasn't wrong. But he didn't budge. No way was she laying this on him. Family wasn't in his future. In order to survive, he'd had to shut down his emotions. It was a lesson too well learned to change. Plus, he'd force no one to share his secret shame. All in all he sucked at relationships, lacked the skill set as one woman told him. When he hit thirty, he quit trying. He'd found Excursions about a year later.

So no, no family for him. And he was fine with that. He'd come to terms with the notion long ago, had made it clear to all who knew him. Jethro wasn't prepared for that to change now.

Certainly not on the whim of a woman he barely knew. Even if she turned him so upside down he'd practically jumped her as soon as he'd walked inside the door. What had he been thinking?

The problem was he hadn't been thinking; he'd been feeling. Further proof emotions couldn't be trusted.

"You have the wrong man."

Lexi slid from the stool and held the picture frame up in front of him. "She has your eyes."

Don't look. It's a ploy. She just wants a rich baby daddy to support the orphan and you're the lucky dupe.

The warning blasted through Jethro's brain. But not even his legendary restraint proved stronger than the compulsion to look.

The baby was beautiful. A little girl with wild black curls and a smile so big and sweet he felt blessed just seeing it. She danced in the picture, her arms were raised and her tiny butt was cocked to the side and one pink-sandaled foot poised in the air. Jethro spied a smudge on one wrist that could be a birthmark. She had light beige skin, a sharp little nose.

And midnight-blue eyes ringed by lush black lashes.

Yeah, the birthmark was iffy, but those eyes, he'd never seen that exact color anywhere but in the mirror. The shape of her eyes, and her straight little eyebrows also matched his.

"I'm not looking for money." Lexi broke the silence. "And I don't expect you to change your life. I read that you don't want a family."

"Then what is this about, Ms. Malone?" He placed the picture facedown on the counter, the better to concentrate on the woman before him. His life just did a one-eighty. He needed to focus. "What do you want?"

"Can you call me Lexi?" Her cheeks flushed a delightful shade of pink. "We just shared…" She waved her hand in the direction of the bedroom. "…a moment. It seems foolish to be so formal."

"I've been foolish in more than one regard tonight, Ms. Malone—calling me on it isn't your smartest move."

"Why foolish?" she demanded, crossing her arms over her chest.

Her position drew attention to her breasts, which were small but plump. And pert, a detail he remembered in vivid Technicolor. Her stance also caused a thin strip of pale skin to show at her waist. His fingers itched to touch that silky skin again.

"Because you didn't have control of every moment of

the evening?" she went on. "Because you actually enjoyed yourself? News flash, people do it all the time."

"Because none of it was real." Or did her show of attitude indicate otherwise? Was she upset because she, too, had got more caught up in their time together than she'd intended?

So what if she was? It didn't matter. Couldn't matter. She was so off-limits she may as well live on Venus.

"What do you want from me?" If it wasn't money or for him to assume care of Jasmine, which would definitely change his life, then what else was there?

She sighed and relaxed her stance. "I want to adopt her."

He lifted both brows. That was a response he hadn't expected. And why did it give him mixed feelings of relief and disappointment?

"Sounds like you have it all worked out. So why do you need me?"

A look of anguish flashed through her pure blue eyes.

"Even though I'm Jazi's godmother and it's what Alliyah would want, I don't meet the qualifications for an adoptive parent. I'm single and a dancer." She shrugged as if that said it all. "I need you to assume custody and then we can do a private adoption."

Custody. The word sent a rumble of dread down his back. And made him wonder. "Where is she?"

"Child Protective Services took her away. She's in foster c-care." She pressed her lips together and blinked a couple of times. "Alliyah would hate that."

The thought of his daughter in foster care burned like acid through his blood.

Except she may not be his daughter at all. The fact she had a birthmark and his eyes was circumstantial at best. Still, he'd spent too many years in the grueling system to be placid about any innocent being tossed to that merciless grist mill.

"I get to see her and I go as often as they'll let me, but if I don't do something soon, they'll release her for adoption

and I'll never get to see her again." In her eagerness, she
stepped closer bringing the scent of a tropical night with
her. She raised pleading eyes to his. "You have to help me."

"I don't actually." Time to go. This woman got to him.
Had since the moment she walked into his world. If he didn't
leave now, he'd promise her the moon. "I need to consider
what you've told me." He moved to the door, grabbing his
jacket en route. "I'll have my assistant call you for an appointment in the next day or two."

She nodded. Her arms were crossed over her chest again,
but the pose held elements of disappointment and hope, as
if she were holding herself together by a thread.

Damn it. He charged across the room and grabbed up
the picture. "I'm taking this with me."

This time when he left, he didn't look back.

There was no going to sleep after Jethro's visit. She tried.
And failed. She tossed and turned, replaying her conversation with him over and over in her head. After two hours,
she finally gave up and crawled out of bed still not knowing what to think.

She dragged herself to the kitchen and the coffeepot. The
scent of the fresh-ground beans perked her up. She stood
over the machine as it brewed, holding her cup under the
spigot to catch the first stream and then switching in the pot.

She wandered to the couch and curled up with her cup.
Dancers by trade tended to be night people. She used to be
at her peak at this hour. Tonight her brain barely functioned
except it wouldn't shut off.

Jethro had pointed out he didn't have to help her. But
he'd taken the picture. And his assistant would be calling
to make an appointment. Did that mean he believed her?
Or was his comment just a way to get him out of the apartment without a further scene and she'd never see him again?

No. She refused to believe he'd just walk away. She'd

seen the look in his eyes when he'd stared at the picture of Jazi. He saw the resemblance. And he'd act on it.

Wouldn't he?

Stop. She couldn't take this vicious Ferris wheel any longer. She drained her coffee and went to change. She needed to dance.

She'd given up her vocation, but she'd always dance. She needed the release like she needed to breathe. Especially now. The exercise would help her to get out of her head and relieve the tension still lingering in her body from its encounter with Jethro's. There had to be a gym open somewhere at this hour.

Jethro stood staring out the floor-to-ceiling window of his penthouse suite. The lights and flash of the Las Vegas Strip spread out before him in a glimmering kaleidoscope of color and movement. And he saw none of it.

He couldn't get the picture of a dancing baby with midnight-blue eyes out of his head.

He'd resolved to never have a family. But Lexi's announcement shook him. If he had a daughter, that changed everything.

Except it didn't have to.

Lexi wanted to raise the baby as her own. She couldn't be more clear that he wasn't invited to the party. His money and presence were not needed.

A knock came at the door and then Clay Hoffman stepped inside. Tall and blond, the man moved with military precision. You could put the grunt in a suit, but you couldn't take the army out of the man. A foster brother and friend, Clay ran all things security related for Pinnacle Enterprises.

"I got your summons." Clay went to the bar and helped himself to a drink. "What's the emergency?" He dropped down on the brown suede couch and glanced around. "Where are Jackson and Ryan?"

"They aren't coming." Jethro joined his friend in the living area. "This is personal."

"Personal?" Clay's brows rose. "And it couldn't wait until morning? Do you have an incident with one of your other companies? Cause you know the guys are more than willing to help even when it's not Pinnacle business."

"I prefer to keep this private for now." Jethro picked up his abandoned drink and sipped. The burn of whiskey down his throat—just what he needed to loosen his tongue. "It appears I may have a daughter."

"As if." Clay laughed and sipped his drink. "Come on, tell me what this is about."

Jethro simply stared at him.

Finally Clay's eyes went big and he shook his head. "You're serious. You have a daughter?"

"Maybe. Probably." Jethro glanced at the picture frame on the coffee table.

"Is this her?" Clay reached for the picture and stared. "Oh, hell."

"So you see it, too?"

"That she has your eyes? It's hard to miss."

"I'm told she has my birthmark, too."

Clay returned his attention to the photo and squinted. "Hmm. Could be, I guess. I'd want to see it up close to confirm. And we'll need a DNA test. Who is the mother?"

"And that's why I called you." He rarely asked for help. But in this case he knew his friend would direct him through the quagmire discreetly and efficiently. Jethro filled Clay in on all the details. "I need to know for certain she's mine before I make any decisions."

"Of course. I already have a sample of your DNA." The Fabulous Four were all millionaires and after Jackson went AWOL last year Clay had collected DNA samples from each of them as a security measure. "It shouldn't be a problem getting the baby's from the county. And I have a lab that will turn the results around in a day."

"Good." Jethro stood to pace. "I want to see her."

"Whoa." Clay held his hands up in a time-out gesture. "If you're serious about giving her up, that may not be a good idea."

"It's the right thing to do, don't you think? Giving her up?"

"Only you can answer that, bro." Clay's alert gaze pierced through Jethro's ambivalence. "You never talk about family, except to say you never planned to have one of your own."

"Because I don't have any. The foster system was never able to locate any next of kin for me." There was no record of who'd abandoned him. Kind of hard to get info from no one.

"In that case this little girl may be the only family you'll ever know. You should think carefully before you sign your rights away."

Jethro shot his friend a get-real grimace. "I'm not equipped to raise a kid. I don't scare easy but the thought of taking on custody of a little girl outright terrifies me. But I'd castrate myself before I left her in foster care."

"Ouch," Clay flinched, "but I hear you. You know it doesn't have to be all or nothing. You can negotiate the terms."

Jethro shook his head. Sharing custody with the red-hot redhead was not going to happen. Between baby and dancer, he'd never know another moment of peace. "Lexi made her terms clear. I won't jeopardize Jasmine's future."

He hesitated. "Jackson and Grace might raise her."

Jethro had considered the option, but he wouldn't do that to his friend. "They aren't even married yet. I can't ask them to do that. And if she were that close, I may not be able to refrain from interfering, which wouldn't be fair to anyone. No, Lexi Malone is her godmother. She obviously loves the child. It's the best solution."

"Then I recommend you don't see her."

Knowing Clay was right, Jethro struggled with the irrational compulsion. He prided himself on making dispassionate decisions. Not this time. "If she's mine, I have to see her."

Clay sighed. "If she's yours, I'll set it up."

Lexi's day didn't get any better as it wore on. Jethro's assistant called but the appointment had been postponed for a day.

The delay was torture. Every minute dragged. And what filled her head? The feel and taste of Jethro Calder. When she'd sought him out last night, the last thing she'd contemplated was an attraction to the man.

Because it complicated much?

Of course she never could have predicted he'd track her to her apartment and seduce her in her own living room. Thank her lucky stars she came to her senses before he actually got her in bed. But it had been too close, the struggle too hard for her peace of mind.

She hadn't lost her head like that in…no, she'd never lost her head like that. Been so swept away by a man's kiss, by his touch, that she lost all sense of the here and now.

The fact he was her goddaughter's father put him off-limits. Those forbidden moments in his arms were hot enough to give her regrets, but Jazi had to come first.

Desperate and longing to see her little girl, she called Jazi's foster mother about setting up an appointment to see the baby, but it wasn't convenient today. Instead they made arrangements for the next day.

Waiting proved too brutal so Lexi called in to Modern Goddess to see if she could put in extra hours and went into work early.

Between waiting and fighting off memories of Jethro's kiss it looked set to be a long day.

Long didn't describe her day. Try excruciating. Lexi decided she required the distraction of people around her for dinner. She didn't set out for that place to be The Beacon, but somehow that's where she ended up.

And surprise, surprise Calder sat at the bar.

Lexi hesitated, about to leave. They had an appointment for the next day. She should leave him in peace. Instead she slid onto the stool next to his.

"A glass of white wine, please," she said to the bartender. "Mr. Calder."

"Ms. Malone."

"Was your day a living hell? Because mine was."

"This is Las Vegas. It's not unusual for the weather to be warm this time of year."

She laughed. "And here I thought you had no sense of humor."

"I'd like a bit of peace with my drink if you don't mind."

"I do mind. I'm no good at waiting. I need someone to talk to and as I'm trying to be discreet about this whole thing, you're the only one I can talk to."

"You're assuming a lot."

"Not so much." Her wine appeared in front of her. She smiled her thanks at the bartender. "Our appointment tomorrow tells me you acted on the information I gave you."

"I may just want more information."

"If that were the case, the appointment would have been for today. You don't appear to be too good at waiting either."

He sent her a searing sideways glare. "The test results aren't back yet."

"Bummer." She sipped her wine. "I guess we'll have to talk about something else."

"Or you could go away."

"I just got my wine."

He tilted his drink, ice clinking against the glass. "I suppose next you'll want dinner."

"I thought you'd never ask." She snagged a pretzel from a bowl on the bar. "It'll be our second nondate."

"Is that supposed to be funny?" he demanded, clearly annoyed. "Because it's not funny."

"Ah, the stuffed shirt is back. Now he has no sense of humor."

He lifted a finger and the bartender came over. "Sam, a table for two please."

"Of course." Sam went back to serving.

In less than a minute the maître d' appeared beside them. "Sir, your table is ready."

"Thank you." Jethro gestured for her to follow the tall man.

"Do you like salmon?" he asked as they wound through the tables.

"I do."

The maître d' stopped and waved them into a quiet alcove where a large table was set for two. "Is there anything I can get for you?"

"Two specials. Would you care for another drink?" Jethro addressed the question to her.

"No, but I'd like water, please." She unfolded the linen napkin into her lap.

Jethro nodded to the maître d'. The man bowed and acknowledged, "Two specials and two waters. Enjoy your meal."

"Nice." The alcove had the feel of an elegant library with a faux fireplace. Above the mantel Lexi admired the Kittrell picture the artist had given Jethro. The cigar-and-decanter piece fit the area perfectly. "I'm impressed."

Jethro pointed to the Kittrell. "Ethan said you helped pick out the picture he gave me."

"He asked for some advice. I warned him we didn't know each other well, but he insisted. The piece reminded me of The Beacon so I thought you'd like it."

"I do, very much."

Did he? His stoic features were so hard to read. "I'm

glad. He wanted to please you. He was very grateful for what you've done for him."

"Good talent deserves to be recognized." He sat back so the waiter could deliver the water and rolls. "Have you ever eaten here?"

"No, but I've wanted to. I've heard lots of good things about The Beacon, even before I came to the Pinnacle." She grinned at him. "I never would have bet I'd be sitting at the owner's table when I finally made it here."

"The world works in mysterious ways."

"So true." She spread butter on one of the warm yeast rolls. "If I hadn't gone to one more dance class, I would never have met Alliyah, never moved to Las Vegas, never have met you."

He eyed her speculatively. "One wonders if there would still be a Jasmine?"

"I don't know. Alliyah's path might have been different as well. But it didn't happen differently and here we are." She bit into the roll and chewed. And then moaned. "OMG, these rolls are delicious. They practically melt in your mouth. Oh, yum." She pushed the basket toward him. "Keep those over there. Do not let me have another one. Not even if I beg."

"Naturally, I've looked you up," he stated. "But why don't you tell me a bit about yourself?"

He probably hadn't gotten the full report on her yet. She had no doubt whatsoever someone was working on one. "I was a music prodigy as a child. I graduated when I was fifteen, played violin with the Michigan Philharmonic at the age of sixteen while pursuing my PhD at the University of Michigan."

"You have a PhD in music and you're a hairdresser?"

"I burned out in music when I was young. I love it, but on my own terms. And I never had that luxury."

The waiter arrived with plates of salmon served with polenta and roasted vegetables. She leaned back to give him access. The food smelled as good as it looked.

"Playing with the Michigan Philharmonic at the age of sixteen is pretty impressive."

"Yes, and I don't regret it. But I wanted to dance and my mom shut me down every time I asked. At eighteen I came into a small inheritance from my father and I took off."

"Where'd you go?"

"New York, of course. It's where dancers go. But it's expensive. And competitive. And I was so new to it. Thankfully, I met Alliyah."

"And ended up in Las Vegas. You fought so hard to dance, why give it up now?"

She shook her head, poked at the fish. Dance would always be a part of her life. Except now it would only be a form of exercise. She still struggled with the change.

"Dancing is considered high-risk employment because contracts can be limited in term and there's the chance of injury. Plus, most of the work is at night. So it's not a good job for a single woman looking to adopt. I have to agree with the last. If I get custody of Jazi, I want to be there for her. As a hairdresser, I can adjust my hours so I can spend part of every day with her."

She laid down her fork and leaned across the table. "Thank you for listening to me last night. Thank you for considering my request."

Eyes on hers, he shook his head, the dim light playing over his dark hair. "Don't get ahead of yourself, Ms. Malone. We don't even know if there's anything to thank me for yet. If I have my wish, there won't be."

Her heart hiccupped at his declaration. Everything she longed for would turn his world upside down. Impulsively she reached across the table and laid her hand on his. "I'll still say thank you because you've given me something I haven't had in a long time. Hope."

* * *

"Good morning." Clay strolled through Jethro's open office door. He carried a manila envelope in one hand.

Jethro nodded for Clay to close the door and then he tossed his pen on his desk and leaned back in his chair. This better be the test results.

His nerves were so frayed he couldn't concentrate. He'd been a beast all morning. His staff mutinied twenty minutes ago and left en masse for an extended coffee break. He'd be lucky if he saw them before lunch. Nothing got in the way of work, but before she left he finally gave in and had his assistant clear his schedule for the day.

"I heard hell froze over up here." Clay dropped into one of the black leather visitor chairs. "I had to come check it out."

"You'll get a front-row seat if those aren't the test results. I'm about to gnaw off my own thumbs."

"These things take time. I had the lab run the tests twice, just to be sure." Clay held out the envelope. "Fresh off the printer."

"And?" Jethro took the envelope, set it in front of him. He'd look at the reports when he was alone.

Clay didn't leave him dangling. "And congratulations, Daddy."

Jethro narrowed his eyes in a glare.

Clay just grinned. "It had to be said. This is a big deal. And if you have your way, it'll never happen again."

"It's for the best."

"Is it?"

A brief knock sounded at the door and then it opened and Jackson Hawke and Ryan Green walked in.

"You don't look dead," Jackson remarked as he settled into the second visitor's chair.

"No, but he's definitely pale. Pasty actually." Ryan perched on the edge of the credenza in front of the window. "He could be dying."

"Ha-ha." Jethro rolled his shoulders. "I'm fine."

"He's not fine."

Jethro glared at the security executive. "I am fine. I just have something to deal with."

He hadn't meant to tell them all, a foolish assumption. They were almost as bad as a pack of women when it came to ferreting out information about each other. And he'd need Ryan's help with the contract and adoption. No need to keep Jackson in the dark when everyone else knew.

Bottom line, he struggled with the secret he already had; no way was he harnessing himself with another one. He fought the urge to pace. The tension in his shoulders was so tight he feared the smallest move might break a bone. His friends looked at him expectantly, their silence a deafening demand. He cleared his throat. Almost wishing Clay would blurt it out saving Jethro from having to say the words.

As if reading his thoughts Clay lifted one brown brow in question.

Jethro shook him off with a minute shake of his head.

"It turns out." Another clearing of his throat. "I have a daughter."

With the words spoken something miraculous happened. Tension drained out of his shoulders and air flowed freely into his lungs. He hadn't even noticed the shallow breaths he'd been taking. Sharing eased some of his pent-up nerves. Not all by any means, but at least he could think again.

"A daughter." Jackson raked a hand through his hair. "No wonder you're freaking." Sympathy shone out of green eyes. He alone knew Jethro's secret.

Still, freaking was a bit strong.

"Does this mean we get to call you Daddy?" Ryan grinned.

Jethro's heart accelerated and tension racketed back into his shoulders. Okay, freaking summed it up nicely.

"I won't be raising her," he announced and filled them

in on the details. "She's better off with someone who loves her," he finished.

"That's a tough decision." All amusement had vanished from Ryan's strong features. "I'm not sure I could walk away."

"You all know how rotten I am at relationships. I wouldn't begin to know how to raise a little girl. I'm doing what's best for her."

"You're not alone, dude," Ryan reminded him. "Four men and a baby. We could make it work."

"Don't forget Grace and Sierra." Jackson tossed his fiancée and assistant into the mix. "They say it takes a village. Well, we are a village."

A lump formed in Jethro's throat. The unhesitating support amazed and humbled him. He shouldn't be surprised, but he was. It made him stop, made him think. But…

"Thank you, my brothers. Seriously, I love you for offering." The words were rusty yet heartfelt. "But it wouldn't be fair to shake up your lives because of an unexpected development in mine. Not when there's an acceptable alternative."

He had nothing of value to offer an innocent child. He was damaged, with no idea how to manage a lasting relationship. Not even his mother had wanted him. She'd tossed him away like yesterday's leftovers.

He'd been found in a Dumpster when he was three weeks old half-starved and suffering from exposure. Lucky to be alive. He sometimes wondered if anyone actually believed that.

Infants usually adopted quickly. But the exposure had damaged his lungs and stomach so he'd been a sickly child. No one wanted to adopt a sick baby.

He'd learned his history when he was six from a foster mother upset because he'd thrown up on her new shoes. He was quickly removed from the home. But how do you get over knowing no one wanted you? Not even your mom. He got moved around a lot after that. His ailments went away, but they said he began acting out, became a problem child.

No. He'd just been trying to prove he was the biggest, the best, the smartest. That he mattered. Even after thirty-five years, he was still trying to prove it.

Talk about dysfunctional. So no, it was best if he were not made responsible for the care and feeding of a toddler. Even if she was the only family he'd ever know. He'd been told, more than once, that he was self-absorbed, but not ever he was that selfish.

Jasmine deserved someone who fought for her, someone who skipped to watch a fake thunderstorm then watched the show with childlike wonder. Someone who spoke to strangers and thought up ways to pamper new mothers.

Of one thing he was certain, life with Lexi would be filled with light, laughter and joy. She'd make every day an adventure of music and dance. Unlike him. His life revolved around work and numbers, boring, steady, reliable numbers, which suited him fine, but hardly rated against the musical arts.

Lexi would cherish Jasmine and that was the best gift Jethro could ever give her.

"Well, if that's decided," Clay glanced at his watch, "I made arrangements for you to see her this morning."

Jackson and Ryan looked at each other and then at Jethro.

"Do you think that's wise?" Jackson asked.

"Probably not." Jethro slid the manila envelope into his top desk drawer and closed it. "But it's something I have to do."

At least once he needed to hold his daughter in his arms.

CHAPTER FIVE

LEXI OPENED THE GATE and walked up the path toward the door of a two-story house. Before she got to the porch, the door opened and a slightly plump blonde waved.

"Hi, Lexi." She stepped aside and a wild-haired child shot out the door and down the shallow step. "She's excited to see you."

"Lexi!" Jazi called out as she raced as fast as her little legs allowed down the walk.

Lexi's heart overflowed with love and she went down on her knees to catch the tiny fireball when she launched herself into Lexi's arms.

"Lexi!" Little arms wrapped around her neck and soft lips smeared something sticky across her cheek.

"Jazi." Lexi returned the smooches, hugging the baby close for a long minute. "I've missed you so much."

"Miss you." Jazi repeated. She framed Lexi's face in her hands and demanded, "Home."

Lexi's heart wrenched. "I know, baby girl. I'm working on it." She turned her attention to Jazi's foster mom, who had to stay within sight of her during the visit. "Hi, Diana, how are you?"

The court had granted Lexi supervised visitation. She'd argued, but in the end, she'd taken what she could get.

"Fine. But it's turning into a busy day. This little one is quite popular today. I know you like to play with her outside, but can you come inside? I want to do a little more straightening up."

At first Jazi's foster mother had been reserved with Lexi,

almost cold. She'd probably been told Lexi had tried to circumvent the system. But as time went by and she saw Jazi's affection for Lexi, she'd loosened up.

"Diana, your place always looks great, but sure." Lexi followed the other woman inside to the family room. "Why don't you find us a book to read?" she told Jazi as she settled on the love seat. What did company for Jazi mean? Caseworker visits were usually impromptu, so it wasn't that. "Who is coming to see Jazi?"

Diana glanced over to where Jazi pawed through the bookshelf. Keeping her voice low she said, "Her father. The caseworker called me this morning and said someone came forward."

"Really?" Adrenaline spiked Lexi's heartbeat. Jethro. It had to be.

"Yes. They did the tests and he is her father. He asked if he could see her this morning."

"Fishies." Jazi dropped a book in Lexi's lap.

"Oh, yeah, let's look at the pretty fishies." Lexi opened the book and mindlessly pointed at the colorful fish. Thankfully Jazi just liked to look at the pictures and flip the pages so she didn't notice her godmother had suddenly gone brainless.

Her hands shook on the stiff pages. *Angels above* she prayed this was good news and not Jethro deciding to raise Jazi himself. It was her biggest fear. Because, seriously who could resist that joyful smile?

"This is exciting, right?" Diana sat down on the matching striped couch. "I know you were seeking custody. But it's good that she'll be with her father." She mouthed the last word.

"I hope so."

Diana nodded. "It's always a concern, isn't it, putting a child in an unknown situation?"

"Yes." Lexi looked down at the book unable to take the sympathy in the older woman's eyes.

The doorbell rang. For a moment she and Diana locked gazes.

Jazi just took off for the door. She loved company.

"No, Jazi." Diana caught her and brought her back to Lexi.

"Should I go?" Lexi asked.

Diana shrugged. "It's okay with me if you stay. We'll see what they say."

Lexi's heart lodged in her throat. She wanted to believe in Jethro, but the man didn't help build a multibillion-dollar company without having a ruthless streak.

She lifted Jazi into her lap and gave her a squeeze before redirecting her attention to the book. If these were the last minutes Lexi ever had with her goddaughter, she'd make them count. "One little fishy, two little fishy."

"You have reached your destination." Jethro parked his car across the street from a two-story house in a nice middle-class neighborhood. A pretty redhead with a skip in her step opened the gate and started up the walk.

Surprise shook him, along with a healthy dose of desire.

She moved as if she had a constant strain of music running through her head.

Something he understood better now he knew she was a music prodigy.

"The caseworker is meeting us here." Clay reached for his door latch. "That's probably her."

"Hold on." Jethro laid a staying hand on his arm. "That's Lexi Malone. What's she doing here?"

"She has supervised visitation rights."

"Supervised." Jethro watched as the door to the house opened and a blonde woman greeted Lexi. And then a tiny bit of a girl dashed past the woman and flew down the walk to throw herself into Lexi's arms. It was almost painful to watch as the two clung together. "Did you find out the full details of why they've refused Lexi custody? Lexi hinted to me that it has a lot to do with her single status and being able to adequately provide for her, but I get the feeling there might be more to it."

"I'm still working on it." Clay's phone buzzed. "This might be something now." He took the call.

Jethro tuned him out as he watched the scene in the yard until the three disappeared inside. He'd never exchanged a greeting with such intensity in his life. It was an honest, unrehearsed demonstration of love and affection and reinforced his decision. It would be criminal to separate the two.

"I've got the information." Clay tucked his phone away.

"What?"

"The reason they won't allow Lexi custody is partly because of what she told you, that she's a single parent in high-risk employment that requires her to be away from the home at night. But she has a black mark against her because she kept Jasmine without proper authority."

Jethro relaxed. "Red tape. She changed her employment. And I'm sure she was only doing what she thought best in caring for Jasmine after Alliyah's accident," he pointed out.

"That was mentioned, but she has no recent employment history as a cosmetologist so that actually worked against her."

"Tough luck for her." Especially after the heartfelt exchange he just witnessed.

"Her story holds up," Clay stated. "But she could still be playing an angle."

A dark car pulled to the curb and parked, blocking his view of the house. A plump woman in a gray suit that matched her hair climbed from the car.

"That's likely the social worker. So what are you going to do?" Clay repeated. "Are you changing your mind? Are you going to leave Jasmine in foster care?"

"No way." Jethro opened his car door and stepped out. With Clay at his side he crossed the street. "I'd keep her myself before I let her stay in the system."

* * *

Lexi held her breath as Mrs. Leslie walked in followed by Jethro and a large blond man. If they were here then the blood tests must have come back.

Jasmine was his daughter.

"Lexi." Mrs. Leslie greeted her with a smile. "I didn't expect you to be here." Then the smile dimmed as the awkwardness of the moment hit the social worker.

Lexi liked the woman—she reminded Lexi of Mrs. Claus, always cheerful and looking on the bright side of things. Qualities that had to be difficult considering her profession.

"We made arrangements for the visit yesterday." She stood and set Jazi down. "But I should go. Let Mr. Calder have his visit."

The little girl made a stark cry and lifted her arms to be held. Even the toddler felt the tension in the room. Lexi lifted her into her arms. Jazi laid her head on Lexi's shoulder and eyed the men suspiciously.

"Perhaps it would be best if you continued your visit at another time." Mrs. Leslie didn't bother with introductions. "We do have some business to conduct today."

"Of course." Carefully avoiding Jethro's gaze, Lexi stood and tried to hand Jazi off to her foster mother, but the baby shook her head and clung to Lexi. "It's okay, pumpkin. I'll see you another day. Be a good girl and go to Diana."

"No." Jazi was having none of it. "Jab-da, Lexi!" For all it was gibberish the sentiment was clear. She wanted Lexi. When Lexi tried to pull her little arms from around her neck, Jazi began to cry.

Matching tears blurred Lexi's vision. Leaving Jazi like this was breaking her heart.

"I don't mind if Ms. Malone stays." Jethro broke the tension-fraught moment. "If it makes it easier on the child."

Mrs. Leslie visibly relaxed. "Thank you, Mr. Calder. I do

feel it's for the best. Jasmine is still emotionally fragile. I believe Ms. Malone will be a calming influence for your visit."

"I'll be in the kitchen if you need me." Diana made her escape.

Lexi resumed her seat and rocked Jazi gently. "You're my big girl, my brave girl. You like Mrs. Leslie. And these nice men just want to say hello. Come on, pumpkin," she tickled her ribs, "give me a smile."

The corner of Jazi's mouth twitched up, but she still snuggled close.

"That's my big girl. Everything is going to be all right," Lexi whispered, needing the reassurance as much as Jazi. "I love you."

Mrs. Leslie settled into the corner of the couch and waved Jethro toward the love seat where Lexi sat with Jasmine. "Perhaps you'd like to tell me how you know Ms. Malone."

Jethro's gaze circled the room seeking another seat, but his associate, whom Lexi recognized as Clay Hoffman, dropped into the corner opposite Mrs. Leslie, which left a seat squeezed between the two of them or next to Lexi. He met her stare before sitting. His features were unreadable, leaving Lexi wondering how much he'd reveal to the caseworker.

When he sat down, the roomy sectional suddenly became a tight fit. She tried to move over to give him space—and her some distance—but he just filled in the area she created. From shoulder to knees they were pressed up against each other.

Yeah, this was comfortable.

"It was Ms. Malone who told me of Jasmine. I wasn't aware of her existence until Ms. Malone brought her to my attention."

"Really?" Mrs. Leslie sent Lexi a chiding look. "If you had information regarding Jasmine, you should have given the knowledge to Child Protective Services to investigate."

"Yes, well, it was more a hunch than anything else." Lexi noticed he'd made no mention of giving her custody.

"Hmm." Mrs. Leslie didn't sound convinced but she chose not to pursue it. She smiled and suggested, "Shall we get this visit on the way. Lexi, would you like to make the introductions?"

Drawing in a deep breath, she let it out slowly. Rubbing Jazi's back in soothing strokes, she told her softly, "Jazi, this is Mr. Calder. He wants to say hi. Can you say hello?"

Jazi had her head turned away from Jethro and for a moment she didn't move.

"Please." Lexi insisted.

Jazi gave him a quick peak and looked away again.

"See, he's a nice man." Lexi continued to pet her back. To Jethro she mouthed, "Smile!"

He notched a brow at her but nodded.

Okay, what did she reveal? She hadn't planned to be the one explaining this to Jazi. She didn't want to build Jethro up as Daddy to the rescue because—hopefully—he wasn't going to be sticking around. But she really didn't want to advertise their arrangement either.

"Mr. Calder knew your mama." Best to keep it simple.

The toddler sat up and blinked at Lexi. "Mama?"

"Yes." Just as she hoped Jazi snagged on the mention of her mother. "He and Mama were friends. And he wants to meet you. Can you say hi?"

She looked at him from the corner of her dark blue eyes. The glance lasted longer than the last one but she still shook her head.

"Okay, we'll get to know him better first." Lexi swept Jazi up and turned her sideways in her lap so Jazi faced Jethro. "Lexi likes him." Lexi laid her head on his shoulder to show her acceptance.

He smiled. Okay it was a little thin, but he'd made the effort.

"What is your favorite color?" she asked him.

"Blue."

So he was keeping it simple. Probably for the best. "My favorite color is green and Jazi's is—"

"Pink?" he guessed.

"Nope. It's yellow, like her skirt." Lexi tugged at the hem of the white-and-yellow skirt.

"Yellow," Jazi confirmed with a nod.

"What next?" Lexi mused. "When is your birthday?"

Something dark flashed through his eyes, but was quickly gone. He cleared his throat. "May."

No day given, interesting. "Jazi's is in November."

"What else do you want to know, Jazi?"

"Doggy?" Jazi whispered to Lexi.

"Ah, good question. She wants to know if you have a dog."

He shook his head. "No doggy."

Jazi's little brown eyebrows puckered.

"Do you have any animals?" Lexi asked.

She saw the frantic wish to say yes enter his eyes even as he began to shake his head. "No. No pets."

"He has fish." Clay spoke up and nodded to the story-book on the coffee table in front of Lexi and Jazi.

Jethro's eyes lit up. "Yes, I have fish." He picked up the book. "Do you like fish?"

Jazi nodded and pointed at the book. "Fishies!"

"I like colorful fishies." He absently flipped the pages in the book. "I have some that are blue and yellow and orange and red."

"Pretty." Jazi climbed into his lap and began to turn the pages and point at the fish.

Jethro froze. Lexi felt his whole body go still. But he didn't panic. His hold gentle, his voice soft, he hoisted Jazi to a more secure position and began reading the book. Of course she was more interested in flipping the pages to the ones she liked, but he soon adapted and began pointing out fun things on the pages she stopped on.

Across the way Mrs. Leslie nodded and rose to join Diana in the kitchen. Clay followed, giving Jethro some private time with his daughter. Except for Lexi of course. She'd leave too, except Jazi might freak out.

She hid a smile. Jethro just might freak out too.

After a few minutes, Jazi hopped down to get a new book. Lexi took the opportunity to assure him, "She likes you."

He let out a deep breath. "How can you tell?"

"She went to you with no urging. And she's looking for another book for you to read. If she didn't like you, she'd be tugging on my hand demanding I take her outside to play. It's what we usually do when I'm here."

"She's so small. But she's her own little person."

"Yep, that's the way it works." Lexi checked on Jazi's progress. She was still looking through the toy box for the book she wanted, so Lexi asked the question burning in her brain. "Why are you here?"

He focused those unreadable, dark blue eyes on her. "I wanted to meet my daughter."

"So I was right." She lowered her voice. "Please tell me you're going to let me adopt her."

The darkness flashed through his eyes again. Jazi ran up, black curls bouncing, to hand him a Halloween-themed book with five little pumpkins. He helped her climb into his lap. Over her head, he said, "We need to talk."

Lexi paced Jethro's office, from the beautiful wall of glass that overlooked The Strip to the plush seating area and then back again. What did he mean they needed to talk? He knew she wanted to adopt Jasmine. Hopefully he wasn't stringing her along.

But he could. He was her father. He held all the power.

Lexi glanced at her watch, but barely noted the time. Where was he? After they all left Jazi, Lexi received a text from him telling her to meet him at his office.

She was here. Where was he?

His assistant, a pleasant African-American woman in her midforties, let Lexi into his inner sanctum and advised her he'd be along shortly. Twenty minutes made up a lifetime when her future was on the line.

She plopped down in his big black leather desk chair and surveyed his massive desk made of ebony glass. Because she knew it would drive him nuts, she drew hearts around his laptop which sat in the middle of the pristine white page of his leather blotter.

Twenty-three minutes.

Next she rearranged the items on his desk. No pictures, of course. Just a fancy fountain pen—the most *bomb* pen she'd ever used—a letter-opener and a white marble paper-weight in the shape of a tiger. No clues to his psyche here.

Why had he been at Diana's? Why had he spent time with Jazi, getting to know her, holding her, when he intended to give her up?

It didn't make sense.

Please, God, she prayed he hadn't changed his mind about wanting a family. Jazi belonged with Lexi. She loved her like her own daughter. Already a void existed in her heart because she missed her so much.

Twenty-six minutes. Time had never moved so slowly. Seriously!

She dug into her pants pocket for her cell phone. Where are you? she texted him. You can't say we need to talk and then leave me hanging. Send. And then, for good measure, I'm going to start rearranging furniture if you don't get here soon. Send.

Pushing away from the desk she sent the chair swirling round and round. Light and dark flashed before her eyes to an accompanying beat in her head. It started as a tapping of her toes, a roll of her shoulders, and then she popped to her feet unable to deny the urge to dance, to put her frayed emotions into actual motion.

* * *

In the elevator on the way up to his office Jethro stared at his phone. Rearrange his furniture? Crazy woman. What kind of threat was that? An effective one actually. He liked things a certain way. Not at an OCD level, but he didn't care to have people messing with his things.

"What is it?" Clay asked.

"Nothing." Jethro slipped his phone into his pocket. "Lexi is in my office and she's getting impatient."

"Well, we didn't expect to go by Child Protective Services." The elevator stopped and Clay stepped forward. "Do you want me to go back with you this afternoon?"

"Maybe, I plan to take Lexi. If she agrees to my terms. If not, then I'll give you a call."

Clay nodded and exited the elevator. "Good luck with the wild child."

Wild child? Yes, it fit. The elevator went up two more floors and dropped him on the top floor. Hopefully he made it to his office before it sported a new decor.

"What's she doing in there?" he asked when he reached his assistant's desk.

"Waiting," she replied without looking away from her computer screen.

"You haven't checked on her?"

"No. She's not four."

"Are you sure?" he muttered and opened the door. All thoughts of his furnishings fled at the sight that greeted him.

Lexi moved to a tune only she heard. Arms, legs, body, she threw herself completely into the dance. She wore black pants and a short-sleeved tank that clung to her curves. Emotion thrummed through every movement whether she flung her arms wide or ducked into a crouch where she held herself close and then rolled into a full stretch reaching for something just out of grasp.

Her performance reached right into his soul and grabbed hold. He'd already decided to give her Jasmine. But seeing the power of her commitment, the depth of her emotion reflected in her dancing, he was reassured on an elemental level.

With a flick of long legs she knelt and then flowed to her feet and then to her toes, arms outstretched to encompass the world. Finally, slowly Lexi wound down—she rocked back on her heels, her arms coming in so her wrists crossed over her heart, her head dropped forward and she was still.

He detested seeing such despair in someone usually so filled with life. It made him want to wrap his arms around her, offer comfort. He resisted. "It's going to be okay."

She slowly lifted her head. "How can it be if we have to talk? You've changed your mind, haven't you? You want to keep her."

"I haven't changed my mind."

She swung to face him. "Does that mean you'll let me adopt her?"

The urge to touch won out this time. He ran his thumb over the silk of her cheek wiping away a bit of moisture. He hadn't noticed the tears until now, doubted she'd been aware of them at all.

Curling his hand into a fist, he turned his back on her. If this was going to work, he needed to maintain his distance. No more spontaneous acts of comfort.

"That's what we need to discuss."

He glanced around the office, looking for his visitor's chairs. She hadn't so much rearranged his furniture as pushed it all aside. He fetched one of the leather armchairs and set it in front of his desk.

Walking around his desk, he spotted her shoes. With an arched brow, he dropped the red heels on the corner of his desk. Her nervousness apparent, she perched on the edge of her chair, hands clasped in her lap.

"I'm not looking for money or a commitment from you."

Ignoring the pang her comment caused, he retrieved his

chair, which was pushed back against the window, and sat down across from her.

"Yes. You've made that clear."

She leaned back and drew her legs up, rested her chin on her knees. "Now you want to keep her."

"I haven't changed my mind," he repeated absently tracing a heart with his finger. "But I do have conditions."

"What conditions?" Hope lifted her chin, lit up her eyes. She scooted to the edge of her seat. "I'll do anything."

"Good. Then you'll have no problem moving in with me."

CHAPTER SIX

MOVE IN WITH HIM? Hope deflating, Lexi plopped back in her chair. No. She couldn't have heard what she thought she'd heard. "Can you repeat that?"

"I want you and Jasmine to move in with me." Jethro stated.

Nope, it made no more sense hearing it repeated.

"Are you suggesting joint custody?" The very notion made the muscles in the back of her neck twitch. Under no circumstances did she want to be answerable to this man. He was too closed off, too controlling. Life with him would be filled with rules and schedules and accounting for her every movement.

She'd fought too hard for her freedom to surrender it now.

Only for Jasmine would she hear him out.

"No."

Though he appeared intrigued by the option making Lexi sorry she'd suggested it.

"What then? You want us to be roommates?"

"In a sense, and for a limited time. I need to be sure Jasmine will thrive in your care. To that end I must observe you with her, which requires us to be in the same household."

"So to be clear, you'll let me adopt Jazi, but you want to spy on us first."

"Careful, Ms. Malone." Not looking at her, he tapped his pen against his blotter. "Where I recognize my limitations as a parent, Jasmine's well-being is still important to me. I need to know I'm placing her in good hands."

"So you expect me to move in with you?"

"Yes. I believe it's the most expedient way to observe the two of you together."

Add dispassionate to the list of his traits.

Too bad ugly wasn't on the list. Or plain, plain would definitely work. It would make the concept of moving in with a stranger so much easier to contemplate. No, it didn't make sense, but the mind was often irrational, especially when it came to emotions. And living with a plain stranger lurking in the background struck her as much easier to do than fighting a constant attraction for a gorgeous man who wanted nothing to do with her except to observe her interaction with his child.

Luckily, her attention would be focused on Jasmine.

"For how long?" she demanded.

"Three months."

She blinked at him. Three months? "That's forever!"

"No need to overreact. It's a mere blip of time."

"Because you'll be in the comfort of your home, going about your life. I'll be uprooted and spied on."

"A tad dramatic don't you think?"

"Is it?" she pouted.

"You'll be with Jasmine. Isn't that your goal?"

She gritted her teeth. Whatever it took to be with Jazi. "Yes." And then because her feelings were hurt. "Why so long?"

"I need to be one hundred percent sure that you really are the best caregiver for Jasmine. A child is an enormous responsibility and I need to be certain that Jasmine's welfare will be your foremost concern."

Shock rocked through her. "I love Jazi as if she were my very own. I would never let anything jeopardize her welfare!"

"Then you have nothing to worry about."

The grimness of his tone made her stop and think about his words. Oh, goodness. Had his own welfare suffered as a child? Had he been the victim of neglect himself, or worse?

"I'm sorry," she offered softly.

He shrugged. "You don't spend your whole life in foster care without falling victim to a few bad seeds. I don't care to talk about it."

Jethro had grown up in the foster care system. Did that account for his aloofness? The steeliness just beneath the surface?

"Maybe you should," she dared.

His blue eyes iced over. "Do not presume to psychoanalyze me, Ms. Malone."

"No. It's just I've learned that holding things in can be more harmful then helpful." For years her mother dictated how Lexi should spend every minute of her day. Requests for fun events and dance lessons were steadfastly refused. After a while Lexi stopped asking—she held in her discontent to the point she'd come to detest the very thing she'd always loved so much. She dealt with it by leaving and never looking back.

"So how is this going to work? I don't want to lose my apartment or my job. I'm going to need both once the three months are up."

"I'll cover your expenses. Clay talked to Maggie at Modern Goddess. She's agreed to hold your job. I need you to go with me when I travel."

"Seriously? Why?" Sighing, she held up a hand. "I get it. Because you have to be with me to observe me. But couldn't you get one of the hotel nannies to stay with us while you're gone?"

"No."

"But—"

"I won't trust Jasmine's future to anyone else. Go home and pack, Ms. Malone. We pick Jasmine up at four."

A knock came at the door just as Lexi finished cleaning out her refrigerator. Perfect timing. She grabbed the trash on her way to the door.

"Great, you were able to make it early," she greeted a brooding Jethro. She thrust the trash bag into his hands. "Can you toss this down that chute over there? Thanks." She pointed out the garbage chute and then turned back into the apartment, letting the door close behind her.

After a quick glance around to see everything was closed down for the time being, she grabbed her purse and the box of good perishables and headed out. She ran smack-dab into Jethro, who stood arms crossed right on her threshold. He didn't even grunt at the impact that sent her stumbling back into her apartment.

"Careful." His hand shot out gripping her elbow, saving her from dropping the box.

"Sorry." Catching her balance, she slid past him. "I wasn't expecting you to be standing there."

"Surprising."

"What's surprising?" She carried the box to the apartment two doors down and knocked.

"That you wouldn't be expecting me to be standing there when you left me standing outside."

"Is that what you're pouting about? Because I didn't invite you in? I thought it would be quicker if I grabbed the box while you handled the trash so we could get going faster."

"Hello, Lexi," Mrs. Diego yelled when she opened her door. Her smile lacked a few teeth but danced in her fading brown eyes. Gray curls were held back by a pink-and-white-polka-dot headband. "Come on in. Is this your new young man?" In a lower voice that clearly carried to Jethro she said, "He sure is a looker. Makes me wish I were thirty years younger."

Lexi bit back a grin. "Sorry, we can't stay. I'm going to be away for a few weeks, so I brought you my perishables. Can I put them in the kitchen for you?"

"That's so kind of you. Yes, if you wouldn't mind carrying the box." The older woman followed Lexi around the corner to the kitchen. She poked in the box as Lexi put the ice cream in the freezer. "Thank you for thinking of me, dear." Mrs. Diego took her hand and patted it. "You take care now and remember what I told you. Don't be giving away the milk or they won't buy the cow."

"I'll remember." Not that Lexi appreciated the whole cow analogy. Still, she appreciated the concern. She gave Mrs. Diego a hug. "No wild parties while I'm gone."

Lexi made her escape and once again encountered Jethro waiting for her outside the door. The look on his face did not bode well for the car trip.

She planted her hands on her hips. "What?"

"I am not someone you summon like a puppy, Ms. Malone. Certainly not to take out the trash or act as chauffeur."

Puppy? Try Rottweiler.

"I said thank you. And you're the one that wanted to ride together."

"To the social service offices, not all about town."

"Well, per your instructions your men took my car, and I have a few things I need to pick up before we go to get Jazi. So you're stuck taking me to the store." Seeing his scowl grow, she moved past him to the stairs. "I don't see what the big deal is."

"I'm a busy man, Ms. Malone." The bite in his voice came right on her heels. "Every minute of my day is accounted for."

The hairs stood up on the back of her neck as she remembered days, months, years where every moment of her life was accounted for. Some days had been so bad she couldn't breathe she felt so claustrophobic.

"So you got to break away from the office a little early? You're welcome."

His footsteps stopped, then began again. "I enjoy my work."

And she'd loved to dance, missed it more every day. So she got it. "Garage or street?"

"Street."

Exiting the stairwell, she walked through the lobby and outside to the street where a big black SUV sat at the curb. A beeping as he unlocked it confirmed it belonged to Jethro.

He moved with her to the passenger door, but kept his hand on the handle. "What do you need from the store? I'll determine if we need to stop."

Feeling crowded, she rolled her shoulders. Was this how the next three months were going to go? He demanded and she answered?

Oh, heck no.

"Look, I get that you're annoyed at having your precious schedule disrupted. And I understand, and even admire, that you need to know you're giving Jazi over to a safe and nurturing environment, and I'm willing to go through your test to prove I'm worthy. But I'm not a puppet to dance to your tune. If you're willing to treat me like an adult, we can have a discussion about what I need from the store. Otherwise, I'll call a taxi and meet you at social services."

He stared at her with those dark eyes. Her stomach began to clench with each passing second.

"And if I change my mind about the whole deal?"

Her heart plummeted straight to the knot in her stomach. But she jacked up her chin.

"You're not going to do that. Because you recognize that I love Jazi and you want her to have a loving family. Someone who will fight for her. And that's what I'm doing. Being under your thumb for the next few months wouldn't be a true measure of me as a mother. You're supposed to be observing us, not dictating our every move."

His eyes narrowed and his jaw clenched, evidence he didn't care for that statement. Too bad. She waved an agitated hand toward the big SUV.

"You set this scenario up when you sent your men in here

to swoop everything up so quickly. I haven't unpacked Jazi's things because, frankly, it was too painful to look at it all when she was out of my reach. I saw no point in opening the boxes up to take a few things out. So yes, I need to stop by the store to outfit a diaper bag. And because I didn't think of it before they left, we need a car seat too."

Okay that last part was her fault, but hey, he should have a seat for his fleet of cars.

He opened the door and waved her inside. "If you don't treat me like a dog, I won't treat you like a puppet."

"Deal." She got in the vehicle and hoped for the best.

So maybe he'd overreacted slightly. Jethro followed Lexi around the baby department store. She had a point. He was used to giving orders, not receiving them. And it didn't help that she was responsible for turning his whole life upside down. So yeah, her text telling him to pick her up early had hit a nerve.

He trailed her down a lane with car seats displayed from end to end. Who knew there'd be so many models?

Her insistence that he keep his distance didn't help. It was his decision to give Jasmine into her care and he recognized it was for the best. That didn't mean he felt nothing. Every time Lexi pushed him away it was like hearing his mother had thrown him away all over again. The same shock to the head, the same sense of betrayal, the same pain of loss. And the same determination to matter.

That last drove him to branch out beyond Pinnacle Enterprises to be a success in his own right. And it drove him to give Jasmine what he never had, the chance to grow up in a loving environment.

It didn't make watching from the sidelines any easier.

He paused to read some product notes. "How about this one? It exceeds the safety standards."

Lexi came back to examine his choice. She started shaking her head before she reached him. "This is for an infant. We need a toddler size for Jazi."

"It says it converts."

"Hmm. It is a good brand. But let's look at a few farther down the way. We'd be smarter to get one that's for a toddler that converts to the next stage rather than back."

"Good point." Honoring their tentative truce, he refrained from mentioning they were unlikely to reach the next stage in the next three months. He also ignored the pang that accompanied the thought.

He never second-guessed his decisions. Now was not the time to start doing so.

As he moved down the lane, he saw the differences in the sizing Lexi pointed out and made the decision when she waffled between two choices. He propped the big box in her cart and headed for the checkout.

"Wait," she called out, "I want to look at the strollers while we're here. I lent ours to a friend and never got it back." She disappeared around the corner, giving him little choice but to follow. A glance at his watch showed they had time.

He pushed the cart past three empty lanes before finding her. She stood studying a stroller she'd pulled into the aisle. He saw the appeal.

"Sporty." He observed of the three wheeler.

"Yeah, it can be used for walking and jogging as well as everyday use. I like it."

"Then get it."

She sent him a *you're not helping* look. "I'm considering my budget, trying to justify the expense."

Surprised, he checked to see if she was messing with him. He assumed he'd be paying. But no, she sincerely appeared to be struggling with her decision as if she fully expected to make the purchase.

"What the heck." She finally succumbed. "It'll make for more Jazi and me time."

He applauded her reasoning. "Does that mean we're done?"

"Almost. She's grown so much I want to grab a couple of outfits—just enough to last until I can shop more later."

"We've used our extra time, so while you do that I'm going to get in line."

"Good idea. I'll be right there," she promised and rushed away.

He supposed that meant he was in charge of the stroller too. Looking for a box he spotted a tag instead indicating he'd claim the item at merchandise pickup. All the more reason to move on to the checkout counter.

With his destination set, he rounded the corner. And came to a dead stop. The endcap assaulted the eyes with a kaleidoscope of color in the form of stuffed animals. The one that caught his attention was a little blue fish with a large rainbow tail. Jazi's fish book came to mind.

Keep it impersonal, he reminded himself, *maintain your distance*.

Sound advice, the only true way to navigate his way through this situation. And still he found himself reaching for the pretty stuffed fish. Leaving one home for another was always scary. Hopefully, the rainbow fish would give Jazi something to hang on to while the grownups decided her fate.

Lexi quickly grabbed some outfits for Jazi. The little girl would need them. But more than that Lexi needed the time to think. She'd been scrambling ever since she'd agreed to Jethro's condition to move in with him.

It pained her to think of him being hurt in the foster system. He said it didn't matter but she knew better. Still she couldn't let it affect her. They didn't mean anything to each other.

The searing passion she'd experienced in his arms flashed through her head.

She ruthlessly tamped it down.

Cultivating any relationship beyond parent and adoptee would be foolish and only complicate an already convoluted situation.

Which didn't make it any easier to think of living with him.

But she'd do it. Because he held all the power in this situation.

All she had to do was make a good impression on Jethro.

Challenging him less might be a start, but that's not who she was. She'd spent her childhood acquiescing to her mother's wishes, seeking love and approval. All she got for her troubles was discipline and more practice. She mastered the violin and the piano. But whatever she did, her efforts were never enough to meet her mother's exacting requirements. She was always required to do more, better.

At the age of sixteen she got invited to play the winter season with the Michigan Philharmonic. She loved it and hated it. Loved the sense of accomplishment and working with professionals. What she didn't care for was adjusting to the maestro's version of the music. She played the notes fine, but it jarred so strongly with her musical ear that it actually hurt.

Of course her mother accused her of acting out.

Jethro's earlier complaint echoed of her mother's lectures. His controlling demeanor certainly got her back up. She'd known him all of three days and she already recognized domineering as his default mode. But she'd also seen him be supportive, gentle, vulnerable, traits that made him much more approachable, even likable.

Which was way more dangerous to her peace of mind.

Best she focus on his harsher characteristics and stay as far away from him as possible over the next three months. It would be safer for all concerned.

Happier with a plan in place she headed to the front of the store and the checkout stands. Along the way she spotted a stuffed fish, blue with a rainbow tail just like the character in Jazi's book. She tucked it into her arm, the perfect gift to distract her little ball of energy while Lexi and Jethro dealt with red tape.

At the checkout counter, Jethro was waiting for her. The big items had already been rung up and paid for. He smoothly stepped back into line at the empty counter, took the clothes from her and placed them on it. The fish he handed to the cashier. The teenager smiled and put it under the counter.

"Hey!" It all happened so fast Lexi didn't know what to address first. "I said I was buying." Under no circumstances did she want finances to be an issue for him to reject her. She'd made it clear she didn't want money from him and she meant it. "And I want that fish!"

"He already bought the fish." The teenager giggled as she held out the receipt to Jethro. "You two know your kid."

Another customer started piling items onto the counter forcing Lexi to move along. Jethro's hand on her elbow encouraged her toward the door.

Oh, no. She planted her feet. "I said I was going to pay."

"I said I'd cover your expenses for the next three months. That includes Jasmine's as well. I can afford it, Ms. Malone."

She gritted her teeth. "Stop calling me Ms. Malone. And I can afford to care for Jazi."

"Yes, you've made it clear you want nothing from me but my signature. However, those are not my terms. My reasons for giving my daughter up are my own, but dodging monetary support is not one of them."

"I never thought it was." Clearly she'd struck a nerve. Suppressing a sigh, she followed him to the SUV. "That's not the point."

"I know the point." He loaded the stroller into the back. "I suggest we leave this discussion for when we go over the contract."

"Contract?" Her heart leaped. "You never mentioned a contract."

"I didn't think I had to. Of course there will be an adoption agreement. My financial responsibilities will be outlined within it."

Her teeth clicked together again. Her pearly whites were going to be nothing but nubs at the end of three months.

"You're not supposed to have any financial responsibilities," she repeated.

Instead of answering he handed her the fish.

She accepted the plush toy and realized it was an answer of sorts. The care and insight that went into the gift made her stop and think. He'd only spent a few minutes with Jazi, yet he'd noticed she liked stuffed animals and remembered a character from her fish book.

Lexi had been wrong to think his lack of desire for a family came from disinterest or an emotional disconnect. He may wear an aloof facade, but this trip was not the simple connect-the-dots, collect-the-child exercise for him that she thought it was.

Intense emotions festered below his dispassionate expression.

It made her wonder exactly what his reasons were for giving up Jazi.

The thought disappeared when he started to load the box with the car seat into the back.

"Wait." She stopped him. "Let's open that up and put it in the backseat. It'll be easier to do when we don't have Jazi with us."

He glanced at his watch. She bet he was five minutes early to every appointment.

"It'll only take a few minutes. And it will be worth it, I promise. You learn to think ahead when you're dealing with a toddler."

He looked doubtful but he didn't waste time arguing further. He opened the box and handed her the instructions.

She glanced at them. "On the one we had before, you secured the base first."

"There is no base. There's just the chair."

And that's exactly what the instructions showed. Lexi looked up to see he had the seat strapped in place.

"See? Easy. Now we just need to adjust the straps when we load her in."

He cocked a dark brow at her and wordlessly tossed the empty box in the back. "Let's go get our girl."

CHAPTER SEVEN

IT WAS LATE AFTERNOON before Lexi carried a sleeping Jazi into Jethro's penthouse hotel apartment. Her light weight warmed Lexi with a bone-deep satisfaction. This was where she belonged, in Lexi's arms.

She'd held Jazi the day she was born and these last four months without her had been a living nightmare. Lexi vowed never to lose her again.

The foyer led to a large living room furnished with sleek, modern pieces. Lexi stepped into the room and saw floor-to-ceiling windows made up the exterior wall. On the far end of the area a dining room held a table big enough to seat eight. Bar stools lined up against a kitchen island though the kitchen was out of sight.

An in-wall aquarium behind the bar in the living room held the fish he'd told Jazi about.

"This way," Jethro said. "We'll get her settled then I'll give you a tour."

He'd offered to carry Jazi, but she was too precious for Lexi to give her up just yet.

He led the way down a hall and opened a door on the right. "This will be you." Moving on a few feet, he opened a door on the left. "And this is Jasmine." He scowled at the low, short child's bed. "There's been a mistake. This should be a crib. I'll call down and get housekeeping to send someone up to fix it."

"No." Lexi placed Jazi on the bed and covered her with a blanket conveniently draped over the foot of the bed. "I told them to set up the bed. Diana recently told me Jazi has taken to climbing out of her crib. At least this way if she gets up in the night, she won't have a four-foot drop."

Jethro ran a hand over the back of his neck. "No, we wouldn't want that."

Lexi fussed over Jazi for another couple of minutes, taking off her shoes and tucking Rainbow, her new pet fish, under the blanket with her.

She looked up at Jethro. "Thank you for this," she said. "Thank you so much for giving her back to me."

He went still before slowly nodding. "We need to make it through the next three months first."

"I haven't forgotten." Undeterred she kissed Jazi's soft cheek. "But that's just a matter of time. Soon it'll be the two of us and we can start our life together." She exited the room and pulled the door mostly closed, leaving only an inch open so she could hear Jazi if she woke up.

When she glanced up at Jethro, his eyes were shuttered. He nodded toward double doors at the end of the hall. "That's me."

"Oh. You're close."

He made no comment to that. Didn't really need to. Still, she found it a little unnerving to know he was only a few feet down the hall.

From the desk in her room and the shelves and books, she figured the space must have been his office. "I'm putting you out."

"It's only for a few months." He shrugged her statement away. "I do most my work downstairs. It's no big deal."

He struck her as a creature of habit, so she rather thought it was more of a deal than he made out, but this arrangement was his idea so she was all right with that. She'd do her best to keep Jazi's sticky little fingers out the books but if he suffered a few casualties, it was on him.

He showed her the bathrooms, she and Jazi each had their own, the kitchen—a cook's dream—and the media room. Like the living room, the furnishings were sleek and modern throughout but built for comfort. It was all a tad too minimalist for her tastes but it fit the game the themed hotel was based on so she got it. And the sheer luxury of it made up for a deficit of style.

The apartment exceeded the size of hers by double the square footage yet still seemed small with Jethro standing next to her. The idea of sharing this space with him for the next three months unnerved her on so many levels.

In the kitchen she opened the refrigerator and a couple of cupboards. They were empty except for ground coffee beans and stale crackers.

"I eat out a lot or order my meals from room service." He explained. "I don't expect you to cook, but I understand you'll need to have food on hand. Make up a list and I'll have groceries delivered."

"That's okay. I prefer to do my own shopping." Yep, she was already looking for an excuse to escape for a few hours. "I like to cook."

He lifted a dark brow at her claim, but didn't challenge her. "Tomorrow I'll introduce you to Velveth. She's in charge of the hotel nanny service. We do an extensive background check on the nanny candidates, and they are all trained in CPR and self-defense."

Outrage and hurt lifted her chin. "Are you saying I can't take Jazi out on my own?"

"No." His immediate response took the edge off her rising ire. "But if you need to go out without Jasmine, I want you to use the service."

Shaking off the tension, she nodded. "Okay. That would work when I go to the gym. Is it okay to use the hotel facilities for my workout? Then I'd still be on-site if Jazi needed me."

"Actually—" He stopped and then continued on. "That's a good idea. The gym is on the fourth floor."

"Great." She wondered what had tripped him up but let

it go. They were actually communicating without arguing. All was well.

"I have work. I'll leave you to get settled."

"Okay." Her spirits rose. She'd breathe easier once he left.

"I'll have my assistant make a reservation for dinner. I'll collect you and Jazi at six."

"Sounds like a plan." She followed him to the door, held it open all the while resisting the urge to shove him through it and snap the lock. "See you later, dear."

Little brat. Jethro brooded on Lexi's farewell message all the way to his desk. Too strange having people share his space.

Except for a few rare occasions when he had to host one of his foster brothers, it had been years since he'd had anyone stay over with him. He liked to keep his private space private. One of the contributing factors in why his long-term relationships failed. Long term being nine months and that experience only lasted so long because she'd been in the middle of a merger and too busy to notice the distance he maintained between them.

He foresaw Lexi and Jazi leaving an indelible stamp on his life.

He opened his bottom drawer and pulled out the contract Ryan had sent down. Lexi kept insisting she didn't need financial compensation, but today he'd seen the prices of baby equipment and how much stuff came with a child. And there was Jazi's future to consider—he wanted her to be able to go to a decent college. He needed to do his part. Locating that section, he made a few significant changes.

After booting up his laptop, he sent Ryan a short email outlining the changes. Five minutes later the man stood in his office.

"I thought this woman didn't want any money from you." Ryan dropped into a visitor's chair.

"You know it's not about the money for me. I'm not attempting to dodge my financial responsibilities."

"Obviously not." Ryan held up his phone, where he'd apparently read the email. "What changed your mind? Did Ms. Malone change her tune?"

"Quite the opposite." He told Ryan how appalled Lexi had been when he paid for the few items at the baby store. "I understand the strategy behind keeping money out of the equation when she approached me. But once I recognized Jasmine as mine, the situation changed. I'm not a stingy man."

"Of course not."

"Doesn't she realize by refusing my assistance she's insulting me and doing an injustice to Jasmine?"

"It's not about the support," Ryan stated. "It's about control."

"What's that mean? I've seen her finances—I know she can afford to support Jasmine. But with my help, they'd both have a better quality of life."

"And that monthly payment would be a permanent link to you."

"Why is that a bad thing?"

"Consider if the circumstances were reversed."

Jethro scowled. "I don't see the problem."

"Because you're being stubborn. If you adopted a child and were trying to raise her would you want a monthly reminder going to the child's mother? Wouldn't it make you worry that someday she might decide she wants to be a part of the child's life?"

"That's not going to happen."

"Are you sure? You seem pretty involved."

"Of course I'm involved. They're in my home. But it's temporary." He tossed his pen down on his desk. "When the three months are up, I'll be out of the picture."

"Except for a monthly payment."

"Put it in a trust if that makes you happy."

"It does actually." Ryan nodded his approval. "With a bank as trustee it takes you out of it."

"Glad you're happy. Just know this, the more Lexi protests, the more I intend to add."

Suspicion filled Ryan's eyes. "Maybe that's her game."

The corner of Jethro's mouth quirked up. "No. She's a dancer not an actress. She's made it clear she doesn't want anything from me, but I didn't sign up to be a sperm donor. I intend to make sure my daughter never wants for anything. Ms. Malone will just have to deal with it."

Already imagining Lexi's arguments, he handed the amended document across the desk to Ryan. She'd just have to get over it.

Providing financial stability was the least he could do for his daughter.

Lexi found that both her and Jazi's things were already unpacked. Wow, she could get used to this hotel life. Except it left her nothing to do.

So, of course, she snooped.

She started in her room. Designed in muted greens and beige, the furnishings had the quality and comfort she'd expect in a luxury hotel. No sense wasting time there, she headed straight for the books in the shelves. And discovered Jethro either bought the books for appearances or had a broad taste in literature. The financial books and periodicals were obviously his. There were also mysteries, biographies, nonfiction history books and some poetry.

The poetry had to be for show. Or maybe a gift from some hopeful woman? Lexi just couldn't picture Jethro reading poetry.

Now this book, yes. She pulled out *The Art of War*, by Sun Tzu, and thumbed through the pages. Did he use it for game play or the boardroom? Probably both. A quote popped out at her.

It talked about subduing the enemy without fighting, about evading the enemy if she lacked strength.

Yeah, she could get behind that.

Yep, evade and avoid, that was her plan. Except seeing it put like this made her feel itchy. She didn't care for the concept of being too weak to engage. She dropped the book on her bedside table. Maybe she'd glean a few tips on how to handle the book's owner.

Next she checked on Jazi. No surprise she'd kicked off the blanket Lexi had draped over her. The child hated to be restricted and always had. It was a struggle to keep her properly covered. Blankets, shoes, socks and jacket constantly got tossed aside. Pants and shirts, too, if she had her way.

Except for the child, there was nothing of Jethro's in the room. Totally pink, the staff had taken the time to unpack all the wall art, blankets, lamps, rugs and put the full nursery together. A nice gesture for a temporary situation. Jazi should feel right at home. In this room if none of the others. She'd adapt as she'd already had to do so many times in her short life.

Lexi looked forward to the time when it was just the two of them and they could build a stable life together.

She wandered down the hall to Jethro's room. Maybe she should look for a house during these three months, consider putting down real roots. She hesitated with her hand on the knob knowing he'd see her snooping as a violation of his privacy.

Knowledge was power. Even the few verses she'd read of battles and war had shown her that. Just a peek, she promised herself.

Wow. Where her room was understated luxury, this room shouted penthouse. From the custom king-size bed, to the sunken conversation area with the fireplace, to the glass-and-crystal bar complete with mini fridge and wine cooler, the room offered decadent comfort. The earthy greens and browns grounded the space and offset the futuristic elements to the art and accessories.

Impressive—oh, yeah—but if she hoped to find insight into Jethro she was doomed to disappointment. The art was interesting but similar to pieces in her room. Which meant it came with the room.

He knew his wines; she'd give him that. Okay, that was something. Reading a few more labels she'd even say he was a bit of a connoisseur.

The mini fridge held cola, some nice cheeses, stuffed olives and dark chocolate ice cream. Humming her approval, she closed the door and rounded the corner into the closet. Female to her core, she just slipped down the wall and sat staring. Envy curled her toes.

A new life goal bloomed inside her. Someday she wanted a closet like this.

Forget the bedroom, she'd just move in here. It was nearly as big as her room and included a lounge for her to sleep on. And a chair if she desired company. Racks, shelves, hooks and nooks ringed the room as well as a three-way mirror. In the middle a marble-topped island with a small sink housed drawers.

The beautiful space was wasted on Jethro's black suits and white shirts. Oh, the color she could bring to this room. Shoes there, purses in those slots. Her jackets on that wall, dance gear in the drawers—

Stop. Focus.

At first she didn't think there was any evidence of Jethro in here either.

But she couldn't be more wrong. The order, neatness and overall preciseness of everything broadcast Jethro's need for dominance and control. She pushed to her feet and prowled down the line of black suits and white shirts. Seriously, someone needed to tell him gray was the new black when it came to power suits.

Then again, maybe it was his way of staying in the background. If so, he was deluding himself. His sheer presence radiated power. So she supposed it didn't matter what he wore.

A picture frame caught her eye. On the marble counter

close to the far end were two frames standing back to back so a picture could be seen from either side of the island. A ratty crocheted cap rested between the two photos. The first shot was of a younger Jethro, in his late teens, and a petite woman with short blond hair and some well-earned wrinkles around her eyes and mouth. She had her hand on his shoulder and he wore a huge grin and the crochet cap. In the other picture the Fabulous Four surrounded the dainty woman.

The woman must be Harman, the foster mother who brought the four boys together and made them a family, one of Jethro's foster brother's had told her, Lexi would bet money the woman crocheted the cap. It said a lot that Jethro had kept it all these years and that he kept her picture not just where only he would see it, but where he would see it daily.

It revealed a capacity to care deeply, something his dispassionate facade belied.

She felt him before she saw him. Jethro. With no thought at all she dropped to her hands and knees. As if she could hide.

"Ms. Malone." Shiny black loafers appeared in her view.

"I lost an earring." She felt her ear, removing the gold hoop. She held it out. "Look at that it rolled all the way in here." Popping to her feet she smiled innocently.

He lifted one dark brow. Nope, not buying it.

His strong features were marble hard, his stance set, quite intimidating. She half expected to see steam coming out of his ears. But his eyes were remarkably calm.

He knew he'd caught her snooping, probably came back early for that very purpose.

She hated to be predictable.

"Okay, you caught me. I was snooping through your rooms. But it's your fault."

He crossed his arms over his chest. "Why? Because I brought you here?"

"Yes."

"And I thought it was a given we'd respect each other's privacy. Perhaps we need to discuss the rules of common courtesy."

Heat flooded into her cheeks. "That won't be necessary, no."

"Then explain to me why you're in my closet."

"I was just trying to get to know you. We're going to be living together for three months yet I know so little about you. I was hoping a peek at your private space would give me some insight."

"And what did you deduce?"

"Not much. You have a wide interest in reading, good taste in wine, and this closet is a physical manifestation of your need for control and order. So you needn't worry, your secrets are safe." She stormed past him into the bedroom. "I don't get it. You're a patron of the arts, but you don't even have anything personal on the walls."

"When you have all your possessions stripped from you, you learn not to invest yourself in them."

What a heartbreaking revelation. One he regretted as soon as he said it. She saw it in his eyes and the stiffness in his shoulders. Even she'd had things, in fact, after her dad died, things took the place of affection in her household.

"That had to be a long time ago."

"Some lessons are hard to unlearn."

"I know you grew up in foster care. I'm sorry. It must have been a difficult childhood." She kept her tone matter-of-fact because—

"I don't need your pity, Ms. Malone."

Because of that.

"And you don't have it, Mr. Calder." Leaving the intimacy of the bedroom, she led the way to the living room, checking on a sleeping Jazi, as she walked by. "I feel for the child you were. You aren't that child anymore. You're a powerful man, Jethro. Nobody's going to take anything from you that you don't willingly give up."

"Indeed. I'm glad we understand each other. There will be no repeat visits to my closet."

"No."

"Good."

"So why are you here?" She planted her hands on her hips. "Checking up on me already?"

He mimicked her. "You mean to see if you were messing in things you shouldn't?"

Okay, her insecurities were showing. She so walked into that one, especially when she suspected he'd known she was snooping.

"You didn't answer your phone," he said.

"Oh." She looked around for her purse, which held her phone. She collected it from where she'd dropped it in an armchair. Neither of them sat. "I didn't hear it. What did you need?"

"I've made two appointments for you tomorrow morning. One with the nursery services and one with security."

Definitely hoping to catch her snooping. The message so could have waited.

"I was concerned when you didn't answer. This is a new place to you and Jasmine. Something could have happened."

"Oh." That took the defiance from her sails. The sincerity in his voice too real to be a ploy. "Thanks for checking on us."

"How's Jasmine settling?"

"Fine. She's been asleep, which is a good sign. She tends to have an internal radar that wakes her when things are uneasy."

"Good. I'll get back to work." He turned into the foyer. "Stay out of my room."

She rolled her eyes.

"I saw that."

"Liar."

He glanced at her over his shoulder as he opened the door. "I never lie, Ms. Malone. I don't have to."

Shortly after Jethro made his exit, a sound drew her from her contemplations. Jazi.

Lexi jumped up and rushed to her girl. Sleepy-eyed and clutching Rainbow she stood in the middle of her room. When she spotted Lexi, her little face lit up with a big smile and she reached out her arms to be held.

Heart squeezed tight, Lexi lifted the toddler into her arms. Sweet, sweet moment. "Hello, sleepy girl."

"Lexi! Hi!" Little arms ringed her neck and a tiny bow mouth bussed her cheek. "Love you."

"I love you, too, pumpkin. Uh-oh, you're a wet little girl. Let's get you changed." Lexi made quick work of changing Jazi, listening to her chatter all the while. Lexi only understood the odd word here and there. Didn't matter, she drank in every syllable. Too soon to get Jazi ready for dinner so Lexi put clean pants on her and set her on her feet. "Do you like your new room?"

"Yes."

"Shall we check it out? Find where everything is?"

"Yes." Jazi ran to the bookshelf and began pulling out books.

"Whoa, pumpkin." Lexi smiled at the toddler's enthusiasm. "Let's do this one at a time."

For the next hour, she patiently helped Jazi explore her new environment and unpack the bag Diana sent with the girl. To Jazi's joy she found the fish book tucked into the bag. Of course they needed to read the book right now. Jazi hunted up Rainbow and climbed into Lexi's lap.

After a while it was time to put the book aside and get ready for dinner. For Jazi that meant a yellow dress with black piping. For Lexi it was a royal blue sheath dress.

To keep her occupied until Jethro arrived, Lexi carried Jazi to the media room. Snuggled into a plush recliner with the girl curled on her lap, Lexi giggled to the outrageous antics of a sponge and his starfish friend when Jethro strolled into the room.

Jazi popped up and clapped her hands. "Daddy."

CHAPTER EIGHT

Daddy. THE WORD ROARED through him like fire destroying all resolve in its path. Everything in him longed to claim this child as his. Daughter. Family. Continuity. All he'd ever wanted sat within his reach, cuddled in the arms of the woman who drew him in ways he'd never imagined.

Terror replaced the want. Except for Mama Harman, he'd managed to sabotage every relationship he'd begun, and that one lasted only because she'd refused to give up on him. He didn't know how to let them in, to share. In order to survive, he'd built up walls he found impossible to let down.

Emotionally deficient, Kimberly had called him. And he couldn't refute it.

Though the Lord knew he'd shared more with this impossible woman Lexi than anyone else.

As emotions warred within him, Lexi's raced over her expressive features. Shock, horror, sympathy came and went as she corrected the child. "No, no pumpkin. Remember, this is Mr. Calder. He's the nice man who is helping us."

Clearly Jasmine had not learned the word from her.

"Man," Jazi said.

"Jethro," he stated, his voice huskier than usual as resolve settled in him. He'd given his word and he'd keep it. There was no denying the love between these two. He wouldn't take that from his daughter. "Mr. Calder is a bit of a mouthful."

"Jethro." Jazi mimicked and smiled.

His heart cracked. He cleared his throat. "We should go or we'll be late for our reservations."

"Jethro." Lexi made a step toward him.

He shook his head and stepped back, refusing her pity. "I'll meet you at the door."

Jethro took them to The Beacon where they sat at the chef's table in the kitchen. It was quite the show, loud and chaotic, a dance of creativity and control and heavenly scents.

The noise made up for Jethro's silence. He was quiet during dinner and who could blame him? Lexi knew this was proving more difficult for him than he'd expected. Something flashed in his dark blue eyes and she feared the additional exposure to Jazi had him questioning his decision.

Dang it. He'd brought this on himself by demanding they live with him.

She prayed he didn't change his mind. This was only the first day and Jazi was so sweet, so beautiful, so clever, she made it impossible not to love her. How would he feel three months from now?

Lexi could only trust he'd keep his word. Otherwise she'd drive herself nuts over the next ninety days.

She kept up a constant chatter through the awkward meal, entertaining Jazi and including Jethro, though he added little to the conversation. Lexi wanted to apologize for Jazi's blunder.

She totally should have anticipated something like that would happen. As far as the rest of the world was concerned, Jethro would be raising the child. Someone may well have called him Jazi's father. But there was no way to address the topic in front of the child, so it would wait.

The chef came over to make sure they were enjoying their meal. Jethro unbent long enough to compliment his steak and lobster. And she praised her lamb in cabernet sauce as the best meal she'd ever eaten, a truth belied only by the tenseness at the table that made it hard to concentrate on food. He frowned at the uneaten food on her plate but seemed appeased when she asked to take the leftovers with her.

Back in the penthouse, she took Jazi off for a bath and to get her ready for bed. Jazi loved the water and played gleefully in the tub. Lexi enjoyed the time and allowed the toddler her fun until her knees protested.

"Time to get out," she told Jazi.

"No." The little girl shook her head and dunked her yellow rubber ducky.

"Yep. Stand up now and let me lift you out."

"No." Jazi continued to play.

"Okay. One more minute." Being smarter than a twenty-three-month-old Lexi found the plug and pulled it. Water and bubbles disappeared down the drain and Lexi lifted Jazi out of the tub and wrapped her in a soft towel. Jazi pointed to the ducky and Lexi reached into the tub to grab it.

Jazi took the opportunity to run off giggling as she went.

"Oh, no, you don't." Lexi made a grab for her but caught only towel. And then there was a naked little girl on the loose.

Lexi pushed to her feet and dashed after her. She entered the bedroom in time to see Jazi running out the door. Lexi gave chase, thrilling Jazi. Her shrieks of glee echoed down the halls.

"Got you." Lexi swept her up and swaddled her in the towel. "Wicked child." She tickled her causing her to laugh and scream.

The door at the end of the hall opened and Jethro stood there. "Everything okay?"

"Bath time escapee." Lexi advised. "I have it under control. Say good night Jethro."

"Night, Jethro."

"Good night."

She felt the weight of his regard until she cleared the bedroom door. She sighed her relief but it was short-lived as he came to lean against the doorjamb and watched as she diapered Jazi and dressed her in warm pajamas.

Tucking her into bed, Lexi kissed Jazi's petal-soft cheek. "Night-night, pumpkin."

"No. Book."

"You want a story."

"Yes."

"Okay." Pretending Jethro wasn't observing her every move, Lexi held up a finger. "But only one."

Jazi held up her hand with all the fingers spread wide.

"Five?" Lexi laughed and closed her hand around the tiny digits. "You don't even know how much that is. Two, final offer. Go pick out your books."

She came back with her fish book and then ran to the couch where she'd left Rainbow. With the stuffed fish tucked under her arm she crawled into Lexi's lap. Lexi kissed the black curls and opened the book. A glance at the door found it empty.

Since this was the little girl's first night in a new place, Lexi stayed with Jazi until she fell asleep. A task that took longer than she anticipated due to the toddler's long afternoon nap. Lexi left a lamp on low and pulled the door half-closed. She wanted to be able to hear if Jazi stirred in the night.

She went in search of Jethro to make her apology, but didn't find him in the common rooms. Standing outside his bedroom door she heard music, a slow bluesy jazz and decided not to disturb his peace.

She thought about going to bed because early to bed would be early to rise for her little charge, but Lexi was a night owl. As a dancer in a casino production, her schedule had practically been the reverse of norm. She'd left dancing behind, but old habits were hard to break. Not to mention she was a bit antsy in this new place herself.

After changing into more comfortable clothes, she strolled down to the kitchen and made a pot of coffee. Then she sat at the table and started a list for groceries. From there she made out a menu for the week, adding a few items to her shopping list as she went.

She drummed her fingers on the table. And what about laundry? According to Jethro the hotel handled that as well. Uh-uh. No way was she letting strangers wash her undies. Not to mention a two-year-old went through a lot of clothes in a week. There was a concierge for the penthouse floor; maybe there was a laundry as well. Grabbing her key, she went in search of what she could find.

The floor held two penthouse suites that spanned half the hotel, one on the north, one on the south so they both had views of the strip. The elevators were in the middle. Lexi padded barefoot down the hall until she found an unmarked door. It opened at her touch.

And yes, there was the trash chute and next to it a laundry chute, a good indication there was a laundry on the floor. She kept going trying doors along the way.

"Bingo." At door number three she hit pay dirt. The small room held two industrial-sized washers and dryers, and one set of standard-sized. "Perfect."

"May I help you, Ms. Malone?"

"Oh." Lexi jumped at the cool male voice. She swung around. A slim, dark-haired man stood just inside the door, hands clasped behind his back. "Hello. You know my name."

"Of course. I'm Brennan, executive concierge. Mr. Calder instructed me to assist you as needed, however, I was expecting a phone call not a visit."

"Oh, well, I was looking for the laundry. Do you suppose it will be okay for me to use these machines?"

"That would be highly unusual, Ms. Malone. Most inappropriate." Brennan moved to stand between her and the machines as if to protect them from her. "There are bags provided in the suites. Just place your items in the bags and I shall see they are properly cleaned."

"See, that's the thing. I don't know you well enough to

let you handle my underthings." Lexi smiled to show no hard feelings. "I'm sure you understand."

Pink flushed bright against his pale complexion. "I can assure you there is no impropriety, Ms. Malone."

"I'm sure. I'd still prefer to do my own laundry."

Relief flooded his features as he looked beyond her. "Ah, Mr. Calder."

"Brennan."

Lexi swiveled toward the door. "Jethro."

He stood in the doorway, hands on hips. Except for the jacket, he still wore his suit except the buttons of his white shirt were undone at the neck and the sleeves were rolled up exposing his hair-dusted forearms.

"Thank you for coming." Brennan rushed forward. "If I might explain—"

Jethro held up a hand. "I heard. I think it's best if we allow Ms. Malone to handle her own laundry."

Brennan nearly sputtered in his indignation, but he pulled himself together and nodded. "Very well, sir. Ms. Malone, I'll provide you with a list of times the machines are available." With a nod he departed.

Jethro met her gaze, gestured for her to precede him. He was annoyed.

With good reason. There'd been no need for Brennan to drag Jethro into this. Lucky he had, though, since she hadn't been making much headway.

"I'm sorry you were drawn into this, but I'm used to doing for myself and with the machines right here it seems ridiculous to have someone else taking time to do what I'm perfectly willing to do." Somehow it felt too intimate to bring up her underwear with him.

He said nothing. They reached the penthouse and she used her key to let them in.

"Good night, Ms. Malone."

"Wait." Maybe his reticence wasn't about the laundry at

all. "I was looking for you earlier." She waved toward the living room. "Can we talk for a minute?"

He gave a shake of his head. "I'm in the middle of reading a report."

"Please, it'll only take a moment."

His jaw clenched, but he followed her into the living room.

"Would you like some coffee?" she asked, nervous now she had his attention. "I made a pot earlier, but it's still hot."

"Sure. I take it black."

She half expected him to follow her into the kitchen to prompt the discussion he obviously wanted no part of but he didn't. She poured two mugs, doctored hers with cream and sugar and carried them to the living room.

He hadn't bothered to turn on the lights. He stood silhouetted against the window, the flickering glow of the strip. From this distance she had no view of the hotels, just the brilliance of the lights that rivaled the sunset in color and brightness. And his bold, strong form.

Hands in his pockets, shoulders straight and stiff, he looked so alone it broke her heart.

She set the mugs on the tray on the ottoman and went to him.

"I want to apologize for what happened earlier with Jazi," she said gently. "I know it was a shock and not what you wanted."

"It wasn't your fault. You were surprised as well." He spoke to the window.

"I was." Relief that he didn't blame her steadied the hand she placed on his shoulder. "But I should have foreseen someone would put thoughts of daddy in her head. I'm sorry."

"You're worried this changes things."

She remembered the vulnerability in his eyes and held her breath. "Does it?"

"No."

Oh, she wished she could believe that. "It would be easier for you to make a clean break."

That brought him around. There was no softness in his features now. "My mind won't rest easy until the three months are up."

Her gut compressed. "I'll take good care of her," she promised.

"I know. And still her safety is too important to take chances on."

She nodded. It was the one argument she couldn't fault. For now, she'd put her faith in him.

"Do you mind if I go down to the gym for a while? Jazi is out and I'm too antsy to sleep yet."

He glanced away but not before she saw a spark of panic quickly subdued. He shrugged. "Don't be too long."

"I won't." She bit back a small smile at the show of nerves at being alone with Jazi. "And I'll keep my cell with me. Call me if she wakes up and I'll be right here."

"I think I can handle a sleeping child."

"Hmm." Lexi hoped so. Hoped Jazi didn't wake with one of her screaming fits. The yoga pants and tee she wore were fine for a short workout, so she grabbed her key and headed for the door. "Thanks. And thanks for helping with the laundry. I'll feel much better doing it myself."

"Don't thank me. I did it for purely selfish reasons."

Her brows jumped in surprise. "Really? And what reasons are those?"

"I don't like the idea of any other man touching your underwear."

Jethro wondered when he'd become such a masochist as he watched the awareness pop into Lexi's pretty eyes. The soft blue irises lit up like the sea on a sunny day. Or maybe it was wishful thinking and the reflection of the lights from the strip behind him.

She stood frozen for a moment. And then her gaze raked him from head to toe and back and when those stunning eyes met his, the heat in them had nothing to do with the sun and everything to do with wanting.

His body urged him forward, but his mind blocked the move so he jerked in place.

Desire tightening her features, she stepped back and shook her finger at him. "No fair muddying the waters. I'll be back in an hour."

She practically ran to the door.

Jethro cocked his head unable to resist watching her exit, enjoying the view of her swaying hips in snug yoga pants and the soft bounce of her breasts from the side once she got through the door.

He turned back to the window and the view outside, seeking a diversion from thoughts of long dancer legs entangled with his as he feasted on lush, cherry-red lips.

She tempted him beyond reason.

Because if he were being reasonable, he'd admit she was right and make a clean break from her, from the daughter he was determined to do right by.

The Lord knew he'd gotten nothing done today while brooding about doing just that. He'd used the excuse of being concerned for Jazi's welfare, and he was, but he no more believed Lexi would purposely do anything to harm the child than he would. At dinner she'd burnt her own fingers moving a hot dish out of Jazi's reach rather than risk the girl touching it.

But he wasn't giving them up.

Not one day before the three months was over.

These were the only days he'd have with his daughter, with the bright and beautiful woman she'd call mother. They might be from the point of view of observer, but he'd still have memories to look back on and cherish.

Except for anything work related, he always felt like an outsider, and neither Lexi nor Jazi was expecting anything from him so this should be a simple stroll down the boulevard.

As long as there were no more tantalizing moments like the one they'd just shared. He'd have to control his tongue. And other body parts.

Who'd think laundry would be the thing to trip him up? He'd been annoyed when he got the call from Brennan that Lexi was snooping through the utility hall. What could she possibly want back there? When he heard her mention strange men in the same sentence as her underthings, his agitation spiked from annoyed to red-hot fury. By the time he reached the laundry room door, she'd had his full support.

Brennan better heed Jethro's orders. He'd fire any man who put his hands on any item of Lexi's clothing more intimate than a winter jacket.

"Fool," he muttered. "Pull it together. Time to get back to work."

He spied the coffee Lexi had poured for him and took it with him to his room where he gathered up his tablet. He carried both back down to Jazi's room where he settled in the armchair. Babysitting was new to him. Best he stayed close in case he was needed.

She slept on her side with one little hand under her cheek and the other flung out at her side. She'd tossed her covers aside, but Lexi had dressed her in fleece pajamas with feet, and the room was fairly warm, so he chose not to disturb her and risk waking her.

He reached for his tablet quite sure they'd both make it through this experience better if she remained asleep.

Forty minutes later she sat straight up in bed and looked at him.

He froze, hoping she'd lie down and go back to sleep. What would he do if she didn't? No tears, he prayed. He should have asked Lexi for more instructions before he let her go.

"Jethro." Jazi blinked a couple of times. Then she slid from the bed. She got the fish book from where Lexi had left it on the bedside table and brought it over to him. Holding the book she lifted both arms up, demanding to be picked up.

He set his tablet aside and lifted her into his lap.

"Story." She snuggled around until she got comfortable and opened the book.

Turned out he didn't have to do anything but follow her lead. "Okay, but only for a few minutes and then it's back to bed."

"No bed." She shook her head. She pointed to the blue fish. "Bow."

"Yes, that fish looks like Rainbow." He'd never held anything so precious in his life. She was soft and warm and weighed no more than a feather. He breathed in the sweet scent of baby powder and decided to let Lexi deal with putting her back to sleep when she returned. He feared he'd have a hard time denying her anything. Better delay than defeat. "Shall we name all the colors in her tail? There's blue and green and yellow."

Lexi heard giggles as soon as she walked in the door from the gym. She peeked in the bedroom door and found Jazi curled up in Jethro's lap. He was reading her book in character. His masterful falsetto was what had Jazi laughing. It made Lexi's lips twitch too.

When a laugh escaped, he glanced up, saw her. He lit up with relief. Making no bones about it, he stood up plopped the toddler in her arms, kissed Jazi on the top of her head, kissed Lexi hard on the mouth and escaped out the door.

His taste on her lips, she watched him go.

What a way to end her first day.

The next morning Lexi awoke to find Jazi in bed with her. Moving slowly, Lexi managed to slip out of bed without disturbing the sleeping child. Diana had told Lexi that Jazi had a habit of wandering around at night.

After tucking the covers around her, Lexi slid into the bathroom for a quick shower.

It had taken forever to get the toddler to sleep last night. Best she stay down as long as possible this morning.

Lexi pulled on jeans and a purple sweater that fell to her thighs. Jazi woke up as she was pulling on her socks.

"Good morning, sleepy head." Lexi gathered her up. "Shall we go see if Jethro is up?"

Jazi nodded.

But a quick trip through the suite revealed he'd already left for his office. A plate with toast crumbs and a coffee mug sat in the empty sink, evidence he'd had a little something to eat before he left.

A note on the counter reminded her of their appointment with the nursery manager at eleven. He asked her to notify Clay if she wanted to leave the hotel.

She frowned, suspecting she knew what that was about. But if Jethro thought she was taking a babysitter wherever she went, he had another think coming.

She'd soon find out because she wanted more than toast for breakfast.

"I hope you're hungry," she told Jazi while dressing her in gray knit pants and a lavender-and-gray shirt topped by a soft quilted vest in lavender. "I know a place that makes a great veggie omelet, but it's huge. You're going to have to eat your share."

"Hungry." Jazi nodded. "Jethro?"

"He's at work. It's just you and me, kid." The joy of that caused her hands to shake as she helped Jazi put on the black boots she'd chosen. She'd almost given up hope this day would come.

She remembered the look in Jethro's eyes last night and knew regret that her happiness came at his pain. She pushed the thought away. So it wasn't a perfect situation. The point was they were both doing what was best for Jazi.

That's what she needed to hold on to.

"The good news is there's plenty of time for us to go grocery shopping."

Jazi bounced up and down. "Shop!"

"You know that word, don't you? I think I'm in trouble."

Jazi giggled.

"Make that lots of trouble."

She called Clay and met him in the lobby. Jethro was with him along with a large, fit man in a dark suit.

Just as she feared, Jethro insisted she have a bodyguard when out in public. Hurt slammed into her like a kick to the stomach.

Forget it. She turned and walked away. She'd sit on her butt for three months before she let him make a puppet of her.

"Ms. Malone," he called out, her name a demand to stop and fall into line.

Yeah, right. Not. Going. To. Happen.

"Ms. Malone." He sounded closer.

She walked faster. The elevators were just ahead.

"Lexi, wait." He grabbed her arm and her own momentum swung her around.

She glared at his hand on her arm. "Let me go."

"Just listen to me."

She yanked at her arm. He released her instantly and she backed away. "I thought we agreed to respect each other. No puppets or puppies."

"This isn't about that." He blocked her path to the elevators. "This is about Jazi's safety, about your safety."

"Don't patronize me. Nothing is going to happen to us."

"I'm not willing to take a chance. I along with the other chief officers are worth millions. As long as you're with me, you're both targets."

"I can't." She pictured having to constantly account to someone for her movements and claustrophobia closed in on her. Shaking her head, she yanked at the collar of her sweater.

"Listen, this isn't public knowledge, last year Jackson was attacked and seriously injured in this hotel. It's only for three months," he reminded her, "and it will give me peace of mind."

"Jackson was hurt here in the hotel?" The shocking news got to Lexi where arguments would fail. "Okay."

Jethro escorted her back to where the men waited. Clay introduced the man with him as Damon Gregory, head of security for the casino and hotel. He'd accompany Lexi whenever Jethro or Clay couldn't.

"I don't know why you're doing this," Jethro stated as they walked through the supermarket doors. "I told you to make out a list and Brennan would order the groceries in."

"I like getting out." She helped Jazi into the seat of the cart. "And I like to do my own shopping. Especially this first time. It'll make me feel more at home in the kitchen. Is there anything you want me to add to the list?"

He stared at her for a moment. "I don't expect you to cook for me."

"Don't be ridiculous." She waved that away. "We live together. It only makes sense we eat the same meals. And it's just as easy to cook for three as two."

"I don't want to impose."

"Please." Imposing was asking her to move in for three months. "You're buying the food. You're welcome to whatever I make. So—" she pulled her list from her purse "—anything you want to add to the list?"

"I'm sure I'll like whatever you make."

"Then you get what you get." Honestly, the man's picture should be next to *difficult* in the dictionary. With her list in hand, she breezed through the aisles. Jethro worked on his phone the whole time. She said nothing when he tossed in a bag of chocolate cookies except to ask if there were any other sweet treats he liked. Without breaking off his conversation, he grabbed a bag of peanut butter sandwich cookies and added it to the cart.

Back at the hotel Jethro pulled in to the valet, instructed the captain to have the groceries delivered to his suite and escorted her inside, the package of chocolate cookies tucked under his arm.

"Was that so bad?" he quizzed her.

She wrinkled her nose at him.

The corner of his mouth crooked up at the end in a half smile. He yanked on her ponytail. "Try to give us at least a half hour notice when you want to go out. See you." And off he went.

"Not so bad," Lexi said to Jazi, "but still restricting. And we didn't encounter a single threat."

"Cookie?" Clearly Jazi had other priorities.

"Later, kiddo. We just ate."

The groceries would take a few minutes to get to the penthouse so Lexi stopped off at the Modern Goddess Spa to introduce Jazi to her friends. Of course everyone exclaimed how adorable she was. The little tyke loved the attention, especially when she got a cookie.

But the visit took a wicked turn when Maggie pinned Lexi with a knowing grin and demanded, "So you and Jethro Calder, hum? Spill, girl. I want details, vivid, leave-nothing-out details."

CHAPTER NINE

THE VISIT TO Modern Goddess lasted longer than Lexi planned. Her watch read ten-thirty when she carried Jazi into the suite. She and Jazi both needed freshening up so the groceries would have to wait. She planned to toss the perishables in the refrigerator and organize everything when she got back.

Except everything was already put away.

She set Jazi down and checked out the cupboards and refrigerator. "Okay, I could get used to this."

Jazi helped by opening one of the lower cabinets and pulling out pans until the door opened. "Jethro!" She ran to him and he swept her up. "Hi."

"Hello. It looks like someone got cake."

"A cookie actually." Lexi shoved the pan back in the cupboard and joined him in the foyer. "We were just headed in to get cleaned up. We'll be ready in a jiff."

He glanced at his watch as he handed over Jazi.

"Don't worry," Lexi reassured him. "We won't be late."

He lifted a skeptical brow.

Oh, challenge on. She had to forgo changing her clothes, but she added some color to her cheeks and a swipe of gloss to her lips. Jazi got a clean diaper, a dusting of powder and the soiled vest was replaced with a pretty sweater with bows on the shoulders.

Within ten minutes they were back in the foyer waiting on Jethro.

The meeting with Velveth turned out to be interesting. The hotel nannies were available twenty-four-seven, and could watch a child or children in the guests' room or in their care center which looked like a preschool with all its toys and amusements for the children. There were cribs and daybeds in a quiet chamber and a theater room for TV and movies. For older kids a media room held game consoles and computers with customized parental controls. There was a lounge and a play area.

All the rooms were monitored by cameras and two people manned the control room at all times.

From what Lexi saw, all the kids, from a one-year-old to a young teen, seemed to be having a good time. Jethro let her lead the appointment. She asked a few questions of Velveth and a few of the other nannies and she liked what she heard. If the need arose, she'd feel comfortable leaving Jazi in their care.

At the end of the appointment, Jethro thanked Velveth and escorted Lexi and Jazi out of the nursery.

"I have one more thing I want to show you." A warm hand in the small of her back directed her toward the casino.

He dropped his hand but stayed close through the casino. Just past the cashier cage, they came to a set of double doors discreetly marked Employees Only. A hallway led to a world she knew all too well, backstage of the theater.

Stagehands and crew members scurried about prepping the theater for the evening show. And from the sound of feet slapping wood, dancers were on stage rehearsing. Her senses absorbed the sights and sounds, the very beat of the world she'd left behind. It was a moment of comfort and angst.

Curiosity got the best of her. "What have you got up your sleeve, Jethro?"

He looked up from his phone. "You'll see. Here's Veronica now."

A woman swept toward them. Just shy of plump, she wore a colorful, flowing robe over a leotard and tights and her gray hair flowed over her shoulder in a thick braid. A beautiful bohemian.

Lexi recognized her immediately. Veronica Snow, choreographer of Pinnacle's dance production *Acropolis*. The woman had an Emmy, a Tony, and an Oscar.

"Jethro!" She claimed a kiss on the cheek. "How good to see you. You so rarely visit us."

"Ronnie, you'd never get anything done if you had to chase away all the men who'd like to spend time here."

She threw back her head in a hearty laugh. "This is true. But for the handsome four, we would make an exception."

Handsome four? It fit the Fabulous Four perfectly. Jethro had a fan.

Jazi stirred, disturbed by the talking. Lexi patted her back.

"Ronnie, this is the friend I was telling you about." Without asking Jethro lifted Jazi from her arms and settled her against his shoulder.

"Yes, I see. You didn't tell me it was Lexi Malone. How are you, dear? I've seen you dance. You're good, very good."

"Thank you. That means a lot coming from you. I truly admire your work." She stepped closer to Jethro to make room for a man carrying a large torch to get by.

"And I yours." Used to the hustle and bustle, Veronica ignored the activity. "You dance from the heart but hit every beat perfectly. Such musicality is a gift. If you're looking for work, there was no need to go through the usual channels. The answer is yes, we'd love to have you."

"Oh." Shocked and overjoyed, it was on the tip of Lexi's tongue to grab the offer. How she missed performing. But that wasn't her life anymore. She glanced at Jethro to gauge his reaction. Was this a test?

Was he hoping she'd choose dancing over Jazi, freeing him from his promise?

Not going to work. She loved dancing, but she loved Jazi more. And she'd promised Alliyah she'd take care of her.

His expression gave nothing away. After a moment, he lifted one dark eyebrow prompting a response.

Veronica Snow watched Lexi expectantly.

With the call of dancers pounding in the background it took all her will to say no.

She clasped her hands over her heart. "I'm very flattered. And I would honestly love to take you up on the offer, but I've given up performing. I'm a mother now. I need to be available during the day for Jazi's care."

"There is a wonderful nursery on-site here at the hotel. I'm sure we could work something into your contract."

Though it really did hurt to do so, she shook her head. "I'm afraid I have to refuse."

"So you really just want to practice?"

"Practice? I don't understand?"

Jethro spoke up. "I know you miss the dancing, so I asked Ronnie if you could have access to the practice room for exercise."

"Really?" The gesture overwhelmed Lexi. "That would be so perfect." She turned hopeful eyes on Veronica. "Would it be okay?"

Veronica's thick braid bobbed with her answer. "I think we can figure something out. I'll send you our practice schedule. You understand the process so you know I can't promise the practice room will be empty of dancers at any given point, but you are welcome to use the room."

"Right, someone is always wanting extra practice time. I promise to stay out of the way."

"It's agreed then." Veronica smiled. "I have to get back to work, but I hope we'll have the opportunity to get to know each other better."

"I'd like that." Lexi's feet itched to hit the boards, but it would have to wait until later. She held back until the other woman disappeared behind the curtains before throwing her arms around Jethro.

"Thank you." She hugged him and Jazi too. "Thank you.

Thank you." She pulled back, fought the urge to kiss him smack on the mouth. "This is the best thing anyone has ever done for me. It's so thoughtful of you."

"It's sheer self-preservation." He stepped back to soothe Jazi, who got jostled during the embrace.

"What do you mean?"

"I've seen you dance, Lexi. It's more than an occupation for you. It's an outlet. If you can't dance, you're likely to drive me crazy over the next three months."

"I likely will anyway." She hooked her arm through his for the walk out. "But maybe not as badly. And I'm too happy to care if the gesture has ulterior motives. Thank you."

He held the door open for her and relented a little. "A dancer should dance."

She nearly stumbled over her own feet. It was the nicest thing he'd ever said to her.

Lexi juggled two boxes of cupcakes and a balloon bouquet while trying to insert the key card for the suite. She held the card, she'd thought that far ahead, but she couldn't see what she was doing. Suddenly the door opened and she fell inward.

Jethro reacted quickly, stepping forward to block her fall and catch the boxes. He did a quick juggling act of his own and his arm ended up around her waist and she ended up pressed to his side while he easily handled the two boxes with one hand on the bottom.

For the first time in her life she knew what it meant to swoon. Cradled against him, admiring his quick reflexes and agile movements, while surrounded by his strength and warmth, inhaling the sexy musk of man and soap, she just wanted to melt into him.

Control, Lexi, no jumping the man and burying your nose in his neck.

Instead she pulled away from his support.

"Whoa. Good catch." She let him take the boxes, watched as he set them on the foyer table. "I wasn't expecting you for a while or I would have knocked."

"My meeting wrapped early." He looked handsome as ever in his black pants and white shirt. And as reserved. She followed as he returned to the living room. A big pink box sat on the coffee table. He sat down and picked up a big white bow.

"Good. I can use the help. I'm running a little late." She grabbed a couple of bags from the corner and brought them over. She dropped to the floor across from him and started pulling things from the bags. "I still need to wrap my gifts." She hesitated. "I'm so glad you could be a part of the party."

"It's likely the only birthday I'll spend with her."

Yeah, she hadn't wanted to mention that.

"She'll be thrilled." His words were matter-of-fact so she should take them that way and move on. Except she couldn't. If he was only going to get this one birthday with his daughter, it should consist of more than a party in the nursery surrounded by noisy kids and employees. "I'm going to take her to the arcade for dinner. You're welcome to join us if you want."

"I'll have to see how my schedule looks later."

"Of course." Gathering the balloons floating about the foyer, she anchored them before following him into the living room.

"What's in the box?"

"You'll have to wait and see."

"Okay, be that way, then."

He frowned, eyed her uncertainly. Poor baby. She really shouldn't tease, but she'd never met anyone who needed it more. He took life way too seriously.

"Well, I got her an animated movie. A baby doll with clothes. And a bag of plastic building blocks. When you're done putting your bow on, you can help wrap mine."

"Wrapping really isn't my thing."

"You're doing a great job. And I have bags for mine. You just drop the gift in, put tissue paper on top and you're done. Thank you by the way."

"For what?"

"Authorizing the party. I get the feeling Velveth would have been a lot less cooperative if not for you."

"Having it in the nursery was a smart choice."

"Right? Instant party. Which is perfect for this year. Velveth had a few concerns. Thanks for smoothing the way there. I talked to her a few minutes ago. She's getting parent consent forms as kids are dropped off. Nobody has objected and luckily none of the kids so far have allergies, so she's happy.

"I'll confess I'm glad there will be staff to help with this party. I'm still too new at this mothering thing to be comfortable wrangling a dozen kids."

"I'm sure you'll be fine. You must have plenty of experience with birthday parties."

"Not as much as you think." She focused on the cupcake tower she was assembling. "When my dad was alive he made the whole day special and there was always a big cake with buttercream icing." She licked her lips. "Best icing ever. But when it was just mom and me, it was just dinner out and a birthday sundae. What about you?"

"I wasn't really into celebrating my birthday. Most of the foster families respected that."

"Well, that's sad." She was curious but did not push for more information. She didn't care to expound on her history so she'd give him the same courtesy.

"Mama Harman felt the same way."

"That's the home where you met Jackson, Ryan and Clay?"

"Yeah. She felt life was to be celebrated. She had a tradition for birthdays where she cooked the birthday boy's favorite meal and baked a cake. I was to be no different."

"It sounds like a nice tradition."

"Yes, well the other guys wanted cake, so I went along with it. She made me a present."

"The cap in your closet."

He arched a dark brow at her. Sheepish, she smiled and shrugged.

"It's all I have left from her." Rather than look at her he opened the biggest gift bag and dropped in the blocks.

"She must have been a remarkable woman to take on the four of you."

"There would be no Fabulous Four without her influence."

Mangled tissue topped the gift. Lexi let it go, more concerned with him than his wrapping skills. When he reached for the next bag, she laid her hand over his. "Then the world is truly a better place because of her."

He did look at her then, undefinable emotion darkening his eyes. He nodded. "Thank you."

"Mr. Calder, Lexi, hello," Velveth greeted them. "We got the cart you sent down and we are ready for you." She led them to the meal room where they'd pushed several tables together to make a square big enough for all the kids to sit around.

"This is perfect," Lexi exclaimed. They'd set up a festive table with the party items she sent down. She'd chosen a fish theme in honor of Jazi's favorite book. The cupcakes served as a centerpiece and favor bags waited at each seat.

"Thanks for letting us have the party here."

"We are pleased to be of service," Velveth replied, her gaze sliding toward Jethro. "Shall we call the children?"

"I'm ready if you are." Lexi wandered over to where Jethro leaned against a work counter.

She copied his stance, waiting to see Jazi's expression.

Velveth returned, ushering children ahead of her. Jazi's eyes were huge with wonder and excitement. Lexi snapped a picture.

The kids ranged in age from one to twelve. Three staff members helped to get them settled at the table. The older ones dug into the favor bags, while the younger ones looked at the tower of cupcakes with awe.

Lexi took the top cupcake with the two candles and placed it in front of the little girl. Lexi lit the candles. Everyone sang "Happy Birthday."

The best part, Jazi's grin reached ear to ear. She picked up her cupcake and began to lick off the chocolate icing. Grabbing two from the display, Lexi carried them to Jethro.

"Chocolate or vanilla?" She held one out on each palm. He took the chocolate.

"Time for presents," Velveth announced.

Lexi got her gifts and Jazi tore through them. She insisted on opening the baby doll and hugged it to her. Lexi tucked the clothes away and promised Jazi they'd play with the blocks later. She pointed at the big pink box. Jethro brought it over.

Lexi bent over Jazi and helped her remove the lid.

"Bow!" Jazi exclaimed.

OMG. He'd got her a fish.

Later that evening in the arcade Lexi chuckled at Jazi's antics. Frustrated by the fact the skeet ball kept rolling back, she climbed up on the ball alley and walked it up to drop it in the hole. Then she came back for the next one.

Lexi glanced around to see if they were about to be busted and spied Jethro propping up a column about ten feet away. She waved him over, but he shook his head.

Oh, for heaven's sake. She tended to Jazi, helping her by tossing in a couple of balls, then she gathered her up.

But when Lexi turned around, Jethro was gone.

Lexi came slowly awake. She pushed back the covers and went to the bathroom. Since she was up, she grabbed her robe off the armchair and decided to check on Jazi. They'd been with Jethro ten days now and thankfully there'd been no screaming fits. But Jazi still tended to wander at night.

Sometimes she made her way into Lexi's room and crawled into bed with her. But Lexi had found her in the living room, the media room and, one unforgettable time, under her bed.

Sure enough Jazi's covers were mussed and the girl was missing.

Lexi went looking, and the more she searched the more unnerved she became. She couldn't find her anywhere, not even under her bed. Nothing.

Fear beating through her she headed down the hall. Time to wake up Jethro. It was only when she got close to his door and found it open that she realized Jazi had sought out her father. She slept on her back, arms flung out and he slept on his side half curled around her, one bare shoulder exposed so his hand could rest on her lower leg.

Father and daughter sleeping so peacefully together.

Seeing them together like this made Lexi question her whole plan.

And her distress shifted in a whole new direction. Was she being selfish in wanting to provide a loving family for Jazi when her real family was right here? This was her father. She'd taken to him from their very first meeting. She ran to him whenever he got home. And he always handled her with such gentleness.

He should have taken more time to think before he agreed to Lexi's proposition.

He said he didn't know anything about raising a child, but he cared. He might feel out of his depth raising a little girl, but there was no denying he cared about Jazi. Lexi wouldn't be here if he didn't.

Her gut clenched as her heartbeat went wild. Because the Lord knew she wasn't any better qualified. All she had in her favor was love.

But she also knew with Jethro's affection and a good nanny Jazi would be set.

But he had promised, and Lexi had her vow to Alliyah to honor. Even if she could bring herself to give Jazi up, she owed Alliyah more than she could ever give back. Raising Jazi into a woman her mother would be proud of was the only way left to show gratitude to the woman who'd saved her soul.

Lexi began to back out of the room.

"You should take her back to bed." A husky male voice broke the silence.

Lexi froze, mortified to be caught hovering in his room. Had she given herself away, made a distressed sound to awaken him?

No other choice but to brazen it through.

She went to the bed and gathered Jazi into her arms. Avoiding his gaze, she said, "I'm sorry she bothered you."

"It's still a new place for her. She'll settle in. It's been several days since her last visit."

The rasp in his voice touched her on a visceral level so she almost missed the message in the words.

"You mean this isn't the first time?"

"No. The first time I found her curled up outside my door." He raised up on his elbow and the covers dropped to the bed revealing his muscular chest. Thank goodness for the darkness. "After that I left the door ajar. This is the second time she's climbed into bed with me."

"I'm sorry," she repeated, cuddling the girl close. So the nights Lexi thought she'd slept through, she'd been with Jethro.

"You too?"

"Yes. And I've found her in other places in the suite. I was happy she'd slept a few nights in her own bed, but I guess she was with you. Maybe I should just let her sleep with me."

He shook his head. "I can't think that's a good habit to

start. She's just learning her environment on her own terms. She'll settle down."

"Okay." Time stretched out and Lexi realized she was staring, admiring the way the dim light curved over his muscles. Heat rushed to her cheeks. What an odd night. "Well," she cleared the rasp from her throat, "good night."

"Hey, Lexi?" He stopped her flight from the room.

"Yes." She paused one foot out the door.

"I have an early meeting—" he ran a hand through his already ruffled hair,"—but I wanted to ask if you'll be my concubine tonight?"

She blinked. Concubine?

"There's this charity thing tonight, and—"

"You need a date." She broke in when her brain caught up with the conversation.

"Yes. As we are living together—"

"Of course I'll go with you." Anything to get out of this room and away from the sight of him all sleep rumpled and wrapped in nothing more than a sheet. Sexy much? More than she could handle at three in the morning. "What should I wear?"

"It's a costume deal. I'll have my assistant send you the details."

"Okay. But just so you know, I don't put out on the third nondate." Holding Jazi close, she fled from the room.

CHAPTER TEN

THE INFORMATION CAME along with costumes. The note said the charity event for diabetes started at eight in Pinnacle's high-stakes casino, Sky Tower. The four top executives of Pinnacle would be attending as characters from the game. They'd be battle chiefs and their dates: concubines.

Battle chiefs were like chieftains, their status gained by the number of their kills, and concubines were their lethal mistresses.

Fun. Lexi dug into the first garment bag and found Jethro's battle chief costume, a cross between a modern-day biker and an Old West gunslinger. OMG, with his austere persona and dark good looks he'd look like he walked right out of the game. In fact, the fab four were going to be smokin' hot tonight.

The concubine costume, on the other hand, lacked...a lot, including material. She'd look like a Goth Tinkerbell in the dark green strapless number. And she'd be lucky if the hemline covered the essentials. As a dancer, Lexi was used to skimpy—this dress might work in a video game where it was painted on, but she preferred not to flash the world.

Especially while accompanying Jethro.

Luckily, she knew just what to do.

Jethro pulled on the leather duster that completed his costume and shrugged it into place. The air-conditioning better be cranked up in the Sky Tower or he'd be sweating inside an hour.

At least the black jeans and tee underneath were comfortable. If he didn't count the ammo strapped over his chest or the guns on his hips. Hopefully, he wouldn't have to stay long.

"Hi, lover. I'm ready."

He swung around. And about swallowed his tongue.

Lexi stood propped against the doorjamb squeezed into a green number that clung to every soft curve. She wore black thigh-high boots, black stockings and a knife strapped to her thigh. A leather jacket was hooked over one pale, bare shoulder.

Her beautiful features shimmered under an incandescent makeup, making her eyes huge and her lips a kissable cherry red. All of it framed by an intricate upswept do that ended in a fall of curls over her left shoulder.

So sexy he took a step toward her.

"Lexi." He pulled himself to a stop. "You look stunning."

The compliment earned him a delighted grin. "And you look like a bad boy."

"Then I'd say we're ready to go." He relaxed into the leather feeling less of a fraud. He could be a bad boy when necessary. He offered her his arm. "Shall we?"

She hooked her hand around his elbow. Heck, with her by his side people probably wouldn't even notice him. They'd be too busy eying her.

Instead of going down and across to the other elevators, he swiped his key card and hit the button for the top floor. The doors opened into a luxurious lounge refitted to a banquet room complete with dance floor. Dim lighting provided discretion while a domed glass ceiling and walls displayed the best view in Las Vegas.

Music from the party grew louder as Jethro led Lexi past the bar to the casino. As requested they were early so the casino was empty except for the band and waitstaff.

The ten-thousand-dollar tickets gained the attendee access to the casino where there was an open bar and five food stations, each with a different international theme.

Later there'd be dancing and a raffle. The extravagant gifts included a week's stay at any Pinnacle resort.

A rep from the charity spotted him and came running over. "Mr. Calder, good evening, sir. I'm Clark. Thank you so much for your participation in tonight's event. May I say you both look spectacular?"

Taking that as a rhetorical question, Jethro waited for the plump gentleman in the Mongol costume to direct them where to go.

"Thank you." Lexi spoke into the silence. "We're looking forward to the event. I hope you meet your goal tonight."

"Oh, my." The man clasped his clipboard to his thread-bare tunic. "Haven't you heard? We sold out. Every ticket. And OMG, we got so many calls asking for exceptions. This is going to be the event of the year. And it's all thanks to Pinnacle."

"Glad we could help." Not liking the way the man's gaze lingered on Lexi, Jethro drew her closer to his side. "Where do you need us?"

"Yes, of course. This way please. The doors will open momentarily. We'd like for the executives to greet the guests as they enter. Mr. Hawke is already here."

"Jethro." Jackson greeted him by pounding his back. "Best gala ever."

"I'm sure you think so." Jackson's outfit resembled Jethro's except he wore khakis and had a sword strapped over his leather duster. "Grace, you look lovely. You bring an elegance to the concubine they could never duplicate in the game."

"Thanks," the tall black-haired woman sheathed in a silver concubine dress responded. "That's because I had them add four inches."

Lexi laughed. "Smart."

"You must be the mysterious Lexi. I'm Grace, Jackson's fiancée."

"More temporary than mysterious. It's nice to meet you." Lexi shook her hand.

"Oh, how sweet of you. He hasn't mentioned me has he?" Grace sent Jethro a chiding sidelong look. "He's been very closedmouthed about you and Jasmine."

"And that's not going to change tonight." A pinch on his side revealed Lexi's displeasure. He ignored her. "Here come Clay and Ryan."

Both men had beautiful women on their arms, the concubine dresses clinging to ripe curves. Quick introductions were made and then the doors were opened allowing in the swarm of guests. The next hour flew by. The costumes were varied and inventive, the guests engaged and friendly.

And the soft scent of tropical blooms reminded him of the woman by his side.

When the line began to thin, she leaned close and whispered, "I'm starved."

"Me too. Let's ditch this. We've done our duty."

Across the way Ryan tilted his head indicating they were cutting out too.

Jethro followed the group to the Italian station. Lagging back a bit he leaned down to Lexi. "We have a reserved table so we'll join the others to eat, but I expect you to respect my privacy."

She patted his arm. "Yeah, I got the message. Don't worry. Your secrets are safe with me."

Funny, he actually trusted her. And because he did, dinner turned out to be fun. He had to block two attempts by Grace to get Lexi alone, but he relaxed after Grace groused that he needn't bother, Lexi wasn't dishing any dirt.

Clark appeared at the table asking for the executives to pose for a group picture.

Jethro stood along with his friends and reached for his jacket. "At least the air is flowing up here."

"You're welcome." Clay shrugged into his duster. "I

called housekeeping as soon as I put this thing on tonight. Told them to crank up the AC."

Jackson clapped him on the shoulder. "We can always rely on you to handle the details regarding our comfort."

"Damn straight."

The photographer was set up near an internal 3-D wall depicting the ruins of a city. He arranged them—some standing, some crouching in the ruins—and began taking pictures. Behind him people gathered, taking photos with their phones. They must be a sight—this was not a group easily impressed. Jethro saw Lexi with her phone out and shook his head.

"Enough." He broke pose to a round of groans. Jackson enjoyed this stuff, let him stay and work the crowd.

Grabbing Lexi's hand, Jethro pushed through the throng of people headed for the lounge.

"Where are we going?"

"I thought you might like to dance." This night was not ending before he held her in his arms. One dance and he'd be ready to leave.

The band just started a moody ballad as he reached the lounge. He ditched the duster then took her hand and drew her onto the dance floor. Pulling her close, he moved into a smooth waltz.

After a moment her head went back and she grinned up at him. "You're very good."

"Such surprise." He twirled her, led her through two steps and twirled her again.

She laughed her delight. "Try shock. I never had you pegged as a dancer."

"Tsk-tsk. That's shoddy research, Ms. Malone. I quite enjoy the occasional dance."

She wiggled well—defined eyebrows at him. "Meaning you like holding a beautiful woman in your arms to music."

His turn to laugh. "You've got me there."

The music changed to a slightly faster tune. He flawlessly shifted to a fox-trot. All grace, Lexi kept pace with him step for step. One more dance wouldn't hurt.

"When Mr. Harman was alive, Mama Harman was a ballroom dancer. It's a well-kept secret between the four of us that she taught us how to dance. She insisted we'd be happy she did. She was right."

Another secret revealed. This woman was entirely too easy to share with. Perhaps it was the way she spoke to him, as an equal, even teasing him sometimes when so many were intimidated by him.

"Besides being a closet dancer, what else do you do for fun?"

"Fun?"

"Yes, fun. You know, for recreation."

"I know what fun is, Ms. Malone." He lowered her into a dip.

"Do you? You seemed confused."

Not confused, surprised. People rarely concerned themselves with his amusements. "I like to read. I do some climbing, some sailing."

She eyed him suspiciously. "Please tell me you don't climb alone."

How was it she could read him so easily? A better question might be why did she care?

"I'm touched you care. But you needn't worry. I have a few climbing buddies. We keep each other safe."

"You're very insular, aren't you?" The music slowed again, and she looped her arms around his neck and swayed against him.

"I enjoy my own company." His hands went to her waist, so small he almost spanned it with his fingers.

"Right, it's quite safe isn't it?" she challenged softly.

"I'm a numbers man, Ms. Malone. I believe in playing it safe."

"Do you suppose you'll ever call me Lexi again?"

"Not likely."

"Why not?" Her lush cherry-red lips pursed in a pout.

Temptation pulled at him to lean down and taste the sweetness he knew matched the fruity color she'd painted those pretty lips. Instead he stepped back, ending the dance.

"It's safer this way."

"Hey, Lex." Jessica hailed her from the practice room doorway. "I'm sorry, but I have to bail on you. Toothache. My dentist has an opening so I grabbed it."

"No problem, Jess." Lexi walked toward the tall blonde. She knew Jessica from the Golden Cuff. She'd left to go to the Pinnacle just before Alliyah's accident.

Lexi had been thrilled when Jessica had asked her to help her choreograph an audition number for an upcoming show. It allowed her to dip her toe back into dancing during daylight hours. It was a little bittersweet to start out, because she was used to being the performer, but watching Jessica master the piece filled her with satisfaction and pride.

"Best to take care of it or you'll feel it when you're dancing."

"Yeah, I found that out. Listen, I gave up my time in the practice room, but I'm sure the girls would be happy to share with you. I've had three people ask if you're taking on additional clients."

"Clients?" Lexi laughed. "You're my friend. I'm only taking your money because you insisted."

"And you're worth more than I'm paying." Jessica checked her watch. "I've got to go, but we're definitely on for Thursday. Oh, and I almost forgot—Veronica asked if you'd stop by her office."

Really? "Thanks for letting me know. Good luck at the dentist."

Jessica waved on her way out the door and Lexi went to gather her gear, wondering what Veronica wanted to see her about. She found the older woman in her office adjacent to the practice room. The office was good-sized with a huge old-fashioned teacher's desk, a chaise longue in the corner and two plum-colored visitor chairs.

Lexi knocked on the open door.

"Give me a minute." Gray head bent, Veronica's hands and fingers moved to unheard music as she flipped through a document on the tablet in front of her. She shook her head once, made a change then nodded and set the tablet aside. Only then did she look up.

"Lexi," the choreographer exclaimed, "come in. Thanks for coming by." She rose and indicated for Lexi to take one of the visitor chairs. "Sorry about that." She waved at the desk as she sat in the second chair. "I'm working on a new dance and I had to get the sequence down while it was fresh in my head."

"No problem. We have to respect the process, don't we?"

"Exactly." Veronica clapped her hands and beamed at Lexi as if she'd performed a wondrous feat. "That's one of the things I like most about you, Lexi, you respect the process and it shows. You take what's given to you and make it your own, bringing a refinement to the work so it appears effortless no matter how grueling the piece is."

Lexi flushed with pleasure. "That's quite a compliment coming from you."

"Believe me, I'm not the only one to notice." Veronica turned in the chair to face Lexi, leaning forward solicitously. "It's the very reason I want to talk to you."

"Really?" Curiosity drew Lexi to the edge of her seat.

"Yes. I'd like for you to consult with me on this new dance."

"Consult?" The word came out as a squeal. Shock could do that to a woman. Lexi felt her eyes pop wide and blinked to gain control. "Me?"

"Don't be so surprised. As I said, your talent has been noticed. I've also seen the improvement in Jessica's dancing since you've been working with her. You've earned this."

"Wow, thank you. I would absolutely love to work with

you. Please know that right up front. But what kind of time commitment would you want? I have Jazi to care for." She'd come too close to losing her daughter not to put her needs first, no matter how fabulous the offer.

"Of course." Veronica reached out and patted Lexi's hand. "It shouldn't require more than a few hours a day a couple of times a week. Frankly, at this point that's all the time I have to put into it. It'll pick up once we start practice, but I'm willing to work with you."

"This is such a surprise." Lexi shook with excitement. She'd have been happy to dance for the woman, having the opportunity to work with her blew Lexi's mind. "Let me talk to Jethro." Okay, she never thought she'd say those words. But he was her partner, of sorts, for the time being. "If he has no objections, I'm in a hundred percent."

"Wonderful. I can't expect he will." Veronica stood. When Lexi also stood, the other woman enveloped her in a fragrant hug. "I'm so excited to be working with you. Call me after you talk to Jethro and we'll set up a schedule."

Lexi's head was still reeling when she reached the penthouse. The unexpected sound of voices coming from the living room drew her in that direction. She blinked at the crowd of strangers sprawled throughout the room. Several held instruments and everyone seemed to be talking at the same time.

A shrill whistle cut through the din and one voice drawled, "Well, hello, sweet thing, who might you be?"

The man had warm brown eyes, dark hair and a trim beard. He looked familiar.

Warm hands cupped her shoulders. "This is Lexi Malone." Jethro stood from behind her. "She lives with me." The message was clearly a hands-off warning. Lexi wasn't sure how she felt about that. But he went on. "Lexi, this is—"

"Jack Rabbits," she finished for him. The crowd turned

out to be two men and two women and one of country music's up-and-coming bands. This was turning out to be quite a day.

"Yes. Pinnacle has just signed them to our label and they were going to show me their new song. I thought you might enjoy sitting in. We can go somewhere else if you prefer."

"No, no. I'd love to sit in." She faced their company. "If it's okay with you? I love your music."

"It's fine with us." The bearded man flashed a friendly grin.

"Fans are always welcome. Hi, Lexi." A slim redhead stepped forward to shake her hand. "I'm Holly. And this is Nathan, Roy and Kate. We're never happier than when we have an audience."

"Goody." She clapped her hands, not even caring she was acting like a teenage girl. Still she made an effort to pull herself together. "Did Jethro offer you refreshments?

"Thank you. We just came from lunch." Holly spoke for the group. "Now we're eager to sing our song for Jethro."

"Then let's get started." Jethro took charge.

Soon the band was situated on the sofa, with Roy in a dining room chair at the end to give him more room to play his guitar. Jethro offered her the chair but she dropped to the carpet next to him and sat cross-legged. She'd left her phone with her gear in the foyer so she glanced up at Jethro. "Can you let the nursery know I'll be late picking up Jazi?"

In response, he pulled out his phone and sent a text. Then he nodded to Roy. "Whenever you're ready."

"We'll start with a couple of our hits if you don't mind." Roy strummed the strings of his guitar. "Singing something familiar helps to warm us up."

He began the chords to "Sunshine and Roses," one of Lexi's favorites. She started to sing along and covered her mouth to stop herself, but a nod from Kate told her it was okay. With a grin she joined in.

For all Lexi's years of studying music, she'd never participated in a jam session. She rocked to the beat as the music flowed through her. This felt like a rite of passage in some ways. So much fun, she couldn't stop smiling.

After a couple of songs, Roy began to pick a slower tune.

"We're still working out some of the harmonies," Holly warned them. "But we think this has the potential to go to number one on the charts."

Lexi hugged her knees as the band began to sing. The song portrayed a single mother learning to trust in love again. It was a lovely ballad with a heartfelt chorus.

When the band finished, they started discussing the harmony changes they were considering. Lexi heard the same stresses they did and she longed to share her ideas, but it wasn't her place. She pressed her lips together and listened.

Jethro sat back and observed. The song was good. He agreed with the potential the band predicted. It sounded fine to him, but the band all agreed something in the chorus needed fixing, they just didn't agree on what.

The corner of his mouth ticked up when his gaze moved to Lexi. She sat at his feet practically vibrating with the need to join the conversation. He appreciated her discretion—the band probably wouldn't appreciate her unsolicited advice. On the other hand as one of the owners, he had more leeway.

"Lexi, what do you think?"

All chatter stopped and five sets of eyes landed on him.

"She has a doctorate in music," he said easily. "I've never met anyone with a finer ear."

The band members looked at each other and then at Lexi. She sent him a glance that was half accusation half gratitude.

"I do have a couple of suggestions, if you're interested," she offered.

"Sure." Nathan spoke for the group. "We don't promise to use them, but we're willing to listen."

"The transition you're stumbling over might benefit from a change of a two-syllable word over a three-syllable word, maybe *tough* instead of *difficult*. Something that simple can give you the extra beat you're missing. I also thought it might add a spark of interest to speed the chorus up a few of beats."

The band's reaction was a mix of thoughtful and skeptical. To demonstrate Lexi began to sing. She had a few pitch problems but overall she recalled the lyrics of the first refrain and nailed the chorus. Before she finished, the band was nodding and they jumped in and continued the song.

At the end they all started talking at once, excitedly drawing Lexi into the conversation. Holly whipped out a tablet and noted changes. She passed the device along and each member of the band nodded.

"Let's try it one more time." Roy played the opening chords.

At Jethro's feet Lexi closed her eyes, her fingers tapping to the beat. A serene smile lifted the corners of her mouth. He heard the difference too, and nodded. He preferred not to contemplate the fact he took almost as much satisfaction in her joy as in the betterment of the song.

As the last verse faded away, a hushed silence filled the room.

Nathan jumped to his feet with a whoop, his fist punched to the ceiling in triumph. "That was sweet, sweet music." He stepped around the coffee table and swept Lexi up into a big hug. "Now it's a number one."

Jethro tensed, ready to intercede. But he was the only one uncomfortable. She laughed and hugged the big, barrel-chested man. Then she went on to hug the rest of the band. Jethro relaxed back in his chair until Holly came over and demanded a hug. Maybe he was the one who needed saving.

He survived it, barely, egged on by Lexi's teasing smile. Still he breathed easier when the band announced they needed to leave for their next engagement. "I'll walk you out."

Unsettled with himself—he never got jealous—he wandered back into the room and suddenly found his arms full of warm woman.

"Thank you. Thank you. Thank you." She nearly strangled him in her enthusiasm and still he pulled her closer. It had been too long since he'd felt a woman's curves against his body. Too soon she pulled away. He suffered a kiss on the cheek.

"It was so sweet of you to include me." She hooked her elbow around his and led him back to the living room. "This has been the best day ever. Let me get you a drink and I'll tell you about the offer Veronica made me."

"Don't tell me you're joining the troupe?" Now there was a temptation he'd find hard to resist.

"Even better, she wants me to choreograph a dance with her."

Lexi poured a glass of chardonnay and carried it along with the baby monitor to a comfortable chair in the living room. She set down the baby monitor and used a remote to open the drapes to the fabulous view. She put on an album by one of her all-time-favorite female artists and turned the volume down low. With a sigh, she sank into the soft cushions and took her first sip. Nice. Peace at last.

Jazi finally slept. She'd been a handful tonight as she'd been cranky from the lack of a nap. Jethro was out at a dinner meeting.

Another week down. That made three.

A second sip made it easy to admit it hadn't been that bad.

In fact, time flew by. She loved all the Jazi time. And after the first week, she'd settled into a rhythm. Unless he had an early meeting, Jethro ate breakfast with them. He joined them for dinner three or four times a week though he checked in with her several times a day.

In the morning she taught Jazi baby yoga and read to her or they played songs on Lexi's electric piano. Mostly that meant she made up songs while Jazi played with her toys. She'd actually started composing a lullaby she really liked. Jazi liked it too. It put her to sleep almost every time. Tonight was the first time it had failed.

Jazi liked to go to the nursery in the afternoon. Time Lexi took advantage of to get in a dance workout or work with Jess or Veronica. Then it was back to the suite where Lexi put Jazi down for a nap while she started dinner.

Something she never expected from this arrangement was a resurgence of her dancing career. She loved working with Veronica choreographing a piece with multiple dancers. It was bigger and more challenging than anything she'd done to date.

And it was all due to Jethro.

She didn't know how to feel about that, so she didn't dwell on it. Surprisingly, he managed to be present without being obtrusive.

The one thing they clashed on was Jazi's bedtime. Lexi had a more open policy. She put Jazi down between eight and eight thirty every night, but if she didn't stay down, Lexi let her stay up until she'd tired herself out. Part of that was fear of the screaming fits coming back and part came from Lexi's determination not to force the restrictions on Jazi that she'd had forced on her.

Jethro believed Jazi should have a set bedtime that was enforced. He stated children craved structure and discipline and that required a set schedule.

She didn't totally disagree—she felt love, affection and a semiset schedule provided a sound foundation for Jazi without stifling her creativity and individuality. It wouldn't be an issue except for Jazi's little jaunts in the middle of the night. So Lexi was trying to set a schedule. Obviously there'd be a learning curve.

The only true blot so far was having to be escorted anytime she went out with Jazi. Clay generally took her wherever she needed to go. He never rushed her or acted as if the trip was unwarranted. And still she felt diminished and claustrophobic.

She felt like she was a teenager again and back under her mother's control. Mother never let Lexi have any independence. She always had to have friends, classmates, teachers or someone with her wherever she went, as if she didn't have the intelligence to be let out alone.

The lack of freedom and refusal to let her have dance in her life was what drove Lexi to leave home as soon as she turned eighteen. She felt sad over the way she left but she never regretted her decision.

She kept telling herself it was only three months—less now—but it didn't help. Something had to give, and it was Jethro.

Today she asked Clay what would change Jethro's mind about her having an escort and his response had been, *Nothing.*

Lexi didn't accept that.

She relaxed a little when Clay added, "He'd have bodyguards on the three of us if he had his way. Only the fact we'd insist he have one too keeps us safe from his overprotectiveness. But I won't lie—I sustain a high level of security on the executive floors, both office and sleeping. And I'm personally overseeing the security at Jackson's new house."

Okay, she understood a lot of money equaled a lot of risk. And it helped knowing she wasn't the only one that needed to take care. She still didn't like it.

Because more than her itchiness bothered Lexi. If Jethro truly feared for Jazi's safety and Lexi's ability to keep her from harm, would he use that as an excuse to keep her?

Everything she'd read and come to know about Jethro revealed him as an honorable man. Severe at times, but honorable. The only thing that trumped honor was loyalty. She could see him justifying breaking his word if he convinced himself it was in Jazi's best interest.

After all, that was his only reason for giving her up.

Which meant she needed to find a way to protect Jazi from harm. A smile slowly bloomed inside her and she uncurled to fetch her phone. She sent Clay a text and then toasted her brilliant idea and finished her wine.

Lexi slowly came awake. Eyes closed, she took stock of what she remembered. Man, the wine really knocked her out. She stretched her body, turning one way and then the other moaning softly as she worked out the kinks of slumbering in a chair.

She blinked her eyes open. A man loomed over her.

"Eee!" she screamed, pushing back in her chair to get away.

And then she was on her feet, fist flying. She had a daughter to protect.

In the next instant she recognized Jethro. He caught her hand in his, pulled her off-balance, swung her around and wrapped her in his arms. It happened so fast her head spun and she may have screamed again.

"Let go," she demanded, wiggling to be set free.

"It's Jethro," he said, his breath warm against her ear.

"Yeah, I figured it out." She tried twisting side to side, but found no give in his strong arms. "After you nearly scared me to death."

"I live here," he pointed out. "Who else would it be?"

"Oh, I don't know, assassins, kidnappers, zombies? Whatever else you believe can make off with Jazi or me."

"You're spooked. Is that why you want Clay to give you self-defense lessons?"

"I'm not spooked."

She stopped her efforts to be released. All she'd succeeded in doing was rubbing her body against his, which she liked way too much. And it distracted her from arguing with him. Holy tomatoes he smelled good.

"You're the one who is spooked. I freaked out because I woke up to find a strange man standing over me."

"I'm not strange."

"That's debatable."

"I meant I'm not a stranger."

"That's debatable too. Are you going to let me go or should we put music on and dance?"

She felt an odd shaking behind her and glared at him over her shoulder. "Are you laughing at me?"

"Would you hate me if I was?"

That made her stop and think. "No. But only because you don't laugh enough. Are you going to release me anytime soon?"

"I like you where you are."

She sucked in a breath. So he felt it too. The awareness between them that never really went away. The heat and sizzle that caused her skin to tingle whenever he was close. Like now.

"All the more reason you should."

"You're right, of course." And still he held her.

After a moment, his grip loosened and she forced herself to step away. She needed more wine. She picked up her glass and held it up. "Want a glass?"

"Sure." He followed her to the kitchen. "Zombies?" he asked.

She shrugged expressively. "It seems as likely as the other options."

"The other options are viable threats. I have letters to prove it."

"OMG." She handed him his wine. "You have letters threatening you? Why?"

He sipped his wine, hummed his approval. "I don't explain the crazies. I take steps against them." He gestured to her with the glass. "If you're not spooked, why do you want Clay to teach you self-defense?"

She carried her glass back to the living room, but his

question riled her too much to sit. "Because I feel like a delinquent teenager whenever I go out of the hotel. If I know how to defend myself, and Jazi, then you won't have to send an escort with us every time we leave the casino grounds."

He shook his head. "You won't be proficient enough in two months to be effective."

"I might surprise you. I'm a dancer, which makes some men think I'm easy." She flexed her biceps. "I've learned to handle myself."

"Really?" He cocked a brow. "Because you'd have broken your thumb if you'd landed that punch."

She frowned. "Okay, I forgot about the thumb. I just need a refresher on some things." Getting into the mood, she bounced on her toes. "But I'm light on my feet and a quick study. You'll be surprised at what I can learn in a month when I'm motivated."

"Okay." He shrugged out of his jacket, tossed it over the sofa. "Let's see what you've got." He pushed the sofa back and then picked up the ottoman and carried it into the foyer.

"What?" She landed flat on her feet. "Now? Right here?"

"Yes." He moved her to the middle of the room and shoved the chair back against the wall. After shifting a couple more items out of the way, he faced her. "Here. Now." He curled his fingers at her. "Come at me?"

Narrowing her eyes, she looked him over. She was awake now and thinking clearly. He wanted to see her moves? She'd show him.

The black yoga pants she wore along with an oversize tee over a white tank were perfect for this exercise.

Bouncing on her toes, she shook out her whole body, arms, fingers, legs. And then she bent at the waist and stretched, keeping her legs straight as she touched her toes. Next she turned her back to him and spread her legs a bit, stretching down to touch her right foot, then up, and down to her left foot. A peek between her legs showed an upside-down version of Jethro with his feet shoulder-width apart and arms crossed over his chest.

But, oh, yeah, he was watching her butt.

Just the distraction she wanted.

"Are we going to do this tonight?" he demanded.

"Just loosening up," she responded. She faced him again and drew the oversize tee off over her head. His dark gaze zeroed in on her unfettered breasts. Normally she'd want a bra for any workout. Tonight, it worked to her advantage not to have one. Or so she hoped. "I don't want to strain anything."

Tossing the tee on the floor behind her, she did a few more stretches, twisting at the waist to the left and then the right, watching Jethro' eyes follow the movements. Now she was ready.

She prowled across the room, slowly approaching him. "So you want to tangle?" she asked, her voice breathy. All soft curves and subtle hip action, she moved closer, invading his space to whisper in his ear, "You want to dance?"

His hands circled her waist. Check. His head lowered. Check. He pulled her closer. Double check.

Her knee flew up aiming for a vulnerable target. At the last moment she pulled to the right meaning to hit him in the thigh instead, only he was already countering her move. Instead of blocking her, their weight went in the same direction, taking them both down.

Jethro tried to catch her, to save her the brunt of his weight. His effort kept her from landing hard. The plush carpeting helped. But then his body slammed down on top of her, and she lost all the air from her lungs.

CHAPTER ELEVEN

LEXI GASPED, BUT no air went in. Unable to breathe, she grabbed at Jethro.

He pushed up on his arms, starring down at her. "It's okay. Stay calm. You've had the air knocked out of you."

She knew that, wanted it back. Every instinct screamed breathe in. But she could only gasp, the breath sticking at the back of her throat. This happened to dancers all the time. She knew what to do but couldn't think.

She was going to die choking on her own air.

"You're okay—" Jethro brushed the hair off her forehead "—it takes a minute. Breathe out first then you'll be able to breathe in."

It went against every action her brain was sending her way, but she was desperate so she followed his instructions and pushed air out. Immediately air flowed back in. She drew in deep breaths. She just may live after all.

The tension went out of him and his body settled on hers again. He laid his forehead on hers. "You scared me."

"I scared me."

"Is that how you fight zombies?"

"No, that's how I fight sloppy drunks except I hit my target. I was trying to save you."

"Thank you."

"You didn't fall for my act." She cringed at the pout in her voice.

"Oh, I enjoyed the performance. I just didn't let it distract me from your purpose."

"Your enemy's goal," she muttered.

He reared back. "You know *The Art of War*?"

The action ground his hips against hers, providing proof his equipment survived the altercation just fine.

She found herself gasping for air again. "There was a copy in my room." The man probably had the book memorized.

"Are you looking to use my library against me, Lexi?"

She noticed he hadn't moved. Why wasn't he moving? Why wasn't she pushing him away?

"I don't want to be at war with you."

"What do you want?" He finally rolled to the side. He leaned on his elbow and gazed down at her. "Why do you really want to learn to fight?"

She sighed and stared at the ceiling. "I told you, I detest having a babysitter when I go out of the hotel."

"I remember. It makes you feel like a delinquent teenager." He ran his fingers through her hair. "Bad memories?"

"I know you have a file on me," she challenged him. "It probably says I had a privileged upbringing. I did."

"The outside picture doesn't always show all the facts."

She met his dark gaze, trying to read what he felt. "I suppose someone who went through the foster system would know that better than most."

"Privileged doesn't mean happy. You mentioned your life changed when your father died."

"Yes. He was a genius, but he knew how to have fun. Mother wasn't so bad back then. He was a professor and he and my mom homeschooled me. He made learning interesting and he'd take me to class with him sometimes."

"What did he teach?"

"Math. I was twelve when he had an incapacitating stroke. Mother couldn't handle it. She hired someone to care for him and focused all her attention on me. I spent as much time with him as I could. He died when I was fifteen. I'd just graduated from high school. My mother immediately enrolled me at the university. Because of my dad's connections, I was able to do most of my work at home and email in my assignments. Except for piano. I got to go to class for that."

"It sounds like you led a sheltered life."

"It didn't feel like it until it was just mom and me. She loved my dad. He and music were her whole life. When she lost him, first to the stroke and then for good, she focused on the music and I was part of that. She wanted more, bigger, better for me." Lexi picked at the material over her knee. "At first I welcomed the attention. I was missing my dad and the music was something we could share. Until it became clear that what I wanted seemed to matter less and less."

"You wanted to dance."

"Yes! I loved making music, but for me it's more about feeling it. The beat and rhythm connect with something in me and my world comes alive. Mom couldn't—wouldn't—understand that. She saw dance as an unnecessary distraction."

"You got your doctorate at the age of twenty-two." His comment confirmed he'd read the reports given to him.

"A slacker by genius standards. I had to work to support myself the last few years."

"Because you left home when you turned eighteen."

"I couldn't stay any longer. I felt smothered in that house. She was the only family I had so I kept hoping she'd see reason. But the more I pushed for freedom to do things I liked, the tighter she got on the reins, until I felt like a prisoner in my own home." She reached up and pulled the band from her hair, sighed at the release of tension.

"For her it was always about playing, about the performance. Not for me. I had a hard time with the symphony because the conductor's version of the music jarred with what I felt. I played it, but it always felt off to me. That's not the career I wanted."

"And not what your mother wanted to hear."

Red strands of hair fell in her face when she shook her

head. "No. And as long as I was in her house, I had to do things her way." She lifted one shoulder, let it fall. "So I left." She met Jethro's dark gaze. "I had to dance. More than the hidden moments I stole for myself. I longed to learn, to know what my body could do. When she did allow me to go somewhere, it was only with an approved companion. As if I couldn't be trusted out of her sight."

A low growl sounded in the back of his throat. "You know my escorts are there for your safety."

"Yeah, that's what my mother said too. They were just there in the event something happened I wouldn't be alone. It all boils down to a lack of faith in me."

"Lexi, that's not true."

She shrugged. "It's what it feels like."

He swept her hair behind her ear. "How'd you manage on your own?"

"I had a small trust fund my father left me. I rented a room from one of the professors and added cosmetology to my curriculum. I can play most instruments so the symphony hired me as a backup artist. That was kind of fun. Between that and a few other pickup jobs, I managed until I got my doctorate. As soon as I finished my last course, I bought a bus ticket to New York and never looked back."

"The Big Apple. You didn't stay there long."

"I couldn't afford to. That is one expensive burg. And you need to be good, I mean seriously good, to dance in New York. I didn't have the chops or experience they wanted."

"You met Alliyah there."

She nodded. "In a dance class. She was the teacher. Now, she was good. I'd watch her and burn with envy. Not because she'd already been in a couple of off-Broadway productions and was working her way up, but because she made it look effortless. She was so beautiful, so graceful. I wanted to be her."

"How did the two of you end up in Las Vegas?"

"We became friends and then roommates. She got the

chance to do a music video with a hip-hop band as the lead dancer. She talked the artist into using me as a background dancer. The choreographer wasn't too pleased, wanted me to pay for my own flight. It was a tough decision, but I'd be getting paid and it would be my first credit. I went for it. Turned out the choreographer liked us, so we got more work and then he offered us spots in the show he was starting for the Monte Carlo. The money was good so we decided to stay."

"And it wasn't long before the student outreached the teacher."

"Never. Alliyah was a headliner well before me and would have continued to be, except she got pregnant. Jazi was the most important part of her life. She dropped back into the chorus because it was less demanding and allowed her more time with her child."

"If the money was good, why was she moonlighting?"

A sense of aggravated fondness lifted the corners of Lexi's mouth. "Alliyah liked to shop. For herself, for others. Her lack of discipline in that area was the only thing we ever fought over. She had no real money sense. More than once I had to cover the rent because we all had new pretties."

"I'm sorry."

Lexi shook it off. "I didn't mind. We were a family. I just wanted her to be more responsible with her money. For Jazi's sake."

"You cared."

"Well, yeah. Of course. She was my best friend. And I loved Jazi from the moment she was born."

"It shows." He ran his fingers over the back of her hand. "Thank you for everything you've done for her. Knowing you'll be her mother is the only thing that keeps me sane about this whole arrangement."

A wash of emotion flooded her, relief, gratitude, affection and so much more. She turned her hand over and curled her fingers with his. "That's the nicest thing anyone has ever said to me."

"I mean it."

"I know—that's what makes it matter. Goodness." She swiped at the tears leaking out of the corners of her eyes. "I'm a mess." She waved toward him. "I've spilled my guts and now you know my whole life story. What about you? How did you end up in foster care?"

"My mother threw me in the garbage when I was a few weeks old."

Something, maybe the way he looked away, kept her from laughing at his comment. Because surely he couldn't be serious. People didn't throw infants away as if they were trash.

Except sometimes they did.

"I'm so sorry. Did they find her? Did you ever get to know her?"

"No."

That was it; he offered nothing more.

His stiff posture shouted his discomfort. Knowing how reticent he was she imagined he rarely, if ever, spoke of this. She'd always wondered what put him off having a family. He was such a strong, intelligent, competent man. Sure he was overprotective and autocratic at times, but he could also be kind and gentle. No one would ever look at him and see a lost little boy.

This was at the heart of the vulnerability she occasionally glimpsed. Why he allowed so few people to get close.

So why spill his guts now? Why to her?

Duh! Because in spite of his desire to remain autonomous, he was a father and he was struggling to find his way.

Her heart bled for him, but she didn't know how to help him. What she did know was keeping it bottled up solved nothing.

"How do you know it was your mom?"

He went still and a scowl darkened his features. "Who else if not my mother?"

She leaned forward, kept her tone soft, gentle. "Maybe your father, or a grandparent?" Neither were acceptable substitutes, but slightly less traumatic than being rejected by your mother.

How often had she angsted over why her mother didn't love her?

He pulled away from her touch. "Is that supposed to make me feel better—that my whole family threw me away?"

"No." Not letting him push her aside, she wrapped her arms around one of his and propped her chin on his shoulder. "I'm saying you don't know what happened. It takes a lot for a woman to abandon her child."

"Then where was she?" he demanded. "Why didn't she fight for me?"

And there was the little boy.

"Maybe she couldn't. Maybe she died and your dad panicked. Maybe she was a runaway forced to work the streets and her pimp threw you away. Or maybe someone from another town stole you and then couldn't live with what they did so they left you somewhere on the way home."

A heavy sigh lifted his chest. "Oh, that's nice."

"I'm sorry, but an infant in the garbage is ugly. What led to it is going to be just as ugly. Maybe whoever threw you away thought you were dead."

"You're just full of colorful scenarios. Maybe it was a zombie."

"Ha-ha. Haven't you ever made up stories imagining what happened?"

He shook his head. "Being thrown in the trash seemed a pretty clear message to me."

"Not to me. How about this? High school sweethearts very much in love. She gets pregnant at sixteen. He stands by her, but her parents kick her out of the family house. It still happens. His parents refuse to take her in so the young couple leaves for the big city. He'll get a job, they'll get an apartment, everything will be fine. Instead they end up on the streets. They have no money, no insurance. You come early. Your dad tries to get your mom to a hospital, but you come too fast. He has to deliver you himself, and then your mom hemorrhages, and he can't stop it.

"Someone finally comes to help him. They call 911. She's dead and you're crying. He's seventeen and afraid. All he can think is if the authorities come they'll take you away. He grabs you and runs. But he has no resources, no way to feed or clothe you. He tries his best, even robs a convenience store, but those supplies don't last long, and it's cold, and you're sickly."

Into the story, Lexi cleared a lump from her throat. Jethro sat still as a stone next to her.

"He wants to take you home except he can't. It was because of his parents and hers that she was gone. He can't go back to that life, to the people who saw honor in death over morals. He needs more supplies so he hides you in a trash can a safe distance away and attempts to rob another store. This time the owner has a shotgun under the counter and your dad is shot and killed. Sometime later you're found in the trash can but the two incidents are never linked."

Silence followed the end of her story. Lexi bit her lip, waiting for Jethro's response, which remained unvoiced for long minutes.

"You do realize," he finally said, "in this version I'm responsible for the destruction of my parents."

"Oh, come on." Frustrated with his pessimism, she reared back and socked him in the arm. "Clearly this was a story of two people who loved their son so much they'd give anything for him, including their lives."

He hooked an arm around her waist and pulled her into his lap. He lifted her chin on the edge of his hand. "What makes you such an optimist?"

"Choice." She gave the easy answer. Then, because the moment called for honesty, she sighed and admitted, "And maybe a touch of defiance. At home it was a form of rebellion and when I left home I wasn't going to let my mother's predictions of failure pull me down. Optimism was my only option. I chose to believe in myself. I chose to believe everything was going to work out. And mostly it does."

His dark eyes roved over her face. "I wish it were that simple."

She cupped his cheek. "It can be that simple. Stop letting the past rob you of a future. Create a story you can live with and make it your reality. You're an amazing man, Jethro. Choose to look to the future with hope."

"I'm too old to change now."

She shook her finger in his face. "You wouldn't say that if we were talking about a business deal."

"Business is different."

"Why?"

"Business doesn't involve emotions."

She laughed, letting him lead the conversation away from his past. "How can you be so successful and believe that malarkey? Business is totally ruled by emotions."

"Business is based on facts and numbers."

"Yes, and once you have the facts and numbers, what guides the decision? Emotion. If you want to call it your gut or instinct, go ahead, but bottom line it's all about how those facts and figures make you feel that shifts the balance when it comes time to make the decision."

He ground his teeth together. "Has anyone ever told you you're a pest?"

"No." She postured and patted the hair at the back of her neck. "I'm perfect."

"Really?" His fingers threaded through her hair and he drew her to him. "Let me taste to be sure."

His mouth claimed hers, his tongue surging inward to tangle with hers. He tasted of man and mocha. And he smelled fabulous. She wrapped her arms around his neck and let sensation carry her away.

Jethro shifted, tilting Lexi's head to deepen the kiss. She was no longer in his arms but sprawled on the floor with him above her. She savored his weight, his warmth, his strength. Pulling him closer, she held on tight, afraid he'd come to his senses. She'd waited for this, wanted this for so long. Since the night he broke into her apartment and demanded the truth.

Her head binged a warning, but her heart sang and her body soared so she let reason go fly.

She panted, his talented fingers and hungry lips driving her into a frenzy of need. Always so cool, so controlled, but not now, not here. He divested them of their clothes in mere seconds. Then his hands were everywhere stroking, caressing. And squeezing. Exquisite.

Who knew?

She tried to reciprocate, longing to taste him, to explore the hard body pressed to hers, but all she could do was cling to him as he played her body like a fine instrument. Smoothing fingers over slick skin, she dragged heavy lids up to see him. Her whole body clenched to find all his brooding intensity focused on her. His eyes darkened to a blue deeper than midnight and blazed with the heat of passion. His features were drawn tight with the primitive drive to claim the woman in his arms.

"So beautiful." He trailed a finger along her jaw, down her neck and lower. "So soft, yet I feel the strength in you. So sexy." He lowered his head and his tongue followed the path of his finger.

Lexi shivered, thrilled to be the target of his intense regard. The look in those dark eyes cherished her, telling her he was with her mind, body, and spirit, that he hungered for her above all others. Touch reinforced the message, building anticipation, heightening the senses, seducing her when there was no need for seduction.

"Jethro." Beyond thought, she arched her dancer's body into his hold, offering him everything. And he caught her, lifting her to the heights until he roared his satisfaction. And she shattered in his arms.

CHAPTER TWELVE

SPRAWLED HALF ON Jethro and half on the lush white carpeting, Lexi had barely caught her breath when a scream echoed down the hall and from the baby monitor. And then another, and another.

She went from boneless satisfaction to alert mother in a blink.

"Oh, no." Despair rolled through Lexi. "Jazi."

She hopped to her feet, realized she was naked and looked frantically for her clothes. The few items she'd worn were scattered all over the room. As another scream sounded, she gave up looking and grabbed Jethro's shirt, pulling it on as she raced down the hall.

Jethro yanked on his dress pants and followed on her heels.

She'd prayed Jazi had outgrown her screaming fits. The lack of them over the last few weeks had made Lexi hopeful they were a thing of the past.

She reached the bedroom, her heart shredding at the sight of Jazi sitting straight up in the middle of the bed, body rigid, tears streaming down her face, shrill screams pouring from her throat.

Lexi wrapped the baby in her arms and rocked her. "It's okay, Jazi, you're safe. I'm here. I've got you."

The little girl hung limp in her arms; the screams continued. It was like she didn't even hear Lexi. Still she held the little girl and rocked her, talking softly to her.

Jethro paced next to the bed.

"What's wrong? What set her off?"

"I don't know. Maybe a dream. She was cranky when I put her to bed. Maybe my screams disturbed her earlier and she woke up scared."

Lexi hummed softly for a few minutes and Jazi stopped screaming. She panted, drawing in deep breaths. And then she started screaming again.

Her distress broke Lexi's heart. Jazi was so tiny, so fragile and nothing Lexi did helped. She felt helpless and near to tears herself. Worse, Jethro was a witness to all of it.

"You should call Clay—" she cleared her throat, forcing the words past the lump sitting there "—and assure him she's okay in case someone complains."

"No one is going to complain." Jethro ran a hand over her head. "The penthouse suites are built to withstand wild parties. They're pretty much soundproof."

Rocking Jazi, she swallowed hard. "Thank you."

"Let me try." He held out his arms.

Lexi tightened her arms around Jazi, hating to give her up, but the need to ease her distress was stronger, so she lifted her up and Jethro gathered her into his arms. He laid her head against his shoulder and placed a hand in the small of her back.

"Breathe with me, Jazi." His chest rose and fell, Jazi moving with each breath. He breathed deep and steady, talking to her until she started breathing along with him. Slowly she calmed and the screams lessened and then stopped. Jazi snuggled against his bare chest, seeming to take comfort in his warmth.

Her breath hitched a few times but she appeared to be past the storm.

Lexi let out a breath she hadn't known she was holding. Thank goodness.

Jazi held out her hand to Lexi. Love welling up, she leapt up to take her, but Jazi had other ideas. She wanted Lexi, but she wasn't letting go of Jethro. He solved the problem by pulling her close with Jazi between them.

Lexi wrapped her arms around his waist, letting the tension slip away. These fits of Jazi's were so hard on the little girl. They were tough on Lexi too. It tore her up to see the toddler so upset. But this time she hadn't been alone. She'd had help.

She laid her head on Jethro's shoulder and leaned on him, an indulgence she rarely allowed. Soaking in his warmth, like Jazi took comfort in his nearness, in his company. She felt as close to him in this moment as she had in the throes of passion.

It occurred to her that parenting with a partner might have some merit to it. Dangerous thoughts, because something happened to her while she watched him soothe Jazi. Something that changed everything for Lexi. She'd fallen in love with Jethro Calder.

That night the three of them ended up in Jethro's big bed. She fell asleep wrapped in his arms and dreamt of them becoming a real family. Jethro smiled more, Jazi thrived under her father's devoted attention and Lexi found the perfect balance between commitment and independence.

In the dream they were walking through a house with a white picket fence in a pretty neighborhood. Jazi exclaimed over a room with a pink canopy bed, an aquarium, bookshelves full of books and an artist easel. She ran inside and began to play. Farther along there was an office for Jethro and in the back a long room had a dance floor and mirrors on one end and a piano and assorted instruments on the other. Lexi wanted to explore but Jethro pulled her down to the master bedroom, a beautiful retreat she couldn't remember because dreamy Jethro tugged her into his arms and the dream took an erotic turn.

Contentment lured her into sleeping longer than usual and she woke to find Jethro gone. She lay there curled around Jazi wishing he'd woken her, wishing they could have talked.

Waking up in Jethro's bed gave her the perfect opportunity to indulge herself in his grotto shower. Water rained down on her, hot and steamy. She stood on smooth rocks while green fronds draped over the top and sides of the glass partition.

But the luxury failed to distract her from her dream. It didn't take a massive IQ to see what her subconscious was telling her. She'd fallen for the hard-headed Jethro so now her heart wanted the daddy-makes-three mix with a flip side of picket fences and rose gardens.

That so wasn't her.

She hadn't had a lot of relationships. She liked to keep things light and loose. Fun while it lasted and friends down the road. No baggage, no obligations. No one telling her what to do. Just being with each other while it felt right.

And that was the problem. The dream had felt right. She'd woken up happy. And she couldn't shake the desire to know that feeling every day. She lifted her face to the rainfall spray and wondered how that was possible when Jethro came with a load of baggage, untold obligations and a fine-tuned art of telling people what to do.

But he'd also given her free reign in the kitchen, which allowed her a sense of comfort in a strange home. He'd found her a place to dance, which was necessary to her well-being. And he'd encouraged her to work with Veronica, an opportunity she'd never have had if he hadn't introduced them.

He got her like no one else ever had.

How did she walk away from that?

Lexi canceled her morning meeting with Veronica to spend extra time with Jazi to make sure she felt secure and suffered no lingering upset from the night before, but the little tyrant demanded to go to "school," as Jazi called the nursery.

Relieved to see Jazi being her usual spirited self, Lexi

took her down to the nursery. She swung by Veronica's office but the door was locked and it was obvious she was out. Lexi returned to the penthouse where she spent the morning brooding.

Last night had been in turns earth-shattering, devastating and sublime.

She'd give anything to know what he was thinking today. So of course she'd texted him.

Twice.

Still no answer.

What she really wished was to go back to the time before Jazi had started screaming. How would it have played out? Never had she been more open with a man, physically or emotionally. And there wasn't a doubt in her mind it was the same for him.

Had the intimacy been too much for him? Is that why he hadn't answered her text or called?

He'd been so patient with Jazi last night, so gentle in the face of her hysteria. It had been him, not Lexi to soothe Jazi. Lexi did not look forward to dealing with those episodes on her own.

And so ended one loop as another began.

No more.

Needing a distraction she decided to make herself lunch. She'd just started putting together a sandwich when a knock came at the penthouse door. She opened it to find a tall dark-haired man standing before her.

"Lexi."

"Ryan."

Handsome in an exotic way, she recognized him from the charity event. If Jethro and his foster brothers ever lost their fortunes, they could take up modeling and get it all back.

"Can I come in for a moment?"

"Sure." She stepped aside, curious as to what had caused Pinnacle's general counsel to seek her out. Before she moved in, Jethro had mentioned a contract, but that was nearly a month ago. Was this his response to last night's intimacy? His way of telling her nothing had changed? "Will Jethro be joining us?"

"No. Something came up in New York and as our offices are closed all week for Thanksgiving, he's handling it."

Right. Jethro had mentioned the office would be closed. "But you're working?"

He shrugged. "I'm happiest when I'm working. I'm a lot like Jethro in that way. Or how he used to be."

Used to be? Lexi latched on to the phrase. Did that mean Jethro had changed in some way?

"Be thankful Jethro is occupied—he's in a foul mood today."

News to her. Since she hadn't heard from him, even though she'd texted him.

"I'm making lunch." She led Ryan to the kitchen where sandwich makings were spread over the counter. "Would you like a ham and provolone on wheat?"

"Actually, that does sound good." He slid onto a stool at the counter across from her and set a folder on the granite countertop.

She waved at the condiments and veggies in front of her. "What do you want on it?"

He surveyed the options. "No tomato."

"Coming up." She added lettuce, pickles and mustard to the ham, cheese and mayo, cut the sandwich in half, plated it with a pickle spear and handed it to him. After she passed him a napkin, she started on a second one for herself.

"Thank you. I can't remember the last time someone made me a sandwich." He took a bite and nodded. "It's good."

She licked mustard from her thumb. "What can I do for you?"

He wiped his mouth. "Nothing. I have something for you." Ryan reached for the folder and pulled out some papers.

"The contract about Jazi." Lexi's heart skipped a beat. "Jethro told me he'd want one."

"No, Jethro is still making changes to that contract. Ask him about it would you? Then we may get somewhere." There was a sardonic tone to the comment that suggested the men were at odds over the issue. "This is something totally different. This is for your contribution to Jack Rabbits song."

She eyed him, ignoring the pages he shoved toward her, wondering instead about what changes Jethro could be making to the adoption contract that had Ryan concerned.

"The band asked me to thank you again for your help. They really enjoyed working with you."

Lexi blinked at him, not following until she recalled he'd mentioned the band Jack Rabbits. "Oh, yeah." Remembering the jam session, she smiled. "It was fun."

He nodded at the papers. "And profitable."

"What do you mean?" She reached for the pile of papers. On top was a sizable check with her name on it. "I don't understand. What's this for?"

"It's a consultant fee for your contribution to the song. Your name will be in the credits and you'll also get royalties from the sales."

Weak-kneed she walked around to sit next to him at the counter. "This is crazy. I didn't do anything. I mean it was just a few simple comments at an informal gathering. I didn't expect anything from it."

"Jethro is big on people getting the proper credit. He called me that night and gave me the terms. All you have to do is sign the contract and the check is yours."

"Terms?"

He finished chewing his last bite before answering. "You should read it before signing, but he negotiated well for you. It's better than standard. And the band was happy to sign, said they'd like to work with you again sometime. They're positive it's going to be a winner."

She stared at the check. "I don't know what to say."

"No need to say anything." He reached across to set his plate in the sink. "Let me know if you have any questions, otherwise sign both copies, keep one and I'll give you the check when you drop the other off at my office."

"Thank you. You didn't need to go out of your way to bring it to me. I could have come to your office."

He shrugged. "It's what I do." His gaze roamed over the open space. "And truthfully, I was hoping to meet Jasmine."

Of course. He was curious about Jethro's daughter. "Sorry, she's down in the nursery. Craft time is her favorite part of the day."

He stared at her for a moment, giving her the impression he wanted to say something. But he thought better of it. He simply nodded. "Happy Thanksgiving."

And he left.

Lexi stared at the papers in her hands. So many emotions roiled through her veering wildly from love to fear and everything in between. She'd spent the whole morning brooding, her mind running one vicious loop after another. Worrying about her and Jethro. Worrying about her and Jazi. Worrying about the past. Wondering about the future.

Papers in hand she returned to the kitchen and her abandoned sandwich. She carried the plate along with the papers to the table and sat. While she ate, she read. For a contract it was fairly straightforward. Her simple suggestions earned her royalties in the song, a partial amount to be paid up front; the rest to be paid quarterly. She felt like a fraud accepting the money. She'd just been happy to be included in the jam session, wouldn't even have spoken up if not for Jethro.

Still, she signed the contract, considered it as a down payment on a house. No more apartments for her and Jazi.

She'd never expected he'd push a contract on the band.

Why had he? Ryan said Jethro had a thing about people getting credit for their work, but the situation had been so informal she'd had no expectation of receiving any credit. Plus the band sang for Pinnacle's label. It seemed odd he'd put her welfare above the band's.

Unless he cared for her.

Which brought her back to the one question she kept shying away from. Did they have a future together? Could her dream become a reality?

A month ago she would have panicked at the thought of giving up her independence. Taking on Jazi didn't count because Lexi remained in control. She got to make all their life decisions. At least until Jazi got older. Allowing a man into the mix was a whole different matter. Especially one who was overly protective and used to taking charge.

Now she panicked at the thought of leaving.

She wondered if he still felt the same way about not having a family now that he knew what it felt like to have one.

Did no response mean he didn't want to talk or was he just busy?

Lexi chewed her lower lip, torn between the need to know what last night meant to him and proceeding cautiously. The last thing she wanted was to make Jethro second-guess his agreement to let her have Jazi. If she suggested mutual custody, he might take it as an opportunity to take back full custody. And then she'd lose both of them.

Ryan's mention of Thanksgiving prompted the realization that the holiday was only a few days away. Traditionally people spent the day with friends or family or both. She and Alliyah always made a point of inviting other dancers also away from their families.

Would Jethro spend the day with his family or with her and Jazi?

She rubbed her shirt right over her heart, surprised by how important the question was.

It would be nice if they could all celebrate the day together. His foster brothers were curious about Jazi. Jackson stopped by one day on the pretext of looking for Jethro.

He actually got to see Jazi, though she'd been down for her nap. And now Ryan had found a reason to come to the penthouse. And of course Clay had become one of Jazi's favorite people.

They were Jethro's brothers and after hearing his story, she knew what that meant. Lexi longed to get to know them better. And for them to get to know Jazi.

But Jethro had looked grim when she'd mentioned Jackson's visit, and he'd made it clear he preferred to keep the two sides of his family separate. Lexi understood he was trying to save heartache for all concerned.

Maybe that was the answer to her dilemma. If he asked her to join him and his friends for Thanksgiving, she'd know he was open to a relationship.

Jethro tapped his pen against his desk. Rage roiled under the surface of his calm facade. Fury at himself for allowing temptation to win over his will, an unwanted distraction when he needed to be at his sharpest.

Luckily he had Jackson's assistant, Sierra, to help him throughout the day. A Harvard attorney, she made the Fabulous Four look good. She lived in the hotel and had been the one to take the call from the New York office.

He wasn't purposely dodging Lexi's texts. He needed his focus to deal with the distribution issue in New York. Pinnacle had a new game releasing on Thanksgiving. They'd chosen the date to maximize sales on Black Friday. The problem with their distribution center had the power to negate those sales if he didn't resolve it in the next two days.

After his third two-hour call, he could no longer deny the need to fly to New York. Part of him experienced relief at having a reason to get away for a few days. It would give him time to think about what had happened and what he wanted to do. The other half of him hated to lose even a moment of his time with Lexi and Jazi.

Waking up with Lexi in his arms rated as the sweetest

moment of his life except now he'd have the taste of her in his head for the rest of his life.

He'd wanted her from the minute she'd walked up to the bar in The Beacon. Setting up house with her under those circumstances boardered on insanity. He might fool others with the excuse that he needed to be sure Jazi would be safe, but he knew the truth. He'd been indulging himself, pretending he was part of something special, the family he'd never have.

He didn't deserve it, but he'd wanted the time with his daughter. And Lexi.

He'd known from the beginning he'd need to control himself. To keep it in his pants.

So much for his famed self-discipline.

"I'll make our flight arrangements. Jet or commercial?" Sierra closed her portfolio.

"Jet." He hated to pull the pilot and crew from their vacations, but they were paid to be on call and the situation warranted it. "There's no need for you to go and ruin your time off."

"It's okay," she assured him. "I'll visit family."

Something in her tone brought his attention around to her. "Everything okay? You don't sound too enthusiastic."

She sighed. "It's complicated. I wasn't going to go this year, but this seems to be a sign I should."

"You don't believe in signs."

She gave a half laugh. "Not usually, no." Then she changed the subject. "Should I leave the return date open?"

"No. Whatever happens with distribution, good or bad, we'll be back for Thanksgiving."

"Works for me." Her fingers flew over her phone as she texted the pilot. "I've been looking forward to a traditional turkey dinner at Jackson and Grace's new house."

"Yeah." The couple had invited the group, including Lexi and Jazi, to join them for the holiday.

Jethro had yet to make up his mind on whether he'd attend or spend the day at home. He'd like nothing better than to bring Lexi and his daughter with him to the celebration, but he couldn't—wouldn't—do that to himself or his friends. Once Jazi left his life, every future Thanksgiving would be haunted by the memory of the one holiday he got to spend with his daughter.

Sierra's phone pinged and she announced, "Wheels up in an hour. Meet you downstairs in thirty minutes?"

Didn't leave much time to pack and say goodbye. "Perfect."

Rocked by Jethro's news, Lexi followed him down the hall. "Thirty minutes isn't long to pack. You should have called me." She turned into her room, her mind already occupied with what to take.

"You're not going." Jethro stood in her doorway.

She swung to face him. "I thought you wanted Jazi and me to travel with you."

"Not this time. There's no point. I'll be tied up in meetings until this is resolved." His features were set in hard lines.

"Oh." She should be relieved. Instead she fretted at the timing of his absence.

He headed for his room. She followed, watched as he pulled down a suitcase in his closet.

"I was hoping we could talk."

"We will." He assured her. "When I get back."

She crossed her arms over her chest. Why wasn't she reassured by his promise? "How long will you be gone?"

"I'll be back for Thanksgiving." He packed quickly and methodically.

Some of her tension eased. At least he wasn't skipping out on the holiday. "Good. What are we going to do? Shall I plan to cook?"

"I'll let you know." He zipped his bag and set it on its wheels. And then he was in front of her.

She placed a hand on his heart. He was dressed in jeans and a lightweight black sweater. "You're leaving already?"

"I want to stop by the nursery and say goodbye to Jazi." He cupped her cheek. "Will you miss me?"

"Maybe. Probably." She lowered her eyes. "A lot." His lips caressed her forehead. "Will you think of me?"

He made a sound low in his throat. "Too much." Lifting her chin on the edge of his hand, he claimed her mouth in a long, hard kiss. "I'll call you." And then he was gone.

Weak-kneed, she dropped to the floor and buried her face in her hands. As far as goodbyes went, it left her breathless. If only it didn't feel so final.

Ten minutes later a knock sounded at the door. Lexi swiped at her cheeks and climbed to her feet.

She opened the door to Velveth and a totally distraught Jazi. The woman gave Lexi an apologetic look as she cradled Jazi to her slim chest. "Mr. Calder wanted to bring her up, but I convinced him it was better not to prolong the farewell."

"Of course." Guilt slammed into Lexi. Some mother she was, moping in self-pity when her daughter was suffering. She should have considered how upset Jazi would get hearing another goodbye when she'd already lost her mother, Lexi, and Diana and family. She was too young to understand the difference between a temporary parting and a permanent one.

And Lexi was old enough to know it was just a matter of time.

"Mama!" Jazi reacted to the sound of Lexi's voice by launching herself out of Velveth's arms and into Lexi's. Little arms wrapped around her neck while sobs racked her tiny frame. "Daddy, bye-bye!"

The words stopped Lexi cold. Her heart clenched. First because it thrilled her to be called Mama. It implied a long-term acceptance that validated the connection between them. But her use of Daddy concerned Lexi for the same reason. Especially under the circumstances.

She cleared her throat. "I know baby, he'll be back."

Jazi just cried harder.

Sympathy stamped the nursery manager's soft features. "Mr. Calder looked as devastated as she is when he left. He's quite devoted. He comes to watch her play every day."

"Every day?"

Velveth nodded, her short black hair flowing to and fro with the gesture. The nursery manager placed her hand softly on Jazi's back for a moment and then turned and left.

Lexi cuddled her daughter close and turned into the apartment. She carried her to her room, climbed into bed with her and pulled the throw over them. She hummed softly, determined to be strong for her daughter.

CHAPTER THIRTEEN

Two DAYS WENT BY. Lexi sat in Jazi's room with the fish book in her lap. She watched Jazi play and brooded about not hearing from Jethro beyond exchanging a few texts.

She supposed she should be happy he was making headway with the distributors, but she'd prefer to know what he planned for Thanksgiving.

Giving up on getting a direct answer from him, she'd decided earlier that she and Jazi deserved a turkey dinner regardless if Jethro joined them or not, so she'd made up a shopping list and sent it to Brennan. She couldn't dredge up the enthusiasm to shop when she knew she'd spend the whole trip pouting or brooding. Or hounding Clay for details of the Fabulous Four's holiday plans.

She'd save herself that humiliation thank you very much.

She looked up to see Jazi had dragged a stool over to the dresser and she held the fish food in her hand.

"No, pumpkin, we already fed Fishy."

"More."

"More will make him sick." Lexi took the fish food away. She tapped the bowl. "Say, *Hi, Fishy.*"

"Hi, Fishy." Jazi hopped down, ran out of the room. She came back a moment later with Lexi's phone. "Mama." She handed the phone to Lexi. "Daddy. Say hi."

Lexi closed her eyes briefly. She was still calling Jethro Daddy. Nothing Lexi said dissuaded her. In fact, if Lexi pushed too hard, Jazi went into another weeping fit.

"He'll be home tomorrow." She set the phone down on the book.

"Tomorrow?" the girl parroted as if she knew what it meant.

"Yes, after you go to sleep and then wake up, he'll be home." But would it be to stay?

These past few days had convinced Lexi of the need for a change. She loved Jethro and the more she contemplated their time together, the more she believed he'd changed. He hadn't wanted a family. Because of his past, he believed he wasn't worthy of one.

"Daddy!" Jazi insisted, pushing the phone toward Lexi.

He couldn't be more wrong. As his daughter's demand illustrated.

He may be stoic in nature and protective of his privacy, but he'd put Jazi's needs first over and over. And he'd done everything possible to make Lexi feel welcome and comfortable.

She'd never felt more cherished in a man's arms. There was a difference between making out and making love. And she'd been well loved. Both raw and elemental, the connection between them burned so deep it touched her soul forever imprinting his essence within her.

"Okay." She picked up the phone and hit the speed dial for Jethro. Expecting it to go to voice mail the same as the other times she called, she put it on speaker for Jazi to hear. "But Jethro's very busy, baby. He may not be able to talk to us."

Uncaring of the warning, Jazi climbed into her lap as the phone rang.

"Hey," his deep voice came on the line. "I'm headed into another meeting so I only have a couple of minutes. It looks like we'll have to burn the midnight oil to get this resolved. I may not be back until Thanksgiving."

"Daddy!" Jazi grabbed the phone. "Hi!"

A brief moment of silence followed.

Lexi wished she could have warned him. "Someone has been missing you. She insisted we call to say hi."

"Hey, Jazi." The words were gravel rough. A rumbling sounded on the other end, perhaps the clearing of his throat. His voice was clearer when he continued. "I miss you too."

Encouraged, Jazi chattered on. Her vocabulary suffered under her enthusiasm, so only a few words made sense. But Jethro engaged her with questions and she rattled out answers until he indicated it was time for him to go.

Her response was more than clear. "Love you."

"Baby." The gravel was back. "I miss you both. I… I'll see you soon."

Lexi woke on Thanksgiving to a sunny day in Las Vegas. Sliding into her robe she went down the hall to see if Jethro made it home. She gave his door a brief knock and opened it. The room was empty.

Disappointed, she checked her phone. There was a text from him advising his flight was delayed due to storms in New York.

She checked the weather in New York and found forecasts for thunderstorms for the whole day. She hoped he somehow found a way out. Jazi would be very disappointed if he didn't make it home.

Who was she fooling? *She'd* be disappointed if he didn't make it home.

She hopped into the shower and then dressed. She peeked in on Jazi and decided to let her sleep. Over her first cup of coffee, Lexi saw she'd missed a call from Jethro. He'd left a voice mail that was garbled and a bit broken up.

"We just got appr…for liftoff. Wanted to talk…you…but…can't wait…storms. Clay will…going… Jackson's… bye."

Okay, that was as clear as jelly beans. She played it again and learned nothing more. The call came in a little before nine and the flight was about three hours, plus an hour to get home from the landing site, which would put him home around one.

But was he coming here or going to Jackson's?

And what was Clay doing?

She knew no more now than she had before. Back to waiting.

She sipped her coffee and tried not to let it get to her. Tried not to worry that he preferred to spend the day with his friends than with her and Jazi. Tried to pretend everything was fine. Tried and failed. Add frustration to worry, longing, hope.

She could call Clay, but she imagined how pathetic she'd sound and decided against that conversation.

So she got busy instead. She pulled out apples, sugar and flour and began paring. She'd start dinner by making dessert. The apple pie sat cooling on the counter when she heard Jazi stirring.

Lexi got her up and dressed while fending off questions of when Daddy would be home.

"He's on his way but it takes a long time to fly from New York to here."

"Long time?"

"Yes. Hours and hours." How did you explain time to a two-year-old? "He'll be here later."

"Later? Daddy come later?"

"Yep, later. Are you hungry?"

She looked so sad, Lexi lifted her up and pretended to eat her tummy. The childish giggles soothed her own sadness.

"I'm hungry." She ate some more tummy.

"Stop!" Jazi tried to push her shirt down so Lexi couldn't get to her belly. "I hungry."

"You're hungry?" She met Jazi's laughing blue gaze. "Do you want tummy for breakfast or pancakes?"

"Pancakes." Jazi clapped her hands.

Happy she'd distracted the child, Lexi carried her to the kitchen. "Mama wants pancakes too."

* * *

A little before eleven a knock sounded at the door.

"Daddy!" Jazi raced to get there before Lexi.

"No, baby. Daddy will come later."

She glanced through the peephole, warned herself not to get her hopes up and opened the door to Clay. "Hi."

"Clay!" Jazi wrapped herself around his leg.

He looked down at her and then up at Lexi obviously bemused by the show of affection.

She shrugged. "She likes you."

"She does?"

"Oh, yeah. She thinks you're funny."

His brow wrinkled as his bemusement increased. "All I do is drive you."

She lifted a brow. "Have you heard yourself when you drive? Plus, you call her jelly bean."

The corner of his mouth lifted in acknowledgment. He swung Jazi up into his arms. "Hey, jelly bean." He carried her inside.

She kissed his cheek. And he flushed.

Lexi smiled and headed into the kitchen. "What can I do for you?"

"I've been instructed to pick you up."

She went still. "And do what with me?"

"Take you to Jackson's. We're having Thanksgiving dinner at his new place."

She swung around. "By Jethro?"

"Grace is cooking."

"You know what I'm asking, Clay." It would be easy to assume Clay was here at Jethro's urging. The garbled message could have meant Clay will pick you up. But she wouldn't be tripped up. This was too important to risk assuming anything. "Was it Jethro who instructed you to pick me up?"

"Everyone agreed. Jazi is family." He set the little girl on her feet and she ran off to the media room. "You deserve to be with the family for Thanksgiving."

Leaning back against the counter, arms crossed over her chest, she demanded, "Everyone but Jethro?"

"You are relentless." He lifted a lid on a steaming pot of carrots.

"I love him, Clay."

"Then fight for him, Lexi." He clipped out the demand.

"I want to." No, that wasn't right. "I'm going to. But this isn't the way."

He propped his hands on his waist. "Why not?"

"Come on." Needing movement, she grabbed a dish towel and wiped up the water the lid had dripped. "You know how he is about Jazi. He hasn't stopped any of you from meeting her, but he hasn't shared her with you either."

"He's a private man. But I've seen the way he looks at you. And he's changed these past few weeks, found an inner calmness. It's good to see him happy. He just needs a nudge."

A nudge? To get through Jethro's thick skull she was going to need a wrecking ball by four. But calm was good, happy even better. She soaked in the words of encouragement. All the more reason to stand her ground.

"It's more than that. He's very protective of all of you. He doesn't want anyone to become attached to her, to be hurt when I take her away."

"You mean he doesn't want us trying to change his mind."

"That may be part of it, yes."

Enough already. Didn't he know how much she longed to go? To spend time with Jethro and the people he held so dear? The fact that he hadn't invited her festered like a raw burn. It didn't help that she knew all the reasons why he hadn't; she wanted to celebrate with him. But only if he wanted her there.

"I just know surprising him with our appearance isn't a good idea."

"Well then, let *us* have some time with her. Come over for an hour. Jethro isn't due until one." He ran a large hand through thick blond hair. "I don't want to put your relationship at risk, but she's essentially our niece and we want to get to know her.

"I'm pretty sure that's what he's trying to prevent."

"We're adults. How much damage can happen in an hour? If Jethro objects, I'll say I shanghaied you."

"Mama." Jazi came running in on bare feet. "More juice."

While Lexi refilled her sippy cup, Jazi tugged on Clay's pant leg. "Daddy?"

Clay shot a questioning glance Lexi's way.

She cringed as she shrugged. "She started in when he left and I can't get her to go back to his name."

Clay hunkered down to talk to Jazi. "He's on his way, jelly bean. He'll be here soon."

"Later?"

He swiped her nose. "Yes. Later."

Jazi looked so sad Lexi sighed and gave in. It felt like they'd been holed up for the last three days, constantly waiting for Jethro's return. Jazi had been so good, but she could really use the distraction.

"Okay, you win. We'll go. But only until twelve thirty. I want to be long gone by the time Jethro gets there."

Though he argued, Lexi insisted on driving her own car. Really there was no need for him to break up his celebration to take her home. As for her required escort, she'd be following him there and she promised to go straight back to the hotel with no stops and no passing go.

Jackson and Grace Black lived in an extravagant trilevel mansion in the hills of Henderson overlooking Las Vegas. The building had a majestic presence with beautiful stone finishes and white columns. A large palm tree shaded the circular drive.

There were no near neighbors. On the way down in the elevator Clay told her Jackson had bought the ten lots surrounding his to ensure his privacy. The only people he'd consider selling to were his foster brothers.

"Do you think you'll build here someday?" she asked Clay as they walked to the door.

"Maybe. We used to joke about having a compound. At least here we'd get to spread out. And I can always travel or buy a second home somewhere else if I feel crowded." He gave a hard knock but didn't wait for the door to be opened. He walked straight in. "I heard Jethro was looking at plans."

Lexi had no time to think about the pang his announcement struck in her heart. People came from all directions to welcome her and Jazi. Or so it seemed. There were actually only the four of them. Clay, Jackson, Ryan and Grace, who came forward and wrapped Lexi and Jazi in a warm hug.

"Welcome to our home. I'm so glad you came. And this is our beautiful Jazi. I'm Aunt Grace."

Jazi peeped up shyly.

"Will you come to me?" Grace held out her arms.

"Grace," her fiancé admonished her.

"Pooh." The slim brunette waved him off. "If I only get an hour, I'm making the most of it."

"Pooh," Jazi echoed and giggled.

"See—" Grace grinned "—she agrees with me." She held her arms out to Jazi. "Won't you come to me? I have treats for you downstairs."

Suddenly shy, Jazi laid her head on Lexi's shoulder.

"It's okay," she whispered, then loud enough for all to hear, "These are Daddy's brothers. You know Clay." She moved so Jazi had a view of Clay, starting with him because she already knew him. "And this is Ryan. Jackson and his fiancée, Grace. Can you say hi?"

"Hi."

Progress.

Once Lexi finished the intros, she set Jazi on her feet. "Can you take Grace's hand and we'll go see what treats she has?"

Grace held out her hand and Jazi took it, earning a bright smile.

"This way," Grace led them past a lovely cream-and-dove-gray living room and a grand curved staircase to a game room down a short set of stairs. TVs were mounted on every wall. Plenty of large comfortable chairs hugged the walls offering a view of the huge table in the middle of the room currently dressed in the colors of fall and set for a formal dinner.

"Is that a billiard table?"

"It is. I had it custom-made to be converted into a dining table for bigger events. It's tapered on the sides so people can sit at it. I was hoping you would be staying, so I set us up down here."

"I'm sorry you went to extra trouble."

"I'm not. I enjoy a pretty table. And the guys can watch the game." She continued through the large room to a table on the far side with so many cookies, pastries and candies displayed it looked like a bake sale.

"I hope you don't mind—" Grace softly touched Lexi's arm "—but since we missed her birthday and I didn't have time to get a gift, we all have a little something for her."

Jackson stepped into the adjacent media room and came back with a plethora of colorful gift bags.

"Goodness." Lexi was overwhelmed with their generosity. Jazi, she had no doubt, would love it. "That really wasn't necessary."

"We wanted to." Grace called Jazi over. "She's a part of Jethro, a part of us."

Jazi squealed when she saw the packages. She came running and tissue went flying. The first bag, from Clay, contained a colorful book of butterflies. Jazi sat right where she stood and began to flip through the pages.

Lexi glanced at Clay. He beamed and bent to point out Violet the purple butterfly. "Jethro said she liked books."

"I think this will be a new favorite." Lexi climbed down on the floor next to Jazi. "This one is from Ryan."

Jazi dug into the bag and pulled out a toy almost as tall as she was. It was a magnetic drawing set, with a pen attached for drawing. She started to play while Lexi lifted her gaze to Ryan. "Thank you. She's going to love this."

Lexi directed Jazi to the next gift. "From Uncle Jackson."

"Unka Jackson," Jazi repeated.

"That's me, kiddo." Jackson dropped down beside her as she pulled out an eight-inch porcelain cylinder hand painted with pink flowers. Jazi shook it.

"No, sweetie, it's a kaleidoscope. You look in it." He took it and put it to his eye to show her how it worked. Then held it to her eye and turned it.

"Ooh." There was wonder in the childish exclamation. She insisted on showing Lexi.

"It's beautiful." Lexi glanced at Jackson over Jazi's head. "I've never seen one with such pretty colors."

"It's made with real precious gems."

"Jackson! She's two."

"And it may be the only thing she ever gets from me."

She had no answer for him, so she carefully wrapped the extravagant gift. "I'll keep it safe for her."

"It's a toy," he protested. "It's meant to be played with."

"We'll bring it out on special occasions until she gets a little older."

"This is from me." Grace joined them on the floor, leaning against Jackson as she held out a small square box gaily wrapped in red, a tiny white bow propped on top.

"More?" Lexi watched Jazi tear into the pretty paper. "What do you say to everyone, Jazi?"

"Thank you."

The two-year-old showed no delicacy for the packaging and soon held a slim silver bracelet from which five filigreed hearts dangled. Each heart held a gemstone.

"Pity." Jazi held it right in front of Lexi's face to show her.

"Very pretty." And way too expensive. Just another example of these people's easy wealth. But also of their affection for this child they cared for simply because they loved her father. "Shall we put it on you?"

Jazi held up her wrist. She loved to play dress up. Lexi set the latch and Jazi wiggled her wrist delighted with the flash of the gems.

"They're our birthstones," Grace said, "so she'll always have something to remember us."

Jazi hopped up and threw herself into Grace's arms. "Thank you."

Grace hugged the small body to her, tears shimmering in her eyes. "Please stay."

Jazi wiggled free and went off to play.

Grace's comment was both encouraging and heartbreaking. And required a conversation with Jethro before Lexi could commit.

"What's going on here?" A harsh male voice demanded from across the room.

"Daddy!" Jazi ran to the man standing at the bottom of the stairs. He swept her into his arms and kissed her curls.

A slim blonde, presumably Sierra, slipped past him and moved discreetly aside.

Lexi pushed to her feet along with everyone else. Dread swamped her at the displeasure stamped into his stone-hard features. Betrayal blazed in the gaze he leveled on her. This was why she wanted to be gone before he got here.

Clay stepped in front of her. "We invited them. We wanted to meet Jazi."

Eyes, sharp as black ice, cut to Clay. "And no one thought to call me? My daughter. My decision."

"You were in the air." Lexi slid forward, drawing his attention back to her. She wouldn't sacrifice his relationship with his brothers because of her decision. "And I wasn't staying for dinner, just for an hour. They had birthday presents for her."

"Oh, well then." Sarcasm dripped from the words. He set Jazi on her feet. "Can you go play with your presents? I need to talk to Lexi."

"'Kay." She ran over to Grace and the stack of packages.

"Jethro." Jackson strolled over and clapped Jethro on the shoulder. "Why don't you relax? Have a drink and some food. You just had a long flight after a couple of long days of meetings. We can work this out."

"There's nothing to work out. I just need to talk to Lexi."

Jethro grabbed her hand and led her up the stairs, through the foyer and out the front door.

"I can't believe you went behind my back to bring Jazi here. You knew I didn't want them involved in this business."

Business?

Anger came off him in waves, hotter than the desert sun shining down on them. She crossed her arms in front of her, but held her ground. "They weren't taking no for an answer."

"They didn't have to try too hard, did they? You've been angling to come here all week."

"That's not true." Her ire jacked up to match his, mixing with the hurt and betrayal she fought to contain. No way was she going to pay for his inability to communicate a simple response. "I've been asking what your plans were so I could make mine."

"You're not dense. You knew I didn't want you here."

"Which is why I gave up asking." She tried for calm. "I have a whole meal prepared for Jazi and me back at the hotel. Did I want to come spend the day with your friends? Yes. So when Clay came to get us, I may have put up less of a fight than I should have. But only because these people care about you and they think of your daughter as their niece."

Attempting to breach the gulf between them, she reached out a hand toward him. He jerked away from her touch.

"They want to know her so they can support you."

"There is no knowing her. Not when she's leaving." He slashed a hand toward the house. "These people are my family. I won't let you take them from me too. Won't let you destroy my life any more than you already have."

Every word shattered her heart more until nothing remained but pieces.

Devastated by his rejection, she retreated a step. Hope trickled away.

She closed her eyes, momentarily blocking out the world, but there was no blocking out the pain, no blocking out the sense of loss.

She opened her eyes, focused on the face she loved so dearly, and choked back a sob. He deserved so much more than he allowed himself. He just didn't know how to open himself to others so he drove them away. As he was driving her away.

"I feel so sorry for you. You're so worried about protecting your friends you don't see you're hurting them."

"You don't know what you're talking about."

"I know they love you. And it's their right to stand by you and help when you're suffering. When you refuse their support, you're telling them they don't matter."

"You're wrong. It's because they matter too much. I don't want them to suffer with me. And now they will. You brought Jazi here and now they'll love her. And they'll lose her too. That's on you."

"Oh, Jethro. You don't get to choose what people feel. They wanted to know her because she's a part of you. And even if she's not with you they can share your memories of her. Show them they matter. Introduce them to your daughter."

His features hardened to the point of granite. "I no longer have the option, do I? You've already done that."

"I haven't destroyed your life. You'll do that all on your own by pushing people away, the people who care about you. You say it's to protect them, but it's really to protect yourself. The problem with that is you'll be the one who loses out and the future is likely to be a very lonely place."

He cocked an arrogant brow. "I was fine until you came along."

How sad. He actually believed that.

"You want to know why I came here today? The truth?" Why not go out big? "I came because I hoped it didn't matter anymore. Fool that I am I fell in love with you. Making love with you was the most incredible thing I've ever done. I felt connected in a way I never have with anyone else. And I thought it was the same for you. That maybe we could be a family together, you, Jazi and foolish, foolish me."

Her throat closed up, cutting off her words. She shook her head, began backing away.

"You want to save them from being hurt? Quit pushing them away."

Heart rending, she turned her back on him and walked away.

Hard fingers wrapped around her elbow and swung her around. "Where are you going?"

"Anywhere but here. I'm leaving Jazi here. She loves you. If you care for her at all, you need to let her into your life or let us go."

"You're in no position to offer an ultimatum."

"You know me well enough to know I'll love her and care for her to the best of my ability. Unless you can come up with a new plan, the longer we stay, the harder it's going to be on her when we leave."

Yanking her arm from his grasp, she walked away.

Jethro stood in the driveway and watched Lexi storm away, knowing it was just for show. She'd said Clay came for her so she'd ridden here with him, and she didn't have her purse. No way she'd walk away without it.

Weary beyond belief, he rubbed the back of his neck. The break gave his tired mind time to catch up with the conversation. He needed a moment to breathe, to think. Lack of sleep dragged at him. A pounding headache reminded him he'd only gotten eight hours in three days.

Her statement about letting Jazi into his life confused and angered him. Something she excelled at. She had no business trying to change the terms of their agreement at this stage. From the beginning, she'd made it clear she wanted to take Jazi and leave. *He* wasn't invited to join the party. So why should she be surprised that he wanted to keep his family out of it?

She loved him? She wanted them to be a family?

He couldn't wrap his head around those possibilities.

Maybe he should have taken Jackson's advice to have a drink and settle down.

He'd been too hurt, too angry to listen. When he saw Lexi ensconced with his family, he saw red. He knew she longed for an invitation to Thanksgiving. He'd even considered it, because the thought of having all his family together appealed to him clear down to the bone.

But he knew he'd be a basket case when Lexi left with Jazi. From the beginning, he'd made it a priority to save his friends the same pain. Why was that a bad thing?

Lexi reached the last vehicle in the long drive. Stubborn woman, when was she going to give up this pretense? The sooner she returned, the sooner they could resolve this. Raw from walking in on a betrayal, he'd said some harsh things. Things he regretted. They'd talk more calmly when she came back.

Wait, he frowned, he didn't recognize the sporty little SUV. Panic set in when she stopped and pulled keys from her pocket.

"Lexi!" He started down the drive. Too late. She climbed

in, met his gaze for a brief second and then she threw the gear into Reverse, and was gone.

He trudged to a stop, hung his head. Something wrenched in his chest; the pain in her eyes ripped him in half. No telling how long he stood there before Jackson came out and fetched him. The others were gathered in the living room off the foyer. Grace wrapped him in a warm hug.

"Where's Jazi?"

"Sierra is with her in the game room. We want to talk to you." She led him to a cream sofa. "To say we're sorry. We pushed Lexi to bring Jazi here. She told Clay it wasn't a good idea, but we insisted. Jazi is your daughter—we wanted to know her."

Jethro perched on the edge of the sofa, stared down at the plush cream carpet. "Lexi said I was hurting all of you by not letting you see her. Was she right?"

Silence met his question. He looked up, met their gazes, shook his head. "Seems I'm the one who should apologize."

Grace laid a hand on his arm. "We don't understand why you won't let us help you."

"It's not about me. It's about you. All of you. I knew having Jazi stay with me was going to be tough. The truth is it's been brutal, harder than anything I've ever gone through. I wanted to spare you."

"Noble, but unnecessary," Ryan said. "Family stands together no matter how tough it gets."

A round of ascents echoed through the room.

"I should have known when you all tried to sneak by the penthouse and meet her that you weren't going to stay out of it."

"You knew about that?" Jackson grinned, clearly unrepentant.

"Lexi told me everything."

"I like her," Clay announced. "I didn't think I would, but I do."

"The problem is I do too. More than I should."

"Why is that a problem?" Grace demanded.

Back to scrutinizing the carpet. "She's leaving. Plus, you all know what a disaster I am at relationships."

Clay humphed. "You've never been in love before."

That brought his head up. "What are you talking about?"

"You love her." Ryan seconded Clay's declaration. "You look at her the way this poor sap looks at Grace. What's really telling is you've had the adoption contract for a month and can't bring yourself to sign it. Maybe I should be writing up a prenup instead."

Marriage to Lexi? Surprisingly the concept didn't throw him into a panic. Not like watching her drive away.

He'd missed her. He never missed people, taught himself at a young age not to bother. It didn't bring them back so it was wasted emotion. Worse, it was wasted energy. There'd only been one exception until now. Mama Harman. He still missed her.

And he'd missed Lexi. Missed her smile, the sweet smell of her hair, the exchange of glances when Jazi did something new. He missed how she teased him and the way she made him laugh. Most of all he missed the feel of her in his arms.

She'd spoken of a connection. He felt it too, the closeness, the chemistry, the bonding. With her he felt a sense of togetherness that chased the loneliness away. He just hadn't known what to call it.

"She said she loves me."

Jackson clapped him on the shoulder. "Then why are you still here?"

"Because I'm an idiot." He surged to his feet, pointed at Ryan. "You can forget the prenup."

"I'm not one to talk, but dude, don't deny yourself a chance at happiness."

"Oh. I'm going after her. And when I catch up with her, I'm never letting her go."

* * *

Lexi didn't remember the drive to the hotel. Between fighting off tears and struggling to breathe around the constriction in her chest she was lucky to make it back at all.

But she did make a decision. As painful as the confrontation had been, it revealed to her exactly what she needed to do.

She let herself into the suite and absorbed the quiet, the emptiness. Smelled the turkey and dashed away fresh tears. She set the key card down on the foyer table. She wouldn't be using it again.

Everything had changed. Just not as she'd hoped.

She loved Jethro.

Her breath hitched as she fought back unwanted tears. He didn't deserve them. She'd offered him her heart, told him of her dreams of becoming a family. Okay, she threw the words at him. But they'd been out there hanging in the balmy November day. And how did he respond? With harsh words and distrust.

In her room she went right through to the bathroom and splashed water on her face. The cool soothed the burn in her eyes. She began opening drawers and emptying them.

He'd accused her of destroying his life.

The woman in the mirror was the one shattered. Not only by his rejection, but because she knew in her heart of hearts that Jazi belonged with him.

Meeting her eyes in the mirror, she admitted she'd known it for a while. But today drilled the fact home. The look on his face when Jazi flew into his arms said it all. For that instant love broke through the anger and betrayal like the sun through rainclouds, lighting him up. Which made the ice he turned on her all the more devastating.

She dragged her suitcases out of the closet, opened them on the bed.

Her promise to Alliyah had become more of a crutch

than a motivator. Father and daughter loved each other, and much as Lexi would like to take Jazi and run, she couldn't justify it. The biggest thing she had to offer Jazi was love. And now she had that with her father.

Plus an aunt and a whole slew of uncles, all waiting to spoil her.

Uncaring of wrinkles, she began throwing things into the suitcases. Her heart couldn't be more broken; it only made sense to leave now. Make one big break. Let Jethro and Jazi begin their life together.

She swiped at her cheek, and stuffed her boots in the bigger case before zipping it. She had to lean her weight into it but she got it closed. Back in the bathroom she gathered her toiletries into a cosmetic bag. What didn't fit, she dumped in the other suitcase.

She wanted to be gone before Jethro got here. Which could be any minute considering how exhausted and angry he'd been. If he came home with Jazi before she left, Lexi feared she wouldn't have the strength to walk away.

And being in his life but not a part of it really didn't work for her. As painful as this was, it revealed to her exactly what she needed to do.

Silence met Jethro when he let himself in the suite.

He'd made a point of introducing Jazi to his friends. Lexi was right. They were his family and he wanted them to know his daughter. He wished Lexi had been there. As Jazi's mama, she was family too. Whether he got her to forgive him or not.

The place smelled of Thanksgiving. He stepped into the kitchen; it sparkled. But in the refrigerator a full turkey took up one shelf, and he saw carrots and potatoes. He hadn't answered her repeated queries about what they'd be doing, so she'd taken matters into her own hands. Had she planned for it to be just her and Jazi? Or had she hoped he'd join them?

He'd meant to. The stop at Jackson's was only to give a report and wish everyone happy Thanksgiving. And then he was going home. Because that's what Jazi and Lexi were to him. Home.

The pain and disappointment on Lexi's face continued to haunt him. Lord, help him, he needed to make this right.

But the silence told him she wasn't there. Just to be sure he checked her room. Dread burned through his belly, filled his heart. Her things were gone. Closet and drawers were empty. The bathroom cleared out. All that lingered was her scent, haunting him like a ghost.

Where would she have gone?

He headed out determined to find her. He'd try her apartment first. Then start tracking friends. Clay would help if needed.

That was when Jethro saw the note. On the foyer table right next to her key card.

Dearest Jethro,

I'm sorry for giving you an ultimatum today. That wasn't fair to either of us and I've come to cherish you as a friend.

You are a good man. I don't know what horrific circumstances forced your mother to give you up. But I can only think she'd be proud if she could see you today. Not for your financial success, though that's impressive, but because you are a man with a good heart.

Jazi belongs with you. She's happiest when you're around and she deserves to grow up with at least one of her parents. And you deserve to know the gift of your daughter's unconditional love.

You've restored balance to her world and she's brought joy to yours. I love the two of you too much to take one of you away from the other. So it's my place to bow out.

Forgive me for leaving this way. I don't think I could do it face-to-face.
Hugs and kisses to you both,
Lexi
P.S. Maybe you could bring her to see me dance some-day. I'd like that.

Raw emotion choked him. Lexi loved him. She'd told him so, but he hadn't believed her. Others had said the words and then left because he'd failed so miserably at communication, at sharing himself. He shared with Lexi without even thinking about it. And she'd left, too, but by God, the sacrifice of it astounded him.

She thought his mother would be *proud* of him. Even after he tore her heart out and chased her away. Her crazy attempts to explain why he'd been in the trash had niggled at his psyche, causing some of the hostility to fade. He would never know the truth but it helped to contemplate a reason other than flat rejection by his mother.

Lexi thought she could tell him that and just walk away? That she could profess her love as if it didn't matter? Oh, no.

And suddenly he knew just where to find her.

Lexi's eyes stung from sweat and tears. Her image in the mirrors blurred from the moisture. But the music blasted, the beat rolled through her and she danced. She pushed all her sadness, her pain, her loneliness into each heart-felt motion.

She felt like she'd never be happy again, that she'd left her heart in the penthouse so far overhead.

She needed to get away, to make plans. Maybe she'd go to a new city, try out for a musical on Broadway. She was free, wasn't she, to do anything she wanted. That's what mattered. Right?

So why did her precious independence suddenly burn like acid in her belly? Why did having someone accept her for who she was suddenly seem like the true meaning of freedom?

Jethro had seen her, done things he didn't have to do. He found her a place to dance because he'd known she needed to dance. He'd introduced her to Veronica which gave her access to her world, and a chance at a new aspect of it. He'd arranged a jam session for her, negotiated for her to get credit for her participation.

Sway, pivot, lunge. Down, up, kick extend. Fast then slow and then faster still. Her feet pounded over the floor. Glided. Lifted her into the air. She danced until her legs shook and every breath became a labored effort.

Fatigue dragged her to a halt. Head down, chest heaving she finally let the tears come.

A moment passed, two when warm arms closed around her, holding her to a hard male body. Jethro's scent surrounded her.

"I'm sorry."

She went still. He'd come. He'd known where to find her. Everything in her longed to turn to him, to wrap around him. But he'd hurt her. She wasn't looking for pacification. She wanted love, a future.

"So sorry. I didn't mean the things I said. I was angry and tired from my trip. God's truth I don't remember half of it."

"Then why say it?"

He rested his chin on her head. "I don't know." His body went taut the full length of hers. "No, that's the old me. I want to do better with you." The words were flat as if squeezed through a tight throat. "When I came down the stairs and saw you there, I had this moment of absolute joy. Here was everything I'd ever longed for. And in the next instant it was wiped out because I'd promised to give it all up. And everyone I cared about was at risk."

"You lashed out."

"And you were the convenient target. I'm sorry. I don't remember much of what I said, but I do remember the hurt on your face." He rubbed his hands up and down her arms. Turned her to face him. With a gentle touch he wiped the tears from her face.

Heart pounding she stared up at him, half fearful, half hopeful. And, oh, my, she was so afraid to hope. What excited her was his effort, his openness. He was talking to her, a huge step for him. But would he make it all the way to a commitment?

"I take it back, all of it." Contrition stamped his features. "I talked to the guys after you left. You were right. They were feeling left out. They didn't need me to protect them. I took the time to officially introduce them to Jazi. Because family stands together."

"That's nice." She was happy for him. But it didn't change anything between them.

"I love you." Blunt. Declarative. Absolute. And so unexpected.

No way to doubt what she'd heard. To question his resolution. Happiness bloomed from her heart, warmed the chill from her blood, gave strength to her legs. She threw herself into his arms. He caught her, swung her around, sealed his lips to hers.

"I love you," she said against his mouth, "I love you. I love you."

He set her on her feet and stopped her talking in the best possible way. He pulled back, framed her face with hands that shook just a little.

"I want a family with you and Jazi. I want to give her a sister or brother, maybe both. I love you. Will you do that with me?"

She clasped his wrists, angled her chin up. "Are you going to require me to have an escort everywhere I go?"

His jaw clenched and his posture stiffened. Oh, he wanted to say yes. The fact he stopped to think showed his love as nothing else could.

"Were you serious about learning self-defense?"

Ah. Compromise, a relationship essential.

"I am if it gets rid of the babysitters."

"Then, no," he conceded. "Unless there's an imminent threat, you're free to roam at will."

Sweet, sweet words. She looped her arms around his neck. "Are we talking marriage? It's not a deal breaker for me, but it's probably best for the kids."

His eyes lit up. "You'd give your freedom up for me?"

See, he got her. "You and Jazi are my freedom. You don't contain me, you fulfill me."

"Then, Lexi Malone." He went down on one knee, held her hand in both of his. Looked up at her with such love. "Will you marry me?"

She cocked her head, pretended to consider? "Can we build a place by Jackson and Grace?"

He stood and yanked her into his arms. "This is not the time to tease me, woman."

"There's the man I know and love." She cupped his cheek, kissed him softly. "Yes, I'll marry you."

"Good." A huge grin broke across his face, revealing a dimple in his left cheek. "I already picked out the lot."

* * * * *

"I'm a private person."

"You used to be, but not anymore. Not since your book hit the bestseller lists and stayed there."

"Drip, drip, drip," he said.

"What does that mean?"

"You're like water on a rock, wearing it down."

She lifted her chin. "I like to think that's one of my best qualities."

"It's good." Jack's gaze dropped to her chest, and the glitter was back in his eyes. "But not your best."

He didn't miss much, so she was pretty sure he could tell that the pulse in her neck had just gone from normal to racing. There was only one way to interpret those words and that look. He moved closer and she held her breath, hoping that he was going to kiss her. Heat from his body warmed her skin when he stopped right in front of her.

* * *

The Bachelors of Blackwater Lake:
They won't be single for long!

A WORD WITH
THE BACHELOR

BY
TERESA SOUTHWICK

First Published in Great Britain 2016
By Mills & Boon, an imprint of HarperCollins*Publishers*
1 London Bridge Street, London, SE1 9GF

© 2016 by Teresa Southwick

ISBN: 978-0-263-92017-8

23-0916

Our policy is to use papers that are natural, renewable and recyclable products and made from wood grown in sustainable forests. The logging and manufacturing processes conform to the legal environmental regulations of the country of origin.

Printed and bound in Spain
by CPI, Barcelona

Teresa Southwick lives with her husband in Las Vegas, the city that reinvents itself every day. An avid fan of romance novels, she is delighted to be living out her dream of writing for Mills & Boon.

To educators Andrea Verga Pascale
and her husband, John Pascale.
The influence of a good teacher can never
be erased and you guys are the best!
When I sit down to write, I'm so grateful
to my former teachers for giving me the
necessary tools to do what I love.
Never doubt that every student you meet is
all the better for having had you in their life.
You touch the world. You teach!

Chapter One

She'd been warned that Jack Garner would be difficult but no one had prepared her for his overwhelming sex appeal.

If Erin Riley had known the author was more buff and better-looking than the guy on the cover of his action-adventure novel, she wasn't sure she'd have taken this job as his book coach. Quite possibly she was in over her head. She'd already failed the first test by not researching the man she would be working for. He'd just answered her knock on his door and all she could do was stare.

"Are you selling something?" He glanced at her wheeled suitcase.

"No. Sorry." She took a deep, cleansing breath. "I'm Erin Riley. Cheryl Kavanagh sent me."

"My editor." His dark blue eyes narrowed. "Cut the crap."

"Excuse me?"

"You're here to babysit me." He glanced over his shoulder and called, "Harley!"

Moments later some black-and-white creature ran outside, stopped beside Jack and looked up adoringly. Erin could respect the feeling.

Jack closed the front door and proceeded down the three steps. "Walk."

She wasn't sure if he meant her, but left the suitcase on the porch and hurried after him. That's when she realized the creature was without a doubt the ugliest dog she'd ever seen. It looked like a four-legged elf, a mythical being straight out of *The Hobbit*. The thing was small with a hairy head that didn't look substantial enough to hold up the ginormous ears. Stick legs had tufts of fur by the paws and some kind of garment made of camouflage material covered the skinny, hairless body.

Fascination with the dog would have to wait. She moved quickly to catch up to the man. For him and his long legs it might be considered a walk, but she nearly had to jog to keep up. He was headed toward Blackwater Lake—the body of water from which this small town in Montana took its name.

"Mr. Garner—"

"Jack."

She assumed that meant he was giving her permission to call him by his first name. "All right. Jack."

They passed a building on the dock that said Blackwater Lake Marina and Bait Shop. Almost all of the slips in the natural bay were full, and held small boats and some that looked more luxurious and big enough to sleep on.

The scenery was nearly as breathtaking as trying to keep up with Jack. Dark blue lake water stretched ahead of her as far as the eye could see and bumped up against some impressive mountains. Overhead, the blue of the sky was only interrupted by wispy white clouds. It was quiet and serene, a place that on the surface looked to be a perfect writing environment. But if that was the case, she wouldn't be here.

"So, Jack—"

"Harley, stand down."

The small dog stopped chasing and barking at the little brown birds that had been pecking in the sketchy grass beside the lake. They took off and the homely animal instantly moved into step beside his human as ordered.

"Girl or boy?" she asked.

"What?" Jack gave her a wary sideways look.

"Is the dog male or female?"

"Male."

"That's unexpected."

"Meaning?"

"I would never have figured a guy like you to have a dog like this."

"Are you insulting my dog?"

Oh, boy. How did she put into words that she'd been profiling and figured a manly man like Jack Garner would have a big, burly guy dog. Pit bull. Rottweiler. Bulldog. The problem was the ugly little animal didn't seem compatible with a man who'd spent a good number of years in the United States Army Special Forces Operations, Ranger Battalion. She only knew that from reading his book and the short bio in the back.

Finding the words was like trying to navigate a minefield. "I just… The two of you are—" She sighed.

"What's wrong with him?"

"Nothing." Aside from not being very attractive. Unlike his owner, who was so attractive her toes were curling. There were a lot of things she could say. *Beauty is in the eye of the beholder. Beauty is only skin deep. Don't judge a book by its cover.* She finally settled on a question. "Why did you pick him?"

"It's classified."

He could tell her, but he'd have to kill her? He looked like he wanted to do that anyway.

"Okay," she said. "What kind of dog is he?"

"A Chinese crested."

"I see. Sounds noble." She knew very little about dogs.

"Don't judge a book by its cover."

Did she get points for not saying that? At least it was the segue she'd been waiting for. "Speaking of books—"

"Cheryl wants to know where mine is." Anger and frustration were wrapped around the words.

"Look at it from her perspective. Your first book is incredibly successful. Even more amazing because there was no promotion." He'd refused to do any. "Word-of-mouth has been unbelievably effective. And it's been optioned for a movie. That's an impressive springboard for a second book."

"The manuscript is a little late," he conceded.

"Nine months late. You could make a baby in that length of time." Did she really just say that out loud? "Not judging," she added.

The look he shot her was as black as his hair. In worn jeans and a faded olive-green T-shirt, his toned and muscular body was displayed to perfection. She'd read that it was instinctive for a woman to mate with a strong male who could protect her and any offspring she produced. Right this second her female instincts were going nuts.

"Meaning what?" His voice was low, just north of irritated, and creeping into superannoyed territory.

It was an alpha-male tone meant to intimidate, but if Erin let him get to her now, this book-coach thing was never going to work and she really wanted it to. She wanted to help. To do that, she had to stand up to him right now.

"Don't play games, Jack. You know why I'm here.

You're late on your deadline and refuse to take your editor's calls. Or your agent's, for that matter. Everyone wants to build on the momentum of your phenomenally successful first book. Cheryl said you have the most raw talent of any writer she's seen in a very long time. So, she sent me here to help you focus."

"Why?"

"You know the answer to that question, but I'll spell it out anyway. There's a lot of money at stake. Millions," she said. "Your editor is in your corner. She'll do whatever she can."

"No, I meant why you?"

He was asking for a resumé so she'd give him a verbal one. Harley walked over and started sniffing her so Erin stopped and bent to scratch his head. "My cousin is an editorial assistant at the publishing house and recommended me."

"Why?"

"I have a master's degree in English and literature. And I've taught high-school honors English, AP classes and community-college writing courses."

"Why aren't you in school now? It's after Labor Day."

"I'm a substitute. That means I can tell them when I'm available." The arrangement had worked when her fiancé, Garrett, was terminally ill. The money was good and after his death a year and a half ago she hadn't changed her status to full-time. "Do you know Corinne Carlisle?"

"No."

"She's one of Cheryl's authors, a cozy mystery writer. This summer she was having trouble finishing her manuscript. Through my cousin I was hired to—"

"Babysit."

"Focus her." Erin had really enjoyed the job and wanted to do more. She and Garrett had talked about traveling the world, but he got sick and they never had the chance. Assignments like this let her go places she might not otherwise see and, if asked, she wanted to do more of this. "She was a delightful lady to work with."

Harley stood still at his feet and Jack picked him up. It was automatic, instinctive, as if that was their rhythm. "I'm not delightful."

"Harley might beg to differ."

Under Jack's big, gently stroking hand the unattractive animal looked to be in doggy heaven. Erin had the most erotic sensation, as if his hand was brushing over her bare skin. Shivers hopped, skipped and jumped down her spine.

"He'd be wrong."

"Look, I was able to help Corinne finish her book. I can do the same for you. I'm good at research. I can critique and edit and brainstorm story ideas. And Cheryl strongly suggested that I make sure you eat three times a day. Your home is ideal for this arrangement with the separate upstairs and downstairs apartments."

A good thing, too, because Blackwater Lake was small. There was a lodge close by, but it had been completely booked and there wouldn't be more in the way of accommodations until the resort under construction was completed.

The look on Jack's face showed a lot of regret and it was probably about the fact that he'd shared details of his duplex home with his editor. "My office is up. I live down."

Erin was very aware that he was trying to scare her off but the technique was useless on her. Jack didn't know that when you faced cancer with someone you cared about there wasn't a lot left to be afraid of. "I won't take up much room."

With Harley in his arms he started walking back the way they'd come. "I got a message from Cheryl."

"Oh?"

"If I want a deadline extension you're the price I have to pay for it."

"Great."

"Not." He stopped walking and stared at her.

"Okay, I get it. You don't want me here."

"If I could fire you I would," he confirmed.

"You could give back the advance."

The glare he shot her almost made his eyes glow. "Abandoning the mission isn't an option."

She studied the brooding man. The sight of the dozing, completely trusting ugly little dog in his arms was so at odds with the hostile, confrontational image he was projecting to her. Somewhere inside him was a guy who'd chosen and was good to a small, homely animal. That was a man she wanted to know. And then there was the powerful, startling, confusing and off-putting attraction she'd felt from the moment he'd answered his door.

"I'm here to be of service."

He stared at her and his mouth tightened. "We're not sleeping together if that's what you're thinking."

"I'm sorry— What?"

Holy smokes! Her cheeks burned and it had nothing to do with the sun shining down from that big, blue sky. How did he know? She hadn't exactly been thinking about sex, but close enough to be humiliated by what he'd said.

"I didn't— I never—"

"I need to know if you can do this job and not look at me like that."

"I'm not looking at you any way," she protested.

He shook his head. "Your face is so easy to read."

"No, it's not."

"And you're a bad liar." He looked closer. "Have you even been with a man?"

That question was getting awfully close to the one nerve

she had left and she figured it was a deliberate attempt to get on it.

"Yes, I've been with a man." She looked up and met his gaze. If she was really that easy to read he would see her defiance and determination. "I was engaged."

"That's need-to-know and I don't need to."

"Okay then. I guess we understand each other."

Jack didn't understand Little Miss Perky at all. In the less than twenty-four hours since her arrival he'd been nothing more than barely civil and yet she was still here. Like an eager puppy.

"So let's talk about the book," she said, putting a mug on his desk in front of him.

Jack looked at it and didn't miss the fact that there was now a coaster for his cup that covered the circular coffee stain he'd grown fond of. That was kind of like shutting the barn door after the horse got out.

He leaned back in his cushy leather chair, a splurge from the unexpectedly astounding royalties on his first book, and met her gaze. "Let's talk about my office instead."

"What about it?"

He could actually see the oak top of his desk, whereas before only that circular spot had been visible. Pens, pencils, Post-its, a highlighter, et cetera, were…annoyingly organized. His mug with the army insignia on it that was for display purposes only was conspicuously full of writing implements. Yesterday, before she'd shown up, there were yellow legal pads scattered on the ratty chair and thrift-shop tables in this room and now they were nowhere to be seen. He didn't know where anything was.

"Things aren't where I put them."

"I tidied up. I was awake early and didn't want to start

breakfast too early in case you liked to sleep in." She shrugged. "So I made myself useful."

"In what universe? A man's office is sacred ground." The up and down apartments on the property were identical floor plans with two bedrooms and bathrooms. In addition to the isolation out here by the lake he'd liked the idea of separate spaces for work and living. Now Erin Riley had invaded both. Last night she'd slept upstairs in the spare room with unfettered access to his office. That was going to change. "I like my stuff out so I can find it."

She sat in one of the chairs facing the desk, clearly not discouraged by his inhospitable reception and intending to dig in. "Understood."

Jack squirmed a little, unable to shake the sensation that he'd drop-kicked a kitten. She was trying to do her job and he wasn't making it easy. Because he didn't want her here poking into things. All he needed was time to work through his creative speed bumps.

"If you want to be useful," he said, "I need supplies. Like you said last night, there's not much food here to work with."

But she'd proved to be resourceful and managed to make dinner. With some eggs, a few vegetables and ground beef she'd whipped up a tasty skillet dish. This morning was grilled cheese sandwiches. When he'd reminded her it wasn't lunch yet, she'd said his stomach didn't know what time it was. As if he didn't already know that. Special Forces training highlighted the need for nourishment to keep the body in tip-top working order and sometimes that meant making do with what was available. He'd just been messing with her because that sandwich tasted pretty darn good.

The thing was, her perky disposition never slipped. Like yesterday when he'd said he wouldn't sleep with her, she'd calmly handled him. The only clue that he'd made her uncomfortable was the high color in her cheeks. Women weren't top secret to him; he knew when one liked what she saw. And from the moment he'd answered the door to Erin Riley, she'd looked at him that way. If she could see inside him, she'd run in the opposite direction.

Maybe this attitude of his was a way of initiating her, like boot camp, to see if he could get her to crack. If so, that made him a son of a bitch and he felt a little guilt, but managed to ignore it. Her insertion into his life hadn't been his idea. But like he'd said—he couldn't fire her. All he could do was discourage her.

So far that was a negative on dissuasion. Her sunny disposition made him want to put on his shades. Looking at her was like coming out of a pitch-dark room into light so bright it made your eyes hurt. Even her shoulder-length brown hair had sunlit, cheerful streaks running through it. And flecks of gold brightened her pretty green eyes. She wasn't extraordinarily beautiful, not like his ex-wife. But she was vulnerable, yet strong—a compelling combination somehow and he didn't want to be compelled.

"Jack?"

Hearing her say his name snapped him back. "What?"

"Talking about your work-in-progress might get the creative juices flowing."

"That's not my process," he said stubbornly.

"Okay." She thought for a moment. "Then let's talk about what your process is."

"You're like a pit bull." Harley was in his bed beside the desk and he reached down to scratch the dog's head. Instantly the animal rolled onto his back and Jack almost smiled. "Once you sink your teeth in you don't let go."

"Nice try." Those flecks in her eyes darkened, making them more brown than green. She looked like a teacher who'd just figured out someone was attempting to pull a fast one. "You're trying to deflect attention from yourself. Let's get something straight, Jack. This isn't about me."

So that flanking maneuver didn't work. Time for a contingency plan. "I have the situation under control."

"Good. All you have to do is give Cheryl a firm date for manuscript delivery."

He couldn't exactly do that. "I'm still working out some plot details."

"Okay. So let's talk about that."

"Look, Erin, my name and mine alone is on the front of the book. The content is my personal responsibility and I take that very seriously. I don't write by committee."

"Ah," she said, as if just understanding something.

"What does that mean?" He was pretty sure his facial expression wasn't easy to read, unlike hers.

"I had a similar conversation when I worked with Corinne Carlisle. She was uncomfortable in the beginning of our cooperative efforts. A clandestine collaboration, she called it. I thought that was a personal quirk of hers, or a chick thing."

"It wasn't?"

She shook her head. "I believe it's a writer thing."

"Call it what you want. I just prefer to work alone."

His gaze was drawn to her legs when she crossed one over the other. The jeans she was wearing were a little loose and left too much to the imagination because he suspected the hidden curves would be well worth a look. Probably a good thing the denim wasn't skintight. It would only be a distraction that he didn't want or need.

"Alone." She nodded her understanding of his statement. "I heard you were a loner."

"Oh?"

"Cheryl explained the downside of this assignment. She made sure I knew that you don't play well with others."

The words hung in the air between them for several moments. Jack couldn't tell whether or not that was a criticism. It really didn't matter. On the upside, maybe she was finally getting the message.

"By definition a loner needs to be alone."

"I understand." Her tone was soothing, like a shrink would use, or a hostage negotiator.

"Don't patronize me," he said.

"I'm sorry you feel I'm doing that. It wasn't my intention." She stopped for a moment, thinking, as if to come up with the right words to make him understand. "I respect your commitment to responsibility in writing the book you want to write. But I have undertaken this assignment and Cheryl is expecting tangible results. I'm not backing down from the challenge of you. It's best you accept that. So, we have to start somewhere."

"And you think talking about the story is the way to go."

"It worked for Corinne." She folded her hands in her lap. "If you have a better idea that would be awesome."

"Look, I appreciate your willingness and enthusiasm." Although he could think of better uses for it. "But I write action-adventure. A woman like you has no frame of reference for that so talking is a complete waste of time."

"I haven't been in the military or gone to war if that's what you're saying. But I read extensively and go to the movies. I can help you dissect the plot. I have ideas and that can be helpful."

He'd started his last book as a therapeutic exercise to work through all the crap life had thrown at him. Pulling that stuff up was like exposing his soul. Doing that with her just wasn't going to happen. For reasons he couldn't explain, he didn't want her to see the darkness inside him.

"Ideas?" He leaned forward and rested his forearms on the unnaturally tidy top of his desk. "You're Pollyanna. No offense, but you can't possibly have suggestions for what I write."

"Really?" She sat up straighter in the chair, almost literally stiffening her spine.

"In my opinion, yes."

"It's hard to form an opinion without information and you don't know anything about me if you truly believe I've had no life experiences."

"So you were engaged. There was a proposal. Probably a ring. Not a big deal." He saw something slip into her eyes but it didn't stop him. He'd been engaged once, too, even took the next step and got married. It didn't work out for a lot of reasons, but mostly he wasn't very good at being a husband. "Since you used past tense I guess you broke up with him. Still not gritty—"

"He died. Whether it happens in a war zone or the home front, death is not pretty. It's raw and painful. I think that qualifies as life experience."

He studied her and realized his mission, real or invented, had been successful. He'd managed to put clouds in her eyes and make the sunshine disappear.

Damned if he didn't want to undo what he'd just done.

Chapter Two

Erin sat in the passenger seat of Jack's rugged jeep trying to figure him out. First he'd said he had no use for her, then later in the afternoon offered to take her into town. She had a long-term rental car from the airport and was prepared to shop on her own, but he'd insisted on driving. His excuse was that they might as well buy supplies together, but she had a sneaking suspicion there was another reason. One that would tarnish his tough-guy image.

"So, Jack," she began, "I think your ogre act is just that. An act."

He turned right onto Lakeview Drive, then gave her a quick, questioning look. "I have no idea what you're talking about."

"You were all gruff and abrupt earlier. Patronizing me about a ring, a proposal and a broken engagement being the equivalent of a hangnail in the action-adventure world."

"It is." His profile could have been carved in stone on Mt. Rushmore. It was all sharp angles and hard lines.

"But when I corrected your assumption that I was shallow and typical by revealing that I lost someone close to me, I think you felt bad about jumping to conclusions and invited me to go shopping to make up for it."

There was another glance in her direction before he returned his gaze to the road. "In the army I operated on gut instinct and never second-guessed my actions."

"That was training for combat situations. In the regular world you replay a conversation and sometimes regret responses. It's normal. You asked me to go shopping because you can't take back what you said and are trying to be nice."

"Are you serious?"

"Completely." She adjusted her sunglasses. It was a beautiful day in late September and this road to town went around the lake. The surface of the water sparkled like diamonds as the sun sank lower in the cloudless blue sky. "The problem is that your nice muscles haven't been stretched in a while."

"You know what I think?"

"Not a clue," she said, wishing she could see his eyes behind those too-sexy-for-words aviator sunglasses. "But I bet you're going to tell me."

"Damn straight." He looked over, his mouth pulled into a straight line. "I think you're a fugitive from fantasyland."

That would be a step up for her after nursing Garrett through cancer and watching him take his last breath. "Oh?"

"I'm not a nice man. If you were smart, you'd ditch this job and get the hell out of here. Away from me."

"Hmm."

"What does that mean?"

"You think I'm fragile and I think you're a fraud. So what we have here is a standoff."

"Guess so," he said. "Sooner or later one of us is going to blink and it won't be me."

"Sounds like a challenge or a treaty to me. Maybe both." It was going to take a lot of convincing to make her believe he was as unfeeling as he wanted her to think he was.

"For the record, it makes good sense to coordinate shopping since you'll be doing the cooking and don't know what Harley likes."

That made her smile. Big bad warrior was hiding behind the world's most unattractive dog. But she just said, "Understood."

"You hungry?" The words were unexpected, but they were nearing the Blackwater Lake city limits.

"Starving."

"Me, too. Let's get something to eat." He glanced over quickly as if checking to see whether or not she'd noticed him being nice. "Grocery shopping will go easier that way."

"I think so, too." And that's the first time they'd agreed on anything in the last twenty-four hours.

He stopped the jeep at a stand-alone building near the end of Main Street, not far from city hall. There was a sign on the outside that read Bar None, with crossed cocktail glasses on it.

"Don't tell me," she said. "I'm driving you to drink."

"You said it, not me." But his teeth flashed in a fleeting smile before he got out of the car.

Erin opened her door and slid to the ground, then met him on the sidewalk. The wooden exterior was reminiscent of a miner's shack and the heavy oak door had a vertical brass handle. Jack grabbed it and pulled the door open for her.

The pulse in her neck jumped as she passed him and walked inside. Heat from his body was enough to sizzle her senses and short them out. That was probably the reason it seemed to take longer than usual for her eyes to grow accustomed to the dim interior after being outside.

"This looks nice," she finally said.

"It's okay."

Lining the walls were booths with leather seats and lantern-shaped lights. Dark beams ran the length of the ceiling and old wooden planks covered the floor. An oak bar with a brass footrail commanded the center of the room.

"Table or booth?"

She scanned the bistro tables scattered over the floor. "Where do you usually sit?"

"At the bar."

She should have guessed and would have if she wasn't standing so close to Jack. Worn jeans, gray hoodie over tight black T-shirt, scuffed boots. This was as much a uniform for him as the camouflage he'd no doubt worn in the military. He'd been so right about what she was thinking yesterday. Not so much about sleeping with him, although she'd gotten as far as wondering what he looked like naked. But she found him incredibly hot and was mortified that he'd been able to see that.

Now she needed to conceal the fact that her instantaneous attraction had not yet run its course, or she'd be risking losing this job.

"The bar it is." She followed him across the room.

It was closing in on five o'clock and there were only a handful of people in the place. Jack headed for the bar and took a seat on one of the stools beside a tall, broadshouldered, handsome man in a khaki uniform.

"Hey, Sheriff," he said. "I see you changed your mind about leaving town."

The man smiled and held out his hand. "Good to see you. Been a while, Jack. If you came around more, you'd know that my dad retired and I'm now the head lawman in town."

"I've been busy."

Erin managed to haul herself up on the stool next to him. Her legs were short; the chairs were high. It wasn't graceful. Jack looked at her then at the sheriff, but said nothing.

"Hi," the man said to her. "Haven't seen you around before."

She reached an arm in front of Jack and shook the sheriff's hand. "Erin Riley."

"Will Fletcher," he said.

A beautiful blue-eyed redhead walked over to them and stopped on the other side of the bar. "If it isn't Blackwater Lake's famous author."

"Hi, Delanie."

The woman looked from Jack to Erin and waited expectantly. Apparently she got tired of waiting because she asked, "Who's your friend?"

"Erin Riley." He rested his forearms on the bar. "And we're not friends."

"Nice to meet you, Erin." Delanie stared at Jack. "So, if you're not friends, what are you?"

The silence grew as all of them stared at Jack, waiting for clarification. He finally shrugged and said, "That's a good question."

Erin jumped in. "I'm his research assistant."

"Okay, then. What can I get you two?" Delanie asked. "Food? Drinks?"

"I'd like to see a menu, please. And a glass of chardonnay would be lovely."

"You got it." The woman grabbed two plastic-covered sheets containing the food choices and set them in front of her and Jack. Then she opened a bottle of white wine and poured a glass, putting it on a napkin in front of Erin. "Beer, Jack?"

"The usual."

"How long have you been in town?" Sheriff Fletcher asked.

"A day. So far I haven't seen much except the lake and marina. And Main Street. But Blackwater Lake is the most beautiful place I've ever been."

"Where are you from?" Delanie used a rag to wipe non-existent spots from the bar.

"Phoenix." The bar owner and the sheriff were nodding as if that explained a lot. "Don't judge. There's a beauty in the Arizona desert, too, it's just different. I actually haven't done much traveling, though, but I've always wanted to."

"So, you're a research assistant?" Sitting at the bar, the sheriff leaned his forearms on the edge of the oak. "Is that a permanent arrangement?"

Erin looked at Jack and he didn't seem inclined to answer so she was forced to wing it. "Not permanent. Just for the book in progress. I freelance and in between assignments I work as a substitute high school English teacher."

"So you're overqualified to read that menu," Jack said.

She got his point. He was hungry and wanted to get this over with. After scanning the list of options she said, "I'd like a club sandwich and side salad."

Jack never even looked at the choices. "Burger and fries."

"Coming right up," Delanie said, then disappeared in the back.

The sheriff stood and dropped some bills on the bar. "Good to see you, Jack. Don't be a stranger. Welcome, Erin. I hope you enjoy your stay here in Blackwater Lake. It is a pretty place. Take it from me. I left for a lot of years, but couldn't stay away. There are good people here."

"I look forward to meeting them."

"What's your hurry, Sheriff?" Jack hadn't been particularly social so the question was unexpected.

"I have paperwork to finish up at the office. Then I'm taking April out to dinner."

"Is that your wife?" Erin asked.

"Fiancée." Will Fletcher's rugged features softened when he smiled. "But us getting married is long overdue. We're making plans to rectify that. Can't be soon enough for me."

"Congratulations," she said.

"Thanks. Good luck with the book, Jack."

Erin had a feeling she was the one who needed luck *helping* Jack with the manuscript. His cooperation would be a good place to start. "He seems nice."

"I suppose."

"He said people are friendly. Have you met a lot of folks since you've been here?"

"No."

"Have you made an effort?"

"No."

"I'm going out on a limb here and say that everyone you've become acquainted with has been a customer here at Bar None."

There was a challenge in his eyes when he met her gaze. "So?"

"Have you ever heard the saying that 'no man is an island'? You have to reach out and meet people halfway. On top of that, writing doesn't happen in a vacuum. You have to fill up the creative well. That happens with experiences and to have those, being sociable helps."

"I'll keep that in mind."

"Good," she said.

"And, Erin?"

"Yes?"

"It occurs to me that the armed forces of the United States don't need to stockpile weapons. All the brass needs to do is turn you loose on the enemy to talk them to death."

She wondered whether or not to be offended by that, then decided one of them needed to be an optimist. "I'll take that as a compliment."

The morning after taking her to town, Jack went upstairs to his office, leaving Erin in the kitchen, cleaning up after breakfast. She was a good cook. If his editor ever spoke to him again he'd have to thank her for that. The omelet, fruit, toast and coffee was the best morning meal he'd had in a long time. Whatever he threw together was maybe one step above the army's MREs—meals ready to eat.

He turned on his laptop and opened the file "Mac Daniels," which was the name of his ex-army ranger, Special Forces hero. After reading through the pages he'd written, he said, "This sucks."

If the pages had been printed out, he'd have wadded them up and tossed the balls of paper across the room. They weren't and he deleted them. Right now he'd take a black ops mission over this. But army rangers never quit and he was literally on borrowed time with this project. After he'd left the military and his wife left him, he'd been pretty sure that being a soldier was the only thing he was good at.

Then he wrote a bestselling novel and the publisher wanted the second book on the two-book contract he'd signed, but he was late turning it in. What if he was a one-hit wonder? Maybe he *was* only good at soldiering. If he had to throw in the towel on this book, that would prove he'd been right.

The sheriff's words from yesterday drifted through his mind.

"Work in progress, my ass," he mumbled. He didn't need luck as much as inspiration.

There was a knock on the door and since he used the living room of the upstairs apartment for his office, technically the knock was on the office door. If he said nothing, would she go away?

Erin opened it and poked her head in. "Reporting for duty, sir."

Nine on the dot. It was as if she was punching a time clock. Harley ran inside and settled in his bed next to the desk. Little traitor had been hanging out with her.

Instead of inspiration, what he got was another challenge. "I work alone."

"Not any more" was what he expected out of her but that's not what she said.

"Let's talk about the book." She moved in front of the desk.

It was exactly what she'd said yesterday. "I'm a writer, not a talker."

A look crossed her face that said she'd noticed. "Tell me about the story. This is the sequel to *High Value Target*, so the hero is Mac Daniels."

He nodded an answer, if only to prove that he was telling the truth about the writer-versus-talker thing.

She tilted her head and shiny, gold-streaked brown hair slid over her shoulder. "I'm curious. When you named this character, did you mean for it to rhyme with Jack Daniel's, the whiskey? An inside joke? Or was it coincidence?"

Sharp girl, he thought. But the only answer he gave her was a small smile.

"Okay then. Moving on." She settled a hip on the corner of the desk and met his gaze. "I read the first book. Mac was a reluctant hero and took down the bad guys. What is his goal in this book?"

Jack wanted to squirm and this is where Ranger training came in handy, other than a war zone, of course. He'd learned how to stay in one position without moving for hours. "Mac is trying to stay alive."

"It's a good goal." She thought for a moment. "So who or what is standing in his way?"

"You mean who's after him?"

"*Is* someone after him? If so, why?"

Jack was still working out those details. It was what he did. On his own. This was *his* work-in-progress. His office. And that reminded him. "Look, Erin, there's something I'd like to talk to you about."

"Okay. That's what I'm here for."

"I'm not comfortable with this arrangement."

"And I'm not leaving." Her eyes flashed and her expression was locked and loaded on stubborn.

"No. I meant you bunking down up here." With unfettered access to his office. On top of that, the whole place was now filled with the scent of sunlight and flowers. And…her. How was he supposed to concentrate when his work space smelled like a girl?

"If you'd like I can pitch a tent outside," she said with more than a little sarcasm.

Jack wondered if that look on her face frightened the teenage boys in her English classes. It sure didn't work on him. For over ten years his job had been about dealing with life-and-death conflicts. Erin Riley didn't intimidate him at all.

"That won't be necessary." Although the idea was interesting, she didn't look like an outdoors kind of woman. More a hotel-and-happy-hour type. When she'd shown up and made it clear she wasn't leaving, he'd figured the spare room up here would be best. It wasn't. "I'd like to move you into the spare room downstairs."

"I don't want to throw your routine off—"

"Too late." He leaned back in his chair. "The thing is, if I want to work during the night, I wouldn't want to wake you."

"Whatever you want."

Jack happened to be looking at her mouth when she said that and the words turned into something that was a very bad idea. "Okay, then. Your job is to move your things to the spare bedroom downstairs."

"And afterward?"

"Isn't that enough?"

"I don't have much. That won't take very long. I'm here to assist. Tell me how to do that."

Yesterday at Bar None she'd introduced herself as his research assistant. That gave him an idea. "You know, it would help if you looked some things up for me."

"Great." That put the splashes of gold back in her green eyes. "What?"

"Why don't you go ahead and pack your stuff up and take it downstairs. I'll have a list ready when you're finished."

"Okay."

Erin disappeared down the hall but unfortunately the scent of her skin lingered in his work space. Later he would figure out how to man this place up again, but right now he had to do something to keep her busy and out of his hair.

Jack searched *gold* and *diamonds* on Google, figuring either one could put Mac Daniels's life on the line. As he browsed, something caught his eye. *Diamonds are a girl's best friend. Say it with diamonds.*

Erin came back into his office with her rolling suitcase and a bag she held in her hand. He had a sneaking suspicion that whatever made her smell so good was in the little one.

"I've got everything," she said cheerfully.

"That didn't take long."

"Told you it wouldn't." She headed for the door.

"Do you need help with those bags?"

"No. You keep working. I'll be back shortly to help."

Jack waited for the door to close and noted that Harley stayed where he was in his bed. "Good move, buddy. Never bite the hand that feeds you."

He typed in some more search words and scrolled through articles, information and sources for all the material. It was interesting stuff, not relevant to his writing, but she might get something out of the research. He printed out a list of topics then went back to his Mac Daniels file.

"What am I going to do with you?" he said to the blank screen, where his fictional character waited for a story. "You've been out of the military for a while and all you're good at is war and training for it. In the first book an old girlfriend sucked you into using those skills. You can handle yourself in a fight because you're trained to beat the crap out of bad guys. Now what?"

Except for the ex-girlfriend-rescue part that pretty much described himself, not Mac Daniels. Jack made a disgusted sound then leaned back in his chair. He was a piece of work, talking to himself. Well, not technically, since Harley was here, but too close for comfort. At least he knew his own flaws and keeping them to himself was the best way to control them.

There was a knock at the door then Erin poked her head in the room and smiled. "I'm back."

"Like the Terminator," he mumbled.

"I love that movie."

"Really?" He pegged her as more of a romantic-comedy type.

"Yes. You know romance is at the heart of the story."

"No pun intended."

She smiled. "What woman wouldn't want to hear, 'I came across time for you, Sarah.'"

Jack had never met a woman he'd want to time-travel for. But that was the best segue he could have hoped for. He pulled the sheet from his printer and held it out. "Your research topics."

"Right. I can't wait to get started." She took the paper and scanned it. To her credit, her perk factor only slipped a little.

The average person probably wouldn't have noticed. Jack was surprised that he had.

Her gaze settled on his and the vivid green was back. "The fine art of romantic talk?"

"Dialogue."

She glanced down at the paper. "A hundred and one ways to be romantic?"

"Mac spent a lot of time in a war zone." He shrugged as if to say that explained all.

"Understanding the female mind?"

"If he ever wants to get lucky, Mac might need some help."

There was a skeptical look on her face—she was suspicious and just a little annoyed. "These topics are important for an action-adventure book...why?"

Jack realized she'd already given him the answer to that question. "The Terminator effect."

"As it happens, women don't typically understand the male mind, either. I need more than that to connect the dots."

"You said you like the movie because there's a romance at the heart. It crosses genres and broadens the appeal."

"And?" One eyebrow rose.

"Maybe if Mac has a relationship it could expand my readership to women."

Her eyes narrowed and the I've-got-your-number look was back. "You don't fool me, Jack."

"I wasn't trying to." Did a half truth make something an out-and-out lie?

"Oh, please. This is you patting me on the head and telling me to run along."

"Not true."

"So in all of your own experience you've never sweet-talked a woman? Never made a romantic gesture? Or two?"

"Hard to say. I tried." With his ex-wife. But he didn't think she left him for lack of romance because she stayed for years while he went through numerous deployments. She left when he didn't re-up with the army. "But does a guy really know if he hit it out of the park with a woman?"

"You really don't know how to read people?"

"Hence the research for understanding the female mind," he pointed out.

She made a show of folding the paper and sticking it in the pocket of her jeans. "I'll do the research. But don't for a second believe that I don't know what you're up to. This is all about keeping me at a distance."

Jack didn't get a chance to respond because she turned and walked out of his office. Just as well. He needed to get to work. And she was wrong about his goal. The phony research wasn't to keep her at a distance, but to keep her in the dark about the fact that he didn't have a story. With luck he could fix the problem before she figured out what was going on.

The good news was that it was now quiet enough to work. And the bad news was he had to put some words on that blank page. And, damn it, he could still smell the scent of her skin. That brought to mind images of her smile and the fact that as hard as he'd tried to make her, she wouldn't back down from him.

Harley stood in his bed glancing from him to the door where Erin had exited. "Yeah, I know, buddy. I'm as surprised as you are that it's not so bad having her around for a distraction."

Chapter Three

In her new room Erin lay on her back trying to get to sleep, but the sound of pacing upstairs was distracting. So much for not waking her if he couldn't catch some z's and decided to work. Hard to type when you weren't sitting in front of a computer.

She was on the futon in the spare bedroom downstairs and it was surprisingly comfortable. That wasn't to blame for her restlessness; that was Jack's fault and not just on account of his walking back and forth, hitting that one squeaky board every time. Earlier he had opened the futon to make it flat and she'd been mesmerized by the play of muscles underneath the smooth material of his snug T-shirt.

Then she thought about one hundred and one ways to be romantic. Bring a woman flowers. Make her breakfast in bed. Surprise her with a B and B weekend. Picturing Jack doing any of those things made her smile. Forget romantic. He was barely civil.

A different sound caught her attention. The door to the

upstairs apartment closed and heavy footsteps sounded on the outside stairway. Erin tensed, waiting to hear him come inside. She could feel him when he was nearby and every cell in her body seemed to say "notice me." Which, of course, was never going to happen.

A few minutes passed and she still didn't hear him come inside. Wide-awake now, she tossed the sheet aside and turned on the light. The room was pretty big but had no personality. Unpacked boxes were stacked on the opposite wall. A lamp sat on what looked like an apple crate turned on end.

Erin grabbed the lightweight summer robe that matched her white cotton nightgown and slipped her arms into it. She pulled the pink satin tie tight around her waist, then let herself out of the room. It was time to find out if there was anything wrong. Then maybe she could get to sleep. One needed all of one's strength to deal with Jack Garner.

The house was dark and she felt for the hall switch to turn on the light. Brightness spilled into the empty living room. Cool air from outside washed over her and she realized that the front door was open. Looking through the screen, she saw Jack on the porch, staring out at the marina and Blackwater Lake beyond. She turned on the lights in the living room.

Barefoot, she walked outside and let the door close behind her. Between the lights and the screen door it was enough to guarantee he wouldn't be startled. "Is everything all right, Jack?"

He didn't flinch in surprise or bother to look over his shoulder for that matter. "Fine."

"It's late." Duh.

"Not for me."

She moved forward a couple of steps. Earlier when he'd asked her to move downstairs, she'd figured it was about keeping her away from his office space. The part about him working at night didn't ring true, but apparently she'd been wrong. "So you're up at night a lot?"

"Yeah." He finally turned to look at her. "You learn to sleep light, one eye open, waiting for something to happen."

"Doesn't sound restful."

"It's not." He slid his fingertips into the pockets of his worn jeans. "But you get used to functioning on little to no sleep."

"I suppose."

She could see a nearby full moon just above the dark silhouette of the mountains beyond the lake and there was a sky full of stars. The air was filled with the scent of pine and man, but she wasn't sure which was more intoxicating. One hundred and two ways to be romantic, she thought.

"Okay, then. I just wanted to make sure there was nothing wrong."

Before she could turn away, he asked, "Why aren't you asleep?"

Now wasn't that a valid question for which she had an embarrassment of answers. No way she'd confess to being distracted by his broad shoulders, muscular back and the romantic notions his research had stuck in her mind. And she didn't want him to feel bad about pacing. This was his home and moving around at night might be his creative process. She also didn't want to imply that moving downstairs had been a problem and make him feel guilty. But he'd already told her she was a bad liar.

So, she gave him the truth with a twist. "I was thinking."

His mouth curved into a slow, sexy smile. "Why doesn't that surprise me?"

"I don't know," she hedged. "Why doesn't it?"

"Because you're the kind of woman who thinks too much. Shakes things up."

"In a good way? Or bad?"

"Both," he said.

She had a feeling he wasn't just talking about the job she was sent here to do. That maybe he was hinting at something a little more personal. The thought made her heart race and she had to stop herself from pressing fingertips to the pounding pulse at the base of her throat. He'd know why and that would show him her vulnerability and give him more of an upper hand than he already had.

"I've been thinking about you." Oh, dear God, that was no better and she desperately wanted the words back.

"Oh?"

She saw the gleam in his eyes and felt a shiver clear to her bare toes. "Now that I have your attention—" She drew in a breath. "What I meant was, I've been thinking about what the military must have been like."

"Civilians don't have a clue."

"You're right, of course. But there are basics. You're expected to follow orders."

"From a commanding officer," he pointed out.

"Right. I'm not giving orders. But I was getting at the discipline factor. You're told where to go, when to report for duty and what job to do."

"Chain of command is followed," he admitted. "If not there would be chaos in the ranks."

"In civilian life we call it a schedule."

The look on his face said he was bracing himself for whatever she had in mind. "What's your point?"

"A schedule."

He moved his shoulders as if they'd tensed up, then stared at her for several moments. "Oh, you mean me."

"Actually I mean both of us." She curled her toes into

the wooden porch. "You had discipline in the military and it would behoove you to establish that in your writing life."

One corner of his mouth quirked up. "Who says *behoove* in actual conversation?"

"An English teacher."

"Right." He folded his arms over his chest. "What did you have in mind?"

"Breakfast first. Your mind and body need fuel." She had not expected him to be even this receptive. "Then we meet in your office for a…let's call it a status meeting. We discuss what you're going to work on and you can give me a list of research topics for anything necessary for the story. Think of it as punching a time clock."

"Don't tell me. This status meeting would be at nine in the morning."

"Yes. How did you know?"

"Just a guess."

"So, what do you think of the idea?"

"Do you really want to know?" he asked.

"Of course. This needs to work for you. It's all about fine-tuning your process. You're the author." She watched him watch her, his gaze flicking over her body, and wished she was wearing jeans and a big, bulky sweatshirt. A thin cotton nightgown and matching robe came under the heading of Didn't Think It Through. Where was a girl's body armor when she really needed it? "Sometimes it's just about putting your butt in the chair. Sheer boredom will force you into doing something."

"Doing something—" His voice was husky, deeper than normal.

Erin sensed tension in him but had a feeling it wasn't about her suggestions for his work schedule. "Anyway, that's what I was thinking about. Give it some thought and let me know in the morning—"

"Okay."

She blinked. "What?"

"Permission granted. We'll try it your way."

"That's great, Jack." She was oddly happy that he'd actually listened to her. "Thank you for meeting me half-way on this."

"This isn't halfway," he said, staring at her. "It's damn near all the way."

"What? I don't understand—"

"For the record, it's not fair to dress like that when you're asking for something." There was a ragged edge to his voice and his gaze never left her.

"There's nothing wrong with what I'm wearing." That was sheer bravado since moments ago she'd wished for body armor. Then she looked down at the eyelet cotton robe with pink accents and her cheeks suddenly burned with mortification. She realized that with the light behind her, the material was nearly transparent. "Oh, God—"

"Yeah." A muscle jerked in his jaw.

Erin's knees got weak and that was a first. No man had ever made her weak in the knees before. "I'm going in now. You should get some sleep."

"Right."

There was a mother lode of sarcasm in the single word, yet she felt it like a caress that touched her everywhere. The look in his eyes sharpened her senses and she tingled in places that might not have ever tingled before.

"Good night, Jack." She tried to make her voice deci-sive, authoritative, unwavering, but was afraid the words came out weak, wishy-washy and just the tiniest bit wanton.

With all the dignity she could muster, Erin backed up to the door then quickly turned and opened it. She went to her room and shut herself in, then sagged against the door.

"What just happened?" she whispered.

There had been a moment. She was sure of it. Until just a few minutes ago, no man had ever looked at her as if he wanted her more than his next breath. Not even the man she'd taken an engagement ring from. But Jack Garner did.

She didn't know whether to high-five herself or crawl into bed and pull the covers over her head. Then an even more off-putting thought struck her. Was that the way she'd looked at him when they first met? When he'd said they weren't sleeping together as if that's what she'd been thinking.

How was she going to face him tomorrow morning?

Jack sat across from Erin at the kitchen table and finished his omelet. It was becoming clear that she was very good at making them. Spinach, tomatoes, mushrooms and cheese—he couldn't say he'd ever had a better one. The eggs were fluffy and filling. The company…not so much. Since he'd come downstairs for breakfast, the cook had barely looked at him.

Barely was most probably the reason why.

She'd been practically naked on the porch last night and his gut still hurt from the effort it took to keep his hands to himself. The high color in her cheeks was a clue that she was still embarrassed about it. She'd admitted to having a long-term relationship, but there was an innocence about her that was inconvenient. Since coming downstairs for breakfast he hadn't done anything except eat. There had been nothing to take the edge off the tension. If he left it alone and let her feel uncomfortable, maybe she would take off back where she came from.

He sneaked a look and there was something sweet and vulnerable about her that made him feel like a buffalo at a tea party. Damn it. Probably he was going to regret this, but…

"Breakfast was good." There, silence broken.

Erin stopped pushing the food around her plate without eating it and looked at him. "Really?"

"Yeah. Coffee's good, too."

"Thanks, I'm glad you liked it. Some guys think vegetable omelets aren't very...well, masculine."

"What guy?"

"My fiancé."

Jack bit his tongue to keep from saying this fiancé was an idiot. Not only was it bad to speak ill of the dead, but a remark like that would also undermine what he was trying to do in erasing her embarrassment. All he said was "His loss."

"That's nice of you to say, Jack."

"Not really. I'm not a nice guy. It's just the truth."

Whatever else he was, wasn't, or had done, he always tried to be honest. Mostly he was successful, but probably not always. "You're a good cook."

"It's just something I like to do. Guess that's half the battle. When I was a little girl, I stayed with my grandmother a lot because my mom worked. Grammy let me help when she cooked or baked. I got to roll out dough, cut out cookies and help make soup." There was a faraway look in her eyes and the corners of her mouth curved up in a small smile. "Those are good memories."

"I never knew my grandmother." Now, why the hell had he said that?

"Singular? You only had one parent?"

He looked at her for a long moment, kicking himself for going soft and letting that out. It was too much to hope she'd miss the slipup. "Obviously at a certain point I had a father, but he was nothing more than a sperm donor."

"You never met him?"

The pity in her eyes made him want to put his fist

through a wall. "She always said he was a magician. When he heard my mother say the word *pregnant*, he made himself disappear."

"I don't know what to say."

"That's a first. But if you feel compelled to comment, just don't say you're sorry. I never needed him." Jack learned a code of honor in the military and did his best to be honest, but that statement closed in on the line that separated truth from deceit.

"You are many things, Jack, but I would never describe you as someone to be pitied." Then she pointed a warning finger at him. "And don't tell me I'm patronizing you because I'm not doing that."

Since that's exactly what he'd been about to say, he almost smiled but caught himself just in time. That was annoying, one more way she tempted him. Enough of this. After pushing his chair back from the table, he said, "I have to get to work."

She glanced at the funky pink princess watch on her wrist. "Oh, wow. It's getting late."

Only if one was on a schedule, which he'd agreed to in a weak moment when he'd been unable to look away from her practically naked body. "Yeah. It's closing right in on nine."

"I'll clean up the kitchen."

Jack knew he should offer to help but this time was able to hold back the words. Washing dishes with her was domestic and he didn't do domestic. Not anymore.

Without another word he walked to the front door and Harley followed from wherever he'd been dozing. They went out onto the porch then up the stairs to his office.

Jack sat down in the chair behind his desk and looked at the blank computer monitor for a while. He patted his leg and said, "Harley, up."

The dog did as ordered then made a circle before settling on Jack's lap. He scratched the animal's hairless back and hoped the mindless activity would stimulate something creative or useful. Ten minutes later he still had nothing.

There was a knock on his office door before Erin stuck her head inside. "Rough commute. Am I late?"

If only. "Nine o'clock on the nose." Damn it.

She took a seat in front of the desk. "Okay, let the status meeting begin. Where are you in the book?"

"Where am I?" he repeated. Harley chose that moment to desert him and jump down and pad over to her. "Well, let me think. That's kind of hard to say."

"Yeah. I can see where it would be. Why don't you start by telling me what you have so far."

"What I have… Let's see." He leaned back in his chair and linked his fingers over his abdomen. "Wow. Where do I begin…?"

Really, he wanted to say. *Where?* Did he open the story with unknown assailants ambushing Mac and leaving him for dead? Or with a mysterious stranger who contacts him for help because word of his exploits in rescuing the ex-girlfriend's kidnapped kid from a vicious drug cartel had spread? The best first line would be something like "The pretty, green-eyed woman with sun-streaked brown hair smiled seductively before telling him to forget the book and take her to bed."

Erin waited patiently for him to speak. When the silence drifted into awkward territory she said, "You know, Corinne Carlisle had a hard time talking about her story, too. It could be an author thing because you're more comfortable with the written word than the spoken one."

Helpful of her to gift-wrap an excuse for him. "Yeah, I think you just nailed it."

"Are you a pantser or a plotter?" she asked.

"I have no idea what you're talking about."

"Do you write by the seat of your pants? Or do you know every detail ahead of time when you sit down at the computer?"

Right this minute he wished to be a plotter but was pretty sure the first one described him best. "That's really hard to say."

"Okay." She nodded thoughtfully. "Then let's talk about your characters."

Oh, boy. He could really use an interruption about now. A phone call, package delivery, or a little rocket attack. "The thing is, I don't have all the characters set in stone yet. Still trying to flesh them out."

"You have Mac," she pointed out.

Good old Mac. "I do have him."

"What's happened to him in the time since we left him at the end of book one?"

"That's a good question. I'm glad you asked." Not.

She waited for him to elaborate. So it was safe to say she wasn't an interrupter. Boy, did he wish she was.

"So," Jack said. "He's been kicking around."

"In Los Angeles? Or has he gone to Dallas, Topeka, or Micronesia?" The perky, trying-to-be-helpful tone was missing in action from her voice.

"He hasn't moved." And that was Jack's fault because he hadn't moved his main character.

"In the last book he had just left the army and had no plan for his life before being pulled into that case involving his dead buddy's younger brother, who was married to his ex-girlfriend."

"Yeah." Funny how the no-plan-for-his-life part sounded a lot like Jack.

"How is he supporting himself?"

"Odd jobs. This and that." And in a military operation

when you wanted to avoid direct confrontation with an enemy that had superior firepower, a good soldier created a diversion. He took a piece of paper from the printer tray beside him. "I put together some things for you to research."

Erin's eyes narrowed as she took it from him, then scanned the list. "Meteors? Dinosaurs?" She met his gaze. "You probably already know that *Jurassic Park* has been done." She looked down again. "Jet Skis?"

"All things I'm considering incorporating into the story."

With careful, precise movements she folded the single sheet several times before slicing him with a look. "What's going on, Jack?"

"I need you to look stuff up."

"No, you don't. You're trying to distract me and it's time for you to cut the crap."

"Is that any way to talk to your employer?"

"Technically I work for the publishing house, specifically your editor. So, yeah, it's a very good way to address a man who is not forthcoming."

"What makes you think something's going on?" Besides the fact that he kept dodging her direct questions?

"Classic avoidance. And to quote Shakespeare—'let me count the ways.'" She held up her fingers. "You won't talk about the story, characters or what your hero has been doing. I'm pretty sure that means you have no idea. And every time I push for information, you come up with a distraction. Some ridiculous research stuff that has nothing to do with your genre. One hundred and one ways to be romantic—really, Jack? You even threw me out of my room and kicked me downstairs." She took a breath. "So call me paranoid and neurotic—"

"Don't forget punctual," he added helpfully.

"—but I'm suspicious," she continued without missing

a beat after his interjection. "Your editor would welcome an outline of the project. Not details, necessarily, just the beginning, middle and end of the story. Possibly a one-line characterization of the hero."

Jack met her gaze, stare for stare. Her perky, cheerful interrogation might have given him a sense of her being a pushover. Now he saw the error of that assumption. She was sunshine and steel.

Still, he couldn't resist trying one more time. "There's nothing to be suspicious about. I'm in the process of pulling all the threads together."

"Then let me see your pages." She suddenly stood and moved around the desk to look at his computer monitor. "It's not even turned on."

"That's easy to rectify."

"Okay. Let me see the work you've done so far."

This time Jack did squirm, and Harley had disappeared down the hall so there was no way to keep Erin from noticing. "The work needs editing—"

She held up a hand. "There's something wrong and I want to know what it is. I'm here to help you finish this manuscript and I can't if you're hiding something."

Her relentless questions were like water dripping on a stone, wearing away the outer protection. Jack was at a crossroads. He knew what it looked like because he'd seen it before in the heat of battle when there was no wiggle room left. Almost always a course of action revealed itself and this situation was no different. Her counteroffensive left him no choice. He had to tell the truth or lie to her and he couldn't do that.

"So quit stalling and turn on the monitor, Jack. Let me see your work."

"I haven't started it."

"Of course not today. The laptop isn't even on yet. I want to see what you've got so far," she stressed.

"You don't understand." He met her gaze.

"Then enlighten me."

"I have nothing. There is no book."

*Of course you know what I think, Rafaella. It's on your
worried when I left. Where are you now? Maybe tomorrow
won't seem quite so awful. I'm thinking of you.

Then continued on.

I wish nothing else in particular.

Chapter Four

Erin blinked several times, letting the words sink in,
while slowly lowering herself into the chair. "What do you
mean there's no book? What do you do up here all day?"

"I write pages. Every single day. Then I delete them
because they're all crap."

Oh God. Oh God. Oh God. The chant went through her
mind as she desperately tried to think of something helpful to say. "Is everything deleted?"

"I have about twenty pages."

"Let me see them." Was her voice even and unemotional? She hoped it didn't show the panic that was slowly
creeping in as the magnitude of this situation became clear.

Jack turned on the computer and pulled up a file, then
hit the print button. When the last page came out he handed
them to her.

Erin started reading and with the turn of every page her
heart sank a little more. There was nothing wrong with the

writing and there was a wry, masculine voice to the work, but it was all internal dialogue from Mac Daniels's point of view. Nothing particularly exciting was going on. Quite frankly there was a very high boredom factor but no way could she tell him that. His instincts, however, were right about the quality of these pages.

She looked up and met his gaze. "I have to agree with you. This isn't your best work."

"Since you showed up we've disagreed on almost everything. I was hoping that streak would continue." His mouth pulled tight for a moment, then he rubbed Harley's head when the dog jumped back into his lap and looked at him. The animal apparently felt his tension. "So you think it's crap, too."

"I didn't say that. Don't panic."

Jack looked the opposite of panicked—cool, calm collected. And she needed to be that way, too. This was why she was here. But she needed to think.

"I'm going for a walk."

Instantly Harley jumped off Jack's lap and began to whine. "Now you've done it."

"What?"

"You said the *w* word. If you're not prepared to take him it's best to spell. *W-a-l-k*." There was amusement in his eyes. "There's very little he likes better. Except maybe raw hamburger. But the *w* is in his top two."

"Sorry. I won't make that mistake again." She headed for the door, wincing at the sounds of doggy protest behind her.

After going outside, the yelping got worse as she hurried down the stairs. Moments later she heard the door open and in seconds the dog was happily dancing at her feet. He ran several yards away then came back, repeating the exercise several more times.

"You're not subtle, Harley." She looked at Jack, who'd come up beside her. "Neither are you."

"I think that's the nicest thing you've ever said to me, Miss Riley."

Instead of rising to the bait, she decided to comment on the fact that it wasn't his usual time to walk and he'd given in to Harley. "You know you're spoiling that dog."

He met her gaze and shrugged. He was either avoiding work or didn't care. "Harley, walk."

Jack started after the dog, who instantly ran down the path that skirted the lake. She stared at his back, the man's, admiring his broad shoulders and muscular back that tapered to a trim waist and really nice butt, wrapped with just the perfect amount of snugness in worn denim. How the heck had those two hijacked her walk?

She could go in the opposite direction but since the whole purpose of her being here was to get his book finished, probably talking to him would be a good idea. Even though she was furious.

His long legs had chewed up a fair amount of distance by the time she'd made up her mind and she hurried to catch up. When that happened, she fell into step beside him. Her mind was spinning from his revelation and she needed to organize her thoughts. If she'd been alone that wouldn't be a challenge, but the manly scent of his skin combined with the smell of pine effectively made thinking difficult.

Apparently Jack didn't have any thoughts to organize because after a few moments he said, "You're uncharacteristically quiet."

"I didn't think you paid enough attention to me to know what's characteristic for me."

"In the army you learn pretty fast that paying attention to your surroundings means survival."

"And you see me as a threat to that?" She was being petulant. He could just sue her.

"Not my personal safety, no."

"Then you think your way of life is at risk by my being here? You're wrong, Jack. I'm only trying to help you." As they walked she met his gaze and tripped over the uneven ground. Instantly he grabbed her arm to steady her. Being touched by him easily scattered the few thoughts she'd managed to gather. She mumbled under her breath, "Pigheaded…stubborn—"

"Harley—" At his voice, the dog turned and headed back. "I heard that."

"Ask me if I care."

"Let me take a wild guess. You're mad."

"Give the man a prize." She refused to look at him and only heard the surprise in his voice. "I am so ticked off. You have wasted so much time. Why in the world didn't you say something when I first got here? When I tried to have a conversation about what was going on? You had numerous opportunities to come clean, yet you shut me out. Why?"

When Harley sniffed at his boots, Jack squatted down and rubbed his head. He looked up and said, "Because I'm used to being the guy who's inserted into a hot zone to fix whatever is wrong."

Holding her breath, Erin waited for him to say more. When he didn't, she figured that was as close as he'd get to admitting he wasn't used to needing or asking for help. She sensed he almost never did it and the fact that he had took all the irritation out of her. Or maybe she was just a pushover because of her acute attraction to him, but that didn't change anything. There was a problem and they had to find a way to fix it.

"Okay, we know you can write a successful book. You

wrote a bestseller." She knew she'd hit a nerve when his jaw tensed and a muscle jerked. "There's no reason you can't do it again."

"Says who? Maybe I only had one book in me." He watched Harley sniff the side of the path then pick up a stick, which he dropped at Jack's feet. He picked it up and threw it as far as he could.

"Your creativity just needs a jump start."

He tilted his head and looked at her. "What happened to if you stared at a blank screen long enough you'll get bored and write something on it?"

"I did say that." She thought for a moment. "But it helps if you know what you're going to write."

He snorted. "Are you going to give me the pantsers-and-plotters speech again?"

"That was a definition, not a speech. But I'll remind you what I said about talking out the plot. Discussing the hero's goals. His mind-set since we last saw him."

"Any thoughts on that?" He all but growled those words, as if his asking-for-assistance muscles were rusty.

"Yes. But feel free to tell me I'm full of it. The point is to toss out ideas and see what feels right in your gut." She slid her fingertips into the pockets of her jeans. "Mac had no emotional growth in the first book because he went into fight-or-flight mode almost right away."

"So he's still aimless."

"Right. Unless he's independently wealthy, he has to have been thinking about what he'll do to support himself since leaving the military." Her mind was spinning. "Come to think of it, we don't really know why he left. He was a career soldier and his reasoning could be explored in this book."

Jack nodded absently. "Yeah."

That was encouraging, she thought. An affirmative instead of sarcasm. She dipped her toe in a little further. "When we get back, it might help to just talk it through and you could take notes. Or record the conversation if you'd rather. Instead of jumping straight into the writing, you can figure out the inciting incident that sets the story in motion, then some loose turning points as a structure for the story."

"And tomorrow there will still be a blank screen."

"Give yourself permission to write badly," she suggested.

His look was wry. "Yeah, because that's what I learned in the army. Permission to be a screwup, sir."

"Maybe it sounds crazy, but you might find it surprisingly freeing."

"And that's supposed to be creative?" he asked skeptically.

"Won't know unless you try." She thought for a moment. "Some authors start their day by jotting down stream-of-consciousness writing."

"You mean gibberish?"

"Probably not something you'd publish," she admitted.

"Then I guess you could say I've already done that. The pages you read are unpublishable and probably fall into the stream-of-consciousness category," he said sarcastically.

"That's not what I meant. You just write whatever pops into your mind," she explained.

"Sounds like a waste of time if you ask me."

"It's just an exercise."

Erin glanced up at him and felt a little flutter around her heart, the one that made it hard to take a deep breath. The way his biceps strained against the material of his black T-shirt made her want to touch and find out for herself what they felt like.

It was obvious that Jack was in excellent physical condition, which meant he'd retained habits from his time in the army that kept him in shape. She knew he ran three or four times a week. There was workout equipment in the upstairs bedroom. One didn't just jump into a fitness regime. Maybe she could explain this to him in a relatable way.

"What do you do before a run?" she asked.

His gaze narrowed on her. "Why?"

"Bear with me. I have a point." Their shoulders brushed as they walked. Personally she was glad the bushes and trees around them weren't tinder-dry because the sparks would have ignited them. She drew in a breath. "What's your preexercise routine?"

"I stretch out. Warm up."

"Exactly."

He looked at her as if she had a snake draped around her neck. "I thought you had a point."

"Stream-of-consciousness writing is like stretching your muscles for work."

"Shouldn't I put that energy into something productive?"

"The point is to not think about work. Free your mind and let the ideas flow."

His expression was still skeptical, but he asked, "What should I write about?"

"Like I said. Anything that pops into your mind."

Jack looked down at the dog, who had thrown himself on the ground at his feet. Automatically he picked up the animal and rubbed his hand over the hairless back. "I still say it's a waste of time."

This man was results-driven. He'd spent over a decade in an organized, mission-oriented environment. The creative process was the polar opposite. But if she could give him a focus, he might be more inclined to give it a try.

As they headed back to the house, she watched him with

the dog. His protectiveness with the animal. The way he automatically picked up Harley when he got tired. Jack had done the same thing that first day when she'd arrived. There was a bond between the two and that homely little creature might just be what he cared about most in this world.

"Write about Harley," she suggested.

"What?"

"Stream-of-consciousness warm-up exercises. Think about your dog and jot down whatever comes into your mind."

With the dog curled happily in his arms, Jack stared at her for several moments. She wondered how it would feel to be safely tucked against his wide chest, wrapped in his strong arms.

Then he shook his head. "It's official. You're crazy."

About you, she thought.

For a moment Erin was afraid she'd said that out loud. Fortunately, the words stayed in her head, where they belonged. He already knew she was attracted to him. If she confirmed it he would say I told you so and send her packing.

Erin didn't want to get out of bed after a lousy night without much sleep. And that was all Jack's fault. He was a bundle of contrasts. Gruff and argumentative with her; tender and protective of his unattractive pet. He measured out a quarter cup of organic chicken or grass-fed beef for Harley's meals! He was a really off-putting combination of macho and mush.

And she knew very little about him. Was there a girlfriend? Wife? But those questions fell into personal territory, which technically made it not her business. And don't even get her started on the geographical situation here. Last night she'd heard him pacing like a predatory tiger.

Back and forth. Back and forth. At least an hour. Maybe more.

Then it got quiet and she'd waited for him to come downstairs to bed. That kept her tense and wide-eyed for a long time. Her body tingled and her skin was hot whenever he was in the master bedroom just across the hall from where she slept. She would challenge anyone to try sleeping when every nerve ending was sparking like a live electrical wire.

After starting a reread of his bestselling book, she finally fell asleep sometime after one o'clock. Now it was six in the morning. Soon she'd need to start breakfast, then meet Jack at nine in his office. If she hauled her hiney out of bed there was just enough time to get in some yoga. Maybe some flexibility poses would flex thoughts of the difficult man out of her mind.

She put on her nylon-and-spandex capris and the stretchy, racer-back tank top she wore for workouts, then rolled out her mat. Mountain pose was first. Standing straight, heels down, shoulders directly over hips. Breathe. Then raised arms. Grounded in her heels, shoulders away from ears and reaching through her fingertips. She held that for the required time and went into the standing forward bend. Exhale and fold down over legs. Let head hang heavy with feet hip distance apart. That was followed by the garland pose, which she hated.

For the lunge pose she started with the right leg forward and the left straight and strong, the heel reaching. She repeated switching legs. About an hour later she'd gone through her routine and worked up a sweat. She rolled up her yoga mat and stood it in the corner next to the unpacked boxes stacked there.

After leaving her room she listened for sounds of Jack and heard none. His bedroom door was opened, meaning he wasn't there, and she thought he'd either slept upstairs or gone for an early morning run. In the kitchen she pulled a bottle of water from the refrigerator and started to twist off the top when she heard the front door open and close.

Jack walked into the room and his shorts and sweaty gray T-shirt told her she'd been right about the run. He looked her over from head to toe and there was a dark sort of intensity in his eyes.

Erin felt the power of that look slip deep inside, tapping into a place where she wanted to be just a tiny bit wicked. He didn't even have to say a word to make her respond to him. When she felt as if she could speak without stammering, she said, "Do you want water?"

"Yeah."

She opened the refrigerator and pulled out a bottle, then handed it to him. "So, *exercise* is the word of the day."

"Apparently."

"Do you want coffee? I was just about to make a pot."

"Affirmative."

"Okay."

She turned away to start the process and resisted the urge to look over her shoulder. The thing was, it didn't matter whether or not she looked. He was *there*. Right on cue her nerves started that electrical arcing thing. Her hands shook as she performed the familiar, ordinary task of filling the coffeemaker reservoir with water and measuring grounds into a filter. Then she pushed the power button and heard the heating element start to sizzle. Or was that her? It was hard to tell if she was hot all over from yoga or Jack's scorching look.

She turned to face him and instantly his gaze lifted to her face. It wasn't possible to be sure he'd been staring at her butt, although the look in his eyes had turned smoky and a muscle jerked in his jaw. That was the same expression he'd worn when she stood on the porch in her cotton nightgown with the light making it practically see-through. Her exercise clothes stretched over her body like a second skin. Did he like what he saw?

She had to break the silence and said the first thing that popped into her mind. "So, I heard you pacing last night."

"Yeah. It helps me think." He leaned a broad shoulder against the wall just inside the doorway.

"Do you want to talk about it?"

"Thinking?" One corner of his mouth quirked up, softening the hard lines of his face. "It just sort of happens on its own."

She folded her arms over her chest. "Would it kill you to answer a question in a serious, straightforward way?"

"It might." He lifted a shoulder in a shrug.

"Well, from what I heard there must have been a lot of thinking going on. That made me wonder if you might have had a breakthrough to discuss. I'm happy to talk about it."

"You're a good talker. I've noticed that about you."

"And you're not."

Right behind her the coffee continued dripping into the pot and the warm, cozy aroma of it filled the room. If anyone saw them now, they could be mistaken for a couple starting out their day. Which they were, but not as a couple. He looked as if sleep had been hard to come by. There were lines on either side of his nose that were signs of fatigue and a supersexy dark scruff on his jaw. Her palms tingled with the urge to brush her hands over his face.

Finally he said, "There's not much to say."

"I disagree. I've told you practically everything about me, but you're a mystery."

"You know all there is to know about me."

"Hardly." She glanced around the kitchen. It was functional, serviceable, but without any cozy pictures or touches that were evidence of this being a home. "I know that you wrote a bestselling action-adventure book. You were a member of army Special Forces, Ranger Battalion. And you have a weakness for strange-looking dogs."

The dog in question padded into the room and looked at his dish then up at Jack. Staring at the animal he said, "What do you want to know?"

"Do you have a girlfriend?"

"No."

"Are you married?"

"No." But something flashed in his eyes. Anger? Hurt? Regret?

"Does that mean you're not married now? Or that you've never been married? Because you know what they say about a man your age who's never been married." She shrugged, hoping he would fill in for her.

"My age?" One dark eyebrow rose.

"Seriously? That's what you got from what I just said?"

"You implied I'm old."

She shook her head. "Either you're deliberately missing the point or you're dense as dirt."

"I don't think so. You specifically said a man of my age."

"Who's never been married," she reminded him.

"What do they say?" he asked, suddenly pretending to be interested.

"That there's something really wrong." She had the sense that he was enjoying baiting her. "You know what I think? You're focusing on minutiae to avoid answering my question."

"You could Google me."

"I have."

"Should I be flattered that you went through the trouble?" He was laughing at her.

"Trouble? That I was trying to find out more about you because we're working together? Or the fact that you've quite successfully managed to not reveal any personal information for public consumption?"

He moved farther into the room and leaned his back against the granite-topped island. "Why do you want personal information?"

"I just do." She wasn't going to tell him it was because she needed a good reason to put the brakes on this crush she had going on. Plus, the more he dodged, the more determined she was to get the truth. "So, have you ever been married? What possible reason could you have to avoid answering that question?"

"I'm a private person."

"You used to be but not anymore. Not since your book hit the bestseller lists and stayed there."

"Drip, drip, drip," he said.

"What does that mean?"

"You're like water on a rock, wearing it down."

She lifted her chin. "I like to think that's one of my best qualities."

"It's good." Jack's gaze dropped to her chest and the glitter was back in his eyes. "But not your best."

He didn't miss much so she was pretty sure he could tell that the pulse in her neck had just gone from normal to racing. There was only one way to interpret those words and that look. He moved closer and she held her breath, hoping that he was going to kiss her. Heat from his body warmed her skin when he stopped right in front of her.

Their shoulders brushed and gazes locked. Sexual tension crackled in the air between them and seemed to push the pause button on everything around them. Was it now? Surely he would touch his mouth to hers now.

Then he looked up and over her head, shattering the moment. He reached into the cupboard behind her and said, "Do you want coffee?"

Erin blinked and managed to answer in the affirmative, but for as long as she lived she would never know how she did it. She stepped sideways and let him get out mugs and pour coffee into them.

Mug in hand, he headed for the doorway. It was as if that click between them had never happened. "I'm going to take a shower."

"I'll start breakfast."

"Good. I'm starved." He stopped and sent a look over his shoulder.

Then he was gone and Erin could breathe again. If anything positive had come out of what just happened, it was that she had a little bit more information about him. No girlfriend and no marriage meant he was single. A bachelor. Available. And he hadn't taken advantage of the opportunity to kiss her. There was only one conclusion to draw. He wasn't interested in her.

Maybe thinking he was attracted had been her imagination. All her concentration on the writing process had her subconscious creating character motivation where there was none. But tell that to female hormones all revved up with no place to go.

From now on she was going to dress like a bag lady. *That* was her best quality.

Chapter Five

After breakfast Jack went to his office and sat behind his desk while the clock ticked ever closer to the 9:00 a.m. status meeting. The truth was that his status was tipping into chaos and confusion. When he saw Erin in those workout clothes, he felt as if he'd been sucker punched. The tight pants left almost nothing to the imagination.

It was the *almost* that really tied him in knots because he didn't want to imagine. Erin Riley was trim, taut and tempting. More than almost anything he wanted to touch her bare skin and taste it, too. And *take* her—

There was a knock on the door and he braced himself for her pert and perky personality. "Come in."

She did and assumed her position in the chair facing his desk. "Ready to get to work?"

"Raring to go." And work had nothing to do with it.

"Okay. Let's talk about the book."

"Is it really necessary to remind you that there is no book?"

"I meant the already published one," she amended.

Geez, he never knew what to expect from her. One minute she was innocent and vulnerable, the next showing off curves that would test the willpower of a man trained to resist even the most aggressive interrogation techniques. She kept him off balance and he didn't like being off balance. Any more than he liked her attempt to find out personal information. What in the world had made him tell her to ask whatever she wanted to know? He regretted that as much as seeing her in those skintight yoga clothes.

"Jack?"

"Hmm?"

"Are you with me?"

"Yeah." He sat forward and rested his forearms on the desk. "I just don't see how discussing *High Value Target* is going to help with this book."

"You never know what will trigger a creative leap forward."

Since he had nothing to show for all the time he'd put in, what did he have to lose? "Okay. What about it?"

"I reread the book."

"Why?"

"Besides the fact that I was having trouble sleeping—"

"Wait." He held up a hand to stop her right there. "You thought my book would put you to sleep?"

"Of course not. I was just trying to put that awake time to good use. And I really enjoyed it the first time, Jack."

"Then why the second read?"

"For ideas."

"And?" he persisted.

"Let me tell you what I did and didn't like."

That got his full attention. "There was something you didn't like?"

"I'm a tough crowd. An English teacher always is." She

shrugged. "Critiquing requires a delicate balance. It's just as important to highlight what works as what doesn't."

"Okay. What did you like?"

"The hero."

It was hard to keep from grinning. Jack had based Mac Daniels on himself. After retiring from the military he'd read that journaling helped put into perspective things you were trying not to think about. That's how the book had started in the first place. For Ms. Tough Crowd to like *him* felt damn good.

"So, you think Mac works."

"Incredibly well," she said. "Men want to be him and women want to be with him. That's why there's such cross-over appeal and the book did so well."

This critique thing wasn't so bad after all. "What else did you like?"

"The action was realistic and suspenseful. It makes the reader feel right there—in the moment. When Mac slaps another magazine into his pistol, you can practically hear the sound of it."

Jack didn't have to hear it; he would never forget that distinctive sound. "Good."

"Clearly you know your protagonist and his strengths. Also his weaknesses. It's incredibly appealing that he's well-rounded. But—" She crossed one leg over the other, apparently pulling her thoughts together.

The movement completely destroyed his ability to think clearly. He couldn't seem to take his eyes off her legs. Or eject the image of black spandex outlining the luscious curves and tanned skin of her calves just before he took off those tight pants and she wrapped her legs around his waist.

If his editor had really wanted him to concentrate on the project, she could have sent someone older. And not pretty. Better yet, a guy. How was he supposed to concentrate when all he wanted to do was leap over the desk and kiss Erin? He was feeling creative, all right, but it had nothing to do with writing his book and everything to do with what they could accomplish in the sack.

"Since you didn't ask, I guess you don't want to hear the *but*," she said.

"No one ever wants to hear the *but*. Worst word in the English language. It always goes something like this. 'Everything's fine, but you lost your job. The decor is beautiful, but the food sucks. You're going to live, but the leg has to be amputated.' No one wants to know what comes after the *but*. Guaranteed you're not going to like it."

"You're right. Of course. And remember this is only my opinion."

"But—" He filled that word with as much sarcasm as possible.

"Mac is well-defined and the action is compelling and believable. But the secondary characters are one-dimensional, a little clichéd. Take the villain—"

"I did. Or Mac did. Took him right out."

"Fairly spectacularly, too. But the guy was all evil weasel with no redeeming qualities. No one, even the bad guys, is that simple. They had parents, possibly siblings or significant others. Children. All of that shapes them into the person they are."

Although Jack didn't want to admit it, she had a point. In war it was more black-and-white. You took out the guy trying to take you out. Survival. As simple as that.

"Okay."

"And remember, the hero is only as heroic as the adversary he faces."

"So the stronger and more formidable the bad guy, the better Mac looks."

"Exactly."

The smile she gave him was like a slice of sunlight riding a rainbow straight through him. "Good point."

"Real people have flaws, a gray area. They're human. The baddie might be completely in love with an innocent, vulnerable woman yet he can do despicable things." Harley stood, got out of his bed and walked over to her. She reached down and scratched his head, then laughed when he rolled onto his back and exposed his belly to be rubbed. "Could be that he has a soft spot for animals."

"Or the villain is a woman." He had a lot of material from his ex to channel into a character like that.

"Speaking of women—" She stopped and met his gaze. "There wasn't a real woman in the story."

"How can you say that?"

"They were either like robots, completely unemotional and too sticky sweet. Or overly emotional and hysterical. There was no middle ground."

"Give me a for-instance," he said defensively.

"Okay." She thought for a moment. "Got one. When Mac breaks up with Karen, who's been waiting for him to come home from Afghanistan, and she starts punching and slapping him, that seemed out of character for someone who'd been so patient."

"She was ticked off at being dumped. But he didn't want to lead her on."

"And rightfully so. But because she was so long-suffering and colorless it didn't feel real."

"What would have been right? In your opinion," he said defensively. In his case, he'd been the one dumped and the only blows had been on the inside, where they wouldn't show.

"She might cry. Struggle to hold back tears. Try to talk

him out of it. Or let him have it with words. But she probably wouldn't attack him physically."

He wasn't ready yet to concede the point even though his gut was telling him she was right. "It could happen."

"But probably not." She gave him a wry look. "Your response makes me wonder if you have issues with women."

"What are you talking about?"

"Maybe you don't like them."

"I like women just fine." And that was the truth. But he wasn't very good with them. If he was, he'd have sensed his wife's detachment before she made the distance real and permanent.

"All I know is that you don't have a girlfriend and you're not married. Maybe you're gay."

"I'm not."

"And in denial," she said.

Just a little while ago he'd taken the high road and passed up the opportunity to show her he liked women just fine. But during that second or two in the kitchen, when he'd reached into the cupboard for a mug, he'd accidentally brushed against her. That barest of touches had sent his blood rushing to points south of his belt.

In spite of what she thought, he knew a little something about women. He knew when one would melt against him if he kissed her. And that's exactly the way Erin had looked in that moment when their bodies had touched.

"I know exactly who I am," he said. "And I don't have issues with women."

"If you need help with the female point of view, I'd be happy to provide feedback."

"I don't need help understanding women."

"Really? Then you would be the first man in history who didn't," she said pertly. "Look, Jack, all I'm saying is that you can make your characters do whatever you need them to, just give them a backstory to support the behavior. Readers want real characters, get to know and root for them."

"Understood."

"Maybe Mac Daniels needs a love interest. A woman, or man," she said with a grin, "who will tell him the things he really doesn't want to hear. Someone to keep him honest. Because right now he really has nothing to lose and it means the stakes for him are pretty low."

"I need to get to work." He took a sheet of paper from the printer. "And I have some serious things for you to research."

"Right." She stood and took the paper. "Later, Jack."

He watched the sway of her hips as she walked to the door and didn't realize he was holding his breath until she was gone and he let it out.

Had she been pushing his buttons to get him to open up?

Off balance. There it was again. And he had another reason to regret missing the opportunity to kiss her. Besides the fact that he still didn't know how she would taste, she was accusing him of pitching for a different team.

If he hadn't so adamantly and, let's face it, obnoxiously, told her on the very first day they met that he wouldn't sleep with her, he would gladly show her how much he liked women in general.

And her in particular.

Jack had barricaded himself in the office all day and actually got some decent pages written. Although he wasn't ready yet to admit that his editor had been right to send Erin, the chip on his shoulder was wobbling.

He glanced at his dog, sitting in the bed and looking long-suffering and loyal. "Walk?"

Instantly the animal hopped up and eagerly trotted to

the door, waiting patiently for Jack to save the work and shut down the computer. He turned the knob and let the dog precede him outside and down the stairs. A view of towering mountains and pristine blue lake was, literally, a sight for sore eyes. And the fresh air felt great.

He jogged down the path after Harley and saw Brewster Smith outside the marina store. The sixtyish man had a full head of silver hair and a beard to match. Come to think of it, he'd be perfect for a mall Santa. Jack normally walked by but today he stopped.

He stepped onto the wooden walkway and under the awning over the store's entrance. The older man was moving racks of sale clothing and summer clearance merchandise back inside. "How's it going, Brew?"

"Good." Blue eyes assessed him. "You're looking better."

Jack wanted to ask better than what, but wasn't sure he'd like the answer. Then curiosity got the best of him. "Better than what?"

"Before Erin showed up."

"I have to admit I had a productive day. It feels pretty good."

"A fruitful day's work is good for the soul," the man said. "And that cute little writing coach you got there doesn't hurt, either. She's a piece of work."

"You'll get no argument from me." Jack wondered how the other man knew that she was a piece of work. "Does she come down here?"

"Every day," Brew confirmed. "Darn near talks my ear off."

"That sounds like her."

"But it's worth it because she makes the best buttermilk spice muffins I ever tasted." The other man pointed at him. "And if you tell my wife I said that I'll deny it."

"I won't breathe a word of it." But Jack felt the same way about her cooking. Her muffins were really good. "And you're right. Erin Riley can be a challenge."

The older man's silver eyebrows drew together as he scratched his beard. "What's wrong with her?"

"I'm not used to having anyone around. Being alone is more my thing."

"That so," Brew said.

"It works for me."

"Whatever blows your skirt off. But for now you should enjoy that little firecracker." The older man smiled. "And she's cooking up something special for tonight. If I wasn't taking the missus out to dinner, I'd have finagled an invite."

Jack heard "something special" and got an instant image of Erin after her workout then wondered if she would be wearing those skintight pants tonight. And just like that he was in a hurry to get Harley's walk over with.

"Later, Brew. Have a good evening."

"You do the same."

Jack whistled and Harley came running back from wherever he'd disappeared to and the two of them walked the path by the lake. As the sun dropped farther behind the mountain the chill in the air took a firm hold. Labor Day was over and Halloween was just around the corner. Before long it would be winter. Some people dreaded the isolation but he wasn't one of them. He was okay with his own company.

In spite of that he found himself rushing the dog through their routine, working him a little harder until Harley plopped at Jack's feet to be carried home. Jack complied and picked up his pace back to the house, then set the dog down at the foot of the steps leading up to the porch.

Jack stood there for a few moments, looking at the lights

glowing in the window. Someone was waiting for him. The realization stirred memories, not all of them good. Once upon a time he'd expected and anticipated a greeting after working all day but that dream had bitten him in the ass. Military training taught him a man didn't stay alive by making the same mistake twice. You might get lucky the first time, but your survival odds went down by a lot after that. In personal relationships, he hadn't even survived the first time.

Now that his head was on straight, he walked up the steps and in the front door. The fantastic smell of cooking food coming from *his* kitchen made his mouth water. Harley just trotted straight to where it was coming from and checked out what was going on.

Jack followed and his gaze was drawn to Erin, who was bending over to check something in the oven. She wasn't wearing the yoga pants, but her snug jeans were a close second in the framing-an-outstanding-ass department.

She looked at Harley, who stopped beside her. "Hello there, handsome. Be careful. This is hot."

Yes, it was, Jack thought, and he didn't mean the oven.

"He knows," Jack told her. "Animal instinct."

Stay away from anything hot because it's going to hurt. Good advice. Jack made note of that just in case his own instincts needed the reminder.

She closed the oven door and straightened. "Hi."

"Brew said you were cooking up something special tonight."

"Did that blabbermouth spoil my surprise?" She planted her hands on her hips and gave him a faux stern look.

"Hey, don't give me the stink eye. I didn't reveal any top secrets." He couldn't think of a single time that anyone had ever tried to surprise him. That gave him a weird feeling in his gut. "And, no, he didn't tell me what you're cooking if that's what you're asking. But it smells awful darn good."

"Fried chicken. Macaroni and cheese. From scratch, mind you. Not out of a box. Green beans. Biscuits, also from scratch. Pure comfort food."

"Why? Do you need cheering up?"

"No, but I thought it would be good for you. Your editor said there's more to a writer than typing words into a computer. Cheryl was adamant that it wasn't just your creativity that needed cultivation. It's about mind, body and spirit." She shrugged. "Makes sense if you think about it. How can your brain work efficiently if it's not fueled properly?"

If she'd done all this cooking for his body, Jack couldn't wait to see what she had planned for his spirit. There were a lot of things he could think of that had nothing to do with food.

He had to get his mind off how she looked in those tight pants and on to something more unexciting. "There's fuel and then there's fuel. I've had MREs that kept your body going. Basic. But this is carb-heavy."

"It's good for the imagination," she said.

The hell with imagination and creativity for crying out loud. He could think of some other parts of him that hadn't had any attention in a very long time. But before he could figure out how to verbalize a segue to that, or even how bad an idea it was to go there, the stove timer started signaling something.

"Mac and cheese is done." Erin smiled brightly and grabbed some heavy-duty oven mitts, then pulled a big, oblong glass dish out of the oven. She set it on a hot tray to keep it warm. "Dinner is officially ready. Have a seat and I'll set everything on the table."

Jack did as ordered, but damned if he didn't get the

strangest feeling. Not woo-woo, déjà vu weird, but regret. After marrying Karen this was how he'd pictured their life when he was finished with deployments for good. He'd go to work and when he got home she'd be cooking dinner. Mouth-watering smells would be coming from the kitchen. They'd have a little wine, some conversation about their respective days. He'd help her with the dishes, then make love to her. Eventually have kids. It would be everything he'd never had and always wanted. What happened was the exact opposite of that and taught him life was a whole lot harder if you had dreams.

"Are you okay, Jack?" She stood staring at him with the mitts still on her hands.

"Why?"

"You have the oddest look on your face."

"I'm good." He'd believed those memories had no power over him anymore but obviously he was wrong. Something about Erin had stirred them up. Forewarned is forearmed and he shook them off. "What can I do to help?"

"You can open that bottle of wine if you want some."

"I'll open it for you, but I'm more of a beer guy."

"Okay. Then you can handle beverages. I'd love a glass of chardonnay."

"On it."

Jack did as requested and set a wineglass in front of her and got a longneck bottle for himself. In the middle of the table was a platter of golden fried chicken, macaroni and cheese still bubbling and slightly brown on top, green beans and a cloth-lined basket filled with fluffy, flaky buttermilk biscuits. "This looks good."

"Sit down and dig in before it gets cold," she advised.

He'd never been quite so happy to follow an order and filled his plate. The chicken was crisp on the outside, tender and juicy in the middle. The mac and cheese was creamy and cheesy and a party in his mouth. And the biscuits? Holy mother of God—don't even get him started on the awesome, warm wonderfulness.

And that's when Jack had an epiphany. He had an attitude and was aware of it. He took great pride in his attitude, nurtured and cultivated being aloof and sometimes abrasive if necessary. Or, as he liked to think of it, succinct. But his attitude just couldn't stand up in the face of this feast.

"Erin, this is really good."

She smiled and the pleasure of his compliment glowed in her eyes. "I'm glad you like it."

"This is pretty much the perfect meal in my opinion."

"I thought it might be." She took a sip of wine.

"Why?"

"Well, who doesn't like fried chicken or macaroni and cheese?"

"Please tell me this isn't about that stupid saying—the way to a man's heart is through his stomach."

"Oh, please, Jack. We both know you don't have a heart." She laughed. "This is about how hard you've been working. Night and day as far as I can tell. I just wanted to make you something good."

"Mission accomplished. And you really nailed the menu." He took another golden brown chicken leg from the platter and bit into it, barely holding back a groan of pleasure.

"I'm no stranger to cooking for a man and tackling his taste buds." She forked up a bite of green beans.

"Your fiancé?"

"Yeah." The glow in her eyes slipped some. "He battled cancer and had chemo and radiation. His appetite dropped off to almost nothing and he was a big guy. He needed calories in order to fight the disease and it didn't matter whether or not they were the healthiest. Kale smoothies or chicken and dumplings. Which would tempt you more?"

"The second one. Hands down."

"The sicker he got, the harder it was to get him to eat. Toward the end it took what felt like hours to get a meal into him."

"Sounds like it was a tough time."

"Yeah." Then her perky hat fell off and she sighed. The sound was full of all the sadness and heartbreak she obviously had inside.

Again Jack kicked himself for throwing sarcasm at her personal life that first day she'd shown up on his doorstep. "How long was he sick?"

"Three years."

"A long time. And he proposed before the diagnosis?"

"Yeah."

"But you never married."

She pushed macaroni around her plate without looking at him. "There was a lot going on and the time never seemed right."

Jack had proposed to Karen just before he left for his first deployment because there was an instinctive need to be connected to someone and something from home. It wasn't a completely rational thing and was more about spirituality and not being alone. A man got pretty damn spiritual when he was facing the possibility of dying. And with her guy it was more than a possibility. He knew his shelf life had an expiration date.

"But he wanted to get married." It wasn't a question and a shadow slipped into her eyes. "He got weaker and weaker. Couldn't manage to do that."

He, not we, Jack thought. There was something she was keeping to herself and that seemed out of character for her. Something she was holding back.

But still, he couldn't help admiring her loyalty, which was more than he could say about his ex. She'd walked out and flatly refused to even try working on the marriage. Erin had never taken the in-sickness-and-in-health-till-death-do-us-part vow, but had lived it anyway.

He respected her for that, along with her determination. Unless she decided to direct it at him. She deserved someone as good at thinking about someone besides himself as she was.

Jack wasn't that guy.

Chapter Six

"How are you coming with those research topics?"

Erin was almost getting used to Jack Garner syndrome, which was what she called the way her heart skipped when he walked into a room. She had her computer set up on the kitchen table and looked away from the screen when he got her attention. Although, technically he'd gotten her attention when he appeared in the doorway looking very Jack-like. Which was to say that his animal magnetism was on full display. But he'd asked a question and it required a response, even a sarcastic one. Sarcasm was the only place where she could hide.

"Research? Really?" She leaned back in the chair. "You're suddenly in a hurry because you can't write the next scene in the book without knowing the mating habits of the blue-footed booby?"

"Fascinating creatures." His lips twitched.

"You're not fooling anyone."

Harley padded into the room and looked expectantly at Jack. He looked at the dog, then her. "I'm not trying to."

"Right." And she was the Duchess of Doubtville. "This research is nothing more than a distraction to keep me from bugging you."

"I think of it more as a flanking maneuver."

"Ah." She nodded. "An end run around your editor. Battle of wills. Cut off your nose to spite your face."

"You said it, not me."

"Very mature."

"Let's just call it my process." He leaned a broad shoulder against the doorjamb, folded his arms over his chest and grinned.

Erin's mouth went dry. She'd been there for over a week and thought she'd seen the best that Jack could throw at her. But she'd been so wrong. His scowl brimmed with sex appeal but the oh-so-masculine and tempting smile on his face right now could flat out make a woman's clothes come off.

Insert change of topic here. "Speaking of your process... How did the pages go today?"

"Oh, you know—" He lifted one of those swoonworthy shoulders in a shrug.

"Actually I don't. That's why I asked." The brooding look was back and that made her nervous—on a number of levels. But she focused on work. "Please tell me there are pages."

"Okay. There are pages."

His tone was flat with shades of mocking and she didn't know whether or not to believe him. "Let me look at them."

"They're not prime-time ready." He reached down to rub Harley's head when the dog put a paw on his leg.

"I'm not asking for Pulitzer Prize quality," she said.

"Just let me take a quick look. Make sure the story starts off with a bang—"

"No one gets shot in the first paragraph."

"Don't be so literal. That's not what I meant."

"I know what you meant." He moved farther into the kitchen. "But I'd rather talk about you."

"What about me?" she asked warily.

"Your loyalty. It's admirable."

This was about Garret and she didn't want to discuss anything more about her fiancé. She'd said enough last night. Apparently comfort food loosened her tongue. She'd danced around why there'd been no marriage and the truth was that he'd wanted it very much. Erin was the one who'd found excuses not to take the step. It was inherently dishonest not to have explained to the man she'd agreed to marry why she couldn't go through with it. And that wasn't admirable.

"I have a better idea," she said. "It's after two. I have no idea what you've been doing all day but this is the first time I've seen you. That equals hard work as far as I'm concerned. And you need a break. Let's go into town for groceries."

His blue eyes narrowed like lasers on her. "Now who's employing a flanking maneuver?"

She decided to take a page from his book, so to speak, and ignore that question. "Do you remember what I said about filling up the creative well?"

"Yes, but—"

"Keeping yourself isolated isn't the best way to cultivate inspiration. Besides, we're almost out of coffee."

"Uh-oh. Threat level goes to DEFCON five." But the expression on his face said the diversion hadn't worked and he wasn't quite finished with her yet. "I'd like to know more about the kind of man you accepted a proposal from."

This guy was mission-oriented and he had his sights set on her. But she just might have the mother of all flanking maneuvers. "Harley. Walk?"

The animal barked and started dancing around Jack. He ran to the door and back yipping excitedly. Jack met her gaze and saluted. "Well played."

It was her turn to grin and she didn't even care that he had her number.

A half hour later, after walking the dog, he drove the jeep up Main Street in Blackwater Lake. It was rush hour, if you could call it that here in this small but growing town. Chalk up the traffic to people from businesses along the main drag getting off work. For Erin the slow pace was an opportunity to check out Jack's stomping grounds a little more thoroughly.

They passed the Harvest Café with the adjacent ice-cream parlor beside Tanya's Treasures, the gift shop. Then there was the Grizzly Bear Diner, with its life-size statue of a ferocious-looking bear standing on rear legs with teeth bared and claws primed.

"I want to go to the diner sometime," she said. "Is the food good?"

"Never been there."

She couldn't believe that. "You've lived here how long?"

"A year and a half—give or take."

"And you have not once stepped foot in that restaurant?"

"No."

Erin waited but it seemed there wouldn't be an explanation coming anytime in the foreseeable future as to why so she took a shot in the dark. "Bar None is the extent of your social networking?"

"Didn't we already establish that loners tend to be alone?"

"Yes, but Jack—"

"What?"

"That's just so—" She struggled to come up with a word that wasn't quite so harsh, then decided what the heck? "It's so lonely."

"Not if that's what I want." He glanced over then, but the darn aviator sunglasses hid his expression. Apparently he saw something that deserved a comment. "And I order you not to feel sorry for me."

"That's just ridiculous," she scoffed. "You can't command someone how to feel."

"Has anyone ever told you that you'd make a terrible soldier?"

"Yes."

They were stopped at a red light and he gave her a long look. "Really?"

"No. I was just messing with you."

The corners of his mouth curved up. "That's what I thought."

Up ahead Erin saw a little storefront called the Photography Shop. In the window there were cardboard figures of an old west dance hall girl and a gambler with the faces cut out for tourists to pose for a picture. Behind that were what looked like framed photos of local scenery.

She pointed. "Stop there. I want to go in."

"You're messing with me again, right?"

"No. I want to look around."

"I don't."

"Then wait in the car with Harley." She glanced at the dog, who sat quietly in the rear seat. Then she looked at Jack and noted the muscle jerking in his jaw. "Or, you can throw caution to the wind and take a social field trip."

Erin really thought he was going to pay no attention to her request, but when the light turned green, he made a left turn and went around the block in order to pull up in front of the place. The lettering on the window said April Kennedy was the photographer. She remembered Sheriff Fletcher saying he was engaged to April and since his office was right across the street, she figured his fiancée owned this place.

She opened the car door and said, "I won't be long."

Just before she got out, Harley whined and she felt a little guilty about leaving him behind. The little guy didn't understand that his beloved human was calling the shots.

When she opened the shop's door an overhead bell tinkled and the two very attractive women inside looked at her. Both were in their twenties, one a strawberry blonde, the other a brunette.

"Hi. I'm Erin Riley."

"Jack Garner's research assistant." The brunette held out her hand. "April Kennedy."

The April who was engaged to the sheriff, which explained how she knew who Erin was. "Nice to meet you."

"Lucy Bishop." The other woman gave her a friendly smile. "Co-owner of the Harvest Café."

"I saw it. Looks like a nice place," Erin commented.

"It is. Lucy cooks all the food and it's really good," April said enthusiastically.

"I look forward to checking it out."

"So, is there something I can help you with?" April asked.

"I saw the photos in your window. Looks like scenes of the lake and mountains around here." Erin settled her purse strap more securely on her shoulder.

"They are."

She studied the breathtaking shots of twilight, when the mountains were backlit by the setting sun. And other scenes of the lake at different times of day. "Any for sale?"

"Not many," Lucy said, only a little rueful. "I've bought quite a few."

"My best customer."

"That will change once the walls in my new condo are decorated. Then you and Will need to be regulars at the café so I can pay for it all."

"Like we aren't in there all the time now," her friend scoffed.

That was probably where the sheriff had taken her after announcing to her and Jack at Bar None that he had a dinner date. "So you have a new condo?" she asked Lucy.

"Yes. Brand-new. Barely moved in. It's just at the foot of the mountains. Awesome views in the summer and winter."

"That's exciting."

"It is." But Lucy's attention shifted to the window that opened onto Main Street. "But maybe not as exciting as that dog."

Erin figured the animal's whining had gotten Jack out of the car. She glanced over her shoulder to confirm. "That's Harley. He's a Chinese crested."

"Is that Jack Garner with him?" April asked.

Erin smiled at the man standing guard over his pet. "Yes."

"I'd like to meet him," Lucy said.

"Me, too."

"He's a little shy. Be gentle with him."

The other two laughed, then April went behind the counter where the cash register was sitting and pulled out a camera. "I have to take some pictures of that dog."

Erin and Lucy followed the photographer outside, where she was introducing herself to a wary Jack. He was giving her camera the death glare.

"Do you mind if I take some pictures of your dog? He's

quite unusual. And I promise to make copies and give you some." April gave him a hopeful look.

He thought for a moment then said, "Okay."

She held up the camera and Harley froze as if he was posing. He even moved his head a little to the left and right as she snapped away. Then he turned sideways, as if for a profile picture.

"He's a natural." Erin laughed. "Jack, you should get him an agent."

"He's very unusual," Lucy said.

"Yes, but he grows on you," Erin told her. She looked at Jack, who was still watchful and alert. On guard. "I've heard that dog owners take on characteristics of their pets."

April studied him as if trying to confirm the truth of the words. "Would that be a good thing?"

Jack shrugged. "Harley is a better man than me."

The two women laughed but Erin got the feeling he wasn't entirely joking.

"So, how do you like Blackwater Lake?" Lucy asked him.

"Nice place."

"Didn't you buy Jill Stone's property on Blackwater Lake Marina?"

"Yes."

"It's beautiful out there. Quiet. Good spot for a writer," Lucy said.

The guarded expression on Jack's face told her it was time to change the subject. "This town is really different for me. I'm from Phoenix."

"I've been there," Lucy said. "I liked it a lot."

"Thanks for not making a crack about the dry heat."

"She's a little touchy about that." Jack almost smiled and gave her a look. He seemed to relax a little now that the focus had shifted away from him.

She could take one for the team. This couldn't have gone better. They had dragged him into a conversation but he was still socializing. She liked being a bridge.

"Well," Lucy said, "I managed to sneak away after the lunch crowd cleared out, but it's time to get back to the café for the dinner rush. Nice to meet you, Erin. And Jack, I hope you'll come by and check out the food at my place."

"Never know," he said.

"I really liked your book. I'm sure the next one will be even better than the first. I can hardly wait until it comes out."

"Don't hold your breath." Without another word he turned his back and got in the car.

Erin couldn't help feeling that the bridge she'd patted herself on the back for building moments ago had just collapsed on her head.

"Okay, so you've had a good brood. Now it's time to stop sulking and get it off your chest."

Jack turned off the jeep's ignition after pulling the vehicle to a stop at the house. They'd barely spoken while grocery shopping and neither of them had said anything on the drive back from town. Now the first words out of her mouth were that he was in a mood?

He released his seat belt and glared at her. "What happened to you supporting me?"

"That's what I'm doing." She wasn't the least bit intimidated by his look.

"If this is being supportive, I think I'll take my chances solo."

She took off her seat belt and angled her legs toward him. "Do you want to talk about what happened back there and why it made you crawl back into your man cave?"

For purposes of this conversation it would help him out

a lot if she didn't smell so damn good. Like flowers and sunshine. And look at him being all poetic. That proved his point. He couldn't think straight when her particular brand of soft skin and spirited push-back was so close he could grab her up and kiss her.

"I have no idea what you're talking about."

"I mean the way you went all strong, silent type on poor Lucy Bishop. She's obviously a supporter and the last time I checked, the goal was to sell books. It's hard to do that when you alienate your fan base."

"She started it."

Erin actually laughed. "You acted like a petulant little boy."

Probably some truth to that. He didn't much care right at this moment. "She said my next book is going to suck."

He expected a rapid-fire return from the copilot's seat and it was a couple of beats before reality sank in that he wasn't going to get one. He looked over and found her staring at him. "What?"

"I was warned that you would be difficult."

"Good to know I lived up to advance billing." That remark might have come from his inner, petulant little boy.

"But," Erin continued, "no one told me you were a diva."

Jack wasn't entirely sure about the definition of a diva, but thought it might involve outrageous demands for white-rose-petal-covered sofas and organic water from Bora Bora. That's not what this was about.

"It was the subtext of what she said," he argued.

"You know they say if you give twelve writers the same idea you'll get twelve completely different stories."

"What in God's name is your point?" he asked.

"You and I heard the same words and came up with two opposite interpretations. I believe she paid you a compliment, and is genuinely looking forward to reading your next book. You heard her say that you're going to fall on your face."

Harley jumped on the console between them and started to whine sympathetically. Almost as if the dog sensed Jack's inner turmoil. Erin didn't come right out and say it, but she was probably thinking that he projected his internal conflict by twisting innocent words. Could be some truth to that. And it made him a whiny toad, which was a rung or two lower than a son of a bitch.

"Understood." He looked at her and the sweetness in her face did not bring out the best in him. It made him want to push back harder. "Next time you decide social networking is just the thing, do me a favor."

"What?"

"Don't."

"But, Jack—" She looked down for a moment. "Creativity needs to be fed, watered and cultivated."

"I'm not a plant."

"I'm aware. It's a metaphor. You might have heard of them." She sighed, as if pulling her tattered patience together. "What I'm trying to say is that everyone needs contact with others."

"There's a reason I prefer being alone."

"And what is that?"

"People."

"You don't like people?" she asked.

"Roger that."

"So you don't trust anyone?" There was something awfully darn close to pity in those green eyes of hers.

"My army buddies. They're like my brothers. Closer. They had my back and I had theirs. I'd have taken a bullet for any one of them and they would have done the same for me." He met her gaze to make sure she was getting this.

"If any one of them needed help, I'd drop everything and be there to do whatever I could for them."

"And they would do the same for you." Her voice was hardly more than a whisper and it wasn't a question.

"Damn straight." Harley put a paw on his arm as if he understood all about duty, honor and loyalty. Jack almost smiled. "So, yeah, there are people I trust."

"But only a select few. No one else. And I'm pretty sure I fall into the no-one-else group."

"You said it." Even as the words came out of his mouth he realized she didn't deserve that.

"Okay." She nodded for a moment. "But here's something to think about, Jack. Trust happens for a lot of reasons. One of them is going into combat situations and finding out who you can count on." There was a lot less sunshine in her eyes when her gaze met his. "I suppose you could say life is combat. And telling someone only what they want to hear isn't the best way to have their back. If someone isn't afraid to lay the bad stuff on you, it's a pretty good bet that when they tell you something good, you can believe it's the truth."

Damn it, why did she have to make sense? He just wanted to be ticked off and he wanted to do it alone. She would call it crawling back into his man cave and frankly, hoo yah to that. It had been a bad idea to let her talk him into going to town and it was a bad idea to sit here now and listen to her being rational. And she smelled so good he wanted to bury himself in her.

He opened his door. "Harley. Walk."

The little guy let out an excited yip and jumped into Jack's lap then out of the car. He raced toward the marina. Without looking back at Erin, Jack followed after his dog.

Brewster Smith was breaking down today's sale display setup just outside the store. There were a few summer things left but the rest was fishing stuff. And it was getting pretty close to quitting time for the older man.

There was a chill in the air that had a lot to do with summer being over, but Jack also felt it inside himself. Probably it had been there for a lot of years, but he hadn't noticed until Erin's warmth showed him the difference.

Brew smiled when the dog bounded up the wooden steps and stopped beside him. He rubbed the animal's out-of-proportion head. "Hello there, Mr. Harley. You're looking fine today."

"Hey," Jack greeted him.

The older man gave him an assessing look, not unlike a military inspection searching for any breakdown in discipline. "Afternoon. You are not looking as fine as your dog."

Everyone was a critic. "Thank you."

"In fact," the man went on, clearly not getting that "thank you" meant don't go there, "you look like something's eating at you."

"Thank you again."

Brew nodded, indicating he got the message this time. "How are things?"

"What is it with everyone wanting to talk about the damn book?"

"Well, now, I can't speak for everyone. And I can't say I'm not curious about how it's coming along, what with your research assistant giving you a hand. But I sure did like the first one." Brew rubbed a hand over his beard. "That said, I wasn't askin' about the book so much as that pretty lady who's stayin' there with you."

"Oh." Jack was just about ready to admit the pretty lady stayin' with him had a point about him hearing something innocent that his subconscious turned into a negative. His only comment was "Erin is many things."

"I'd put talker at the top of the list." Brew laughed. "That little thing could babble the ears off a bull elephant."

The imagery made Jack laugh. Mostly because it was true. She turned out to be nothing like he'd first thought when she'd turned up here. The small, eager-to-please woman he'd believed he could torment into leaving had turned out to have a steely, stubborn streak. If anything she was the one pushing him around. How else did he explain getting him to go to town? And she spoke her mind whether he liked what she had to say or not.

Mostly he didn't *dis*like it.

"You're right about that, Brew. She's perky."

"A firecracker, that one."

Jack wondered if those washed-out blue eyes studying him so closely could see inside, what he was thinking. He sure hoped not.

"So that dinner she made the other night was pretty special," the old guy said.

"You mean the chicken, and mac and cheese?"

"That's the one. She brought some leftovers down to me for lunch the next day."

Because sweet and thoughtful was how she rolled.

"Yeah," he admitted. "It was good."

Brew nodded sagely. "Careful with that one, Jack. You know what they say about the way to a man's heart being through his stomach."

"I do. And no worries. Erin already told me I don't have a heart."

For some reason Brewster thought that was hilarious and laughed until Jack was afraid he would choke. He didn't think it was funny at all. And he had a sneaking suspicion that shrewd Brewster Smith was sending his own message. Jack figured his take on her was need-to-know and no one needed to know that she'd gotten his juices flowing, none of the ones that had anything to do with the creative process.

Jack had been between a rock and a hard place before, but this was different. Putting a move on her was pretty damn tempting, but he'd told her the very first time he laid eyes on her that they wouldn't be sleeping together. Besides not looking like a hypocritical ass, it would be dishonorable to compromise an employee. He was a lot of things—whiny toad and son of a bitch immediately came to mind—but a jerk who would put her in that kind of position wasn't one of them.

The burning question, and he did mean burning, was how the hell was he going to keep from being that jerk?

Chapter Seven

Erin was fed up with Jack's silent treatment.

Oh, there had been grunts and grumbles, a shrug here and there, but none of that counted as actual communication. It had been going on for a couple of days now, since his snit following their visit to town. Afterward he'd practically barricaded himself in his office.

They had meals together but very little conversation. The daily status meetings he'd agreed to had been aborted but that was about to change. Because she was useless this way and she was going to make him talk to her or die trying.

She grabbed her file folders with the bogus research acquired from the ridiculous subject matter he'd assigned to her. One of the topics caught her eye and was particularly ironic considering the way he'd clammed up.

"Erotic talk, my ass," she mumbled.

It was getting close to dinnertime and no way was

she putting up with his stonewalling for even one more meal. She was going to do her job. If he didn't like it, he could fire her and explain to his editor why the book wasn't turned in. Erin walked out the front door onto the porch, then turned right and stomped up the stairs to his office. Taking a deep breath, she knocked on his door. He had never given her permission to enter so, as usual, she opened the door and stepped inside.

Jack was at his desk typing on the computer as if he hadn't heard her. She wasn't sure she'd ever seen him from this angle, working. He had a very sexy profile and that was not a comforting thought as she prepared to jump into this confrontation with both feet. But she had to take a stand. She refused to be ignored.

"Hi, Jack."

His fingers stilled over the keys and he looked at her. "Do you want something?"

So much, she thought. "We haven't had a status meeting for a couple of days. I wanted to see how the book is progressing."

"You mean the one that's going to be better than my first book?"

"Wow, there's not a lot of forgive-and-forget in you, is there?"

"No."

She stared at him, hoping he would expand his answer, possibly explain what it was about Lucy's innocent remark that had hit a nerve. But he stared back and said nothing.

With a confidence she wasn't even close to feeling, Erin walked over to his desk and sat down in one of the chairs facing it. "How's the book going?"

"Fine."

"Great." That was a lie and she knew it, but she smiled

anyway. That deepened the frown on his face. "I'd love to read what you have so far."

"That's not part of my process."

She was this close to telling him what he could do with his process. Just in time she stopped herself because she had an epiphany. He was doing his best to goad her into losing her temper. This was him reverting back to his behavior from the beginning, trying to get her to go away.

"It's not going to work, Jack. And I'm a little disappointed in you."

"Now what did I do?" The words were defiant, the tone bored, but it was all to cover the fact that she'd surprised him.

"I thought we were getting along swimmingly and now you're trying to get me to quit again. And I have to say the surly act isn't very original. You're a creative guy. Surely you can do better than this."

He swiveled his chair away from the computer monitor and gave her his full attention. "What are you talking about?"

"This disappearing act of yours. We agreed to touch base once a day and you've violated our truce."

"I saw you at breakfast."

"That's not what I mean and you know it. We had a routine and for some reason you've gone rogue."

His lips twitched. "Gone rogue?"

"You're doing things alone. Not playing well with others. Shutting me out."

"Not true."

"Oh, please. I dare you to tell me how I'm involved in the work."

"In case you've forgotten, I leave you a list of research topics every day."

There was an air of self-righteous superiority because

he thought he had her on a technicality. As if what he gave her to do was seriously a job and the material he had her look up was important to what he was supposed to be working on.

"Really, Jack? Medieval weapons. South American coups and the history of orchids? We both know it's a smokescreen, throwing me a bone to keep me out of your hair."

"That's harsh. Mac Daniels could be a key player in the disruption of a South American political power grab."

Erin got the feeling he was enjoying his own power grab just a little too much. He was holding all the cards and that wasn't okay with her anymore. In a physical contest he could take her down with both hands tied behind his back. The man had training. He knew three hundred ways to incapacitate an opponent with a Q-tip.

All she had was her wits. Charm and feminine attributes could be weapons, too, but she wasn't sure she had a sufficient amount of either.

"Name one topic you've ever given me to investigate that you actually plan to use in your story."

He leaned forward and rested his elbows on the desk. "What do you have there?"

"These?" She held up several folders. "It's everything that I've worked on since I got here."

"What's in the top one?"

She'd been around him long enough to know a bluff when she saw it. Jack couldn't remember what he'd had her looking in to. That's how important it was.

Erin opened the file folder. "How to tease, tempt and tantalize your lover with words."

"That was on the list?"

"Technically the focus of it was how to talk dirty. But I fine-tuned the theme."

"Ah." He nodded. "How about the next file?"

"Don't you want to know what I found out about this?" She pointed to the material that had put a hitch in her breathing and shot a look in his direction that dared him to hear her out.

"Sure. What have you got?"

"Okay. Let's start with the language of love." She felt a stab of satisfaction when the smirk on his face disappeared. "There's talking dirty, which is simply a graphic account of lust, and then there's listening to your lover express pleasure in how attractive, special or sexy you are."

"I can't see Mac doing either."

"You haven't heard everything yet." This was where she got even with him for all this research. "Moving on to voice. The tone you use with your partner can be more arousing than what you say. I found out there are exercises one can do to develop a richer, more pleasing pitch to make your voice sound naturally sexy. In my opinion the most effective ones are for the jaw, tongue and lips."

"Good to know, Erin. Great job. You are incredibly thorough—"

"I'm not finished." And speaking of jaws, the muscle in his was tight, as if he was gritting his teeth. *Take that, Mr. Action-Adventure.* "You're going to love this. I need to tell you about sexual communication during a first meeting." And the first one she'd had with him didn't count. The one where he'd flat out told her to not even think about sleeping together because that wasn't going to happen. "Some of this just might come in handy for Mac."

The amusement on his face was now missing in action. "He can handle himself just fine."

"Still, he might meet a gorgeous woman with the figure of a goddess and instead of complimenting a particularly well-endowed body part, it's more effective to express appreciation about a standout quality in a person."

"So instead of Mac saying to a woman 'you must work out a lot because your—'" he stopped for a second, let his gaze linger on her chest, then met her gaze "'—muscles are nicely developed,' he should compliment her persistence?"

"Exactly."

"Okay, Erin, you've made your point. Let's not—"

"I haven't gotten to the best part yet." She flipped through her notes and something caught her eye. "Let's talk fantasies."

"Let's not." His voice wasn't resonant or modulated. It was practically a growl and filled with warning.

"Just hear me out." In for a penny, in for a pound. She was poking the bear and couldn't seem to stop. He'd shut her out of the work. In her mind she had nothing left to lose. "Imagine a scene where Mac says to Bianca, 'I want to make love to every inch of your body. I want to discover your most secret fantasies, the part of your soul that you've never shared with anyone else before. Let your erotic imagination go wild—'"

Was it getting hot in here? Or was she heating up because his eyes were almost certainly focused on her mouth?

"Mission accomplished. Research rebellion understood."

The words were barely a whisper but Erin swore his breath caressed her naked skin. She felt tingles everywhere—there wasn't a place on her body that wasn't touched. Her heart started to pound and she was sure he could hear.

That was the problem with unintended consequences. This was supposed to get to him, but she'd turned herself on.

What was it they said about revenge being a double-edged sword?

Erotic talk was intended for your partner, which technically Jack wasn't. She couldn't swear to it, but his breathing seemed to be more uneven than when she'd started reading from her notes. That was just her own wishful thinking. It would be too humiliating if he saw that she had the hots for him. She needed to get out of here before this bad idea turned into a disaster.

"General rule of thumb, Jack. Don't punish your reader and put all the research into the book." They both knew he wouldn't use any of this. She leaned over and put her folders on the corner of his desk, then stood to make her escape. "I have to go."

She made it to the door before Jack reached her and she hadn't even heard him move.

He put a gentle hand on her arm. "Wait—"

Erin could feel him behind her—the heat and danger. His body barely touching hers. He didn't need to do any exercises to make his voice more appealing, at least not for her. The deep sound was soft, sexy and seductive. A single word had her hesitating.

"I need to go." She turned and caught her bottom lip between her teeth.

Jack's eyes darkened with intensity and he blew out a long breath. "When you do that— God, Erin—"

"What? I'm not—"

He touched his lips to hers and she realized this was the definition of irony. Half her mission was accomplished. He was using his mouth, all right, but not for talking.

One thing was clear—she hadn't gotten over the attraction she'd felt the first time she saw him. This man, this awesomely hot guy, was kissing *her*. Miss Nobody. The touch was soft and sweet, and suddenly getting enough air into her lungs was a challenge—in the best possible way. It was hard to think straight, but one thing she knew for sure—this extremely wonderful, mind-boggling moment could end in a heartbeat so she was going to enjoy the heck out of it while she could.

She pressed her body to his, stood on tiptoe and slid her arms around his neck. He groaned again against her mouth, but she could feel the vibration in his chest, which was pressed to hers. His fingers slid into her hair, cupping the back of her head, and he cradled her in a way that made her heart race.

With his arms wrapped around her he half lifted her and moved a step, backing her against the door. She could feel his muscular thighs, her breasts snuggled to his broad chest and—oh, God—how much he wanted her. *Her!*

She brushed her palm over his cheek and jaw, smiling at the way his stubble scraped her hand. "Jack—"

"No—" He braced a forearm on the door and studied her with dark, smoky eyes. His breathing was ragged and she sensed he was just barely holding on to his control. She slid her hand down his chest and to the belt of his jeans, tugging his T-shirt from the waistband.

He put a gentle hand over hers. "That's a dangerous game you're playing."

"What if I don't care and want to play anyway?"

"If you were smart you'd walk out that door."

"That was my plan." She could barely get the words out, what with having so much trouble breathing. "I'm not the one who prevented me from leaving."

"Yeah. About that—"

She touched a finger to his lips, stopping the words, and stared straight into the raging storm in his eyes. "Don't you dare say it was a mistake. I don't want to be someone's blunder."

"No. Not you." He hung his head for a moment, then his gaze blazed into hers. "It's me. I'm not a good risk. This isn't smart—"

"You're telling me the sensible thing is to stop this right now. And frankly that just made up my mind."

"Good. It would be best—"

"Stop right there." She jabbed her index finger into his chest. "I don't want to come to my senses. Just once I want to do something without planning it to death. No more making a decision because it looks good on paper. Live life to the fullest everyone says. Grab on with both hands and enjoy it. Without regrets."

Erin knew with every fiber of her being that if she walked away now she would deeply regret it forever. For a long moment Jack studied her and she felt as if she could reach out and touch the conflict churning through him. Finally he sighed, and she was almost sure he'd surrendered.

Jack took her hand and the lead, heading toward the doorway that led to the bedroom. Stopping by his desk, he opened the bottom drawer and pulled something out of a box. She caught a glimpse of a square packet and realized it was a condom. Thank goodness he'd been thinking because she was still in not-coming-to-her-senses mode, the one where rational thought wasn't allowed.

He tugged her down the hall into the bedroom where she'd spent her first night under his roof. It was dark outside now, but he didn't turn on the light. There was enough coming from the hall. As soon as they were through the doorway, he kissed her with a desperation that matched her own. With his mouth and hands on her, all she could think about was how good this felt.

He stopped long enough to drag his shirt off in one easy, quick movement and she tried to do the same with hers. But the material got hung up on her hair and Jack seemed eager to help her out, then tossed her shirt into a shadowy corner of the room. With the light to his back, she couldn't see his eyes when he cupped her breasts, but his hands were shaking slightly.

He brushed his thumbs over the tips of her plain white bra and she wished for an estrogen miracle that included pretty, feminine underwear. Kissing her neck and shoulder, he reached behind her and unhooked that plain white bra, letting it drop to the floor between them.

He straightened and settled his gaze on her, drawing in a quick breath. His voice was a little hoarse when he said, "Pretty."

Somehow lacy lingerie didn't seem quite so important all of a sudden. She rested her palms on his chest and wanted to say something, but she had no idea what. Instead, she just felt…the dusting of hair. The contour of muscle. The taut abdomen. It gave her a moment of pure clarity—the last one for a long time.

Lacy, matching bra and panties didn't make a woman feel feminine. What did that was the way a man touched her. A gentle, commanding caress that activated every nerve ending in her body and made her hormones snap to attention.

Slowly he backed her toward the bed and when she felt the mattress behind her legs, she kicked off her shoes and sat. He dropped to one knee and undid the button at the waist of her jeans. Without conscious thought, she lay back on the bed and let him draw the zipper down, then lifted her hips so he could slide off her pants.

A moment later he dragged off the rest of his clothes and slid in beside her, pulling her into his arms and kissing her into a frenzy of need.

His fingers traced the edge of her panties as he slipped his hand between her legs, not quite touching her where she most wanted to be touched. Then he hooked a thumb into the waistband and dragged them off. When he touched her where she wanted him to, she arched her hips and shamelessly pressed herself into his palm, where he cupped her.

His breathing grew increasingly harsh until finally he left her long enough to take the condom out of his jeans pocket. He put it on, then kneeled on the bed, gently nudging her legs apart before covering her naked body with his own. He took most of his weight on his forearms so as not to crush her. The warmth and sheer wonder of being skin-to-skin washed over her.

With one hand he brushed the hair away from her face. "You're looking at me like that."

Like she had the first time they'd met. And he was looking back, his eyes dark with heavy-lidded desire. No man had ever looked at her like that before. The realization shattered her control and she reached for him, arching her hips again, letting him know she wanted him.

He slid inside her slowly, deeply. It was a delicious sensation as she felt herself close around him. He rocked into her and she wrapped her legs around his waist, hanging on for dear life as she came apart in his arms.

He held her close as pleasure rolled through her, tremors in its wake. When they stopped, she pressed her mouth to his neck and nibbled kisses down his chest. With a groan from somewhere deep inside, he buried his face in her hair as he thrust one more time and followed her into release. She held him as he'd done for her and they stayed locked in each other's arms for a long time. Frankly, Erin didn't ever want to move, but that wasn't an option when her stomach growled. It was dinnertime.

Jack smiled tenderly. "Someone needs to be fed."

"Something tells me I'm not the only one."

"I'm not saying you're right, but with my training I can get by longer on less."

"Nuts, berries and bugs?"

"If necessary," he agreed, his lips twitching.

"Gosh darn, we're fresh out of survival provisions."

"Bummer."

"What about steak, baked potato and salad? If it would make you feel better I can lie and tell you I picked the greens in the forest."

His stomach rumbled right on cue. "As you might imagine, I don't much care where the greens came from."

"Okay. Then you have to let me up."

"Roger that." Surely there was reluctance in his eyes.

Before she could decide whether or not it was real or imagined, he rolled away and grabbed his clothes off the floor before leaving her alone. The sound of the bathroom door down the hall was her cue to get up and she dressed as quickly as possible.

A few minutes later they were both back in his living room/office. Erin noticed that the bottom drawer of his desk wasn't all the way closed. She glanced at Jack and saw that he'd been looking in the same place. After her remark about survival rations she must have provisions on the brain because she couldn't resist asking. "Office supplies?"

"There's a legend in the writing world that a well-stocked office makes one a better writer." He lifted one broad shoulder in a shrug.

She'd seen that shoulder without a shirt and the simple, masculine gesture was now a major turn-on. That was her signal to leave. "I'll go get dinner started."

"Okay. Meet you downstairs."

She nodded and walked out the door. If she didn't miss her guess, he had no desire to talk about what just happened. That worked for her. The problem with coming to your senses was the return of rational thought.

On the first day they'd met Jack had said in no uncertain terms that he was never going to take her to bed. Erin didn't know whether or not to be pleased that she'd made a liar out of him. Or completely shocked that she'd crossed a professional line. When his editor had hired her to look after him mind and body, she probably hadn't meant for Erin to sleep with him.

She had a strong work ethic so that made her feel bad enough. Even worse was the guilt she felt toward the man she'd agreed to marry, then didn't before he died. Sex with Jack Garner was the best she'd ever had.

And she had no idea where things went from here.

Chapter Eight

The next morning, Jack stepped out of the shower, grabbed a towel from the bar beside it and dried off. It was an ordinary start to the day—or it would be if he hadn't slept with his research assistant the night before. The same assistant he'd once asked whether or not she'd ever slept with a man. Now he knew for a fact she had, because he'd been there.

That was bad enough, but the part that made him feel as if he was living in an alternate universe was where she hadn't talked about it. During dinner she didn't bring it up even once.

He'd waited, alert and ready, and had been braced for anything. Had an apology all rehearsed in his head. Along with a promise that it wouldn't happen again. It was no lie that he was a bad risk. He had the juvenile record and bad marriage to prove it. Erin was the kind of woman you protected so she could find the guy who deserved her and would make her happy.

Jack wasn't that guy.

The thing that messed with his head was that she acted as if it never happened. Or in any way let on that she had regrets or felt used. But now she'd had a whole night to think things over. This morning at breakfast she was going to hit him with the rocket-propelled grenade of what happens now.

After shaving, combing his hair and putting on the usual jeans and T-shirt, he took one last look in the mirror. "I'm ready for you, little Miss Sweetness and Light."

Jack opened his bedroom door and was immediately hit by some mouth-watering smell coming from the kitchen. Coffee mixed with sausages and potatoes. He was hungry and knew it was probably too much to hope she would wait until after he ate to launch her verbal offensive.

Following the smell of food, he walked down the hall to the kitchen. As usual Erin was there and the coffee had been brewed.

She had her back to him and was whipping something in a bowl with a wicked-looking metal thing. Probably she was pretending that stuff being worked over was his face.

Jack braced himself and tried to put on his not-a-care-in-the-world hat. "Morning."

Her body jerked and she glanced over her shoulder. "Good grief, you startled me. I didn't hear you. But I guess when you're army Special Forces, you get pretty good at sneaking up on people. Obviously your training stuck because I had no idea you were there."

"Understood." He was trying to decide if her cheerfulness was forced and she was prattling more than usual. It was hard to tell.

"I'm making omelets today. And there's sausage." Apparently Harley was helping by standing guard at her side.

"Sounds good." Jack studied her eyes, which were bright green and so clear and beautiful it was hard to look away.

His gut told him she didn't have a deceptive bone in her body and if there were any hard feelings the evidence would be right in front of him. His assessment was a complete blank on negative feelings, which should have been a relief, but wasn't. That didn't mean she wasn't planning a discussion over breakfast. Best keep up his guard and repeat that apology one more time in his head.

"Do you want coffee?" she asked.

"Does Harley like walks?" He laughed when the little dog yipped and scurried over to him, doing his level best to follow orders and not whine. Jack squatted and scratched the hairless body. "Sorry, buddy. Didn't mean to say the *w* word. It's going to have to wait. I have a scheduled meeting this morning."

Erin poured the beaten eggs into the hot pan, then glanced over her shoulder and smiled. "Nine o'clock sharp."

His comment wasn't about time confirmation as much as giving her an opening for that discussion. She'd been locked and loaded when she came upstairs to reestablish a perimeter around the status meeting she'd insisted on having, then proceeded to bust his chops about the research he'd given her. After that...

He was so turned on.

And that's where military training had deserted him. You couldn't always be in command of a hotspot, but you learned discipline over your own actions at all times. Last night this woman took him down without firing a shot. Thus the need to establish rules of engagement—if she brought up the subject.

While she stood watch over the cooking eggs, he poured

coffee into the mug she'd set out for him. His favorite mug, he noted. The one that read, Go Big or Go Home.

"Can I help?" he asked.

"Yeah. Make toast. The bread's already in, just push it down."

"Roger that." He did as requested and buttered the slices when they were ready.

A few minutes later they were seated at the table across from each other, just like every morning since she'd arrived on his doorstep. His plate was loaded with a spinach-and-cheese omelet, fried potatoes, sausage links and toast. Hers looked the same but with significantly smaller portions. She dug into the food like someone who'd been marooned on an island for weeks. Was it his imagination, or could she be avoiding conversation?

She chewed a bite of toast and swallowed. "So, I'm curious."

Okay, not avoiding talk. Here it comes, he thought. "About what?"

"How did you happen to choose a dog like Harley?" She speared a potato with her fork. "Not that he isn't a sweetheart. But, let's be honest here, he's not really your type."

Did he have a type? If they were talking women, the one across from him was the polar opposite of the kind he usually favored. The looser their standards, the better he liked them. With Erin, her standards had standards. But she'd asked about Harley. And he was so relieved that she hadn't brought up close encounters of the sexual kind that he didn't even consider not answering.

"I saw Harley when I walked by an animal shelter in California. He was standing at attention in the window and wearing a camouflage T-shirt. He was, hands down, the least appealing animal in the place. Pretty much the ugliest dog I'd ever seen in my life."

"So why did you take him?" She cut off a bite of egg and put it in her mouth.

"I didn't. Not then, at least."

Erin stopped chewing for a moment and stared at him. She swallowed quickly, then said, "So you went back for him? On purpose?"

"I went back," he said, "but not for him. My mission was to talk myself out of any imaginary attachment. My fall-back position if that didn't happen was any dog but him."

"A more handsome one who would complement you?" One of her delicate eyebrows lifted, daring him to contradict her.

He wished he could, especially because there was a flattering subtext in the question. She apparently thought he wasn't so bad to look at. Jack wasn't particularly vain, but hell, how did he fight that?

"I was sure one of those other dogs would grow on me," he admitted.

"But that didn't happen and you took him home," she persisted.

"Nope. Not that day, either."

She set down her fork. "So, what happened? Obviously this story has a happy ending because he's here. Did he escape from the shelter and stow away in your car?"

"I think he would have if he had opposable thumbs and was tall enough to reach the door handle." He laughed at the image. "No. Third time was the charm."

"Ah, so he wasn't an impulse buy. The acquisition was premeditated."

Jack didn't have a snappy comeback to that so he was honest. "There was something about him. Every time I saw him he stood proud and dignified. Like a good soldier who was presenting himself for inspection to a superior officer. The next thing I knew, I had a dog."

"Oh, Jack—" She smiled. "That's a great story."

He looked at her, waiting for a zinger to follow the praise, but those eyes of hers went all soft and gooey, as if he was some kind of hero.

That wasn't good.

The dog had plopped himself beside her and she reached down to rub his head. "You chose wisely."

"You were not one of his groupies the first time you saw him," he reminded her.

"I was hasty. He's a keeper."

"You think?" Jack honestly wanted her opinion.

"I do. He's proof of all those sayings. Beauty is only skin deep. It's in the eye of the beholder. Don't judge a book by its cover."

"Yeah," he said dryly. "That."

"This little guy has grown on me," she admitted.

"I think the feeling is mutual." And there was a lot of that going around, Jack thought. Because she was growing on *him*.

That was the only explanation for why he'd compromised his principles and slept with her when he'd sworn it would never happen. He'd told her that to her face before asking if she'd ever been with a man. He'd tried his damnedest to ignore her and she'd destroyed his willpower with her erotic talk.

"Thank you for telling me that, Jack." She had that mushy hero thing going on again.

"No big deal."

"That's where you're wrong. I think opening up about something so personal means you're starting to trust me." And she looked ridiculously happy about it.

Suddenly things had gotten even more complicated than a simple clarification of where they stood after sex. Erin was the kind of woman who wanted promises, the white picket fence, a family. She'd been engaged, for God's sake. But Jack knew that a promise wasn't worth the powder it would take to blow it to hell. As much as he wished it could be different, there would not be a repeat of last night.

No discussion necessary.

He was counting on the discipline he'd learned in the army to keep him from disobeying his own direct order.

Jack had apparently received her message loud and clear about the folly of assigning her absurd research topics because today's list *could* be relevant to an action-adventure story. Erin had compiled some information on search-and-rescue, bullying and drug-sniffing dogs. But her favorite, by far, was diamonds. As in fencing stolen ones.

She looked at the pictures on her computer and sighed. "Definitely a girl's best friend. Men can break your heart, but a diamond will never let you down."

"Should I be worried that you're talking to yourself?"

Erin jumped, then saw Jack in the doorway. "I wish you'd stop doing that!"

"What? Worry?"

"No." She pressed a hand to her chest, over her pounding heart. At least she told herself it was pounding because he'd startled her. It was probably something more serious than that but she wasn't going there. "Quit sneaking up on me. Wear a bell or something. I'm not a covert op that requires stealth protocols."

"Someone is crabby."

"Someone was just dandy until you scared the stuffing out of her."

"Understood."

The word was crisply spoken, all military discipline, but the grin was a targeted weapon that did nothing to return her heartbeat to normal and everything to rev it up again. Darn him. It was like some kind of mind control. If he grinned and ordered her to take off her clothes, she'd be naked in a hot minute. But that was just wishful thinking. Going to bed with him again was like eating a whole bag of potato chips in one sitting. Giving in to temptation might be satisfying in the moment, but the process of getting rid of the negative consequences would be long and ugly.

On the other hand, maintaining the status quo was practical.

She knew it was late afternoon but not what the time was. Diamonds tended to make a girl lose track of everything. The sun getting lower in the sky said it was inching toward the dinner hour, which meant she should cook soon.

"Why are you here?" she asked.

"It's my house?"

"What I meant to say was, are you finished working?" she asked.

One dark eyebrow rose and he leaned a broad shoulder against the wall. "Are you?"

She was going to lob that ball back in his court. "I could be. Or not. Because I'm not the one who's at the beck and call of my process to write a book."

"I see." He nodded thoughtfully. "Well, let me put it this way. My process is getting cabin fever."

"So you're finished working?" she persisted. "I need a simple, direct answer."

"Yes. I'm going into town," he added.

Erin was almost sure they'd had a conversation about filling up the creative well, an idea he'd mocked. She couldn't resist rubbing it in a little. "That will be good for your process. Have fun."

"You're going with me."

"Oh, you don't want me." She was sure about that. He'd never said a word about them sleeping together, which told her how much she mattered. That slipup was a one-time thing. "I'm quite certain they keep your chair warm at Bar None. There's probably a sign on it. You should go make another new acquaintance."

"It's not Bar None I have in mind."

"Grizzly Bear Diner, then." She nodded. "Looks like a fun place. You should check it out."

"Another time." He straightened away from the wall and there was something in his eyes that was almost vulnerable. "I'm going to the Harvest Café."

"Wow." A vivid image of his last encounter with the café's co-owner was still fresh in her mind. "Are you going to talk books with Lucy Bishop?"

"Actually it's her partner, Maggie Potter, I want to see. And this is long overdue."

Erin tried to be on her toes with him at all times, but that one she really hadn't seen coming. "Why?"

"I could tell you, but…"

"You'd have to kill me," she said wryly.

"You're very dramatic."

That was ironic coming from the man who went all wonky and weird at the mention of his second book, or she should say work-in-progress. At least she hoped there was forward momentum. But she decided to take the high road and not point out that he was the pot calling the kettle black.

"Okay, then. When do you want to leave?" she asked.

"Now."

"What about Harley?" Come to think of it she hadn't seen the little guy all afternoon.

"I think the health department frowns on animals in restaurants."

"Smart-ass." She shook her head. "I meant, he'll need to be fed."

"Already done. He had a walk and is in my office. Probably sound asleep after exercise and wolfing down his dinner."

She couldn't come up with any other excuse. "I'll go get a sweater."

When the sun went down it was pretty dark and isolated out here by the lake. Besides the lighting down at the marina, the one on the front porch was all that cut the shadows. As they walked down the front steps together and headed for the jeep, Erin fought the feeling of intimacy the twilight created. This wasn't a date. It was her job.

She wondered if this was how Stockholm Syndrome worked. Forced confinement created feelings you wouldn't ordinarily feel for the person you were cooped up with. Yeah, that's all it was.

She climbed in to the passenger seat at the same time Jack slid behind the wheel. A shiver went through her and she wouldn't let it be about anything personal.

"It's getting cold," she said.

He turned on the car and instantly headlights sliced into the night. "That happens in Montana when it gets to be October."

"Halloween is just around the corner. Before you know it the holidays will be here."

"So? It's the same as any other time of year. Except colder."

"How can you say that? Everything is decorated. There are parties. And presents." She sighed. "Family."

"Yeah, that's my point."

She could see his rugged profile in the glow of the dashboard lights. He didn't look happy. "You don't have family?"

"Didn't say that."

"So you do have relatives."

"Singular," he explained. "Mom."

Erin remembered him saying his dad had disappeared. "Where does she live? Around here? Do you see her often?"

"Don't see her. That's the way she wants it."

"You can't be serious."

"According to her, I was trouble from the moment I was born. Didn't sleep much, got into everything, then I turned into a teenager and the trouble I got into was the against-the-law kind."

"You were arrested?"

He nodded. "Fell in with a bad crowd. Always looking for the next kick and got caught breaking and entering."

"What happened?"

"I was almost eighteen and still a juvenile. Lucked out with a sympathetic judge, who figured this was my first offense and I might benefit from structure and discipline."

"Since you joined the army, I'm guessing you took his advice."

"No one was more surprised than me at how well the life fit. I even went the extra mile and joined the army Special Forces, Ranger Battalion." The words were positive but there was a raw note in his voice. "The downside is we train for action, but when we're sent in bad things happen to good people. There's a price to pay."

"Yin and yang."

"What?" He glanced at her.

"Up and down. Ebb and flow. Good and bad. It's the balance of life." She tried to keep her voice light, but wondered why he was suddenly telling so much about himself. "You just go with it."

"As easy as that?" he asked.

"Didn't say it was easy. That's just the way it is and you make the best of it."

"Doesn't anything get you down?" He started to say more, then stopped. "I mean, obviously losing your fiancé was rough. I don't mean that. But you're always so damn...perky."

"I don't always feel that way." Things with her fiancé weren't what she'd let Jack believe. She would always regret that her feelings changed, but there was nothing she could do to alter his terminal diagnosis. She'd put on a happy face and done her best to keep him from knowing the truth before he died. "I just make an effort to be cheerful."

"You set a high bar."

"It's not about being an example to anyone else. I don't judge."

Jack didn't say anything for the rest of the drive to Blackwater Lake. He drove into town and found a parking place on the street, right in front of the Harvest Café. After exiting the car they walked inside and stopped by a glass-front bakery case. There was a sign that read, Please Wait to be Seated.

They weren't there more than a minute when Lucy Bishop approached them. The expression in her blue eyes could best be described as wary. "Welcome to the Harvest Café. Table for two?"

"Yes," Jack said. "Nice place you have here."

"Thank you. Right this way."

Erin glanced at Jack, a look that said the woman's polite yet cool tone was his fault, but she wasn't sure the message had been received. They followed her to a table in the back corner, a little secluded and a lot intimate. There was a high shelf containing country knickknacks, including a copper pitcher and metal washboard. The tablecloths were shades of gold, green and rust. Coordinating cloth napkins had eating utensils wrapped up in them and were on every empty table.

"Here you are." When they sat across from each other she handed each of them a menu. "I'll be your server tonight."

"I thought you were the chef." Jack's voice was disarmingly friendly. "And, by the way, something smells fantastic. I'll take one of everything."

"I appreciate that." Lucy smiled, revealing a dimple in her left cheek.

"Obviously I can't sample everything. So, what do you recommend?" The man had his charm set on stun. That was as close to an apology as he would go.

"I've heard from more than one person tonight that the meat loaf is particularly good. And we have carrot-ginger soup that's pretty yummy if I do say so myself. But only if your taste runs to that sort of thing."

"I'll keep that in mind," he said. "But I have to ask. You're the chef, so why aren't you in the kitchen?"

"I'm wearing both hats right now. My partner, Maggie, is having dinner with her fiancé." Lucy nodded toward a young couple sitting two tables away. She was beautiful, he was handsome and they couldn't take their eyes off each other. "He's Sloan Holden. A real estate developer. In fact his company built the condo complex where I bought a place."

"I see." He looked over then fixed his gaze on Lucy. "There's no rush, but when she finishes dinner, would you ask her to come over? I'd like to speak to her for a moment."

"Anything in particular?" Lucy's wariness had disappeared but she looked puzzled. "Since you haven't eaten yet, it can't be a complaint about the food. And I've been incredibly gracious so it can't be about poor customer service."

"It's all good." Jack smiled, but it disappeared when he glanced at Maggie. "I knew her husband."

"I see." Lucy's eyes widened just a little. "I'll let her know."

Erin watched her walk over to the table where Maggie and Sloan were having an after-dinner cup of coffee. The dark-haired woman listened, then looked surprised as she glanced at Jack. She said something to the man with her, then stood and came over.

"Hi. I'm Maggie. You're Jack Garner."

"I am." He stood to shake her hand. "And this is Erin Riley, my research assistant.

"Nice to meet you," Erin said.

"Same here." Then Maggie looked at Jack. "Lucy said you knew my husband, Danny?"

"Yes, ma'am. I served with him in Afghanistan. I just wanted you to know that I'm very sorry for your loss. He was a good man."

"Yes, he was."

"All Danny talked about was you and his baby on the way."

Maggie smiled a little sadly. "That sounds like him."

"He also said that Blackwater Lake was the best place in the world. That's the reason I checked it out when I was looking for property to buy."

"How do you like it so far?" the other woman asked.

His gaze slid to Erin for a fraction of a second before he answered, "It's growing on me."

"If he were here, he would be the best tour guide to make sure you saw all our little town's charms." A wistful expression slid into Maggie's eyes. "I'll always regret that our daughter will never know her father."

Jack looked down for a moment, then met her gaze. "I would be happy, if you'd like, to share my memories of Danny with her."

"She's two and a half." Maggie smiled. "But it would mean so much if you could do that when she's old enough to understand."

"It would be an honor."

"Thank you, Jack."

Erin was a sucker for emotional moments and this one got to her big-time. Crusty loner Jack Garner had volunteered to do a nice thing for a fallen brother's little girl. Tears gathered in her eyes and it took all she had to keep them there.

How was a girl supposed to resist him?

Where was a bag of potato chips when you really needed to eat your feelings?

Chapter Nine

Several days after Jack's meeting with his friend's widow, Erin was still regretting passing on that bag of chips in the grocery store. She was confused and uneasy in equal parts.

Confused because she'd been almost sure he meant *her* when he'd said the town of Blackwater Lake was growing on him. But his behavior toward her hadn't changed. If anything he'd become more distant. He was still man-caving in his office and avoiding her as much as possible.

A better book coach would be happy he was writing, and she was. Except that she hadn't seen any pages and he might be working too much. Again last night she'd heard him upstairs during the night. When she passed his room this morning on her way to the kitchen, his bedroom door was open and he was nowhere to be seen. Like the last couple of nights he'd probably slept in the room off his office, the one where he'd made love to her.

No. Not love.

It was just sex. Really good sex, but nothing more than a physical release for both of them. If she repeated that enough, the message might actually become true. She hoped so because she'd never been the type to get intimate with a man just because he was pretty to look at.

While making coffee, she heard the front door open and close, then Jack appeared in the kitchen. He filled a glass from the water dispenser on the refrigerator and started to guzzle.

When he took a breath she said, "Good morning."

His only response was a nod. He'd been for a run already. The shorts and sneakers were a clue. But the deciding factor was his black T-shirt with bold white letters saying ARMY on the front. It was sweaty and clung to his upper body in a very intriguing way. She remembered how good it felt when they were skin-to-skin... And this was a train of thought that needed to go off the rails.

"So, you've been out for a run bright and early."

"Yeah." He finished the rest of the water. "Clears my head."

"Did your head need clearing?" If so, she thought, what had to go?

"Figure of speech."

"Oh. I just wondered. Because you were in your office during the wee hours last night."

"Are you stalking me?" There was amusement in his eyes.

"Only if stalking is defined by hearing you pace at one in the morning."

"Didn't mean to disturb you."

"You didn't." Liar, liar, pants on fire. And the disturbance had nothing to do with being awake. She'd never gone to sleep and he was the reason she couldn't. "So you were working on the book that late?"

"Yeah." But his gaze didn't quite meet hers.

"Be careful, Jack."

"Of work? I thought that's what you wanted."

"Yes. In balance."

"Inspiration and balance aren't always compatible," he said.

"That's a fair point. But burnout isn't the goal." And speaking of burnout, he was looking so hot she might just go up in flames. "You barricaded yourself upstairs all day, barely taking time to eat. Then you put in more time during the night. It's not healthy."

He thought about that for a moment. "Did you mother-hen Corinne Carlisle?"

"I didn't have to. She didn't work day and night, then go running to clear her head."

"Maybe she should."

"She's over sixty."

"Spring chicken. Jogging shakes things loose."

"If you knew Corinne, you'd know that her idea of shaking things loose is a gin and tonic when happy hour rolls around."

"High five, Corinne." There was a gleam in his eyes when he said, "So she took care of the spirits. Your job was body and mind. How did that go?"

"Good—healthy food for the body and talking about her book kept the work fresh in her mind. Speaking of the book—"

"I'm going to take a shower." Abruptly he turned and walked out of the room.

So much for meeting the enemy head-on. There was mischief afoot.

She thought about what he'd said and on the surface it seemed as if he was engaged. But something was off. He was vague, deflecting the questions. Wry, coy, sarcastic and mocking. Similar to the way he'd acted when she first arrived and he'd tried to intimidate her into going away. Before he'd admitted he had no book.

She was into him now and not just because she'd been hired to be. No question he wasn't an easy man, but there was more to him than that. He had a soft spot for a homely dog and came to Blackwater Lake because a fallen brother had told him it was the best place in the world. He'd offered to tell a little girl about the father she would never know.

Erin wanted to help because she'd chipped away at his hard shell and underneath it discovered there was a man she genuinely cared about. They said the way to a man's heart was through his stomach and she was going to find out whether or not that was true.

Ten minutes later Jack walked back into the kitchen and poured himself a mug of coffee. It was annoying and unfair how fast the man could clean up and look as if he'd been through hair and makeup on a movie set to get ready for his close-up. Of course, the not shaving saved time and made him look like the guy most likely to have women falling at his feet.

"What's for breakfast?" He sipped coffee and met her gaze over the rim.

She poured a beaten mixture into the heated pan on the stove. "Scrambled eggs. Sausage. Biscuits and gravy. And blueberries. I hope you're not disappointed."

"Are you kidding?"

"I never joke about breakfast. It's the most important meal of the day."

"Of course, it needs to be sampled first. But judging by the smell, it will beat army chow for sure."

"If I wasn't here," she said, sneaking a look at him while stirring the eggs, "what would you be eating?"

"Coffee. Something out of a can."

"Seriously? That's sad."

"But true," he said.

"What you need is a cooking coach. So you can feed yourself when I'm gone."

His expression didn't change but there was something smoky in his voice when he said, "Did Corinne survive on her own?"

"Yes."

He shrugged as if to say "okay, then." "I'm starving."

"You're in luck."

"Because I'm starving?" One dark eyebrow rose.

"No. Breakfast is ready."

The table was already set and she put the food on it. Jack sat across from her and filled his plate, then wolfed down what seemed to her enough to feed an army. And it hadn't come out of a can. A girl could only hope it was appreciated.

She deliberately channeled conversation to the weather or topics equally innocuous because they were due to meet in half an hour. The questions would keep until then.

When he was finished, Jack actually thanked her for cooking, which kind of left her speechless. Then he refilled his coffee and went upstairs to his office. She did the dishes and cleaned up the kitchen while mentally preparing for the coming conflict. In the last couple of days she'd felt more like a housekeeper than anything else. She'd given him the latitude he'd asked for, but it was time to do what she'd been sent here to do.

One minute before nine o'clock she climbed the stairs and knocked on his office door, then let herself in. "Hi."

He looked up from his computer monitor and frowned. "What are you doing here?"

"Status meeting. Remember?"

"We already had the update. Before breakfast."

"Not even close." She sat on a chair in front of his desk. "That was about the hours you're putting in. I'd really like to see what all that effort has produced."

"You don't trust me?"

"With my life? Absolutely," she said with complete conviction. Meeting his gaze she added, "But you are an expert at evasive maneuvers and I don't have faith that you'll be straightforward now."

"I'm hurt."

"Oh, please. This is me." She was prepared to die on this hill and refused to be intimidated by the glare he shot at her.

"You want to see pages."

"Give the man a gold star." No matter how much she wanted to, she refused to look away.

Apparently he got her take-no-prisoners message because he reached down to open a desk drawer. He pulled out pages, but after glancing at them, he had an odd look on his face then quickly shoved them back. He retrieved another stack of paper from another drawer and held it up. "See? Pages."

When he made a move to put them away she said, "Not so fast."

"What? You see them."

"Very funny. What are you? Fourteen? And trying to pull a fast one because you didn't do your homework? This isn't my first rodeo."

"Do you have any idea how much I hate it that you're a teacher?"

"It's a dirty job but someone has to do it." She sighed. "I'm on your side, Jack. I just want to read what you've got so far."

He didn't hand over the pages, just put them on the desk

in front of him. "I'm asking you to wait until the book is finished."

"I get it, Jack. I understand that every writer has a process and this is yours. But I find myself caught in the middle. Your editor is entitled to reassurance."

"I know. Just tell her I'm putting in so many hours you're concerned for my mental health."

She couldn't help smiling. "Because she'll find that so encouraging?"

"Why not?" There was no surrender in this man. Bravado and bluff was how he rolled.

"She's going to want something tangible. Or at least to know that I've seen hard copy. It's not unreasonable."

"Negative."

Erin wasn't sure if that was a no or an assessment of the request she'd just made. "This isn't negotiable."

"They need polishing."

"Do we need to have the diva conversation again?" She was only half teasing. "Please, Jack. My job is on the line. It's what I was sent here to do."

He looked at her and with every second that passed his eyes grew darker, more defiant. Just when it seemed he was going to refuse, he flipped through the stack of paper and handed it over. When she took the pages their hands brushed and she felt the touch all the way to her toes. That had never happened when she'd coached Corinne.

"Thank you." For the pages or the thrill? She wasn't sure.

"Don't say I didn't warn you."

It seemed she got a warning about him every day, for all the good it had done. But that wasn't what he meant. "I'm sure they're really good."

"I hope you're not disappointed."

He meant his work but she took it a step further. Every

day that went by upped the chances that she was going to experience a deep feeling of disappointment when this assignment ended. Jack wasn't someone who would be easy to forget.

Erin couldn't get downstairs fast enough to read the pages and it left her wanting more, which was the opposite of disappointed. The chapters were really good. Mac Daniels met a mysterious woman with brown, highlighted hair and green eyes. He called her Little Miss Perky and she wasn't extraordinarily beautiful, like his ex-wife. But she was vulnerable, yet strong. A compelling combination. And she talked a lot.

She thought that sounded a lot like her, which was part of the reason she wanted more. And the writing was sharp, intense, like Jack. The good news was he had pages—strong pages. The bad news? He hadn't given her any research topics. It was possible he didn't need any information for the book or was dropping the ridiculous pretense. Either way he was working and that had been her job. Speaking of which, she needed to update his editor.

After making sure about the time in New York, Erin called the publishing house and hoped to get Cheryl's voice mail in order to minimize details. But no such luck.

"This is Cheryl."

"Hi. It's Erin Riley." She paced the kitchen.

"Hey. I was just thinking about you. How are you holding up?"

Interesting way of asking about her well-being. Not "how are you," but "how are you holding up?" "I'm fine."

"Is Jack behaving himself?"

The better question was whether or not Erin was. And the answer would be no. She'd practically seduced him. But that was one of those pesky details better kept to herself. She decided to fall back on the Jack Garner conversational method of evasive maneuvering.

"That's why I'm calling, Cheryl."

"Oh, God, you're quitting. He's so difficult you can't take it anymore."

He was certainly difficult, but leaving had never occurred to her. At least not before her assignment was completed. "He's a complicated man."

There was a moment of silence on the other end of the line. "Does that mean you're not quitting?"

"It means I wanted to let you know he's moving forward on the book."

"That's fantastic. Have you read it?" Relief and excitement mixed together in the other woman's voice.

"I have. It's very good."

"Great news," Cheryl said. "I want to get it in the publishing schedule but I need an idea of time frame."

"He's touchy." Considering Erin had called him a diva that was extraordinarily diplomatic.

"That's not news, Erin. It's the reason you were sent there. How close to finishing is he?"

That was a very good question. It presupposed Erin was in control of the situation. That so wasn't the case. How to not lie and cover for both Jack and herself. "I believe he's seeing the light at the end of the tunnel."

"Can you get him to commit to a completion date?"

Jack didn't seem the committing sort, but that observation was strictly personal. Her best guess was that it wasn't wise to put pressure on him just yet.

"He's clicking along and I'm reluctant to say anything that might get in the way of his progress."

"Okay. I'll hold off on that for a little bit. Obviously you have a handle on the situation since he hasn't sent you packing."

Not for lack of trying. At first what kept her there was the prospect of more assignments and travel. Now she was staying for the man. God help her.

"He wasn't warm and fuzzy when I showed up, but I've seen a lot of layers to him." Naked didn't count.

"Okay, then. I trust your instincts."

She wasn't so sure that was prudent. "I'll do my best."

"Just keep doing what you're doing," Cheryl said. "I've got another call and need to take it. We'll talk next week?"

"Sure. Bye."

Erin clicked off and the best she could say about the conversation was that she still had a job. Even though it didn't feel that way because she didn't have anything to do.

This might be a good time to stock up on office supplies. Based on Jack's modus operandi the last couple of days, he'd be locked in his office indefinitely and wouldn't know whether she was around or not. But she left a note next to her laptop on the kitchen table in case he came looking for her. Then she grabbed her purse along with the keys to her rental car and headed out for the town of Blackwater Lake.

During one of their trips to town, Jack had driven by Office Supplies and More, which was on Blue Sky Street, just off Main. She parked in the lot and entered through the back door. The baskets—hand held and rolling—were kept up front by the cash register. She walked past the counter where a cute, petite teenage girl was standing.

"Welcome to Office Supplies and More," she said automatically.

"Thanks," Erin replied just as automatically.

"Can I help you find something?"

She scanned the aisles and noted that there were signs clearly identifying where things were located. Pens and pencils. File folders. Notes. Calendars. There was nothing exotic on her list so this should be easy. "I'm just going to browse."

"If you can't find something, just let me know."

"Will do."

Erin picked a rolling basket, which would hold more, then decided to go from one end of the store to the other. Step by step and logical, the complete opposite of the way things had gone for her from the moment she'd met Jack Garner.

"Never too late to turn things around," she muttered to herself.

From what she'd observed of his office, Jack did a lot of his writing on legal pads, probably blocking out a scene in longhand while his subconscious churned on ahead and ideas came flooding in. She put a box of mechanical pencils in the basket.

On the paper aisle she found a giant economy package of yellow legal pads and grabbed it. Sticky notes in different sizes and colors were next to go in. Those were all over the place on his desk.

And in the bottom drawer he kept condoms. Probably not purchased from the office supply store. The memory of being with him put a hitch in her breathing and regret in her heart. Everything had changed after sex. He'd opened up about Harley and there was that "aww" moment with his army buddy's widow. Since then he'd been avoiding her as if she had cooties. She even missed obnoxious, abrasive Jack and that was pretty pathetic.

After adding highlighters and file folders to her basket she wheeled it to the check out counter, where a pretty, blue-eyed blonde just beat her in line.

"Hi, Miss Fletcher—" The teenager stopped and shook her head. "I'm sorry. Mrs. Miller."

"Don't worry about it, Glenna. I'm still not used to the married name."

Maybe it was loneliness, but Erin couldn't resist. She asked, "How long has it been? Since you were married, I mean."

"Seven weeks." She smiled dreamily, then looked more closely. "We haven't met. My first name is Kim."

"I'm Erin Riley. Are you any relation to Sheriff Fletcher?"

"He's my brother."

"And more," Glenna chimed in. "He was the man of honor at her wedding."

"Like a maid of honor, only a guy," Kim added.

"I met him at Bar None. Big guy. Major hunk factor. I'm trying to picture him in a bridesmaid's dress and just not loving it."

"He agreed to the job and was absolutely the best. But he drew the line at a dress or carrying flowers." Kim laughed. "Will mentioned meeting you at Bar None with Jack Garner. You're his research assistant."

Sort of. Her job description was kind of fluid at the moment. "I work with Jack."

"Talk about hunk factor—" Kim blew out a long breath. "I've seen him a couple times at Bar None. He's Heathcliff and Mr. Darcy rolled into one."

"If you're saying he's a brooding loner, you would be absolutely correct."

"Sorry. That was my inner literature geek talking. I teach honors English at Blackwater Lake High School."

"So do I. I mean the teacher part. I'm a substitute in Phoenix. My current assignment is temporary." Saying it out loud stopped her cold. The idea of leaving was remarkably unappealing. It's not the way she'd felt when her time with Corinne Carlisle was up.

"Mrs. Miller is the best English teacher I ever had," Glenna interjected. "All the kids want to be in her class."

"I love my job and that helps. I enjoy working with kids, although it's not for the faint of heart. But you know that."

"I do."

"Is that why you're moonlighting? Working for a famous author?"

Erin smiled. Jack was many things but definitely not for the faint of heart any more than teaching. "I just love the written word. The way each one is put together in dialogue and paragraphs to tell a story. And Jack is very good at what he does."

Kim's expression turned thoughtful. "I've got some kids in my honors class who are natural storytellers. They might get some valuable information from Jack Garner. And even for the students who aren't great writers it might spark an interest in reading. It's hard to get across to them how important it is, so anything out of the ordinary might jumpstart them. Do you think he might be interested in talking to the kids about what he does?"

"I can ask."

"That would be so awesome," Glenna said.

"What have I told you about the word *awesome*?" Kim's expression was teasing.

"It's overused. Exercise your brain and come up with something more creative," the teen said, obviously parroting what was preached in class.

"Exactly." The teacher beamed. "But it would be pretty awesome if he would say yes."

Erin didn't want to burst her bubble, but the odds of being struck by lightning were probably better than convincing Jack to give a motivational talk to high school kids.

"I'll mention it to him," she agreed. "But you may have

noticed. He's not particularly social. Please, don't get your hopes up about him."

The words were barely out of her mouth when Erin realized that same warning could apply to her. She was teetering on the edge of having feelings for Jack and somewhere deep inside she wanted him to return them.

She really should heed her own advice and not get her hopes up about that ever happening.

Chapter Ten

Jack was standing outside the marina store with Brewster Smith when he saw the rental car return. Erin got out and something inside him relaxed. He'd come downstairs expecting to see her and found the note she left. It crossed his mind that he'd pushed back a little too hard on her reading the chapters and she'd had enough. Left before he'd learned to cook for himself. That reminder about her being gone soon had struck a nerve.

She glanced in their direction and waved, then set a couple of bags on the front porch before walking down the slight hill to join them. Harley ran ahead to meet her and she dropped to one knee and enthusiastically rubbed him all over.

Jack wouldn't mind if she greeted him that way and his body tightened at the thought of having her in his arms and getting her naked.

Not necessarily in that order.

But there was one problem with the scenario. Another intimate encounter would be like walking into an enemy ambush without body armor or a weapon. That's why he was maintaining a safe zone. Although keeping it up was taking a toll.

She gave Harley one more rub, then stood and walked over to them. "Hi."

"I see you made it to town and back," Jack said.

"Did you get my note?"

"Yes." For some reason it wasn't especially reassuring.

"Then what's the problem?" she asked.

"You were gone for a while" was the best he could come up with.

"Did I make it home before curfew?" She lifted one eyebrow before smiling brightly at the older man. "How are you, Brewster?"

"Fit as a fiddle. Yourself?"

"Fine. How is Mrs. Smith's cold?"

"Stubborn. Like her." He lifted one shoulder in a shrug. "But better. Although she still has a pretty bad cough."

"I'm sorry to hear that. Has she gone back to work yet?"

Brewster shook his head. "Someone is covering for her at the thrift store. She's getting impatient, though."

"That's a good sign. I wish I could do something to help. Maybe a batch of chicken soup?"

"Lucy Bishop already brought some over." His blue eyes twinkled. "But Aggie wouldn't mind some of your macaroni and cheese."

"I don't believe she's ever had it." Erin laughed. "But I'll whip some up for you to take home to her."

"If it's no trouble."

"Not at all. It's easy."

Jack watched her relate to the older man with a potent combination of friendliness and charm. She made it look effortless, natural. Dangerous to him. She'd been in town about two hours and he'd noticed. The house had never felt empty before. Not until her. That was too damn close to missing her.

"So you went to town?" Brew asked.

"Yes. All the stores are decorated for Halloween. Pumpkins, ghosts, skeletons. Spiderwebs up in the windows. It's so cute. I bet Christmas is really something here."

The old man nodded. "We're all about holidays in Blackwater Lake. In fact there's a big costume party at the community center for Halloween."

"Do you and Mrs. Smith go?"

"Wouldn't miss it." He looked at her, then Jack. "You coming?"

"I don't know." She looked as if she wanted to.

"Worried about a costume?"

"Maybe," she admitted.

"Thrift store. Good place to get ideas." Brew nodded then glanced up at the house. "So what's in those bags you brought back?"

"That's what I'd like to know," Jack said.

"Stuff to make you a better writer." She grinned wickedly.

He wondered if she'd read the chapters yet and found what she thought about his writing really mattered to him. "What's wrong with my work?"

"Not a thing," she assured him. "Love the beginning, by the way."

Did she really? Or was she just being nice in front of Brewster? Give him body armor and a tactical mission and he was secure and confident. But coughing his guts onto a page? The doubt made him feel like a teenage boy afraid to ask a girl out on a date. Later he would grill Erin for her real opinion.

"So what did you get that's going to make me brilliant?"

"Sticky notes. Index cards. Pencils. Highlighters."

Brewster scratched his head. "That's just stuff."

"Writers love stuff," Erin explained. "It makes them feel empowered."

"That true?" the man asked him.

"Yes." Jack slid his fingertips into the pockets of his jeans.

"Seems to me ideas come from here." Brewster tapped a finger to his temple. "Taking your head out for a spin now and then couldn't hurt."

"He means filling up the creative well." Erin's tone clearly said "I told you so."

"I know what he means," Jack said.

"Talking to people is fun. You should try it sometime."

Apparently it was too much to hope her needling would be contained in front of the older man. "I have no beef with talking. It's people that are the problem."

She got a funny look on her face. "Have you ever talked to kids?"

"Not if I can help it."

"You offered to talk to Maggie's daughter about her dad," Erin pointed out.

"That's different."

In the waning daylight Jack studied her. Something was up. He knew her and this wasn't idle banter. There was something on her mind and he wasn't going to like it.

"What did you do?" he asked.

"Nothing." She folded her arms over her chest and met his gaze.

"Something's going on. You might as well come clean."

She stared at him for a few moments, then nodded. "It's Saturday in Blackwater Lake—"

"The edited version," he suggested.

"I ran into Kim Miller—"

"Who?"

"She's Sheriff Fletcher's sister. You remember him. Your friend from Bar None, the place where you take your inner writer out for a spin to make friends?"

"I know who he is. It's her I don't have a clue about."

"She teaches honors English at Blackwater Lake High School."

The dots were not yet connected but he had a bad feeling about this. "So you two bonded over teaching Shakespeare. I felt the ripple in the Force all the way out here."

She tilted her head and gave him a you're-going-to-the-principal's-office look. "Sarcasm is so unattractive. And you're going to feel really bad when I get to the good part."

"Regret is my middle name. Go for it."

"Kim is a fan of your work. And a teacher. A good one, according to Glenna."

"Who is Glenna?"

"She works at Office Supplies and More. And she's one of Kim's students."

"And what does her opinion have to do with anything?"

"She's a fan of Kim's. As a teacher myself I can tell you that a good educator never overlooks a teachable moment. She's hoping to highlight the importance of reading. And when you think about it, giving of your time is an investment in job security. You need readers to buy the books you write." Erin glanced at Brewster, who seemed to be enjoying this back-and-forth a lot. "Kim wants you to speak to her honors English class about what it's like to be a career writer."

Jack had his doubts about whether or not he had a career as a writer. He'd sucked at being a son and husband. Soldiering was the only thing he'd ever been good at. And his publisher had sent him a babysitter to get this book done.

How could he talk to kids when he didn't know what the hell he was doing?

"You shouldn't have promised," he told her.

"I didn't. Just said I would ask you."

"Mission accomplished and the answer is no."

"Why, Jack?"

He was an imposter? Had nothing to say to them? A guy like him was not a good role model for impressionable teens? *Pick one of them*, he thought. *Or all of the above.*

"How about I don't have time," he finally said.

"Baloney." She put her hands on her hips and might have been glaring at him. The sun had just disappeared behind the mountains throwing them into shadow so it was hard to tell. "It won't take more than forty-five minutes to an hour. You'd lose a couple of pages but those kids are giving up valuable instruction time. Because their teacher believes it's important. I do, too."

Damn it. Those words turned out to be heavy artillery because, for reasons unclear to him, he didn't want to disappoint her.

Maybe just one more try to back her off. "Now isn't a good time."

"You could live anywhere you want, but you settled in this town." Brewster didn't butt into a conversation unless he had something to say. Apparently he did now and it wasn't good. He wasn't smiling.

"That's just an address," he countered.

"Not in Blackwater Lake. If you're bleeding or on fire folks call 911. For anything else they pitch in when asked. They share what they've learned, what they know."

"What if they don't have anything to share?"

"You'd be surprised. Won't know unless you try," the old man said. "And you try because being neighborly is a way of life here. If you don't get involved, the magic of this place doesn't work."

Jack kept his mouth shut even though he wanted to ask, "What magic?" The grizzled, practical old guy talking about it at all was enough to get his attention. If he said no now it would look like he had a heart the size of a sunflower seed. He knew when he'd been outflanked. "Okay. I'll talk to them."

Erin smiled, a cheerful, satisfied smile. As if she'd known he would give in. "You won't regret it, Jack."

"I'm pretty sure that's not true." The look on her face irked him so he added, "I'll do it on one condition."

"Oh?"

"I'll talk to the class, but you're coming with me."

She saluted, being a complete smart-ass. "Yes, sir."

Her job was to take care of him—body, mind and spirit. His body was pretty happy what with being well fed and the spectacular sex. She'd managed to touch his mind, too, in ways she didn't even know. But he had his doubts about the spirit thing.

Still, he figured the job description included having his back while attempting to communicate with teenagers.

God help them.

And him.

Erin wouldn't exactly say Jack looked afraid to go into the high school classroom, but it was a good bet that facing heavily armed enemy combatants was a more comfortable fit. The two of them stood just outside Kim Miller's room while teenagers swarmed up and down the hall, hurrying to their last class of the day.

After Jack's less-than-enthusiastic agreement to show up, Erin had contacted the teacher and they'd agreed Friday would be best. With the weekend staring them in the face, the kids were restless anyway and they'd probably learn more from Jack. Judging by his dark and brooding expression, he didn't agree.

"Take a deep breath, Jack. The kids are going to love you."

"Why?" He shot her a don't-give-me-that-crap look. "It's too late for a personality transplant and no one has ever accused me of being charming or approachable."

"Doesn't mean you aren't."

"Seriously?"

"Never too late to turn over a new leaf." She met his gaze, trying to infuse him with some of her optimism. The dark look in his eyes didn't falter. "Come on. Embrace the moment. You're just here to talk to them."

"About what?"

"Didn't you prepare some notes?" Now she had a knot in her stomach.

"No."

Oh, boy. The hall was much less crowded now. In a few minutes there would be some kind of signal to let students know they'd better be in their seats. And Jack had nothing ready for the class he would face. She was his research assistant/book coach. This situation was the equivalent of thirty seconds left on the clock in a football game, just enough time for one or two plays to win the game. It came down to coaching and she had to give him something.

"Okay, this is basically the same principle as writing what you know."

He stared at her. "Not even close. Two different things."

"What I mean is, start out by telling them your personal story. You know yourself." Better than anyone, she thought. "Talk about you."

"That will take fifteen seconds."

"Oh, please." She rolled her eyes. This man was complicated. She could talk about him for hours. "Give them the high points. Maybe five minutes or so. Then open it up to questions."

"And if there aren't any?"

"You thank them for not hitting you with spitballs and we leave. It will give us more time to poke through the thrift store for Halloween costume ideas."

"What?"

"We're shopping."

"Torturing teens isn't enough? You want to torture me, too—"

A loud signal broadcast over the school's public address system interrupted his protest. "Saved by the bell," she said.

With the kids in their seats, Kim saw them in the doorway, smiled and motioned them to come in. "Class, I have a surprise for you. The test will be on Monday. Anyone who didn't study just got a reprieve." There was a collective sound of relief. "We have a guest speaker."

Erin nudged him farther into the room, where about twenty teens sat in several rows. The teacher's flat-top desk was in the front with the chalkboard behind her. They walked over and Erin introduced him to Kim.

"I'm a big fan," she said, gushing.

"Thanks."

In a low voice Erin said, "I'm going to sit in the back. You'll be great."

"I'll get even with you," he muttered.

She slipped quietly to a chair against the rear wall, trying not to be a distraction, but there was no worry about that. The guys stared at him in awe and the girls were smitten at first sight. It was like being in the same room with Indiana Jones.

"Everyone," Kim continued, "this is Jack Garner, author of the phenomenally successful book *High Value Target.*

Has anyone read it?" All but one or two hands went up and there was an enthusiastic murmuring as hero worship ratcheted up. "Good. I thought you all might enjoy hearing what Mr. Garner has to say. So, take it away, Jack."

"Thanks." As the teacher moved to the side, Jack stood alone.

He could have looked more uncomfortable, but Erin couldn't see how. Still, the students didn't know him like she did and wouldn't see it.

"Okay. Here's the deal. I figure you get lectured to enough." He glanced at Kim. "No offense, Mrs. Miller."

"None taken."

"So, I didn't prepare notes. I'm just going to tell you a little about myself then open this up to questions." He thought for a moment, then seemed to make a decision. "I was raised by a single mother and never knew my dad. Not a very good student. Didn't have a lot of options beyond high school so I joined the army. After leaving the service, I wrote *High Value Target* and you all know the rest."

He wasn't kidding about his life story taking five seconds. But that was such a skeletal description of him and Erin had been around teenagers long enough to know they wouldn't let him get away with not filling in some of the blanks. When he asked for questions, again nearly everyone in the room raised a hand.

Jack looked surprised, but relaxed a little. He pointed to a dark-haired girl in the front row. "Tell me your name, then ask your question. That goes for all of you."

"Mackenzy Bray," she said. "And this is my question. Mrs. Miller told us there are a lot of options for us when we graduate. I'm wondering why you picked the army."

"The choice was kind of made for me. It's true I was a bad student. But I left out the part about being arrested. Not proud of it and don't recommend the experience. Before you ask, it doesn't matter what I did. The important part is the judge went easy on me because I was just under eighteen and it was a first offense. He made it clear it better be the last and said I lacked structure and discipline. Strongly recommended joining the military in whatever branch would take me. That turned out to be the army."

"Did you like it?" A boy in front of Erin blurted out the question.

Jack grinned and you could almost hear every female heart skipping a beat. "Speaking of discipline and not following orders."

"Sorry." The kid's voice was sheepish. "My name is Blake Hoffman."

"And you want to know if I liked it since there was some arm-twisting to get me there." He nodded. "The answer is that no one was more surprised than me when I took to the life and was good at it."

A girl's hand went up and he pointed to her. Erin recognized the teenager from Office Supplies and More. "Glenna Smith, Mr. Garner—"

"Call me Jack."

"Jack," she said shyly. "The bio in your book said you joined Special Forces, Ranger Battalion."

"Yes. That's how much I liked the life. I wanted to be the best of the best and serve my country."

"So why retire from it?" she asked.

"Good question." There was a guarded look in his eyes. "I just knew it was time. Next question."

"Did you always want to be a writer? Russ Palmer," the boy added.

"No. In fact I wasn't much of a reader until I needed something to do during downtime. And there was a lot of it. A buddy gave me a book and I was hooked. Read everything I could get my hands on."

"Why did you start writing?" Kim shrugged. "You already know who I am and this is my classroom. Rank has its privileges."

He grinned, then half sat on a corner of her desk. "To be honest, along with the positive of joining up, the fact is soldiers train for war. There are some things no one can prepare you for. It leaves a mark. I started a journal and really liked putting words on paper. That evolved into a fictional character with a story." He shrugged. "Against all odds it was published."

"And a success," Kim said.

Erin saw a shadow cross his face and knew it was doubt, the intangible enemy dogging him now. The expression was completely opposite of the way he'd looked when talking about being a soldier. He'd once told her it was all he was good at, but she disagreed. And he couldn't see the way he was connecting with these kids. Until you'd stood in the front of a classroom and witnessed teenage eyes glazed over with boredom, you couldn't appreciate how involved these kids were now.

She was very surprised that he opened up to her about his rocky youth, but chalked that up to progress in their working relationship. Today he'd related some very personal and not very flattering details about himself to these kids—strangers—and it was a huge step for him. For them it was a lesson that there was no single path in life to success. Good information for them to have. He'd been honest about the bad stuff so his message had a profound impact.

"What's your next book about? Chloe Larson," she added.

Erin's stomach knotted again. The last female who mentioned his next book got the cold shoulder. He was touchy about the sequel and wouldn't discuss it. She held her breath, waiting for him to respond. Or walk away without another word as he'd done to Lucy Bishop.

He glanced at the class. "You might remember from the first book that Mac doesn't have a job. And he has a limited skill set. It's either law enforcement or private investigation."

"Which one does he pick?" the girl persisted.

"What do you think?" he asked.

She thought for a moment. "He liked the military, so I believe he'd become a cop."

"A case can be made for that," he said. "But Mac's going into the private sector. Too many rules in police work."

"There are a lot of similarities between you and Mac." That was from Glenna. "Do you break the rules, Jack?"

His gaze met Erin's over the heads of the kids and somehow she knew he was remembering the two of them ending up in bed with tangled legs and twisted sheets. Since they'd both ignored the implied guiding principles of a working relationship, that made them equally guilty of breaking the rules.

He smiled, a mysterious expression on his face. "Let's just say you have to know and understand the rules before breaking them."

"What does that mean—"

The bell sounded and the kids groaned. She caught murmurs of disappointment because some of them still had questions. That had the ring of success to Erin's way of thinking.

"Always leave them wanting more." Kim laughed. "I'm quite sure that's the first time any of us were sorry to hear the last bell on Friday afternoon. Class, let's give Jack a round of applause. If you're nice, maybe he'll come back and talk to us again."

"Count on it," Jack said.

The sound of hands clapping was instantaneous and enthusiastic. He lifted a hand to acknowledge them, then moved to the back of the classroom, where Erin stood waiting. After putting his hand at the small of her back, he quickly ushered her out the rear door before anyone could slow him down with another question.

"That went well," she said, trying to keep up with his long strides.

"Depends on what you mean by *well*."

"You really connected with them."

"That and a buck will get them a soda."

"You underestimate yourself, Jack." She glanced up at him, the tight mouth and tense jaw. "You have a lot of wisdom to pass on. It was enlightening for them to know that the choices they make have consequences—some good, some not."

"Yeah, I'm just a real role model."

"You're determined not to believe that so I'm not going to waste my breath. But I'll tell you this and I believe it with all my heart—books give you the power to reach people."

"Right."

"They picked up on the fact that Mac has a lot of you in him. Through your characters and the truth in your words, you can inspire anyone to do whatever they set their mind to."

His pace slowed and he dropped his hand. For a moment he met her gaze, then the corners of his mouth turned up. "Good try. But I'm still not ready to let you read everything I've got."

"I think what we have here is the lesser of two evils."

"What?"

"Reading your book or the thrift store."

"Never thought I'd say this without a gun to my head, but let's go shopping."

Chapter Eleven

"So, you've made up your mind about going to the community Halloween party." Jack glanced over at Erin in the jeep's passenger seat before driving out of the Blackwater Lake High School parking lot. *Go, Wolverines*, he thought as they passed the mascot displayed on the marquee.

"What makes you jump to that conclusion?" she asked.

"Because we're going to the thrift store where Brewster told you to look for a costume. That implies you're planning to go to the party."

"I am," she confirmed. "It's like Brewster said—being neighborly is a way of life. So, I want to be a good neighbor. At least while I'm here."

He kept forgetting that she was leaving. So much for watching his six. He'd better be more vigilant about protecting his perimeter or there would be hell to pay. He'd managed not to kiss her again, which wasn't easy. But necessary. Kissing would lead to sex and he had no doubt that would be as excellent as last time, but no way was it the smart move.

"So why am I shopping with you?" he asked.

"Because we're already here in town. But if you have things to do, we can go back and get my car." She looked over. "Why? What did you think? That I was going to try and convince you to go to the party?"

That's exactly what he'd thought. "Not if you're smart."

"Oh, I'm smart." Her tone was full of brash confidence. "And I'm still going to make a case for why you should go."

Jack couldn't wait to see what her strategic approach would be. "This is going to be good."

"I don't know about that, but I agree with Brewster. It's important to support the community where you live. To give back and be a part of it."

"You don't live here," he reminded her. And himself.

"For a little while longer, I do." She was quiet for a moment, probably bringing in reinforcements. "I've always lived in a good-sized city and Blackwater Lake is different. Special. It's actually possible to know everyone in town and they're people worth knowing. Your friend Danny Potter was right. This is the best place in the world. And Brewster is right, too. The magic doesn't work if you don't get involved."

Damn. That was some serious ammunition she'd hit him with. "Roger that."

"So, you're going to the party?"

"I'll take it under advisement."

"You won't regret it, Jack.

Although she was right that he didn't regret talking to the high school class, he wasn't so sure about this.

A few minutes later he pulled into the thrift-store parking lot, a stand-alone building on the outskirts of Blackwater Lake. It looked like a barn and probably had been once, but not now. The outside was painted red with white trim. There was a sign visible from the main road that said all donations welcome. All proceeds went to the Blackwater Lake Sunshine Fund.

That was right up Erin's alley. He didn't know for sure, but wouldn't be surprised if Sunshine was her middle name.

He parked the jeep, noting that there were quite a few cars in the lot. That meant a lot of people inside. Super. They exited the car and approached the wide open door.

"Isn't this place cute?" she said.

"Not the word I would use."

By the spacious entrance Erin pointed out half barrels overflowing with flowers. An old wood-and-tin washboard propped up against the outside wall. A piece of wooden ladder because everyone knew you couldn't have too many half ladders that were completely useless.

"Looks like junk to me."

"One man's trash is another man's treasure."

He looked down at the high color on her cheeks, the excitement in her eyes that made her beautiful. The feeling was like a sucker punch. "Don't you ever get tired of being an optimist?"

She shook her head. "Did you know that it takes more muscles to frown than to smile? You should try it sometime."

He'd done more of that since she showed up than he could ever remember doing in his whole life. But that information was best kept to himself.

They walked inside and let their eyes adjust to the dimness before glancing around. In his opinion it looked like a hoarder's garage exploded in here. There were mismatched dishes, suitcases, wall hangings, old bottles, a trunk, furniture. And dust. A whole lot of it.

"This is going to be so much fun."

Jack studied the bright smile of anticipation on her face and decided they should make her president in charge of the Sunshine Fund. He wanted to put on the shades he'd just slid to the top of his head. "Does your cell phone have a GPS tracker?"

"I don't know. Probably. Why?"

"If we get separated, I'll send in search-and-rescue."

"Very funny." She tsked. "Come on."

After moving down a center aisle, where they passed lamps, old toys and more ancient furniture, they found an older woman, somewhere in her late fifties or early sixties, he figured. She was still attractive and had short blond hair and brown eyes. In jeans and a thrift-store T-shirt, she was trim and friendly-looking.

"Erin." The woman's smile was warm. "Nice to see you."

"Hi, Aggie." She looked up at him. "Jack, this is Brewster's wife, Aggie."

"Ma'am." He shook the hand she held out and wondered how Erin knew her when he didn't.

As if she could read his mind, Erin said, "Aggie stops by the marina to drop off Brew's lunch when he forgets it."

"Which is pretty often," the other woman added.

"When she's there, Jack, you're mostly in hunker-down mode. Or being a hermit. Or both," Erin commented.

That sounded an awful lot like a challenge. She'd told him talking to people was fun and he should try it sometime. Now was his chance. He could be friendly and charming. It had happened once or twice before.

"It's nice to meet Brewster's better half. And it has to be said…he's a very lucky man."

"Why, thank you, Mr. Garner."

"Call me Jack." He smiled, just to show Erin he knew how.

"All right. Jack." She looked from Erin to him. "So, what brings you out of your cave today?"

The downside of a charm offensive was you had to be sociable and that meant chatting. He caught the expression in Erin's green eyes that dared him to keep this up. So, he would show her.

"As my assistant would tell you, I should be working, but I took time off to talk to Mrs. Miller's honors English class today about writing."

"Good for you, Jack." The woman nodded her approval. "Did they give you a hard time? I bet a big, strong guy like you didn't have any problem keeping them in line."

"Didn't have to. They seemed interested in what I had to say. Asked a lot of questions."

"That's wonderful."

"Speaking of questions, I have one. What is the Sunshine Fund?"

"It was Mayor Goodson-McKnight's idea." Aggie folded her arms over her chest. "It's an account funded by donations to help out a down-on-their-luck citizen or family. A kid who needs help paying for football equipment so he can participate in the sport. Someone out of work who needs groceries or money to pay utilities. The city council pays me to run the thrift store, accept and organize donations. But all proceeds above and beyond overhead go into the fund. In fact a lot of the money is raised by community events."

"Like the Halloween party?" Erin asked.

"Yes." Aggie nodded. "There's a small admittance fee and it's a potluck so there's very little operating cost. Folks have fun and money is raised for a good cause. A win-win."

"Noble undertaking," Jack agreed.

"You'll be there, won't you?"

"Affirmative." It would have been like saying no to Mrs. Santa Claus.

"Wonderful. You know it's a costume party," Aggie said.

"That's why we're here," he told her.

"Then you're going to want the clothes area," she suggested. "It's in the back right corner. And if you need any props beyond hats and jewelry, just ask."

"You can actually find stuff in here?" Jack was skeptical. "Specific items?"

"It may not look that way, but things are organized and I know where everything is."

"Understood."

"So, are you two going to do a couples costume? Romeo and Juliet? Caesar and Cleopatra? Beckett and Castle? He's that writer who solves crimes on that TV show. Since you're an author…" The older woman shrugged.

"I love that show," Erin said.

Jack was glad she fielded that because he was still trying to wrap his mind around the couples-costume remark. Why would she think that?

"We're just going to look around." Erin grinned, obviously enjoying his version of being a fish out of water.

"Have fun, you two."

In the back corner they found stands of old clothes, hats and coats. Erin started rummaging through the racks along with several other women. Since no one said hello, he was pretty sure she was not acquainted with them.

She pulled out a dress, then walked over to the headgear section. In front of a full-length mirror she put on a 1930s-era hat. Turning, she said, "I could be Bonnie Parker."

A young brunette looked up and checked her out. "That would work. And on the men's rack there's a pin-striped suit. You guys could go as Bonnie and Clyde."

Erin nodded and smiled at the other woman. "Thanks. I'll keep that in mind."

Over Jack's dead body. No pun intended.

The brunette drifted away but Little Miss Perky kept looking. She pulled a pink satin jacket out and said, "Sandy from the movie *Grease*."

A familiar redhead moved in from behind him and walked over to check it out. He didn't think Delanie Carlson ever left Bar None. "Hi, Jack."

"Who let you out?"

"As it happens, I'm the boss. And people who live in glass houses shouldn't throw stones. How did you give your computer the slip?" She smiled at Erin. "He hasn't scared you off yet?"

"I'm made of sterner stuff."

"Sassy." Delanie nodded at the pink jacket. "Then Sandy is perfect for you. All Jack needs is a black leather jacket, white T-shirt and a bucket of hair gel to be your Danny Zuko."

"What makes everyone think we're coordinating costumes?" His charm had one nerve left and this woman had picked a bad time to get on it.

"You're here together, aren't you?" Delanie asked. "That shouts couple to me. Just saying…"

Erin laughed but it sounded strained. "It's not like that. We work together. You could say we're friends. But nothing more."

"Whatever. None of my business." Delanie lifted a shoulder in a shrug.

"Seriously," Erin continued. "I won't be here that much longer."

Couples costumes did not a couple make. They worked together and it was a temporary situation. Yet another reminder was like a bucket of ice water and got his attention. It was easy to slip into complacency but also dangerous. To be a couple you had to live in the same town and they didn't. Geographic distance wasn't an insurmountable problem, but not the only one. It was impossible to be a couple by yourself. He wouldn't participate because he wasn't good at being anyone's significant other. Not even Erin's.

The Blackwater Lake community costume party was on the Saturday before Halloween. Erin dressed up as Sandy from *Grease* with the pink jacket, crisp white blouse and the tightest pair of black pants she owned since the thrift store was fresh out of leather ones. Go figure. Her hair was pulled up into a sassy ponytail and blond enough with the highlights.

Jack had pulled out his inner juvenile delinquent and put it on display. The leather jacket was battered. His white T-shirt stretched across his broad chest tight enough to make the Pink Ladies swoon. And he hadn't shaved, adding an element of danger to his Danny Zuko, a bad boy in a very good way.

He parked the jeep in the lot behind the community center, next door to city hall, where the mayor's office was located. Looking at Erin he said, "So, our deal is that when I'm bored to tears we can leave, right?"

"You won't be bored." Please, God, don't let him be bored. This was supposed to be good for him and if he ended up a wallflower it wouldn't be pretty.

"But if I am we can split." He waited for confirmation.

"There's going to be food, music, dancing. People. Remember them? You're going to have a great time."

"As you're so good at reminding me, I'm a hermit. Hermits know no one."

"*Hermit* might be an exaggeration." But not by a lot.

"No, it's on the mark." He was staring at the big building with light pouring out of the windows and people moving around inside. "A hermit, by definition, avoids large gatherings. We haven't been spotted. It would be easy to turn around and leave. No one would even notice—"

"Bite your tongue, Jack Garner. That's crazy talk. And, dare I say it? Cowardly."

"I can live with that."

Probably he could. He was a hero in the noblest sense and had served his country with distinction. There was nothing to prove. But she wanted this for him. "I already paid for our admittance."

"What if I pay you back?"

"Here's an idea. Take a risk. And look at it this way— when tonight is over you'll realize that no harm was done in this socialization experiment."

"What about my ego?"

"It's so big you won't even miss a little bit if you're dinged."

"Ouch." He opened the driver's side door. "This is a tough crowd. I think I'll take my chances with the hostiles."

"That's the spirit." She slid out, then opened the rear passenger door to retrieve the batch of four-cheese macaroni she'd made. "Love the optimism, by the way."

"Thanks." He was waiting at the front of the jeep for her. "Good talk."

"See? I proved you wrong. I am good for something. There was a time when you didn't want me here."

Spotlights on the outside of the building shone in his eyes, illuminating a sudden intensity. But it disappeared when he said in a teasing tone, "Now it's hard to picture Blackwater Lake without you in it."

Erin stumbled in her black heels but it wasn't about the uneven surface of the parking lot as much as his words.

Did he mean that or was it more to mess with her? Between that and the feel of his hand on her arm to steady her she was in a state that could best be described as flummoxed. When the buzzing in her head stopped she was going to ask whether or not he was serious, but by that time they were approaching the door. Putting the discussion on hold seemed prudent.

A woman Erin had never met was sitting at a table just inside the door. Face paint made it hard to tell her age and the black hair looked sprayed on. She was wearing an orange T-shirt with a spider and web on it and a headband with pumpkins sticking up.

She grinned at them. "Sandy and Danny. You guys look great. Name, please. I'll check my list."

"Erin Riley and Jack Garner."

"The writer." Her eyes grew as big as saucers and no reply from him was necessary since she babbled on. "I'm a big fan. Dory Carter." A little flustered, she glanced down and scanned the sheet of paper in front of her. "Here you are. I'll stamp you."

They held out their hands and came away with an inked pumpkin on the back.

"The table against the wall over there is for food," Dory said. "Just drop off your dish and have a great time. Happy Halloween."

"Thanks, Dory," she said.

The oblong-shaped room was big with long tables and folding chairs set up at one end. The walls had pictures of witches, ghosts and vampires. White cottony web with spiders caught in it was liberally spread over everything. Orange and black balloons decorated the tables. It was cheerful and festive. They took the casserole dish containing a double batch of four-cheese macaroni to the food table and Jack set it down. "Mission accomplished."

"Come on, Captain America, let's mingle." She snapped her fingers. "Now that would have been a fitting costume."

"I don't do tights."

"I'm not sure he does them, either." She pointed. "There's the sheriff. That's a good place to start being sociable. He's already your friend."

"April Kennedy is with him."

"Look at this as an opportunity to show her you're not a temperamental writer."

"I'm not."

"If you say so."

Side by side they threaded their way through the crowd to where the couple was standing. Will Fletcher was in his sheriff's uniform and his fiancée had on an orange jumpsuit.

"Hi," Erin greeted them. She looked at the man's khaki shirt and pants. "I thought costumes were mandatory. You're cheating."

"I'm on duty. Crowd control." He grinned down at the woman beside him. "And this is Shady Sadie, my prisoner."

"Prisoner of love," she said, grinning at him before looking them over. "And you guys look great."

"It's all her." Jack nodded in Erin's direction.

"Thanks goes to the thrift store. The Sunshine Fund is a little sunnier now."

Jack looked around the room that was getting more crowded all the time. "Is it always like this?"

"Yes," April said. "People in this town do holidays right and Halloween is neck and neck with Christmas as the favorite. Who doesn't love to get dressed up and be someone they're not?"

Erin gave Jack a look that warned him not to say that under protest *he* was dressed up and pretending to be someone he wasn't. His small smile said that's exactly what he'd planned to say but he got the message.

"There are some very creative costumes," April said, letting her gaze wander over the people closest to them. "And some…not so much. Seriously? A shirt that says *This is my costume*?"

"Nobody cares." Will was constantly looking, checking things out. "Mostly we just love a good excuse for a party."

Jack was watching the other man, alpha male to alpha male. "Must be hard on you having to work."

"Not so bad. I'm a trained observer and do it all the time whether I'm on the clock or not. This way my staff gets to relax and let their hair down. And tonight I get paid."

"And I get paid to take pictures." April removed a small camera from the pocket of her jumpsuit. "Let's get one of our local celebrity. Say cheese, you two."

Without warning, Jack pulled her into his arms and bent her back, as if getting ready to kiss her. There was a flash and Erin wasn't sure if it was the camera or his grin. Before she could decide, he stood up straight and brought her with him, keeping his arm around her waist. It was very coupley and nice. But she was pretty sure he was messing with her.

April was checking out the shot. "Good move, Jack. Great picture of you both."

"Happy to oblige."

"This one is going to make it into the newspaper," the photographer proclaimed.

"What?" Jack tensed a little.

April looked up. "Like I said, I get paid to take pictures. I do freelance work along with having my shop. The *Blackwater Lake Review Journal* pays me for any pictures they print. I hope it's okay to submit this one for consideration."

"Absolutely." The smile Jack aimed at the other woman oozed charm.

"Good." She snapped her fingers. "Speaking of that… There's someone you need to meet."

Erin watched her disappear into the crowd. "Where is she going?"

"No idea," Will answered. "It's always an adventure when you hang out with a creative personality. But you should be used to that."

Maybe. But she was resisting that feeling because hanging out with Jack was going to end sooner rather than later.

April reappeared with a nice-looking man in his thirties who was wearing a black Stetson, worn jeans, a long-sleeved snap-front shirt and boots. Best guess? This was a cowboy costume, although there were enough people who made their living on ranches around here that it was hard to tell.

"Jack, I want you to meet Logan Turner, owner, publisher and editor of our local paper. Logan, this is Jack Garner and his research assistant, Erin Riley."

"I'm a big fan of your work." Logan held out his hand. "It's a pleasure to meet you."

"Same here."

"Look, Jack…" He hesitated, then barreled on. "I'm just going to put this out there and feel free to tell me to go to hell. I know you don't do interviews. Although lack of promotion didn't seem to hurt the sales of your book any. But I was wondering if you'd make an exception and talk to me for an article. Now that you've put down roots here in Blackwater Lake."

"How do you know I have?"

Logan shrugged. "Heard about the talk you did for the high school kids."

Erin felt a knot in her stomach the size of Montana.

The last time someone with April mentioned his book he turned into an antisocial ass. The expression on his face didn't change but that meant nothing. She had no clue what was going through his mind. This request could come under the heading of being bored and make for a very short evening.

That would be a shame. The batch of mac and cheese she'd made was probably her best ever and she would have to leave before having any.

"What do you say?" Logan stood his ground.

"Okay."

The other man grinned. "I'll set it up."

"Let me know where and when," Jack said.

"Count on it." He looked at the food table. "I hope it's time to eat because I'm going to crash it now."

"Try the macaroni and cheese. It's Erin's best batch yet." Jack smiled at the look she shot him. "What? Someone had to take one for the team and taste it. Just to make sure it's okay for public consumption."

"Comfort food. Yum." April looked up at her fiancé. "Now I'm starving. Are you ready to eat?"

"Always."

The four of them headed over and picked up paper plates and utensils before checking out the variety of food. Somehow potlucks ended up with choices to make a nutritionally balanced meal. Green salad, fruit, potato salad, macaroni and cheese. Everyone raved about it when they sat together at one of the tables. People stopped by to say hello.

Lucy Bishop was friendly and seemed to have forgiven Jack for his snit. Delanie Carlson, who was probably the first friend he'd made, sat and chatted for a while. Brady and Olivia O'Keefe talked to Jack about designing his new website. Maggie Potter and her fiancé, Sloan Holden, slid chairs over and stayed to visit. Aggie and Brewster Smith stopped to admire their costumes and ended up sitting with them.

The best part was that Jack never once made noises about leaving because he was bored.

Chapter Twelve

The party broke up just after midnight and Jack drove the jeep out of the community center parking lot. If this was a fairy tale he would be in a pumpkin right now. Kind of appropriate for Halloween. And it was conspicuously quiet on the passenger side of this pumpkin so he waited for incoming. Some form of I-told-you-so. It didn't take long and he grinned when she cleared her throat.

"So, let's debrief," she began.

"Like a military operation?"

"Yes. Were you bored tonight?"

He knew one-word answers made her crazy and making this easy on her wasn't his plan. "No."

"At any point during the evening did you feel the urge to bail because you were not being intellectually challenged?"

"Does now count?"

"No. This is not bailing," she informed him. "It's called closing the place down."

"Then no." There was silence from the other seat. "What's wrong?"

"I forgot the question." She sounded a little tipsy.

"Then I'll remind you. You asked whether I felt the need to bail because I was bored."

"Right. Did you?"

"No."

"Isn't there something you want to tell me?" she asked.

"Many things." He knew what she wanted to hear and wasn't going to play.

"Don't make me hurt you, Jack."

He laughed. "Bring it."

"Okay. Watching you tonight was like seeing a butterfly escape the cocoon."

"Dramatic much?"

"It's not drama if you're dead serious. And I am. You opened up. Like peeling away another layer of an onion."

"Metaphors must be on sale tonight," he said wryly.

She ignored the jab and went on. "You were downright friendly in there. Could have knocked me over with a feather when you agreed to an interview for the paper."

"I'm always friendly."

There was a moment of stunned silence before she started to laugh. "Oh my God. That's too funny. The first time we met I thought you were going to pick me up bodily and throw me off the porch."

"I thought about it."

"Seriously?"

"Of course not," he said.

"Oh. I get it. That was to distract me, make me lose my train of thought before making my point. But I'm on to you." She scoffed. "You were charming and funny tonight. People like you and you made friends. It's a victory."

"One skirmish. That's all."

"It was more than that. I saw the way women were looking at you."

"Not interested." Because none of them was her. The thought popped into his mind and blew up like an improvised explosive device.

"Okay. Maybe that's pushing the socialization experiment too far." There was a *but* in the air. *Wait for it...* "But you seemed to get along really well with the guys."

"Seriously?"

"I'm always serious." She was thinking. He could feel it.

"Let me list those guys for you," she said. "There was the sheriff. Sloan Holden and his cousin, Burke. Maggie's brother Brady. And don't tell me you were putting up a front because this is me. I know you're not that good an actor."

"They seem like stand-up guys," he admitted.

"And?"

"What?" He wished she would just drop it.

"Just tell me I was right and you had fun." There was frustration in her tone.

"Now whose ego needs a jump start?"

"Jack—"

He laughed. "Okay."

"So you're glad you went," she prompted.

"Don't push it—"

There was a big sigh from her side of the car. "Why do you make it so hard? Why can't you just give it up and admit that I was right? Would it be so bad to open up a little?"

"Because I'm a warrior, trained to resist."

He was teasing, but the words stuck in his head and wouldn't let go. Once burned, you pushed back and established a safe zone to keep from being hurt again.

Outside the Blackwater Lake city limit it was pitch-black without the commercial lights of town. There was nothing but darkness beyond the range of the jeep's headlights. They were alone. She couldn't see his face; he couldn't see hers. And suddenly he wanted to tell her why he'd closed himself off.

"Do you remember when you asked me if I had a girlfriend or was married?"

"Yes. You said there wasn't anyone."

"Not now." Except for the feelings rattling around inside of him for Erin and she didn't fit into either of those categories. It felt like a lie to leave them unsaid, but that's the only way he knew to protect her. "I was married once."

"So, you're divorced." She wasn't asking.

"I think that's what 'married once but not now' means."

He gave her a wry look and didn't know whether or not she could see it in the dim interior.

"Right. Of course." She blew out a long breath. "It's just that was unexpected. More peeling of the onion. My comment was meant to encourage an exchange of information. And I'm officially babbling. Please feel free to interrupt me at any time and continue peeling the onion, so to speak."

She made him smile, which was a minor miracle, what with the dark memories he'd voluntarily given up. "I met a woman in a bar."

"Not a surprise. Apparently that's where you meet all your friends," she said dryly.

"She wasn't a friend. Do you want to hear this or not?"

"Sorry. I'm listening. Please continue."

Jack gripped the steering wheel a little tighter. "It turned into a thing pretty fast. We got married before my first deployment. There's something about facing danger that makes you want to have someone waiting for you when you get back."

"How long were you married?"

"Ten years. But only because I was deployed a lot. When I left the army she left me."

"I'm sorry, Jack. That must have hurt you a lot."

The genuine sympathy in her voice touched him almost as if she'd put her hand on his arm. It was like healing salve to an open wound. "I'm over it."

"Are you?"

"What does that mean?" Stupid question. He knew what she was getting at and was sorry he'd started this in the first place. "Never mind. My question was rhetorical."

"Mine wasn't. You have a point and I'd like to hear what it is."

Jack slowed the jeep for a left-hand turn onto Lakeshore Drive. They were almost home. His home, not hers. She was temporary.

In a few moments the lights from the porch and the marina beyond came into view. He pulled up beside Erin's rental car and parked. When he switched off the ignition there was an eerie silence.

Erin undid her seat belt and angled her knees toward him. "Jack? What is it you wanted to say?"

Without answering he released his own seat belt and got out of the car, then headed for the porch. Sounds behind him indicated she was hot on his heels. She caught up to him just as he unlocked the front door and opened it. Harley barked and bounded outside. He circled them, completely joyful that his humans had returned.

This human wanted to exfiltrate the situation ASAP. He pushed the door wider and started to walk into the house.

"Wait, Jack." This time she did put her hand on his arm.

He wanted to strip off the leather jacket and feel the gentle touch on his bare skin. "Let it go. Trust me, I'm no hero."

"Isn't that for me to decide?"

Who was he kidding? From the moment she first showed up on this very porch she'd proven she wasn't a quitter. There was no reason to believe that had changed. "You're not going to let this slide, are you?"

"Not until you get to the point."

"Okay. Don't forget you asked for it." He saw the concern on her face and it was too damn close to pity for his liking. *Get this over with.* "I was a teenage delinquent. Big disappointment to my mother. I was a crappy husband and my marriage was a bust. So I was two for two. And failure doesn't sit well with me. My point is that I'm no good at relationships, so avoiding them is a win."

"You only fail when you fail to try," she said so softly he almost didn't hear.

"Did you get that from a motivational seminar?"

"From my weight-loss support group, actually. But you were saying…"

"I'm only good at being a soldier. I don't want to let anyone else down. The best way to achieve that goal is keeping to myself."

"Cut yourself a break, Jack. Exercise those friendship muscles. Just do it. You might surprise yourself."

He didn't get her. He just didn't. Anyone else would have given up on him by now. Thrown in the towel and said good riddance. But she was hanging in there and it was both annoying and astonishing. "Why is it so important to you that I insert myself into this town?"

"Because I don't want you to be all alone when I'm gone." Her gaze searched his face as she caught her top lip between her teeth.

The words were like an explosion in his heart and looking at her mouth tore his willpower to shreds. He wanted her more than his next breath and talking was optional. After pulling her inside and shutting the door, Jack took her in his arms and kissed her. He poured all the feelings there were no words for into the kiss…making it one eloquent kiss. Show, don't tell.

Erin melted against him like chocolate left out in the sun. Or ice cream in the oven. He was right. A sale on metaphors tonight. A *fire* sale. This was a bad idea, but when it felt so good how was that wrong?

Jack tasted like pumpkin cinnamon spice—the cake he'd eaten at the potluck. His lips were soft, warm and full of temptation, but part of her was still resisting, right up until he tenderly freed her hair from the ponytail and let it fall over her shoulders. He wasn't fooling around. Well, he was, in the best possible way.

When she stood on tiptoe and settled her arms around his neck, he put his hands under her butt and easily lifted her. She wrapped her legs around his waist and he headed for the hallway where the bedrooms were located. His? Hers? Erin didn't care just as long as it had a bed. She kissed his lips, cheek, neck and earlobe.

The last kiss touched a nerve and he groaned, tightening his arms around her. "You're playing with fire."

"Do I have your attention?"

"Oh, yeah."

He was breathing hard and she hoped it wasn't the extra pounds that refused to budge from her thighs. "I'm too heavy, Jack."

He stopped underneath the hall light and his eyes glittered with intensity. "Let's get one thing straight."

"If this is going to be a long discussion, you might want to put me down first. Your back will thank you."

Very slowly he shook his head. "About that weight-loss support group you mentioned? Waste of time. You don't need it."

"Really?"

"Affirmative." A slow, sexy smile curved up the corners of his mouth. "Your body is perfect."

"Then you have pretty low standards. My legs are too short and—"

His mouth quickly and efficiently stopped the flow of her words and had warmth pooling in her belly. And then he was on the move again, turning right into his bedroom. He stopped beside the king-size bed and set her on her feet before sliding his hands to her waist. He pulled the white blouse from the waistband of her black pants. His fingers brushed the bare, sensitive skin beneath and a moan escaped.

It was like throwing kerosene on a campfire. She pushed at his shirt and her pink jacket ended up on the floor beside his black leather one. In ten seconds flat they were naked and he tugged her to him, settling his big palms on her rear end again. He lifted, letting her wrap her legs around him before bracing a knee on the mattress and gently setting her in the center.

The muscles in his arms and chest flexed, making her want to swoon, so it was a good thing she was already down. He reached into the nightstand drawer and felt around before finally pulling out a condom.

He frowned at her laugh. "Something funny?"

"Who knew condoms are like smoke detectors. You have one in every room." She smiled up at him. "Not complaining, just saying…"

"You talk too much."

"It's a flaw. I'm working on it—"

His mouth silenced her for the second time as he kissed her thoroughly. By the time he moved his attention to her neck, then lower to her breast, she was too caught up in the delicious sensations to say a word.

Jack nibbled his way over her abdomen, hip and thigh until she was writhing with need, her body begging for release. He moved his body over hers, then thrust gently inside and she arched her hips to meet him. Her breathing grew more labored as he slowly moved in and out, taking her higher.

Without warning the tension inside her stretched and snapped, sending shock waves of exquisite pleasure thorough every part of her. She splintered into a thousand points of light and he held her until she came back together.

He rolled to his back, taking her with him so that she was on top. She rested her cheek on his chest, delighting in the way his heart thundered beneath her ear. When she shifted her hips against him, once then twice, he groaned and went still, wrapping her tightly against him while he found his own release. They stayed locked together for a very long time.

The last thing Erin wanted to do was move. She'd never felt this safe with a man, not even with her fiancé before he got sick. That thought opened the flood gates and let the guilt flow unchecked. It also opened the door to all the things she didn't want to face.

"I have to go—"

Jack didn't loosen his hold. "Don't leave on my account."

The warmth of his skin and the security of his arms were intoxicating, like a drug she craved. All the more reason she needed to break the contact.

"Let me go, Jack."

He brushed a big hand down her back before rolling over with her beneath him. Gently he touched his mouth to hers. "I'm going to get up—"

"Okay, then I can—"

He touched a finger to her lips. "I'll be right back. I don't want you to move."

"Okay." But she couldn't look at him.

"Promise, Erin." He nudged her chin up, just enough so that their gazes locked and he could see into hers. "Give me your word."

Good grief he was stubborn. It was a strength and a flaw. Right up there with being too perceptive because she'd planned to make her escape. But clearly it was important to him that she didn't.

She nodded. "I'll stay. Promise."

When he left her and went into the bathroom she felt exposed in so many ways. Pulling the sheet up over her nakedness only helped a little. Before she had time to blow everything out of proportion he was back and lifting that sheet to slide into bed beside her. Then he put an arm under her and folded her next to his warm body. It was a wonderful place to be.

"So, I was thinking—"

"Uh-oh. That can't be good. You might want to shut that down ASAP." She was joking. Mostly.

"Just hear me out."

"Oddly enough, those words aren't making me feel any better."

"Keep an open mind."

"Still not making me feel better," she said, hoping he wouldn't say whatever was on his mind. Somehow she knew it was going to complicate things even more than they already were.

"Sometimes I wish you weren't quite so verbal." The beginnings of frustration tinged his words.

"It's a gift."

"And a curse." But he settled his chin on the top of her

hair. "The thing is, I don't see any reason you can't move into my bed."

Erin's heart skipped a beat, then started up again, pounding very hard. She didn't know how to respond to that. Saying nothing seemed the best way to keep from saying something wrong.

"Or I'll move into your bed," he offered.

That's how he'd interpreted her silence?

"For the duration of our collaboration." He waited for an answer that didn't come. Obviously he noted her less-than-enthusiastic reaction to his suggestion. "Erin?"

"I heard you."

"It makes sense if you think about it." He was going into close-the-deal mode. "We like each other. We're friends."

With benefits. But she kept that thought to herself.

"There's no reason we shouldn't enjoy each other for the next couple of weeks. Until this joint venture is over. What do you say?"

"No."

"Good, I—" The single word seemed to penetrate and he said, "What?"

"Negative on moving into your bed or mine."

She should slip out of his arms now and try to pull her dignity together to make a graceful exit. Or escape. The second option would be more accurate. But she wanted to hang on to this intimacy just a little longer.

"Is it necessary for me to point out that this is the second time we've had sex?"

"I'm well aware of that," she said.

"Okay." Absently he rubbed a strand of her hair between his fingers. "The first time you could chalk it up to…impulsiveness."

"Now who's being verbal. This is very uncharacteristic of you, Jack." The rumble of his laugh vibrated in his chest, tickling her cheek.

"But the second time it's more difficult to make a case for spontaneity. It's leaning toward a pattern," he pointed out.

"I reject the word *pattern*. It comes under the heading of 'moment of weakness.'"

"Twice," he reminded her. "And that tips into pattern territory if you ask me."

"No one asked."

"Erin—"

She sat up and slid away from him. "Look, Jack, we know what this is and isn't. In the long run it's better not to take that step. I've learned not to make decisions in haste."

Before he could say anything else that might weaken her resolve, she got out of bed, gathered up her clothes and left his room. She scurried across the hall into her own and shut the door firmly behind her.

Holding her breath, she waited for him to knock. To follow her and try to change her mind, part of her hoping he wouldn't let her go that easily.

But there was nothing. Only silence.

And when there was silence her mind had the freedom to work overtime. She wasn't ashamed of sleeping with him. But how was she ever going to face him in the morning?

Chapter Thirteen

The next morning when Erin didn't show up for their status meeting by five minutes after nine Jack was officially concerned. Last night he'd had probably the best sex of his life. He would freely admit that blood flow to his brain hadn't yet returned to normal when he suggested changing their sleeping arrangements. It was quite possible he hadn't made it clear that sex wasn't the reason. Not the only one, anyway. He was a guy after all.

But he wanted her close. The smell of her skin, the warmth of her body. Something about her made everything brighter, more peaceful, and God knew there hadn't been enough peace in his life.

If he'd said any of that she would have thought he was crazy. Or laughed at him waxing poetic, which might just have been worse. Instead, she gave him a negative and told him she'd learned not to make hasty decisions. He wasn't

used to hearing no, but ego had nothing to do with anything. At least not much.

What made him uneasy was that Erin was nothing if not
prompt. And stubborn. She'd gone to the mat for her stupid morning meeting. Until she hadn't shown up, he didn't
realize how much he'd started looking forward to seeing
her for those few minutes after breakfast, before he started
working on the book. The one he wrote during the day.

Breakfast had been simple this morning. Eggs, potatoes, toast, fruit, coffee. But the woman who'd cooked it
was stewing about something and no work was getting
done until he made sure she was okay.

"Harley, walk."

The dog yipped out a bark and scurried over to the office door, waiting expectantly, giving no indication that
he'd noticed their walk usually happened a lot later in the
day.

Jack picked up his pet and scratched beneath the furry
chin. "I don't think I've ever told you how much I appreciate the fact that you aren't complicated."

The dog licked his face.

"You're welcome. Let's go find Erin." One bark sig-
naled the animal's solidarity with that plan.

He carried Harley down the stairs and set him on the
porch, knowing he would take off running. Before following, Jack took a quick look in the house, then made sure
her rental car was still parked beside the jeep. It wasn't
gone, which meant she was on foot as he'd suspected. Private eye Mac Daniels had nothing on him.

Jack started jogging down the path beside the lake to
catch up to his dog. About half a mile past the marina he
saw Erin, down on one knee scratching and rubbing Harley, who was in doggy heaven. Not a surprise. What was

not to like? There was no telling whether or not they'd caught her returning.

Jack slowed to a walk, then stopped beside them. "Hi."

She didn't look up but kept lavishing attention on the little beast she clearly had changed her mind about. "Who's a good dog?"

"You didn't used to think so."

"That was before I got to know him."

Jack waited for more. With Erin there always was, but not this time. Her silence was like the quiet in a war zone before the world exploded all to hell. Waiting was the worst part. This time he could call the shots.

"Now that you know him, what makes you like him?"

"He's loyal, obedient, understanding and loves unconditionally. He doesn't expect anything in return."

"So looks has nothing to do with it."

"It's all about character," she agreed.

Jack had the feeling she wasn't talking about the dog anymore. "They say dogs are a reflection of their owners."

"Seems like I've heard that." She looked up then. "I'm not so sure about that in his case. He's not especially abrasive or short—" She laughed when the *he* in question batted her with a paw to let her know he wanted more attention. "That is, he's short but in a noble way."

"He lets you know what he needs. Never have to guess." Last night for instance. She'd implied what they'd done was a moment of weakness. A mistake. He couldn't disagree more and it bugged him that she thought so.

"It's a good quality," she said. "Along with honesty—"

Jack heard the catch in her voice and felt the emotion of it without a clue what was going on. There was a time when her perkiness annoyed him, but not now. He'd give anything for her to challenge him with words and the fire in her green eyes that he'd come to expect when she was making a point.

"What's wrong, Erin?"

"Just tired, I guess."

Frustration tightened in his gut. He was no expert on women, but was pretty sure *tired* was the same as saying nothing was bothering her. "I've seen you tired and this isn't it."

"Really, I'm fine."

He hated that word. Every man on the planet hated that word when a woman looked the way she did and said it in the tone she'd used. Both were clues that she was the exact opposite of fine.

Jack picked up a stick and got the dog's attention. He threw it and the animal tensed, waiting for permission. "Harley, fetch."

The dog took off like a shot, eager to obey the order. If only it was that easy to understand this woman. "You're not okay. Or you wouldn't have missed the nine-o'clock status meeting. The one you insisted on, in case you forgot."

"I didn't." She stood up and met his gaze. "It doesn't seem all that important anymore."

Negative, he thought. Maybe she didn't realize, but that was when he fleshed out and fine-tuned the scene he was working on. He'd taken her suggestion to write about Harley and it had gone in a different direction, one that would never see the light of day. That writing happened at night and was personal in a way Mac Daniels would never be.

Bottom line: their status-meeting chats were responsible for moving the book forward and it was almost finished.

"You're wrong," he said. "They are important."

"I stand corrected. My bad." She looked down for a moment. "Let's go back and we can talk about the book on the way."

"Forget the book."

"I can't. It's my job," she reminded him.

"And it's my career. But I didn't follow you because of some damn arbitrary schedule."

"Then why did you follow me?"

"Because—" He blew out a breath. "I made a suggestion last night after we—"

"Slept together." She met his gaze directly.

He remembered the first day she'd walked with him and the look on her face when he'd challenged whether or not she could do the job without looking at him as if she wanted him to take her to bed. She sure wasn't looking at him that way right now because of what happened last night. And if he had to guess, he would say she looked ashamed. He had to fix that.

"We slept together," he said. "You need to know that meant a lot to me."

"I appreciate you saying that, Jack." The corners of her mouth curved up but it was a sad smile.

Where was the GPS when you really needed it? He was in uncharted territory and could use some coordinates to head him in the right direction. "Do I need to apologize? If I was out of line—"

"Stop. This isn't about you, Jack."

"Well, it can't be about you. You're practically perfect. Never abrasive. A little short maybe, but no one can hold your DNA against you." He was trying to get a smile out of her but with zero results so far. "Look, you're the one who stuck it out with your fiancé after a cancer diagnosis. I don't know any woman who, under those circumstances, would keep the ring. But you did. Until the end."

"Stop," she said again. "I'm not that nice for staying when he got sick. I'm an impostor."

He must be missing a piece of this puzzle. "Let me get

this straight. He was dying and you didn't leave. You loved him until the end. How is that a bad thing?"

She looked more guilt-ridden with every word and winced at the word *love*. "The truth is I wasn't in love with him. I realized it and was trying to figure out how to break the news that my feelings had changed when he got even worse news. I loved him as a friend and couldn't walk out when he needed me."

"Okay. Still not seeing the bad."

"More than once he brought up the subject of a small wedding, but I always came up with some lame excuse. Wait until chemo was over and he would be in remission. Then he was too weak and didn't bring it up anymore." She shrugged. "On paper we were a perfect match. Both teachers who wanted to see the world. That was about having something in common, not love. I jumped in too soon when I accepted his proposal. If he hadn't gotten sick I would have broken it off."

The bleak look in her eyes made Jack want to pull her into his arms, but he was afraid if he touched her she would shatter. "First, you're being too hard on yourself."

"You're wrong, I—"

He held up a hand to stop her. "You said what you had to and now it's my turn."

"Okay."

"Second, let me give you a guy's perspective. It would have been more dishonest to take vows. He probably knew the truth and was pretending, too, because it would have been harder being alone. You call it dishonest, I call it courageous."

There was moisture in her eyes but she blinked it away. "Maybe someday I'll share your opinion."

"Believe it. I do."

"About last night—" She caught the corner of her lip between her teeth then met his gaze. "I like you, Jack."

"So you said last night."

"That was completely honest. With my fiancé I jumped in too fast and stayed for the wrong reason. If I moved into your bed, that would be jumping in too fast when we both know I'm not staying. As mistakes go, that would be the bigger one."

As opposed to the mistake of having sex.

Jack had to admit she had him there. He didn't like it but she had him. Before he could think of a comeback, she nodded and walked past him, heading back to the house. Harley followed her and Jack couldn't blame him.

This was a sneak preview of what he would get on her last day with him. Watching her leave. He didn't much like the view. And now there was the devil to pay. He found out what was eating her, that she felt dishonest for not telling a dying man she wasn't in love with him.

Oddly enough that made Jack trust her more. And want her in his bed even more than that. The problem with what she'd confessed was that it took the wanting to a level he'd never experienced before. A place it wasn't safe to be.

It was entirely possible that he wouldn't survive Erin Riley after all.

Erin put the finishing touches on breakfast and thought about Jack calling her out on missing their meeting yesterday. She had to own taking the coward's way out. It was always the best course of action to face an issue head-on, but she'd headed in the opposite direction. Then he'd tracked her down, kept her honest. Confessing her guilt about not loving Garrett seemed to lift the burden that she'd carried since his death. Jack's words gave her absolution and she would always be grateful. She'd also told him she wouldn't share his bed because she had to leave.

He hadn't tried to change her mind.

What she felt for him was much more than just *like* and if he'd only said "don't go" it would have been enough. But he hadn't. Still, the air was cleared and things went back to normal. Whatever that was. Jack acted as if nothing happened so she would, too. She only had two weeks left so there was no point in rocking the boat.

"What's for breakfast?"

Speaking of the devil, there he was in the doorway. Because winter was coming fast, this morning he was wearing a long-sleeved black T-shirt with his jeans. It was a good look, but then he didn't have a bad one. When he was near, her heart pounded erratically no matter what he was wearing. Or not wearing. Maybe she should rethink that offer to share his bed…

"Erin?"

"Hmm?"

"Breakfast?" He moved closer and looked at what she was doing. "French toast."

"You're quite the detective."

"Not me, but I'm writing one."

"How's that going?" She dragged a slice of bread through the egg mixture and dropped it in the frying pan. The grease was a little hotter than she thought and it splattered. "Whoa—"

"Careful." He hovered, ready to intervene. "You okay?"

"Fine. Watch out or you'll get burned."

"Too late."

Instantly her gaze lifted to his, but he quickly shuttered any expression and she had no idea what he'd meant. Burned by his wife? By her? Or he'd literally felt splashes of hot oil just now. Change of subject.

She'd heard him in his office again last night. He was putting in a lot of time, a good sign about significant progress on his sequel.

She added three more slices of bread to the frying pan. "So, how's Mac Daniels these days?"

"I'll save that for the status meeting. You'll be there, right?"

"Wouldn't miss it." Not again.

She had already put the bottle of syrup on the table along with cut-up fruit. When the toast was evenly browned and crispy, she put a slice on her plate and the rest on Jack's. After handing them to him, she grabbed the platter of bacon. "Let's eat."

"I'm starved."

He always was. She was going to miss cooking for him—because he seemed to appreciate good food. Going back to meals for one was a sad, lonely and pathetic thought so she gave herself permission to run away just this once and made a conscious decision not to face it until she had to.

Erin sat down across from him and picked up her fork and knife. She cut a bite and chewed thoughtfully. "The weather is turning cold."

"You're not in Phoenix anymore."

"I noticed." She spooned some fruit on her plate. "What is it like here in the winter?"

"Cold. Snow. Tourists come for ski season." He shrugged.

"There will probably be more people now with the new hotel opening and the condos for sale near the mountain." She got all the news when shopping for groceries in town. "The newspaper is full of information about business expansion."

"That reminds me. Logan Turner called. I'm going to meet him later for the interview."

"You should let Cheryl know. That will make her happy."

Jack picked up a crispy piece of bacon and there was a twinkle in his eyes. "Maybe we should see how it goes before I tell my editor. If he critiques my characterization of women or talks about the next book it won't be pretty."

"You are many things, Jack, but dumb as dirt is not one of them. I believe you're capable of learning from your—"

"Mistakes?" One dark eyebrow lifted.

"I was going to say missteps."

"Same thing."

"But it sounds so much better. You can trust me on that," she teased.

"Yeah." The words pushed the laughter from his expression and replaced it with a smoky intensity.

"Do you want me there for the interview?"

"To keep me on the straight and narrow?"

"Moral support," she said to clarify.

"It's not technically in your job description, but…yeah, I'd appreciate it if you had my back."

"Of course I do."

While they talked he ate and finished all of his French toast. "Did I mention that this is really good?"

"No." The unexpected compliment from this particular man made her warm and gooey inside. "But thanks. I'm glad you like it."

Because there wouldn't be many more. Erin didn't say that out loud, but the thought stayed in the air between them.

They finished their coffee, but it seemed to take longer than usual. Then she glanced at the time and reluctantly stood and grabbed their plates.

"Time to get to work."

He nodded. "I'll go upstairs and get organized."

"I'll be there by nine," she said.

"Promises, promises." He grinned, then turned and left the kitchen. Moments later the front door closed.

Without moving Erin stared at the place where he'd just been standing. She felt blinded by the brightness of that smile, so different from the hard-faced man he'd been the first time they met. This man was going to leave a mark on her heart.

But there was no time to dwell on what she couldn't change. As quickly as possible she did the dishes then wiped down the kitchen table and counters. When all was as shiny and bright as Jack's smile, she went out the front door and up the stairs to his office.

After knocking once she went inside and saw him behind his desk. She saluted and said, "Reporting for duty, sir."

The corners of his mouth curved up. "The salute needs work."

"So does this room." She frowned at the stacks of paper on his desk and file folders placed haphazardly on every flat surface, including the floor. Had it been this bad yesterday when she came up here after their conversation? She wasn't sure. Apparently that talk had put her in a fog, but she'd bet that it was now officially worse than she'd ever seen. He must have been very busy last night. "You call this organized?"

Jack calmly surveyed the chaos surrounding him. "I know where everything is."

"Hmm." She settled her hands on her hips. "It doesn't strike you as the tiniest bit hypocritical that you were skeptical when Aggie said she knew where everything in the thrift store was?"

"No."

"Of course not." She sighed.

"Don't worry about it."

She moved closer. "Someone has to. How in the world do you concentrate in here?"

"One way to look at this is motivation to be in a world of my own creation."

"I hope your imaginary world is tidier than this one," she said ruefully. "Seriously, it must take you forever to find anything?"

"At this point in the book I don't need to. All the research is in the manuscript and I scroll through as necessary."

"Then why not put it away?"

"No reason. Habit. My process." He leaned his forearms on the desk. "So, are we done with this topic? Mac is in crisis."

"He's not the only one," she muttered.

"I heard that."

"Sorry." She moved a pile of folders to the floor in order to sit in her customary chair facing the desk. "Is he trying to decide whether to go after the dirty bomb or the bad guy?"

"No. He's thinking he made a mistake hiring someone to answer the phones in his new office."

"Since he just set up shop, I'm guessing it doesn't yet look like an office supply store threw up in it."

"Focus." He was enjoying this.

"Okay. What is he questioning about his hire? Is she young? Too young for him? Old? Experienced or not? Pretty? A temptation? In danger?"

"Wow. I'm almost sorry I said anything." He sat back, looking shell-shocked. "All of that off the top of your head?"

"Yeah. That's my job." She crossed one leg over the

other. "The thing is you need to make some decisions about…what's her name?"

He thought for a moment. "Let's call her Winnie."

"Short for Winifred? Seriously? Because you don't like her in particular? Or women in general. No offense to anyone with the name."

"Watch it. There's that whole characterization-of-women thing. The name is arbitrary."

"True, but what you call her can define character."

"Point taken." He rubbed his hands over his face. "So, in your opinion are there any other things I should think about for Winnie?"

"Is she going to be a recurring character? Does Mac have a history with her? Maybe she's a down-on-her-luck stranger with no skills that Mac hired out of the goodness of his heart."

"He doesn't have a heart," Jack said wryly.

She grinned. "Her life might be an open book or there could be skeletons in her closet."

"My head is spinning—"

"Maybe she's an ex-con who did time for manslaughter. Or she—"

He held up a hand to stop her. "Hold it."

"All I'm saying is she can be as simple or multilayered as you want. Just don't limit yourself with too many hard-and-fast facts if you decide that she'll be a recurring character."

He blew out a breath and stood, then started to pace. "That's a lot to think about."

"No pressure, but this is going to be a long-running series. The direction you go is important."

"Yeah. I can see that." He stopped and met her gaze. "I'm going for a run."

She stood to face him. "I didn't mean to complicate this for you."

"No. You're right. I just need to clear my head before it explodes. I won't be long."

"Is there anything you want me to research?"

"Yeah, now that you mention it. Classic literary secretaries. To avoid minefields, better known as clichés. Meet me back here in an hour."

"Roger that."

He grinned again, then went out the door with Harley hot on his heels.

Erin walked downstairs, set up her laptop on the kitchen table and pulled up what she could find on TV and movie secretaries or executive assistants. After an hour, she went back upstairs and knocked once before entering. Jack wasn't at his desk.

"Hello?"

There was no answer, which told her he hadn't returned yet. She'd printed out a lot of research pages for him and looked, without success, for an uncluttered place to put it. Temptation to tidy up his office had her fingers itching even though she remembered what he'd said that very first morning after she'd arrived. About a man's office being sacred. But an hour ago he'd said he didn't need any of this stuff so where was the harm?

She wouldn't do much. Just the little table by his desk. She took the files on top and put them neatly in the corner filing cabinet. There were loose papers underneath and she rifled through them, some of which were drawings. Of a dog that looked a lot like Harley. Jack was creative with more than just words.

Beneath the stack of drawings was another file labeled Adventures of Harley the Wonder Dog. Flipping through it she saw a compilation of charming stories that could only be targeted for children. Tales of a Chinese crested dog who compels a young boy to confront bullying. Other ones about bravery, friendship and loyalty. The writing was completely captivating. And that's the reason she never heard Jack open the office door.

"What the hell are you doing?"

Chapter Fourteen

"Jack—" Heart pounding, Erin stared at the man in the doorway. "I didn't hear you come in."

"Obviously. I repeat—what the hell are you doing with my stuff?"

She glanced at the file in her hand, the one she'd been so absorbed in that she didn't know he was there. "I did the research and printed out a bunch of information. You'd be surprised how much material there is on fictional secretaries." She was babbling. "Anyway, there was no place to put it."

"So you decided to read my private file?" His eyes narrowed and a muscle jerked in his jaw.

Some part of her mind registered that he'd taken a shower after running. His hair was damp and he'd changed into worn jeans and another long-sleeved T-shirt with ARMY in bold black letters on the front. It was as if someone had correctly dressed him for a movie scene. He was in full warrior mode and so not happy.

"You make it sound as if this was premeditated," she said. "It wasn't like that."

"I don't care how it was. The fact is you're looking at something that I didn't give you permission to read."

"The fact is," she countered, "you haven't given me permission to read very much of anything."

"So you went rogue, behind my back, to read this? That's not even part of your job description."

"Okay. Then tell me what it is."

"Nothing."

"Oh, please, Jack. You were an elite soldier trained to remain calm in combat situations when the average person would freak out and come unglued. But you're unglued now over this?" Defiantly she held up the file. "Don't insult my intelligence and tell me it's nothing."

"Don't insult mine by claiming what you're doing is cleaning up." His hands balled into fists at his sides. "You're looking through my stuff. That's called snooping."

"I was putting things in order," she said, defending herself. "Then I snooped."

She was hoping a confession laced with humor would bring his intensity down a notch, but couldn't have been more wrong. He looked angrier, if that was possible. More disturbing was how clipped his voice had been and the fact that now he wasn't saying anything at all. Since she'd first arrived he'd gone from a man of few words to downright chatty. He actually bantered with her, which was her favorite thing. But he wasn't doing it now.

"Jack, this is the truth… I was rearranging the stack of papers beside your desk and I saw this file—Adventures of Harley the Wonder Dog. How was I supposed to resist that? I was curious. So sue me. I read them and the stories are wonderful."

He simply stared at her.

"Every one has a message, a lesson, a take-away. For instance, the little boy with no friends that Harley latches on to, paving the way with other kids. Or the child who's being bullied, then rescued by a small, funny-looking dog." His expression didn't soften. If anything it got darker. "The last one was a real heart-tugger. The boy without a dad who brings Harley home and hides him from his mom—"

"Enough." The tone was razor-sharp.

Erin would have stopped anyway because of the "aha" moment. The light went on. "The little boy in all these stories is you."

"Right," he said sarcastically.

"I suggested you do stream-of-consciousness writing as a creative exercise and even told you it could be about Harley. You took my advice. This is what you've been working on so late every night."

"That's a stretch."

"I don't think so. It makes sense. The covert midnight sessions and your reaction right now prove I'm right. And you're acting as if I stole something from you."

"Your words."

"You're twisting them." Erin shook her head. "The thing is, you claimed not to be good at anything except being a soldier and it has to be said. You're wrong. I love these stories. And I love you."

Erin hadn't planned to say the last part but she'd never meant anything more. It was the honest truth. The only part she wished she could take back was Jack's reaction to hearing what was in her heart. It didn't seem possible, but he looked even more furious. Any second she expected his eyes to turn red and shoot fire.

He didn't move a muscle, until he did. Without warning, he crossed the space between them and took the file out of her hand. With a take-this look, he dropped it in the trash by the desk. "That's cleaning up."

"No, Jack. You need to send these to your agent. To Cheryl—"

He backed up several steps, as if he couldn't stand being so close to her. "I can't work with anyone I can't trust."

No, she thought. *I'm not ready to leave. Don't do it. Don't say it.* "Your editor hired me. You can't do this."

"Watch me." He moved to the door and opened it. "I'm taking my dog for a walk. Don't be here when I get back."

"No, Jack. Calm down—"

"Harley—"

For the first time Erin noticed the dog standing between them. He'd been so quiet and now she could see that the animal knew something was very wrong. He didn't react to the four-letter word that normally made him quiver with excitement. But after whining sadly and a last look at her, he followed Jack out the door.

Erin took the hesitation to mean the little guy cared about her and it was some comfort. Not much, but some.

She'd never been fired before. Certainly not by the man she was in love with. But he'd been quite clear and left her no choice. She was only here for the work and he refused to deal with her during the remainder of her contract. There was nothing left but for her to go.

The file in the trash caught her eye and she reached down to fish it out. She pressed the cardboard folder and its contents against her and whispered to the empty room, "No, Jack, that's cleaning up."

It didn't take Erin long to pack her things and load them in her rental car. She fought the urge to hang around until Jack returned from the walk, to try to change his mind. She didn't because he was in no mood to listen and, frankly, another rejection from him would destroy her.

So, with a heavy heart and a last look at the house and marina, she drove away from it and pulled out onto Lakeshore Drive. It must have been her state of shock, or muscle memory, but somehow she ended up in town. To get to the airport a hundred miles away, she needed to go through Blackwater Lake anyway.

The car needed gas and it wouldn't hurt to pick up a sandwich. The odds of her getting hungry any time in the foreseeable future were slim, what with a knot the size of a Toyota in her stomach. But she forced herself to be practical, even though every instinct she had was advising her to curl into the fetal position.

After filling up the gas tank she stopped at Bar None. It was sort of on the way out of town, at least that's what she told herself. The truth was darker and really more stupid than she'd have given herself credit for. Anyone here would know Jack because this was where he'd made his first friends. And she had an overwhelming need to unburden herself.

She went inside and hesitated, letting her eyes adjust to the dim interior. As it happened the place was empty, except for owner Delanie Carlson. She was standing behind the bar polishing glasses.

Erin walked over and sat on a stool. "Hi."

"Hey, yourself." The other woman looked at the door as if expecting it to open. "You alone?"

Completely, Erin thought, pain slicing through her. "Yes. I'd like to order a sandwich and cup of coffee. To go."

"You mean two, right?"

"No. Just the one." Only that morning she'd thought how lonely cooking for one was going to be, never thinking it would come so soon. Before she was prepared. "Turkey club, please."

"Okay." Delanie set the short glass down on the bar's scratched but gleaming surface. "What's Jack up to?"

"I don't know."

"Isn't it your job to watch him?" That was supposed to be funny.

"It was—" Erin blinked back the emotion that choked off her words.

"Was?" The other woman's blue eyes widened in surprise. "You're leaving?"

"Yes. I was always only temporary." Even though part of her had never abandoned hope that Jack might ask her to stay. What a fool she'd been.

"But this is…sudden."

Erin lifted one shoulder, putting all the nonchalance she could muster into the gesture. "If you have to go… Go."

"I can't believe Jack is letting you leave so easily."

There was a spurt of hope, which was dumb, but Erin couldn't help it. Any more than she could stop the question. "Why would you say that?"

"He was different with you. Lighter, somehow, if that makes any sense. Happy, and I think he hasn't been for a long time, if ever."

"That's nice of you to say." Erin had thought the same thing but found out the hard way how wrong she'd been. "But he doesn't need me."

"I'm not so sure." Delanie frowned.

"The book is nearly finished." *Along with several children's books that he threw in the trash. Idiot.* "My time is up a little early. So I'm heading back to Phoenix."

"Maybe you should stick around a couple days. Just in case he needs something."

"He won't." Not from her. She was untrustworthy.

When she got to the airport, she'd call Cheryl and report. The long drive would give her time to figure out how to explain her early exit. But that's not what was bothering her so much. The reality was that Jack handed back her heart because he didn't want it, or anything else from her. "I really need to get on the road so if I could just have my sandwich—"

Delanie hesitated as if she wanted to say more, then nodded. "Coming right up. And coffee."

"Yes."

The other woman turned away but not before the tears slid down Erin's cheeks. This was so much harder than she'd thought it would be. She was going to miss Blackwater Lake, the community spirit, the people.

Most of all she was going to miss Jack and was pretty sure she would forever.

Jack figured he had a couple more days to put in before the rough draft of his book would be finished. His editor should be happy he was working. After saving the new pages to the computer and a flash drive, he stretched then stood up. It was past dinnertime and he was hungry. The way Harley was looking at him meant the dog was hungry, too.

"Let's go, bud."

He grinned when the little guy raced over to the door. After *walk*, *go* was the word that made Harley quiver with anticipation. Jack, on the other hand, wasn't quivering with anything these days. Erin had been gone a week but he refused to believe he was doing anything but just fine on his own.

He opened the office door and Harley bounded down the stairs, then waited patiently on the front porch for Jack to let him inside. While he flipped on the lights, the dog ran down the hall into every room, as if searching for something. Moments later he came back and gave Jack the where-the-heck-is-she? look.

"Phoenix. Unless Corinne Carlisle needs a nosey book coach."

Jack listened to the sound of silence, the same sound he'd heard for the last seven days. No rattling pans in the kitchen. No closing cupboard doors. No amateur, ladylike swearing over lumpy gravy. If he didn't have Harley he would be talking to himself. The funny thing was that before Erin he hadn't minded that. Never gave a thought to the weirdness of talking only to his dog for long stretches of time. The fact that he thought about it now was annoying.

"Damn it." Harley trotted over as if to ask what was wrong. Jack dropped to one knee and rubbed his furry head. "She ruined the isolation for me."

And that wasn't all. She'd gone through his personal things. More unforgivable was the fact that she'd been right. She figured out that the lonely little boy in the Harley books was him. She'd looked inside him without permission and he couldn't stand the pity he saw in her eyes. Now he would never have to see it again because he'd never see *her* again.

That thought didn't make him feel as satisfied as he wanted to.

Jack opened the refrigerator and checked out its contents. There were multiple leftover containers where alien life forms were growing. This was the last of what she'd cooked for him. He shut the door with a little more force than was necessary.

"A beer and a burger," he said to no one in particular.

Jack put out Harley's food and made sure his water dish was full, then grabbed his keys from a hook on the wall. He felt a little guilty when the dog followed him to the front door. "Don't be inviting your friends over to party, bud."

It was cold outside but somehow it penetrated in a way he'd never noticed before. Just his imagination, he thought, as he walked to where the jeep was parked. The empty space beside it seemed to mock him. How stupid was that? He'd spent a lifetime being a loner and a couple months with a mouthy substitute teacher who got in his face all the time wasn't going to change that.

He would be fine. In a day or two.

Jack drove to Blackwater Lake and followed Main Street to Bar None. He pulled into the parking lot, which had quite a few cars for a weeknight. After settling in a space he exited the car and walked toward the building, with its neon flashing beer bottle in the window. On a sign over the roof proclaiming the name of the establishment there were crossed cocktail glasses.

When he walked inside people sitting in booths and the scattered tables looked up. A couple of them lifted a hand in greeting. That was different.

He recognized Kim Miller and her husband, Luke, teachers at the high school where he'd talked to the kids. April Kennedy sat at a table with Sheriff Will Fletcher. His bar buddy was part of a couple so Jack would have to go solo. That was okay. He was dusting off his loner cred anyway.

He sat on a stool at the bar, the one farthest away from anyone. Delanie Carlson was drawing a beer from the tap and gave him a nod, letting him know she would be right with him. Communicating without words, what a concept. And a welcome change.

After setting the glass in front of a cowboy, the red-headed bar owner walked over to him. "Hey, stranger."

"Hi."

"What can I get you?"

"Beer and burger," he said.

"Coming right up."

After drawing another beer, she set it on a cocktail napkin in front of him. She didn't ask how he liked his burger or if he wanted cheese because she already knew. There was something to be said for no surprises. He liked that.

While waiting for his order, Jack sipped on his drink and looked around the dimly lit interior. He recognized the checker from the grocery store, the one he'd never engaged in conversation until shopping with Erin. The mayor and her husband, who owned McKnight's Automotive, where the jeep got serviced, were sitting at a table with his daughter, Sydney, and her fiancé, Burke Holden.

Before Erin he'd been able to come in here and ignore everyone else. Now he couldn't.

Delanie walked over with a plate containing his food and set it in front of him. "Here you go."

"Thanks."

Instead of moving away, she rested her forearms on the bar, as if settling in for a chat. He hated to admit it but he craved a little company. Nothing heavy, just shallow small talk.

"How's business?"

"Good. Look at you initiating conversation." She smiled as if he was the star pupil.

"I've got skills." He ate a couple of fries.

"Maybe. But not so much with people." Her blue eyes narrowed. "Until Erin."

He grabbed a few more fries, intending to stuff them into his mouth, but stopped halfway there. Hearing someone say her name out loud was an awful lot like a sucker punch.

He didn't want to talk about her. "What's new?"

"Same old, same old." Delanie picked up a cloth and used it to wipe nonexistent spots off the shiny wooden surface of the bar. "So the rumor is that she left town earlier than expected."

Jack knew the "she" in question was Erin and figured the bar owner didn't share his inclination to avoid the subject. He put down the fries and took a drink of beer.

After a sip, he set it on the cocktail napkin and said, "It was time for her to go."

"Really? Are you sure about that?"

"Why wouldn't I be?"

"Oh, I don't know. Maybe because you look kind of lost. A little miserable. I'd have to say lonely."

"Looks can be deceiving," he retorted.

"For the average person. But I'm not easily fooled." She didn't bat an eye at the irritation in his voice. "People are my business. I listen, watch and talk to them every day. I've pretty much seen and heard it all, every story. Breakup, fight and lies. Even when someone is lying to themselves I can spot it a mile away. One look is worth a thousand words."

"I thought that was a picture."

"Whatever." She lifted one shoulder. "The point is I can see right through you. So why don't you tell me the real reason she left."

"Even if I do, how can you trust it? I make stuff up for a living," he warned.

"Didn't I just get finished explaining that I can spot a lie in a lineup?"

"Isn't there someone in this place who needs a refill?" Please, God.

"Touchy, aren't you?" Delanie looked around and seemed satisfied that everyone was happy. "And that was an attempt to distract me. Good try, but not good enough. Tell me why she left."

Jack thought about walking away and a couple of months ago he would have. But not now. And he refused to add "since Erin." "She went through my files."

"You mean writing files?"

"Yeah."

"The ones where you put things about making stuff up?" There was a hint of sarcasm in her voice.

"It's the principle." When he said it out loud his reasoning seemed trivial, inconsequential.

"So you let her go."

Jack wondered at the phrasing. She could have said he fired or terminated her, but didn't. "He let her go" put a very personal spin on what happened.

"She was leaving anyway."

"That's what she said."

"You saw her?" Jack shouldn't have been surprised but he was.

"Just before she left," Delanie confirmed. Her expression turned accusing. "You made her cry."

That one stuck. But he wouldn't let her know. "How can you be so sure it was about me?"

"Oh, please, Jack. Anyone with a brain could see how she felt about you. And you were a son of a bitch to her."

"She was leaving anyway. Sooner was better than later," he said again.

"Was she?" Delanie let the question hang there.

"Yes. She has a life somewhere else. Blackwater Lake was just a pit stop."

"Know what I think?"

"I have a feeling you're going to tell me," he said.

She grinned. "I think you found an excuse to be mad at her."

"Why would I do that?"

"So you could hide behind your self-righteous indignation. That way it wouldn't hurt when she was gone."

That hit closer to the target than he wanted to admit. But not hitting the bull's-eye qualified as a near miss. Which made her attempt off-the-mark. "You couldn't be more wrong."

"Has anyone ever told you that when you bury your head in the sand you leave your backside exposed?"

"Yes."

"And you don't think that's what you're doing?" she persisted.

"No."

"Then you're a jack-ass. No pun intended, Jack."

He'd abandoned being a loner to come here and be insulted? Didn't matter how close to the truth she was. He drank the last of his beer. "On second thought, can I get this burger to go?"

"Sure thing. I'll take care of it." Just before she turned away there was a look on her face that said her work there was done.

A minute or two later she came back with a to-go container for his uneaten food. "Take care, Jack."

"Yeah." Next time he wouldn't turn his back on this woman.

He'd thought a beer and a little trivial conversation would help, but that was his mistake. Another in a growing list.

He drove home and pulled into his space, with the empty one still there beside it. After grabbing his cold, crappy burger in a box, he got out and walked toward the porch. Again he had the sensation of being punched in the gut.

There were no welcoming lights or comfort-food dinners to look forward to. The scent of her skin was still there, but growing fainter every day. No one to plot his book with.

After having Erin, being alone sucked. And there was no hiding from it any longer.

Chapter Fifteen

Jack watched the digital clock on the microwave until it showed 9:05, then poured himself another cup of coffee and sat down at the kitchen table again. If Erin was here he would be late for the status meeting.

But Erin *wasn't* here.

He could do what he wanted to do when he wanted to do it. For the last two weeks he'd been doing just fine without her. The book was finished and he was reading it through one more time before sending the completed manuscript to his editor. He knew something was off, but couldn't quite put his finger on what was missing.

"Erin would know."

Jack didn't realize he'd said that out loud until Harley jumped up and looked hopeful before scurrying out of the room. The animal was going to find Erin, same as he had been for the last two weeks. Moments later the dog came back and stared at him as if to say "Do something to bring her back."

"I know you're missing her, buddy." He reached down and scratched the animal's head. "As much as I'm savoring my self-righteous indignation I understand where you're coming from. But work is waiting."

After grabbing his coffee mug, Jack headed for the front door and Harley trailed after him. He'd waited until after nine every morning for the last two weeks and felt a brief flash of anticipation before reality sank in again. There was no sunshine to look forward to. If she'd never been here he wouldn't know what he was missing.

He opened the office door and glanced around. Everything was just as he'd left it. Because no one was there to move stuff. Irritated, he set down his mug on his desk, right where the coffee stain was. No sissy coaster for him.

The printed-out manuscript was waiting for him and he sat down to finish editing. The action scenes were fine, the dialogue crisp, funny in the right places and moved the story forward. But every time Mac's assistant showed up on the page everything came to a grinding halt. And changing her name wouldn't solve the problem.

She was flat and one-dimensional. Mac's coffee was always waiting. She did exactly as told, never pushed back and was boring as hell. She didn't put pens and pencils in the mug where they belonged or put that coffee on the coaster he hated, or cook the best comfort food he'd ever tasted.

So there was something missing in his work, too. The female character Erin said this story needed wasn't her.

Jack remembered Delanie saying he'd found an excuse to be mad so it wouldn't hurt when Erin was gone. If she was right, the strategy was a complete failure because the pain tearing through him now hurt as surely as if someone put a bullet in him.

And he'd made her cry.

"I'm an idiot, Harley—" Without looking he reached

down, knowing the dog would be there. He rubbed his hand over the furry head and didn't feel the calm that usually settled over him. "A real bastard—"

The phone rang, startling him, and he looked at the caller ID. His editor. He picked up the receiver and hit the talk button. "Hi, Cheryl."

"Jack? Is that really you? Not a voice-mail message?"

"I deserve that."

"After avoiding me for months?" There was just a touch of sarcasm in her voice. "No. Don't beat yourself up. My feelings weren't hurt at all."

"Okay. Take your best shot. Get it out of your system."

"That's just mean. Giving me permission takes all the fun out of it." She laughed. "But I'll do my best. It wasn't hard at all to juggle the publishing schedule or put promotion on hold for you."

"I'm a son of a bitch." He'd just called himself worse and didn't blame this woman for dumping on him even more. "I guess you're wondering about the book. You should know—"

"I'll get to that, but there's something else I need to talk to you about."

Absently he rubbed Harley. "I get it. You're not finished chewing me out."

"No, I am. That's not it." There was a pause. "You've been holding out on me, Jack."

"I thought we already established I'm a jerk and my book is late."

"No. I meant the Harley books."

He went still. "The what?"

"The children's stories with the Chinese crested dog."

"Still don't know what you're talking about." He'd trashed the file.

"Erin sent me a folder with stories about a little boy who triumphs over adversity with the help of his dog."

Jack hadn't realized they were gone. The last time he'd seen them was when he took the file folder from Erin and threw it away. The bag of trash from his office went into the big container at the marina store, where it eventually was hauled off. And that was that. Or so he'd believed.

He waited for the anger to help him camouflage the pain but he was fresh out. That hadn't been the case when he found Erin reading his stuff. He could talk about it rationally because his editor was probably just trying to decide whether or not he had a screw loose.

"Those aren't really stories as much as creativity exercises. Just ignore them."

"Are you crazy?"

He hadn't thought so, but now he wasn't sure. "Why?"

"They're completely wonderful, Jack. Who'd have thought you, of all people, could write like this? With a message for children. Where did that come from?"

Erin knew, he thought. She'd figured out almost right away that the little boy in the stories was him. She saw into his soul and surely couldn't care about him after that. So he fired her. And made her cry.

He was a rat-bastard son of a bitch.

But Cheryl was waiting for an answer. "Like I said, it was something I did to get the writing motor started."

"It worked."

"What does that mean?" he asked.

"I sent the proposal over to the children's division and they love it."

"What?"

"I hope that was all right." She must have heard something in his voice because for the first time she sounded doubtful. "You did send them to be considered for publication, no?"

He hadn't sent them at all. It took someone who believed

in him to pass them along. Where was your self-righteous indignation when you really needed it?

"It's all right" was all he could think of to say.

"Good. Because there will be an offer coming. We'll contact your agent and he'll be in touch."

"You're serious about this? You really want to buy them?" That sounded an awful lot like "you really like me?" But he couldn't hold back the question.

"This is a new career direction. Just in case you decide to kill off Mac Daniels," she said. "A lot of well-known authors are branching into children's and young adult genres. I just never thought you would be one of them."

"Should I be insulted?" he asked.

"I can't stop you and it's not what I meant." She laughed. "It was a compliment. But, fair warning, we're going to want you to do some media."

Before he'd met Erin, he would have shut down the idea. But he'd done the interview for the Blackwater Lake newspaper and lived to talk about it. Logan had told him the issue with the article about their local author had set a record for newspaper sales. And he never would have agreed if Erin hadn't talked him into it. Since she showed up at his door life had done a one-eighty on him and nothing bad happened. If he didn't count her leaving.

"I'll do media," he said.

"Wow." There was stunned silence for a moment. "That's it. Just wow."

"Was that sarcastic?" he asked.

"Maybe a little." Again there was a pause before she said, "About the other book. The sequel to *High Value Target*…"

"It's finished."

"Great. I can't wait to read it," she said.

"About that—"

"Jack, you have to let it go sometime. No one likes a

clean, problem-free manuscript more than me, but I really need to see this book."

"Look—" He leaned back and stared at the empty chair in front of his desk, the one where Erin always sat. If she could hear what he was about to say there would be no living with her. Actually there was no living with her now. Self-righteous indignation completely deserted him and the dam on his pain crumbled, letting it all rush in. "The book needs a little tweaking. Not the story. It's fine. Just something isn't right."

"I don't know, Jack—"

"I know it's a lot to ask and I don't deserve it, but can you give me a couple of weeks for a small revision? I'll send you a detailed outline."

There was a long, tense silence before Cheryl sighed. "Okay. You've got two weeks. Max."

"Thanks. You're the best."

"Yes, I am. After all, I sent you Erin."

"You did."

That was a blessing and a curse. Living the blessing was the best time he'd ever had. The curse part he could do without and had no one but himself to blame.

"She really brought out your creativity, Jack. At the risk of patting myself on the back, I have to say that she's good for you."

If ripping a guy's heart out was the goal, then yeah, she was good for him. But that was information better kept to himself, so he did.

"So what did you do to her?"

The question came out of left field and caught him off guard. Somewhere this professional conversation had taken a personal turn. "I'm not sure what you're asking."

"I don't think that's true. But you're a man so I'll explain. Erin is different since she spent time with you. I sent you an outgoing, cheerful young woman to help with your manuscript and she came back distant and, there's no other way to say it...she's sad."

Jack drew in a breath. He was a writer. Words were his weapon of choice. But he couldn't think of anything bad enough to call himself for what he'd done. And apparently she hadn't told Cheryl about being fired or his editor would have mentioned it.

"Jack? You didn't hang up on me, did you?"

"Still here," he answered.

"I'll say it straight out. I'd like to know what happened because you broke my book coach."

From his point of view she'd broken him. When Erin arrived he'd been a fat, dumb and happy loner. Now he was talking to his dog about plot twists. But this woman deserved something. "What happened is that she brought out more than just my creativity."

"You fell in love with her." Cheryl wasn't asking a question.

And he wasn't going to tell her she was right. His editor shouldn't be the first one to hear the truth.

"I'm sorry for the delay on this book. I apologize for any inconvenience to you and the publisher. It will never happen again. You'll have it in two weeks. I give you my word on that."

"Okay, Jack."

After saying goodbye he hung up. There was a manuscript to deal with, then the real work would start.

He'd made Erin cry and somehow he had to fix that.

Erin sat behind the desk in front of the classroom and monitored the seniors who were taking a pop quiz. They didn't know it wouldn't count toward their grade and was basically busywork. In about fifteen minutes the final bell of the day would ring and she could go home and curl into a protective ball. It had been her go-to coping mechanism since Jack threw her out a month ago.

How long would she feel so empty inside? she wondered, because this funk showed no sign of letting up anytime soon.

The flip side of the final bell was that she'd have to assume her coping mechanism in her lonely apartment. Maybe she should stop at the dog-rescue shelter again and get a pet for companionship. She'd really become attached to Harley. And Jack… Her eyes filled at the thought of him but crying in front of a room full of teenagers wasn't an option. Darn it, why did she have to go and fall in love with him?

She looked at the clock again. "Okay, class. Time is up."

There was a collective groan and automatic protests of not being finished with the test they'd griped about taking in the first place.

"Mrs. Castillo warned you she would do this and instructed me to be firm." She stood. "Please pass your papers forward."

The sound of paper shuffling filled the room and her back was turned, which was why she didn't hear the door opening or see who walked in.

"Who's the dude with the weird-looking dog?" one of the students asked.

Erin whirled around and saw Jack just inside the door with Harley in his arms. After one bark, the little guy wiggled until Jack set him down. His paws had barely hit the ground before he ran to her.

She dropped to one knee and took his noble little face in her hands, scratching him under his chin. "Hi, Harley. You're such a handsome dog. I've missed you."

"Miss Riley? Should we notify the office?" one of the guys asked.

"It's okay," Jack said. "I stopped to see the principal and for probably the first time I wasn't even in trouble."

The kids laughed at his joke and it would have been funny to her under different circumstances.

"I know him," Erin said. "This is Jack Garner, the author of the runaway bestselling book *High Value Target*."

"Why did Mr. Pascale let you in with the dog?" a girl asked.

"I vouched for him," Jack explained. "I have permission just this once. And if anyone asks, he's a service dog."

"I know him, too," Erin said. "His name is Harley."

"My dad read your book." The girl in the first desk couldn't take her eyes off the author.

Erin knew the feeling, but she was in charge here and it was time to take control of the class, at least, even if she was having trouble managing her feelings. She couldn't look at Jack hard enough and her heart was racing, trying to outrun the pain of seeing him again.

She ignored both and took the quiz papers that were passed to her, noting that the bell would ring in a few minutes. She'd make her escape then. "Never miss a teachable moment. Jack, why don't you tell the kids about yourself."

"Just the high points? Maybe five minutes?"

"Yes." That was the advice she'd given him when he'd shown up at Kim Miller's classroom in Blackwater Lake without notes for his talk. He'd remembered and she found that oddly endearing. Foolish, but true.

So, Jack told his personal story again and, like the last time, didn't gloss over the fact that he'd chosen the army over juvenile detention and liked the life so much he joined the rangers. But for every up there was a down. He lost brothers in arms that he cared deeply about and it left a mark. Writing helped him deal with those scars and he got lucky.

Then he asked if anyone had a question and most of the hands in the room shot up. He pointed to a kid sitting in the middle row.

"What's your name?" Jack asked.

"Cameron. How do you know Miss Riley?"

Jack met her gaze. "I was having trouble with my second book. My editor sent her to me to move things along. I'd never collaborated before and it didn't go well at first."

Because he was a loner, she thought. She wasn't sure what he was doing here, but there was no reason to think he'd changed. She watched him answer the kids' questions in a straightforward, humorous way and he had them firmly under his spell. So what else was new?

She recalled the moments before his first time in front of a high school class, when he'd said it was too late for a personality transplant and no one had ever accused him of being charming or approachable. Apparently he was capable of learning because he was both of those things now.

Good God, would the darn bell ever ring?

A girl in front of him asked, "You said you live in Montana. Why did you come all this way to see Miss Riley?"

He looked over at her, but before he could answer the question, the darn bell finally rang. She really wanted to know why he'd come, but this group didn't need to hear the free-at-last signal twice. They grabbed their things and headed for the door.

Jack called after them, "Thanks for not throwing spitballs at me."

And suddenly it was quiet. She was alone with Jack.

Erin moved to the desk and retrieved her purse from the bottom drawer. "That's my cue. I'll just be going—"

"Please wait."

She looked down for a moment, then slid her hands into the pockets of her black slacks. With a deep breath she forced herself to meet his gaze. "I don't think we have anything to say to each other. You made yourself clear the last time I saw you."

"You're not at all curious about why I'm here?"

She was trying not to be and failing miserably. "Okay. Yes. Why are you here?"

He watched his dog wander the classroom, exploring and stopping occasionally to sniff something that caught his attention. "I know you sent the Harley books to Cheryl."

"So you came all this way to yell at me for violating your privacy? News flash, Jack, you can only fire me once. After that, technically I don't work for you anymore and it's—"

He moved closer and touched a finger to her lips, stopping the flow of words. "She loved the stories."

"What?"

"Cheryl passed them on to the editor in charge of children's books and they bought them. Everyone at the house loves the idea of an ongoing series."

"Congratulations." Oh, she wanted to rub that in, but taking the high road seemed... The hell with the high road. She'd already been fired. There was nothing left to lose. "I told you so."

"What?"

"I knew they were good but you wouldn't listen."

He nodded. "I was an ungrateful jerk."

"Yes, you were." There. She'd said it and waited to feel some satisfaction. Unfortunately, there was nothing.

"I came here to explain why I reacted so badly."

"It's not necessary. I get it. You felt vulnerable revealing so much of yourself."

"It's more than that." The easy charm he showed the

kids was gone, replaced by a tightly coiled intensity. The warrior. He was fighting for something. "I believed when you saw the real me you'd be disappointed and—"

"Leave?"

"Yeah." He folded his arms over his chest. "Sending you away first was my way to control the situation. It was knee-jerk."

Gosh darn it, she understood and didn't want to. She was trying to stay mad at him because it was the only protection she had.

"You really didn't have to come, Jack."

"Yeah, I did. Cheryl said I broke her book coach."

"What?" Erin never mentioned what had happened between her and Jack. How could the editor have known?

"She said you were different. Sad." He looked troubled for a moment, then went on. "Delanie said you stopped by on the way out of town and you were crying."

"She was wrong." Talk about knee-jerk. "Bar None is dark. I had something in my eye."

"Liar."

She had seen many expressions cross his face. Anger. Irritation. Passion. Intensity. Tenderness and toughness. But there was a look now that was different from anything else. It had all the signs of self-recrimination. "Okay. I may have shed a tear. But it had nothing to do with you." Now *that* was a lie. "I've never been fired before. It was a shock."

"I'm sorry I made you cry, Erin. It was definitely not my finest hour."

"Understood. But it wasn't necessary to come all this way to apologize. Although I appreciate it and accept your apology. Now I really need to go." She started to reach for her purse again. "We're done."

"I'm not."

"What else could there possibly be?" She wasn't sure how much longer she could keep it together and wished he would leave.

"You never asked about the sequel to *High Value Target*." He held up his hand to stop her when she started to say something. "I thought you should know that I figured out what was missing from the book. And from my life."

"What?" She held her breath as hope twisted free inside her.

"The answer to both is you. I love you, Erin."

She had an imagination and knew how to use it. She'd pictured a scenario where Jack would say those words to her. Never once had she seen herself bursting into tears, but that's what happened. The feelings came spilling out and she covered her face with her hands.

Instantly, strong arms pulled her in close to his body. "Please don't cry. I can't stand it."

She laughed, but it came out more a snort. "You? Big, bad Special Forces ranger?"

"It's our secret. I'd rather face incoming fire than see you cry." He cupped her cheek in his palm and lifted her gaze to his. "I love you. I came to get you and bring you home to Blackwater Lake. I'm asking you to marry me. If you meant what you said. That you love me."

She sniffled, then pulled away just far enough to look into his eyes. "Yes."

He waited, looking increasingly frustrated. Finally he said, "That's all you've got? I expected more."

"Show, don't tell." She shrugged, then stood on tiptoe and pressed her mouth to his. She poured all the pain of rejection and now unexpected joy into the kiss. Both of them had trouble catching their breath when they reluctantly pulled apart.

"Sometimes a guy needs more than a word. Does that mean you'll marry me?"

"I love you, Jack. No one warned me you would be so much trouble, but I fell in love with you the moment we met."

"Love at first sight?"

"Laugh if you want, but it's true."

"I'm not laughing. Thanks to you my career in action-adventure is on target and I'm doing a series of children's books." He lifted one shoulder. "Even I couldn't have made this up. So, who knows? Maybe together we'll break into the romance genre."

"The best part is we'll live it. Nothing would make me happier than marrying you. And I love Blackwater Lake, too. Just try and keep me away." She smiled up at him. "Is that enough words for you?"

"For now. But there's a lot to be said for 'show, don't tell.'"

And he proceeded to kiss her again. Being in his arms was like coming home. Life was funny and wonderful. She'd taken a job looking for adventure and found the most exciting one of all. Love.

A word with the bachelor had turned into her happily-ever-after.

* * * * *

Can't get enough of
THE BACHELORS OF BLACKWATER LAKE?
*Don't miss Teresa Southwick's previous books
in this heartwarming series:*

*HOW TO LAND HER LAWMAN
THE WIDOW'S BACHELOR BARGAIN
A DECENT PROPASAL
THE RANCHER WHO TOOK HER IN*

MILLS & BOON®

Cherish™

EXPERIENCE THE ULTIMATE RUSH OF FALLING IN LOVE

A sneak peek at next month's titles...

In stores from 8th September 2016:

- **A Mistletoe Kiss with the Boss** – Susan Meier *and* **Maverick vs Maverick** – Shirley Jump
- **A Countess for Christmas** – Christy McKellen *and* **Ms Bravo and the Boss** – Christine Rimmer

In stores from 6th October 2016:

- **Her Festive Baby Bombshell** – Jennifer Faye *and* **Building the Perfect Daddy** – Brenda Harlen
- **The Unexpected Holiday Gift** – Sophie Pembroke *and* **The Man She Should Have Married** – Patricia Kay

---

Just can't wait?
Buy our books online a month before they hit the shops!
www.millsandboon.co.uk

Also available as eBooks.

MILLS & BOON®

EXCLUSIVE EXCERPT

Emma Carmichael's world is turned upside-down
when she encounters Jack Westwood—her
secret husband of six years!

Read on for a sneak preview of
A COUNTESS FOR CHRISTMAS
the first book in the enchanting new Cherish quartet
MAIDS UNDER THE MISTLETOE

'You still have your ring,' Jack said.

'Of course.' Emma was frowning now and wouldn't
meet his eye.

'Why—?' He walked to where she was standing
with her hand gripping her handbag so hard her
knuckles were white.

'I'm not very good at letting go of the past,' she
said, shrugging and tilting up her chin to look him
straight in the eye, as if to dare him to challenge her
about it. 'I don't have a lot left from my old life and
I couldn't bear to get rid of this ring. It reminds me of
a happier time in my life. A simpler time, which I don't
want to forget about.'

She blinked hard and clenched her jaw together
and it suddenly occurred to him that she was struggling with being around him as much as he was with
her.

The atmosphere hung heavy and tense between them,

with only the sound of their breathing breaking the silence.

His throat felt tight with tension and his pulse had picked up so he felt the heavy beat of it in his chest.

Why was it so important to him that she hadn't completely eschewed their past?

He didn't know, but it was.

Taking a step towards her, he slid his fingers under the thin silver chain around her neck, feeling the heat of her soft skin as he brushed the backs of his fingers over it, and drew the ring out of her dress again to look at it.

He remembered picking this out with her. They'd been so happy then, so full of excitement and love for each other.

He heard her ragged intake of breath as the chain slid against the back of her neck and looked up to see confusion in her eyes, and something else. Regret, perhaps, or sorrow for what they'd lost.

Something seemed to be tugging hard inside him, drawing him closer to her.

Her lips parted and he found he couldn't drag his gaze away from her mouth. That beautiful, sensual mouth that used to haunt his dreams all those years ago.

A lifetime ago.

MILLS & BOON®

18 bundles of joy from your favourite authors!

Get 2 books free when you buy the complete collection only at
www.millsandboon.co.uk/greatoffers